STARBRI

Rise To Omniscience
Book Two

Aaron Oster

For my baby brother. You are an inspiration. *Woof.*

Prologue

A man sat on a rooftop overlooking the plaza where Morgan had just put on an impressive display of power. Despite the mid-afternoon sun shining high above, he was entirely cloaked in shadow. He had been there for the last half hour and had witnessed the entire fight from beginning to end. Even now, his keen eyes tracked the quickly fading specs that were Morgan and Sarah.

He was about to sit up from his position propped against the chimney, when some commotion from the plaza below caught his attention. He felt a small smile curl the corner of one lip, as the prone body of one of the boys was carried off. *Morgan had been careless. That would undoubtedly come back to bite him in the ass.*

A sudden whoosh of air made him turn his head. A woman now stood on the flat roof next to him, her entire form hidden by a heavy, hooded cloak.

"You look ridiculous in that thing," the man said, gesturing at the garment. "It must be nearly eighty degrees out."

"You're just saying that because you have no sense of style!" The woman had a light, feminine voice that always got on the man's nerves.

The woman flipped her hood back, revealing long, silky black hair, striking green eyes and an unfamiliar face. She stuck her tongue out at him, giggling again, and leaned back in midair where she remained propped up, as though by an invisible wall.

"Why the new face?" he asked, quirking a brow.

"It's best that the people around here don't see me," she replied with a shrug, bringing both arms up and tucking them behind her head.

The movement shifted aside her cloak, revealing a full figured body, with curves in all the right places.

The man just grunted in reply and turned his attention back to Morgan and Sarah, who were no longer visible.

He knew better than to stare. She might be attractive to his eyes, but who knew what her real form looked like. Not that he thought anyone had ever seen her true form…

"Aww, they look so cute together!"

The man gritted his teeth as the woman spoke once again. Clearly, her eyes were better than his, not that it was a surprise.

"You do realize that they're *not* a couple," he replied, inwardly berating himself the moment he opened his mouth.

"And who's fault is that?" the woman said in a sing-song voice, giving him a sidelong look.

"Like I've already told you, several hundred times..." the man said between gritted teeth. "You can't ask for the perfect warrior, and have me leave a glaring weakness- like an interest in women. You do realize that he wouldn't be nearly this effective if he was just a regular, hormonal, teenage boy; don't you?"

The woman pouted at him, shoving off from her invisible wall and turning to face him. She placed her hands on her hips, widening her eyes, and leaning forward to give him a generous view down her top.

The man didn't so much as twitch at the display.

He knew she only did this just to mess with him; and if he showed her how much her displays were affecting him, it would only get worse.

"Can't you fix that part? I know it's a weakness, but I love a good romance, and the two of them would just work so well together!"

The man just shook his head with a snort of derision.

"Not unless you'd like me to fry his brain. Do you have any idea how many years of work went into getting him to this point?! How many months I worked on meticulously changing every aspect, every hormone, and every instinct, to craft the perfect warrior and all while suppressing his abilities? I've already taken the risk of wiping his mind once; if I go in there again, he'll turn into a raging lunatic."

What the man didn't mention, however, was that he wasn't even sure if he could anymore.

The woman puffed out her cheeks and turned to look at the area where the two of them had already disappeared from his view.

"I know," she said, still pouting. "But why does he seem so clueless? That poor girl is practically throwing herself at him and he doesn't even seem to understand why."

The man shrugged.

"The mind is a strange thing. How am I supposed to know what kind of damage has been done, due to all the modifications?"

In fact, he was shocked that Morgan was even functioning as a normal human at all. With all the changes he'd done, he should have been as emotionless as a pile of rocks. He was sure that the woman standing next to him had something to do with that. Perhaps she'd been the one to instigate the meeting between him and the girl. What he couldn't figure out, though, was how she'd managed to turn him into a mostly functional person.

"So, what you're saying is that you have no idea," the woman said, smirking at him in a self-satisfied manner.

The man scoffed at her, not willing to rise to the bait again.

"If it's so important to you, why don't *you* fix him?"

She turned to look at him, cocking her head to the side.

"You know that I can't interfere. That would be against the rules."

"But it's fine to tell me to do it?"

"Exactly!"

The man growled.

"You still haven't told me why you need *him*, specifically. Why put all this time and effort into him, when you can just grab a far more powerful supermage? We know of one in the East Kingdom, in fact. I believe that he actually came into contact with her at a certain point, though he doesn't seem to remember it."

She leaned forward, giving him an indulgent smile and patting him lightly on the head.

"You just leave that up to me. Mortal minds cannot comprehend the thoughts of a god, now, can they?"

She straightened then, pulling her hood up and turning away from him.

"I can feel Sammy snooping, so I have to go. Keep a close eye on him for me, there are way too many interested parties involved for my liking. You'd better not fail me."

Her voice took on a bit of an edge at the end, causing the man to shiver involuntary; and he was very rudely reminded of the powerful, immoral being standing before him.

"Of course," he said, then the goddess abruptly vanished.

The man blew out a long, shaky breath. He then stood and hopped off of the roof, eyes alighting on another group approaching the open square as he fell. After landing in a crouch, he took off at a sprint, following the path that Morgan had taken only minutes ago.

His mind wandered back to the years that he'd spent with Morgan; teaching him, protecting him, and finally, leaving him. He hated to admit it, but he had a bit of a soft spot for the boy after all these years. He just hoped that whatever fate the fickle goddess had in mind for him wouldn't be too horrible.

***

Grub ran through the darkening forest on the outskirts of the Central Kingdom. It was silent, except for his ragged breathing and the rapid pounding of his heart; as well as the sound of crunching leaves underfoot.

He stopped for a moment, pressing his back to a tree and taking in massive gulps of air, as he tried to calm his racing heart.

This was bad! He knew what he'd overheard back at the academy was enough to get him killed. In fact, the Princess had outright ordered the man named Arnold to do so as soon as they left the city. He'd been smart though, pretending not to have heard anything and even going so far as to offer the man a handshake before he left.

As soon as the man was gone he'd made run for it, not even taking the time to gather any of his possessions.

Grub straightened, closing his eyes and listening as hard as he could for any sound of pursuit. It was made difficult, as all he could hear was the pounding in his ears, and his still ragged breathing.

He was pretty sure he'd gotten away clean, but it didn't hurt to be cautious. After all, he had some extremely sensitive information about Katherine's plans to overthrow her father, as well as Morgan being a supermage.

No wonder that little shit was so strong, he thought, taking deep, steadying breaths. It could hardly have been called a fight at all if he'd had to go up against someone like that alone.

Grub smiled to himself as he pushed off the tree and took off running once more.

He might be a fugitive for now, but as soon as he made it home, he would be a hero. His family would reward him handsomely for this information. Hell, they might even promote him early, now that Keldor and Frush were both dead.

Aaron Oster

His good mood soured instantly at the thought of his two dead cousins.

That bastard Morgan and his bitch girlfriend would pay for what they'd done to his family. No one messed with the Merchants Guild and got away with it!

Grub's fists clenched at his sides as his sour mood turned to outright anger, then on to rage.

"I'll kill you all for this! Mark my words!" he yelled into the surrounding forest.

The moment he opened his mouth, he knew he'd made a mistake.

"I think I head something over there!" A voice cried out from some distance off.

Shit! They were following him and he'd just given his position away.

Grub pumped his legs even faster as the sound of pursuit suddenly reached him.

They must have been after him the entire time, but since he'd kept quiet, they hadn't been sure of where he was. He was such an idiot!

Grub heaved for air as the tree line thinned up ahead, then he was running across open ground and heading straight for the border wall.

All he had to do was reach it. Then he'd be in the South, and safe from any of the North soldiers. At least, that's what he hoped.

The North had just declared war and attacked the Central Kingdom. Maybe the South was next?

Grub took a quick look over his shoulder but didn't see anything.

That didn't mean they weren't following, though. All that meant was that he just couldn't see them yet.

His vision was beginning to swim as he approached the border guards and he could see them straightening up from their relaxed positions.

This border outpost was quite remote, so they likely hadn't heard about the war just yet.

As he drew near, he heard the distinct sound of thudding hooves and snapping branches. Taking a quick peek over his shoulder, he saw five riders clad in red and white break through the tree line.

"Shit!" Of course, they would have to have horses.

Grub leaned forward, putting every ounce of strength he had into making it to the border guards, who by now were calling for help as they spotted the riders as well. Grub finally made it to the wall, coming to a stumbling halt before the guards, who both raised weapons at him.

"Who are you?! State your name, and business. Otherwise, we'll run you through!"

Grub was too out of breath to speak, so instead, he held up his right hand; revealing a shining gold ring with the mark of the Merchants Guild stamped on it.

The guard recognized the crest instantly and to his credit, didn't ask any further questions. He moved to the side and motioned him to pass, stepping into the path of the oncoming horses and preparing an attack. As he stumbled up to the large border gates, a group of guards streamed out of a side door and ran to help the others fight off the riders.

Grub reached the border gates and slumped to the ground in exhaustion. He concentrated on filling his lungs with air as he fought against the clutches of unconsciousness, watching through blurry vision as the gate guards fought against the men who were following him.

He knew he really should get into better shape. At his rank, a run like that shouldn't have cost him nearly this much effort.

The guards made quick work of the soldiers, butchering them down to a man.

They must not have been very strong if they'd been cut down that easily, Grub thought, not sure if he should be insulted that they'd sent a group of weaklings after him.

The guards began cleaning their weapons and looting the corpses, as the Captain turned his attention to the still prone Grub.

He groaned, forcing himself back up to his feet, despite the overwhelming urge to just lie there and let himself pass out.

He had an image to maintain, after all.

The captain gave his men a few terse orders, then stepped forward to speak with him.

Aaron Oster

"Can you tell me why a group of soldiers from the North Kingdom were chasing someone from the Merchants Guild; and in the Central Kingdom of all places?" he asked, grounding his staff before him, and grinding the butt into the ground.

"Haven't you heard about the war?" Grub asked, doing his best to retain a sense of dignity, despite his sweat-streaked, and dirt-smeared face.

This statement made the captain take a step back and an audible ripple ran through the other border guards, who by now, had finished what they'd been doing, and had come to join their captain.

"What war?" the Captain asked, now looking quite worried.

Grub quickly recounted the attack on the academy, making sure to emphasize the slaughter of innocent people and the imminent fall of the kingdom.

"I thought I'd gotten away clean, but they apparently decided to send someone after me," he finished.

The border guards looked about ready run off and join the fight, but their captain held up a hand to forestall them.

"If what you're saying is true, then the North may be sending soldiers this way to launch an attack on the South as well." He rubbed at his chin for a moment as if contemplating something, then nodded to himself.

"We can't leave this checkpoint. If more soldiers come this way, then we will be the only ones standing in their way. As a member of the Merchant's Guild; can we count on you to deliver a message of our plight to the nearest outpost? We would gladly supply you with a horse and rations to hasten your journey."

Grub didn't even need to think twice. The journey back home would have taken him several months had he been forced to go by foot. It would still take nearly a month by horseback, but it was far preferable to walking.

"I will gladly carry your message," Grub said, giving the man a formal bow.

The captain smiled then and bowed back. His bow was a bit deeper than Grub's, showing him the respect he was due, as a high ranking member of the Merchants Guild.

In just a few minute's time, Grub was riding through the open gates and into the South Kingdom. A small smirk played around the corner of his lips, as the wall behind him receded.

He'd made it out alive. Now all he had to do was make it home and once he did, Morgan would pay.

***

Lord Simon paced restlessly in his office, as he waited for his guest to arrive. It was nearing midnight and he was expecting them at any moment. His fists clenched and unclenched as he thought of the people responsible for making him take such drastic actions.

That damn Morgan had to steal his daughter away, and the one person he thought he could count on to retrieve her, had failed him.

He stopped his pacing and took a few deep, calming breaths.

He needed to compose himself. Showing any fear in front of these people would be dangerous, to say the least. He would need to project an aura of confidence and self-assurance for this to go smoothly.

A knock came at his door and he nearly lost his composure right then and there. Grumbling to himself, he quickly sat down behind his desk, making sure to clear it of anything he didn't want to be seen. He ran his hand through his hair, smoothing it back into place before calling out.

"Enter."

The door opened a moment later and a man dressed in black from head to toe walked in.

At least he thought it was a man. It was hard to tell, as the only visible part of him were his eyes.

The man stopped before the desk and placed his hands behind his back.

"What's the job?"

His voice was quiet and smooth, with an accent that Simon couldn't quite place.

Southern maybe? This could, of course, be a ploy to make him think that the man was from the South when in reality he was from somewhere else entirely.

Simon cleared his throat, then began speaking.

"I need two jobs done. One will be a retrieval and, the other, an assassination."

"Retrievals are extra. Killing someone is easy, but capturing them alive is a lot more difficult. Especially if they are of high rank."

Simon inclined his head, and reaching into his desk drawer, removed a heavy leather pouch, which clinked audibly as he placed it on the table.

The man swept up the heavy purse and peeked inside. The glint of platinum showed for a moment before the bag disappeared into the man's clothes.

The mask covering the man's face shifted slightly and his eyes crinkled a bit at the corners. Simon took this to mean that the man was happy with the payment, so he laid out the mission.

"My daughter Sarah was last spotted fleeing the academy. My sources believe she was heading to the East Kingdom. Traveling with her is a boy named Morgan. I want them both captured alive and brought back to me."

"And the assassination?" the man asked.

"A man named Arnold. He was supposed to complete this mission over two months ago but has failed me miserably. You'll have to be careful, as he currently holds favor with King Edmund."

"It shall be done as you say. You should expect to hear back from us within the week." The man abruptly turned then and slunk out of his office.

Simon waited a few minutes, until he was sure the man was gone, then let out a deep breath and slumped in his seat.

He'd faced many dangerous men in his lifetime, but that man was undoubtedly one of the most terrifying he'd come up against. The man himself likely wasn't all that powerful, but rather it was who he represented. The Assassins Guild didn't bow to anyone, be they commoner or noble.

Simon allowed his tension to ease as the time passed and, eventually, a grim smile broke out onto his face.

The Assassins Guild had a terrifying reputation, and they never failed to complete a job. Morgan was as good as his, and Arnold would likely be dead in a matter of days. Then he could finally rid himself of all the nuisances and focus on getting in good with the king. After all, there were still other kingdoms to conquer and King Simon had a very nice ring to it.

1

"Duck, you moron!"

Sarah's timely and slightly insulting warning was the only thing that saved Morgan's life. He dropped to the ground and heard a pair of stone shod hooves whistling through the space his head had occupied, only moments before. Then a hail of icy spears flew past him and impacted his assailant, prompting it to let out a scream of pain.

Morgan straightened as Sarah jogged over to him, a wide grin plastered on her face.

"I don't see what's so funny. I almost died just now," he grumbled, as he turned to look at their downed foe.

"Well, the almost dying part wasn't funny," Sarah said, bending down near the beast and retrieving its core. "What *is* funny is that the mighty supermage was almost killed by a freaking donkey!"

Morgan looked down sourly at the now dead donkey, as Sarah walked past him, still snickering to herself.

It wasn't his fault. She'd been distracting him when the donkey was sneaking up on him, and he hadn't sensed the attack coming. She'd done it on purpose; probably to get him back for that comment he'd made about her weight the other day.

Just the thought of Sarah's expression was enough to make his sour mood evaporate.

She might have almost gotten him killed, but it was totally worth it.

They were currently in a *rank 12 beast zone*. This was their first time going through this particular *zone* and, so far, Morgan wasn't impressed. It seemed like Gold had some kind of sick sense of humor, and had given them a key to a *beast zone* filled with a new assortment of farm animals.

So far they'd run into a bunch of insanely aggressive chickens, some sheep that looked to be the evolved form of the ironwool-sheep they'd fought back in the academy, and now this; a donkey that used stealth to attack.

"Are you just going to stand there all day?"

Morgan turned to see Sarah still grinning and staring at him with a raised eyebrow.

"Just thinking about Gold's sick sense of humor," he said, walking over to her.

"Yeah. Only he would send us to a place like this," she said, starting to walk again once he'd caught up with her.

Morgan looked around at the surrounding landscape and wondered how a place this nice could be so dangerous. A massive plain of swaying green grass spread out before them. The sky was clear and blue overhead. A light breeze wafted across, rustling the grass, and bringing the scent of wildflowers along with it.

If he could, Morgan would spend the rest of his life here. It was calm and even peaceful, as though there was nothing wrong with the world.

His illusion of peace was instantly shattered when a mass of feathers and claws launched itself at him with an angry squawk.

"Damn chickens!" he yelled, using his new *gale force* skill, along with *condensed wind blade* at the same time.

He narrowly avoided the stabbing beak of the green and yellow chicken, then brought his swirling purple blade across, cleaving the chicken in two.

"Son of a bitch!" Sarah yelled as she was drenched in feathers and chicken blood.

"Duck!" he yelled, as another one of the chickens launched itself at her.

Sarah didn't duck, though. She whirled on the spot and thrust her hand out with a scream of rage. The chicken didn't stand a chance. It practically exploded in a shower of blood and guts; as she used her upgraded *icicle barrage* skill.

She then turned to Morgan, who was doing his best not to burst out laughing at her appearance.

"Not. A. Word!" she said, turning and stalking away from him.

Morgan bent down near the two chickens and retrieved the cores. He made sure not to dismiss his *wind blade*, as the cost to summon a new one would be too high. Instead, he held his arm out to the side as he worked.

He straightened, clutching two slightly bloody cores in his hand and jogged back to Sarah, who was attempting to wash off the sticky mix of blood and feathers.

Morgan considered asking her to put the cores away but decided that she was best left alone for now, so he instead opened his status to view the core's stats.

Name: Bloodsucker-chicken core
Rank - 11
Total available energy: 1,872/1,872

This core was taken from a bloodsucker-chicken and has no special properties.

Who knew a chicken could be such a good source of energy?

Morgan closed his status, and placed both cores in one of the many pockets of his canvas pants. He looked over to Sarah, who had by now managed to clean most of the blood off herself. He was walking over to ask her if she was feeling better when he caught something out of the corner of his eye. Turning, he saw a break in the landscape off to their left. An open and bare patch of ground in an otherwise grass-covered field.

He held his hand up to shade his eyes and squinted to try and get a better look. It was no good though; the shifting grass, as well as the bright sunlight, made it nearly impossible to make anything out.

There was only one way to get a better view.

"Hey Sarah!" he called out.

Sarah stopped, turning to give him a questioning look. Morgan pointed upward and she nodded, stopping in her tracks and keeping a lookout.

Morgan used his new *enhanced flight* skill and took off into the air, flying straight up so he could get a better view of their surroundings. He stopped when he reached his maximum height of *60 feet* and looked to the area he'd spotted from the ground.

It looks like I'd been right, he thought, examining the beasts wandering around below.

A small flock of sheep was wandering around the clearing, and standing in the center was a massive ram.

Sarah's eyes tracked him as he came down and landed next to her with a grin.

"I found the Patriarch. Looks like it's a ram, just like the other *zone*."

Sarah groaned when she heard that.

"Yet another farm animal. Why was I expecting anything else?"

Morgan shrugged.

"You can stay here if you want. I'll be more than happy to take the core for myself."

"Not a chance!" Sarah said, placing her hands on her hips. "We had a deal. I agreed to take a break from traveling and come into a *beast zone* with you, so long as you gave me the Patriarch's core!"

"Keep your pants on, I haven't forgotten," Morgan said with a dismissive wave.

It had been a challenging few days since they'd left the academy, and he'd thought coming into a beast zone to unwind would do them some good. The only problem was that Sarah had refused. Offering her the Patriarch's core was the only way he'd gotten her to agree to join him, and now he was regretting it.

"Well then, let's go," she said, marching out in front of him once more, and heading in the direction he'd indicated.

Morgan stared after her for a moment, then sighed and followed after her.

This was going to be fun.

2

The ram and his flock of sheep soon came into view and Sarah came to a halt at the edge of his territory. The ram wouldn't attack them, so long as they didn't step out of the grass, which Morgan found quite strange.

The ram could clearly see them, so why wasn't it attacking?

"How strong do you think the ram will be?" Sarah asked, tightening a few straps on her uniform.

"Well, the last few times, the Patriarch or Matriarch was *2 ranks* higher than the other beasts, so maybe *rank 14*?"

"It's going to be a tough fight if it is, especially seeing as the sheep surrounding it will likely all be at *rank 12*."

Morgan snorted out a laugh and Sarah raised an eyebrow at him.

"Sorry. I just never thought that a conversation like this would ever come up," he said, gesturing to the gathered sheep.

Sarah flashed him a grin then, and the two of them prepared their plan of attack.

"I think the best course would be for you to use your new skill to start off," Morgan began. "As soon as the attack hits, I'll move in for an all-out attack. The sheep will probably go down pretty quickly, but the ram will be trouble. Try and slow it down. Maybe pin it in place. As soon as the sheep are dealt with, we'll hit the ram together. It's likely going to be at least *5 ranks* higher than us, so let's try and act before it can use its ability."

Sarah thought on that for a second.

"Do you really think it's a good idea for me to use my new skill now? If I do, I won't have access to it for the next twelve hours."

Morgan nodded.

"I think that we can move up in *rank* after this fight, so I'll finally have enough *RP* for my new extra skill."

"Alright! Let's go murder some sheep!" Sarah said, pumping her fist in the air, prompting him to flash her a grin.

Battles like this always put him in a good mood. Judging by what the ram's rank was likely to be, it would be a good fight.

He took up a fighting stance as Sarah prepared to use the new skill she'd acquired at *rank 9*. Her hands took on a bright blue glow. She brought them up and slammed them into the ground with a shout.

Sarah's new skill was called *icy wave* and it was devastating. A massive wave of jagged spikes spread out in a cone shape from where her hands had impacted with the ground. They covered the distance between her and the sheep in an instant and began skewering them with razor-sharp icicles.

Morgan watched in fascination as one sheep after the next was heavily injured, or outright killed.

Now it was his turn.

Using a whopping *350 RP* Morgan activated *wind blade*. He'd dismissed his earlier one, which in hindsight, wasn't very well thought out. He was then forced to wait for his *RP* to regenerate, then activated it again. His arms snapped to the sides, and two swirling purple blades formed from the air around him. Gravity further compressed them until they were as solid as any blades made of steel.

He'd chosen to go with slashing blades because the ram was likely using a super ability. The blades also cut through the tough wool better than the piercing blade did.

He then used *heavy impact* and *gale force* at the same time. His already diminished *RP* began to plummet at an alarming rate, but all he needed were a few seconds. Morgan braced himself, then launched forward, activating his last skill- *enhanced flight*.

His massive upsurge in both *strength* and *agility,* coupled with his *flight* skill, propelled Morgan forward at an incredible speed. He covered the distance in a flash, making sure to keep his legs well clear of the icy spikes below him and lashed out with a powerful attack.

He sliced through the trapped sheep with the whirling blades of air coated in reiki, making it almost too easy. In just a few seconds, he'd managed to kill every single sheep in the clearing. He grimaced, deactivating his *gale force* and *heavy impact*, then quickly flew back to Sarah, who was trying to hold off an angry ram and landed beside her.

"How's your *MP* looking?" Morgan asked as she used her *icicle barrage*, launching a mass of icy spears at their wooly assailant.

"I've got enough for a few more attacks, but I'll be completely done after that. How about you?"

"Got almost nothing. I'll be fighting with just these," he said, waving the two blades in the air and grinning.

"If I didn't know any better, I'd say you were enjoying this!" she yelled, as the ram finally broke free of the ice and came charging at them.

"I am!" Morgan exclaimed.

Then he activated his version of the mage shield.

Unlike Sarah's, which was made of mana, his was made of reiki. So instead of the usual blue color one expected when seeing a mage shield, Morgan's was a deep purple.

Because of this, he hadn't really been able to use it much, as it would be a dead giveaway as to what he was. Now he could use it without fear of being caught, and he was excited to see what it could do.

The ram glowed an angry red as it used its ability, then it pawed at the ground and charged. Morgan met it head on, running straight at the charging monster - who was nearly as tall as him - with wild abandon.

This was what he lived for. The thrill of the fight, the excitement of facing new enemies, and the opportunity to grow stronger.

The ram slammed into him at full force and Morgan's breath exploded out of him as his shield buckled under the force. He grinned as the ram impacted against him, and he brought his blades across its throat in a pincer attack, slashing through the wool and partway into the skin, but not deep enough to finish it.

Morgan flew through the air, managing to catch himself with his *flight* skill before he hit the ground, and righted himself. He looked over to the ram, who looked both perplexed and annoyed that it hadn't managed to kill him. That was its last mistake.

A massive barrage of icy spears suddenly slammed into the side of its head, and within a few seconds, the ram lay dead. Morgan let out an annoyed sigh and let his shield flicker out.

Aaron Oster

Of course, Sarah would have to steal his fun. Why did she always need to do that?

She jogged over to him and flashed a wide grin as he dismissed his *wind blades*.

"We did it!"

"Yeah, we did it," Morgan said, unenthusiastically.

"Oh, come on. Don't get all pouty on me because I killed the ram in one attack when you couldn't," Sarah said, patting his cheek and laughing. "I think you owe me after treating me to that shower of chicken guts earlier."

Morgan just nodded, turning his attention to the carcasses of the dead beasts.

"Let's see what we got." He said, walking over to the first of the sheep.

He retrieved the core and opened his status to view it.

Name: Steelwool-sheep core
Rank - 12
Total available energy: 2,009/2,009

This core was taken from a steelwool-sheep. As this core was taken from an evolved beast, the amount of available energy has been slightly increased.

At least the energy from the sheep wasn't too bad.

Morgan closed his status and saw Sarah examining the Patriarch's core with a look of delight. He walked over to her as she closed her status and raised a questioning eyebrow.

"See for yourself," she said, handing him the core and walking towards the other sheep corpses. "Just remember that I've already checked how much energy there is. Don't go taking any for yourself."

Morgan opened the core's status and gasped.

Name: Steelwool-ram Patriarch core
Rank - 14
Total available energy: 5,611/5,611

This core was taken from a steelwool-ram. As this core was taken from a zone Patriarch, and an evolved beast, the amount of available energy has been slightly increased.

What the hell? How did this beast give so much energy?!

He closed his status and looked over to Sarah, who twiddled her fingers at him and gave him a wink.

Morgan grimaced as he walked over to another one of the sheep corpses.

That was the last time he'd let her have the core without a fight.

It took them another few minutes to finish collecting the cores, and by then, Morgan was well and truly ready to leave.

Sarah pulled the key from the small leather bag that held all their possessions and opened a portal back to their world.

3

Walking through the portal, Morgan stepped into the utter darkness of the cave where they'd made camp for the evening. Sarah stepped out behind him, cursing lightly as she stumbled into him and nearly fell.

He heard her rummaging around for a few moments before a bright light flared, illuminating the small cavern. Morgan turned and saw her clutching a small lantern in one hand as she rummaged around in the bag. A few moments later, she produced another and placed it on the ground.

The cave was small, barely ten feet deep, but the entrance was well hidden by a small clump of bushes, making this the ideal camping spot until nightfall.

Despite their escape from the academy, there was still a war raging on between the North and Central Kingdoms. From what they'd heard, King Herald had returned from his diplomatic mission and was now leading the war effort to push the North back. The academy had become a ruin and refugees were fleeing to the South and East. There were patrols of soldiers that would pass by every once in a while, and if they ran across the wrong ones they'd likely be killed without a second thought.

"I'll go check outside for the time," Morgan said, stretching and walking over to the low entrance of the cave and peeked out.

The light outside the cave was dimming, but it wasn't yet fully dark, meaning it was likely around six or so in the evening. Another hour and it would be fully dark.

He slid back into the cave and saw Sarah taking off her boots and beginning to work at the straps on the side of her shirt.

That was good. Despite washing herself off in the beast zone, she was still covered in blood, and it would likely start to stink in a few hours.

Morgan began walking over to sit down when Sarah turned to glare at him.

"What?" he asked, reaching into his pockets and fishing out a few cores.

"I'm changing."

Morgan shrugged. "I've changed in front of you plenty of times." He rummaged around for another moment before he came out with the core he'd been looking for.

When Sarah didn't immediately reply, Morgan looked up from what he'd been doing and saw her standing there with a sickly sweet smile on her face.

Oh crap. He knew that look.

"Morgan?" she asked in a terrifyingly calm voice.

"Yes?" he asked nervously, wondering what he could possibly have done to upset her this time.

"Unless you'd like an ice bath, you will leave. *Now.*"

The two stared at each other for a few moments, she with a smile plastered across her face and him, with a look of incredulity.

"I don't understand what the big deal is…" Morgan tried to say but was forced to roll to the side when a ball of freezing water came flying at his head.

"I'm leaving! I'm leaving!" he yelled, diving to the side once again, then ducking quickly out of the open cave mouth.

The moment after he left, a block of ice formed over the entrance, sealing it shut.

What was with this girl?! A group of soldiers could have been passing by!

Morgan quickly looked around, making sure he hadn't been spotted. They were pretty close to the border between the Central and East Kingdoms and planned to go over the wall tonight. It wouldn't do to get caught now, not when they were so close to escaping.

Not spotting anyone, he let out a sigh of relief and sat down inside the bushes near the cave. He fished the core out of his pocket once more and turned it over in his fingers.

He really hoped he'd gotten enough training since his last rank up. It would suck to gain fewer attribute points because he hadn't put in the correct amount of work.

Steeling himself, Morgan opened the core's status and assigned the energy. A shiver ran through him as he felt himself *rank up,* and the core crumbled to dust between his fingers.

This rank up hadn't felt like any of the previous ones he'd had before unlocking his supermage ability. It felt a thousand times better. Like the feeling of eating all the best food, sleeping in the

Aaron Oster

most comfortable bed, and fighting the most dangerous beast, all at once.

Morgan grinned to himself, basking in the after effects of the *rank up*. It faded after a few seconds, leaving him feeling oddly relaxed.

Now for the moment of truth. He had to see if he'd been correct.

Morgan opened his status and looked over the changes from the previous *rank*.

> *Name: Morgan*
> *Supermage: Rank - 10*
> *Energy to next rank - 5,889/20,000*
> *Ability - Divine Gravity & Air*
> *RP - 610/610 (Regen - 6.0 per second)*
> *Strength - 57*
> *Agility - 68*
> *Constitution - 60*
> *Intelligence - 61*
> *Wisdom - 60*
> *Skills - Enhanced flight, Heavy impact, Gale force, Condensed wind blade*
> *Traits - Gravity field, Recovery*
> *Extra - Gravity storm*

So he'd been right. All of his attributes had increased by 3 or 4 since rank 9.

Next, he opened his skills tab to see if there had been any changes.

> *Skills:*
>
> *Enhanced flight - Manipulate gravity and air to reduce your weight and move quickly through the air.*
> *Cost - 10 RP per second*
> *Max. height - 60 Ft*
> *Max. speed - 40 Ft per second*
> *Max. carry weight - 200 pounds (Adding any more weight will reduce speed by 1 foot per second for each additional pound).*

Heavy impact - Manipulate gravity and air to make your blows land significantly harder (Currently X2.25).
Cost - 15 RP per second

Condensed wind blade - Manipulate gravity and air to create a dense whirling blade in the shape of your choice. The type of weapon you create will determine additional effects.
Piercing weapon - Double damage is dealt to mages, or beasts with mage abilities.
Slashing weapon - Double damage is dealt to supers, or beasts with super abilities.
Cost - 350 RP
Duration - Until dismissed

Gale force - Manipulate gravity and air to significantly increase your speed (Currently X2.25).
Cost - 15 RP per second

So no changes. That was surprising to him, considering the way his skills had kept improving when he'd previously ranked up. Maybe this was normal. He would have to ask Sarah once she ranked up just to be sure.

He opened his traits tab next.

Traits:

Gravity field - Your body is surrounded by a dense field of gravity, making all attacks- both physical and magical- 10% less damaging.

Recovery - The spirits of the air have blessed you with the power of healing. If you can survive for 24 hours after being wounded; no matter the injury, your body will be completely healed.

Once again, there were no changes. Perhaps now that he'd gotten past rank 9 they wouldn't change until he ranked up again?

Morgan moved on to the last tab, and the one he was most excited to check.

Aaron Oster

Extra:

Gravity storm - Create a storm of intense gravity, damaging winds, and lighting in a targeted area.
Cost - 600 RP
AOE - 30 Ft
Duration - 30 seconds
Cooldown - 8 hours

Morgan could have jumped for joy.

He had done it! He could now - if only just barely - use his new extra skill. He couldn't wait to try it out on someone, but he would have to be careful when using it. From the way it sounded, gravity storm would be an extremely showy skill, so unless it was life or death, he would only use it in a beast zone. Not to mention the ridiculous cost, as well as the 8-hour cooldown.

Morgan heard a slight cracking sound off to his right and closed his status. A moment later, the ice blocking the entrance exploded outward, showering him in bits of ice and freezing water.

Sarah walked out, dressed in a clean uniform and looking quite happy. Her long red hair was slightly damp and fell loosely down her back, out of its customary braid. Her green eyes sparkled in the dimming light and her cheeks had a rosy tinge to them. Judging by her appearance, Morgan could only guess that she'd doused herself with her own icy cold water and shivered at the thought.

He'd been on the receiving end of Sarah's impromptu baths more than once, and he didn't relish those memories. At all.

"What are you doing?" she asked, walking over and taking a seat next to him.

"Just finished *ranking up*," he answered, brushing bits of ice off himself. "You should probably do so as well. It'll be dark soon and we'll be making an attempt at the wall."

"So you were right?" she asked excitedly.

Morgan nodded.

"All of my attributes went up by three or four each. I know yours work a little differently than mine, but you should be good all the same."

Sarah nodded, pulling a core from the small spatial pouch Gold had provided and quickly absorbed the energy. The core crumbled to dust, and she shuddered lightly as she *ranked up* as well. The next moment, her eyes unfocused and Morgan knew she was looking at her status.

Morgan stood and walked around the cave. Peeking out from behind the large outcropping, he could just make out the road about a hundred yards away. Looking further up, the vague outline of the wall was just visible on the horizon. Squinting his eyes, Morgan could see figures moving down the road.

Most likely a group of refugees hoping to make it into the East Kingdom. Not that they would have any luck. The East began turning people away as soon as news of the war broke out. He didn't blame them. If he were the one in charge, he would likely do the same. He just wished that they would enforce these rules after they had let them through.

They'd already tried to get in the right way the day before, so now it was time to go in his way.

Morgan smiled as he imagined the smug gate guards congratulating each other of not letting them pass, while he was flying in over their heads.

Maybe he'd teach them a lesson once they'd gotten over, like having Sarah dump a bunch of water down on them.

Morgan shook his head as all these thoughts invaded his mind.

Since when had he become so petty? Maybe hanging around Sarah for this long was having a negative effect on him.

Morgan heard the sound of rustling leaves and turned to the girl in question, approaching him. Her hair was once again in a braid, and she'd even taken the time to tuck a flower into it.

"All done?" he asked, turning his attention back to the road.

The group of people he'd seen earlier was heading back this way. They'd likely been turned away by the guards and were now probably heading to the South border, in hopes of getting through there.

"What, no comment on how I look?" she asked, turning her head and giving him a smile.

Morgan honestly didn't know what to say.

He didn't know why, but she'd constantly been asking him about how she looked. At first, he'd just shrugged, then she'd get annoyed at him and walk away. Then he'd tried the opposite, telling her she looked nice, but this also seemed to annoy her, as her face would turn red and she'd walk away. There was just no winning with her, so he would just have to keep his mouth shut.

Sarah stared at him for a few more seconds before letting out an explosive breath.

"I don't even know why I bother!" she said, tearing the flower from her hair and throwing it at him.

Morgan sighed as she stomped off in a huff and he mentally added ignoring her to the list of things not to do.

Maybe next time he would ask her what she wanted him to say. This way she couldn't be mad at him if he gave the wrong answer.

Morgan nodded to himself, content that he'd found a foolproof way to avoid her ire the next time this came up.

Thankfully, Sarah's anger always seemed to pass quickly and just five minutes later she was back at his side.

The refugees had already passed and Morgan had caught a brief snatch of their conversation. Apparently, someone had tried to sneak into the East Kingdom earlier that day and the guards had killed them for it.

They really weren't messing around. If they were willing to kill instead of jailing, then the East must be taking the threat of war a lot more seriously than he'd originally thought.

"Do you think it's dark enough to go yet?" Sarah asked, snapping him out of his thoughts and back to the present.

"Yeah, I think we can risk it now," he said, bending slightly as Sarah clambered up onto his back.

"Hey, I have an idea," Sarah said, as he floated up off the ground.

"Yeah?" Morgan asked, as they rose above the treetops and angled toward the wall.

"How about I drop a bunch of freezing water on those guards as we pass over. I bet it'll be hilarious!" She shook lightly against him, giggling with suppressed mirth.

Of course.

4

Morgan took a long deep breath of the cool night air as he reached the maximum height his skill would allow. From this high up, the wall, about two miles to the east, was clearly visible by the bright moonlight.

He felt Sarah shiver and press herself tighter to him as a gust of wind buffeted them. Morgan didn't mind the wind or the cold in the slightest. Oddly enough, neither seemed to affect him at all.

It probably had something to do with his ability. He still found it interesting that Sarah, who had an ice and water ability, would be bothered by the cold.

Morgan must have been hanging there for too long without moving, because Sarah began squirming in his arms, signaling her discomfort.

They'd decided not to talk until they were well over the border wall. Sound carried far out here, and they didn't want the guards spotting them.

Morgan tightened his grip on Sarah's thighs, then shot forward, heading to the wall. The wind whistled around him as he picked up speed, approaching the border at a rapid pace and it didn't take them long to cover the two-mile gap.

Morgan could feel his pulse pounding in his ears as the wall drew near.

Just five more seconds and they would be over it. Four, three, two...

Morgan's power suddenly cut out; his momentum being halted at the same time. They hung in the air for a few heartbeats. Then, they fell out of the air, heading for a collision course with the ground, sixty feet below.

Sarah lost her grip with a panicked scream and she fell away from him, thrashing and flailing as she fell into an uncontrollable tumble.

Morgan felt his heart rate skyrocket as he fell, trying desperately to reach for his reiki.

What the hell just happened? One second he was about to cross over and the next he couldn't feel his power at all.

Morgan took a deep breath and concentrated.

Aaron Oster

No, his power hadn't been cut off, just partially suppressed. He could do this, all he needed to do was concentrate hard enough and…

Morgan breathed a massive sigh of relief as he felt his power flood back into him. He cast around for a few breathless moments until he spotted Sarah. She was falling off to his left and would hit the ground in just a few more seconds.

He had to act fast. The wall was most likely the reason for his skill being suppressed, so if he got far enough away, he should regain full use of it.

Grunting with effort, Morgan forced himself back and away from the wall. The process took less than a handful of seconds, but with Sarah's life on the line, it felt much longer. Finally, he got far enough away to feel his reiki completely once more. He turned on the spot and used *gale force*, then plummeted towards the ground at more than twice his normal speed.

He saw Sarah, face white with fear, now just thirty feet from impact with the ground. Redoubling his effort, Morgan poured on more speed, as he rushed to catch her before it was too late. Out of the corner of his eye, he spotted movement as border guards began streaming onto the wall. A few of them took shots at him with their various skills, but he was moving too quickly for them to hit.

Morgan pushed harder as he rapidly closed the distance, but the ground was rushing up at an alarming rate, and he wasn't even sure he could pull out of the dive in time once he did catch her. Then Sarah's eyes landed on him and she seemed to calm somewhat. She spread out her arms and legs, stabilizing herself and slowing her fall just enough for Morgan to finally catch her.

She wrapped her arms around his neck as he scooped her out of the air, pulling herself tightly to him. As soon as his arms tightened around her, Morgan cut off his *gale-force* skill and tried to pull out of the dive. He fought desperately for control, but he was still moving way too fast, and the ground was just a few feet away.

Gritting his teeth, Morgan used his *heavy impact*, then flipped in the air so he'd hit the ground feet first. Next, he used his supermage shield, despite the risk that they'd be seen. The wind shrieked around him as he fell, and Morgan gritted his teeth and prepared for the impact.

This was not going to be pleasant.

Morgan crashed into the ground, thrusting his legs down as hard as he could to try and counteract the momentum of his fall. It worked, in the sense that both he and Sarah survived.

Morgan plowed into the ground, his supermage shield instantly shattering, and leaving an impact crater five feet across. He grunted in pain as both his legs snapped, and he lost his grip on Sarah as they both went tumbling, and bouncing along the ground until the momentum of his fall was all used up.

Morgan gritted his teeth against the overwhelming pain.

His legs felt as though a thousand hot needles had been shoved into them, and someone was trying to pull them out by pushing them clean through.

Sarah was at his side in an instant. She had a bloody scrape across her forehead but otherwise looked to be unhurt. She took one look down at his legs and winced.

"That bad?" Morgan asked with a pained smile.

There was a loud shout from the direction of the wall and Sarah spun, using her *condense water* skill to form a wall between them.

Despite the agonizing pain in his legs and just about everywhere else, Morgan had to admire how much stronger she'd become with the skill since her *rank up*. The *condense water* skill hadn't changed when she'd broken through into *rank 9*, rather her control of the skill was what had changed. She could now summon vastly more water then she could previously and controlling it cost quite a bit less.

Sarah squatted down next to him as attacks began hitting her ice wall.

"We have to leave now! I know you're in pain, but can you fly?"

Morgan tried to concentrate through the agonizing pain and managed to rise an inch or so off the ground before he fell back down.

"Guess I'll have to carry you then," she said, taking a quick look at her ice wall as another attack slammed into it. "I won't be able to carry you on my back with the way your legs are, so I'll need you to get at least a few inches off the ground."

Morgan's vision was starting to become hazy as the adrenaline wore off and the pain began to really set in. He shook his head and nodded, concentrating as best he could to get off the ground.

After a few more tense seconds, he managed to shakily hover about half a foot off the ground.

"That's good," she said, grabbing his arm and pulling it over her shoulder. Next, she got a grip on the inside of one of his legs and straightened from the crouch.

The position was far from comfortable, as his frame was hoisted over Sarah's narrow shoulders, but there really was no other way. She adjusted her grip and Morgan winced as her hand aggravated the injury.

"Hold on tight. There's an inn we passed not too far from here. I'll try to get us there as quickly as I can."

Morgan grunted in reply and Sarah took that as a confirmation. She tightened her grip once more, then took off running down the road, and away from the border wall.

***

Arnold was in a sour mood.

He felt like this was becoming his default over the last few months, and he could trace all his misfortune back to the day that he'd accepted the mission to retrieve Sarah for Lord Simon. Now here he was, somehow caught up in a conspiracy to overthrow the king.

Arnold snorted, getting the attention of the small group of soldiers he was traveling with. One of the men gave him a questioning look, but he just waved him off.

He'd been traveling with this particular group of men for the last week and a half. They were heading for the South Kingdom border in the hopes of catching Morgan there. The soldiers didn't know why they were on this mission, and Princess Katherine had threatened him with severe bodily harm if they should find out.

He shivered at the memory of how angry she'd been when he'd told her of Grub's escape.

He'd been sure she'd kill him for it, but apparently, she still needed him to track Morgan down. She'd sent men out after Grub, but he'd left on his mission before they'd returned. He highly doubted that they'd find him, so it was more than likely that his only chance of living to see another year would be to find Morgan and persuade him to meet with her.

She'd been very specific not to force it. She wanted her future husband to view her favorably, so she'd tasked him with making him an offer he couldn't refuse.

Arnold growled lightly as he thought of the ill-fated day when he'd agreed to take that job.

He technically hadn't yet completed it, seeing as Sarah was still on the run. But he was hoping to kill two birds with one stone. Bring Morgan to the Princess and get Sarah back to her father. He would likely be furious that it took him this long, but at least his life would no longer be at risk. At least from Simon.

A light tap on his shoulder snapped him from his thoughts, and he turned to see a group of refugees heading their way.

He was now happy that he'd insisted on dressing in peasant clothes. It would be much easier to glean information if they weren't dressed in the colors of an invading army.

He had his men slow their pace. He slumped his shoulders, taking on the appearance of a travel-weary group who was trying to escape the war. Their decreased pace meant that the two groups didn't actually meet up for another ten minutes or so, but this gave Arnold the time to run over his back story in case they asked any questions.

The two groups stopped within a few paces of one another and Arnold plastered on his best fake friendly smile.

"Greetings to you. Have you any news of the goings on at the border?" he asked, making sure to pitch his voice higher and take on a more Central accent.

"If you're trying to escape into the East Kingdom, you're out of luck, my friend," the man returned with a sad shake of his head. "They're turning everyone away and killing those who try to get in."

He let out a long sigh and motioned to the group behind him.

"I was hoping to get the family out of the kingdom as soon as possible, but now it looks like we'll have to try for the South instead."

Arnold nodded along with the man, plastering a look of concern on his face as he listened to the old man's complaints.

He couldn't care less about the old geezer's griping, but if he had any information, it would be worth it.

Aaron Oster

"So they're turning everyone away? They haven't let anyone in? Not even citizens, or those with the correct paperwork?"

The old man cleared his throat and hacked up a lungful of phlegm. He spat the nasty glob to the side and Arnold had to resist the urge to cut the man in half for the disgusting behavior.

"Nope, not a single person was let through in the last week. You'd best turn around and head to the South. That'd be your best bet."

Arnold pretended to think about that for a moment. His mind was racing with the possibility of finding his quarry, without the need for a long and exhausting chase.

If no one would be allowed in, that meant that Morgan and Sarah would still be in the Central Kingdom. They'd likely already tried for the walls and failed, so where would they be now?

"I thank you for your advice, friend," Arnold said, giving him his best weary smile. "But my friends and I have been traveling for over a week without rest. Do you perhaps know of an inn nearby where we might rest our heads before heading south?"

"Yeah, there's an inn not two days down the road. They'll probably charge an arm and a leg, but it's the only one for miles around."

"Thank you for the information. It was most welcome," he said, turning back to his group and motioning them forward.

"If I were you, I'd skip the inn and head straight south. I hear that the North is circling around this way to try and flank King Herald. It might be too late if you don't go now."

Arnold had to suppress a grin.

There were no Northern troops heading this way. That had just been a rumor he'd asked Katherine to spread to get people out of the area. It had only been a hunch, but he was glad to see that it hadn't been in vain.

"I appreciate your concern, but we are much too weary to continue. We can always hold up at the inn if it gets too bad."

"Suit yourself," the man said with a shrug and spitting once more.

Arnold nodded to the man, then walked past him and continued down the road.

Starbreak

The chances that they were in that inn were very high- if what the disgusting man said was to be believed. Especially if no one was being allowed into the East Kingdom.

Arnold felt a grin tugging at the corners of his mouth for the first time in weeks.

It was about time things worked out for him.

5

Morgan groaned, waking from a troubled sleep and sat up in his bed. A small candle flickered on a nightstand, and beyond that was a small window, thrown open to the cool night air. He was confused for a few moments as he looked around the small, comfortable looking room until his brain caught up with what he was seeing.

He was likely in the inn that Sarah had mentioned before he'd passed out from the pain in his legs. He wasn't sure how she'd managed to explain away a severely injured person slung over her shoulders.

Morgan was rudely snapped out of his thoughts as his legs throbbed painfully once again. Pulling the covers to the side, he winced, seeing the damage he'd managed to inflict on himself. His pants were torn and bloodied, covering up the horribly mangled limbs beneath. Both his legs had swollen up, making removing the pants all but impossible, and Morgan was secretly glad about that.

He'd known that something like this would likely happen, but he was just fine not being able to see the extent of the damage.

He quickly pulled the covers over his legs and leaned back against the wall. Looking over to the side, he saw Sarah passed out in a chair near the bed. Her mouth was wide open and a small line of drool had worked its way down her chin.

In the light of the early morning, he could see that she was a lot more banged up than he'd originally thought. Aside from the scrape on her face, her uniform had torn in several places and he could see bits of steel thread poking through.

He must have hit the ground harder than he'd thought if the tough uniforms had been shredded they way they had. He was just glad to be alive.

He winced as his legs throbbed painfully again and he closed his eyes, trying his best not to concentrate on them.

With his recovery trait, his body should be fully healed by around eight o'clock that night. At least, that's what he hoped. He'd gotten a few bruises and cuts since awakening his supermage ability, but he hadn't yet injured himself this badly. Then again, this could be a blessing in disguise. Better to find out now if it would work, rather than when they were in more dire straits.

There was one upside to this entire mess, though. As soon as he healed, he could likely rank up again and not lose any attribute points. That fall had probably saved him a good week of hard work.

He opened his eyes as he felt the bed shift under him, to see that Sarah had slumped forward and was now lying partially on the bed, still fast asleep. Morgan stared down at her sleeping form for a few seconds, watching the gentle rise and fall of her back.

He wondered why she hadn't gotten into the bed with him. There was plenty of room and that chair really didn't look very comfortable.

Morgan pondered over this for a few minutes until an answer presented itself to him.

Of course! He'd been injured and she was afraid of jostling him in the night!

He smiled to himself, glad that he'd figured it out. He was figuring a lot of things out since he became a supermage.

It most likely had to do with his increased intelligence, that he was becoming so good at social interactions. In fact…

Morgan concentrated for a moment, then levitated a few inches off the bed. The pain had abated somewhat and he was able to concentrate enough to move through the air. As gently as he could manage, Morgan slipped his arms under Sarah's sleeping form. Then he floated up a bit higher and drifted back to the bed.

It only took him a minute to have Sarah arranged comfortably on the bed and he nodded to himself once more.

Sarah would be very happy that he'd been so thoughtful. She might not even yell at him for getting hurt the way he did when she woke up. Not that he really understood why she got angry at all. He was the one who'd gotten hurt, not her, but for some odd reason, she always did get angry.

Morgan drifted over to his side of the bed and pulled the blanket to cover her as well. He watched as she curled up a bit and pulled the blanket up to her chin.

Yup! He'd definitely done the right thing.

With that thought in mind, Morgan closed his eyes and went back to sleep.

***

Six years ago…

Sarah was very excited. It was the day of her tenth birthday, and her father was finally allowing her to leave the manor and explore the city!

She'd never been to the city before.

She bounced out of her bed and went running down the halls to her parents' bedchambers and began banging on the doors.

"Daddy! Mommy! It's my birthday!"

One of the manor maids came rushing down the halls at the commotion and spotted Sarah immediately.

"Lady Sarah! Stop that this instant."

Sarah turned away from the door, as grouchy old Millicent came striding down the halls.

She didn't like Millicent. Millicent was mean.

But even Millicent's angry face couldn't ruin her good mood.

"It's my birthday, and I wanted to tell my parents how excited I am to go into the city!" she said with a wide grin.

Millicent tut-tutted, and took her firmly by the arm, and began pulling her back to her room.

"Well, you can't tell them. They've gone away on business and won't be back until this evening."

Sarah felt her face fall, and her good mood melted away.

Of course, they weren't here; they never were.

"Can I still go into the city?" she asked, eyes beginning to water.

"Absolutely not!" Millicent said. "The city is no place for a woman of nobility. You will stay inside and study."

"But I don't want to study," Sarah whined, feeling her heart sink even more, as all the plans for her birthday vanished in a puff of smoke.

"What's going on here?"

They both stopped as Hint, Sarah's personal guard, came walking through a door, holding a tray stacked high with blueberry pancakes- Sarah's favorite breakfast.

"I wanted to go into the city today, but grumpy old Millicent won't let me!" Sarah exclaimed.

"Young lady…!" Millicent began, but Hint was quick to cut her off.

"You may go now, Millicent. It is her birthday after all, and her parents did promise to allow her out today."

Millicent looked between Sarah and Hint, clearly having trouble with the order. Hint technically outranked her. As Sarah's personal guard, he had the final say on all matters when her parents weren't around.

Finally, she huffed to herself and released Sarah's arm.

"This isn't over, young lady. You will work twice as hard tomorrow to make up for today's missed lessons!"

Then she marched off, back stiff as a board and shoes clicking noisily on the hardwood floor.

The two of them watched her disappear down the hallway, then Sarah turned to Hint with a huge smile.

"Thank you!" she said, running at him and wrapping her arms around his waist.

"Whoa! Easy there!" he said with a laugh. "You'll make me drop your breakfast."

Sarah released him and began chattering animatedly about all of the things she was looking forward to seeing in the city as they made their way back to her room.

"I can see you've been planning this trip for a while," Hint said, placing the tray on a small table and setting the fork and knife down next to it.

"It's all I've been thinking about for the last year!" Sarah exclaimed, plopping down into her chair and snatching up the fork and knife.

She waited for Hint to pour the dark maple syrup over the stack, then eagerly dug in. She squeaked in delight as the first bite hit her tongue, and happily chewed while Hint set out her clothes for the day.

Sarah loved blueberry pancakes, but her excitement at finally going out made her eat just a little faster than she normally would. Within two minutes, she had cleared her entire plate and stood hiccupping as Hint held her clothes out to her.

"It really isn't good to eat so quickly, Lady Sarah," he said, shaking his head in mock disappointment. The smile on his face said otherwise and Sarah grinned back at him, snatching up her dress and dashing behind the partition to change.

Hint let out a long sigh, then set to cleaning up her plate and utensils, stacking them up neatly and leaving them by the door. He knew that the manor staff would be around to pick it up, so he didn't feel too guilty about it.

It took Sarah all of five minutes to change- an almost unheard of record, as she normally fussed and primped before the mirror for over an hour before she was satisfied.

Hint suppressed the urge to laugh at her disheveled appearance and took a few minutes to straighten her dress and fix her hair. Once he was satisfied that she looked presentable, he opened her door and she dashed out into the hallway, hopping excitedly from foot to foot.

"Come on! Come on! Let's go already!" she exclaimed, cheeks flushed red with excitement.

Hint just shook his head once more, closing Sarah's door behind her and heading down the long corridor. She kept running ahead of him, then sprinting back when he didn't arrive quickly enough, only to repeat the process as soon as she returned.

Hint let out a long sigh, wishing he had her energy. In truth, he was getting old. He was an ability user, and one of the strongest in the city, but at *rank 7*, he was never destined for long life. He was nearing his seventies, and would need to retire soon; possibly even by the end of this year.

He smiled as Sarah came dashing back for the tenth time and tried to speed him up, but he stubbornly refused; and after a moment, she dashed off again.

He just really wished she could find a friend. Life as a young noblewoman was lonely, especially with the parents she'd been stuck with; and a friend would make life bearable for her once he was gone.

His thoughts trailed off as they finally emerged from the manor and into the grounds. It was springtime, and the flowers were in full bloom around the garden. Sarah leaned down to sniff at one of them. Her nose wrinkled up and she sneezed from the nose-full of pollen she'd received.

She heard Hint chuckling from behind her and turned to stick her tongue out at him, before dashing down the path, relishing the feeling of freedom that came with being young.

She was forced to stop when she reached the manor gates and had to wait for Hint to catch up with her.

Why was he always so slow?

Hint stopped by the gate, and the guards who'd been blocking her path stepped aside to let them pass. Sarah felt her heart flutter with excitement as she finally walked through the gates and out into the cobbled courtyard that surrounded the manor.

***

Sharp pain in his leg brought Morgan out of peaceful slumber. He slowly cracked his eyes open, blinking at the almost blinding sunlight streaming in through the open window.

He felt something shift against him and pain flared from his legs once again. Groaning lightly, he tried to sit up. It was only then that he felt the weight on his chest. Looking down, he saw the top of Sarah's head just a few inches from his face. Her arm was thrown over his chest and she'd pressed herself into him. He blinked in surprise, as his sleep-addled mind finally kicked into gear.

He'd woken up in the middle of the night and seen her sleeping in a chair, so he'd moved her to the bed. But how had she gotten all the way to his side?

Morgan felt her shift a bit and winced as her knee bumped against one of his legs.

So that was what had woken him.

Morgan tried to wiggle away from her, but the more he tried to move, the tighter she clung. He could now feel every curve of her soft body against his, the lithe strength of her muscles and the soft pounding of her mana-heart.

Why did she have to be so damned heavy?

Morgan tried to shift away from her once more, but it was no good.

Sarah just wouldn't let him go.

Sighing to himself, he began prodding her lightly in an attempt to wake her.

He knew she wouldn't be happy with him waking her up. She looked quite content sleeping on top of him, but he wasn't a bed. He also didn't like the feeling of her knee poking his injured legs.

After a few moments of poking and prodding, she finally began to stir.

"Sarah, can you please move?" Morgan said in a low voice.

Sarah shifted against him, then turned her head, blinking sleepily up at him. Her hair had come out of the braid in her sleep, and it clung to her face in messy clumps. She stared at him for a few moments, squinting and trying to understand what was happening.

"Morgan?" she asked in a confused sounding voice.

"Who else would I be?" Morgan asked. "Now can you please get off me? You keep prodding my leg and it hurts enough as it is."

Sarah stared at him for a few moments more, then she seemed to realize where she was. Her eyes drifted down to see herself halfway draped over him, then she looked back up, her face going beet red.

Oh no. He knew waking her up had been a bad idea.

Sarah let out a loud squeak of alarm and practically dove out of the bed. Her eyes flicked between him and the chair she'd been sleeping in, as though trying to figure out what had happened.

Morgan noticed that the red of her face was now so dark that it nearly matched her hair.

Crap! She really wasn't a morning person.

"I.. I'm sorry... I didn't mean..." she stammered out, biting her bottom lip and looking at the ground.

This was not good. She was so mad that she couldn't even form a coherent sentence.

Morgan tried desperately to think of something to say to save himself from her wrath.

Her eyes had been flicking between the bed and the chair. Maybe he could calm her down by telling her about how thoughtful he'd been?

"I'm sorry I woke you up. I know you're probably tired from having to carry me all the way here. But I did do something nice for you, though. I woke up and saw you sleeping in the chair. It didn't look too comfortable and the bed had plenty of room, so I moved you onto it. I only woke you because you were bumping against my leg."

Sarah's head whipped up as soon as he said this and her already red face turned even redder.

"You what?!" she yelled.

Morgan jumped at the volume of her voice and was quick to try and placate her.

"I'm sorry, okay?" he said, holding his hands up in the air. "If you want, you can climb back in and go to sleep and I won't wake you up this time. You can even use me as a bed if you want!" He tried to plaster a smile on his face, but Sarah's expression made that difficult to do.

She glared at him for a few tense moments before she seemed to deflate, slumping down in the chair and rubbing at her temples.

Morgan breathed a sigh of relief when she did this, now very glad that he'd been so considerate her in the middle of the night.

Finally, she looked up at him. Her face was back to its normal color and she seemed a lot calmer.

"Why did you move me into the bed?"

Morgan blinked in surprise.

"Because you were sleeping in the chair and it didn't look comfortable."

"Of course that's why you did it," she said with a laugh, leaning back in her chair and staring up at the ceiling.

"Are you okay?" Morgan asked after a few more moments of silence.

"No, Morgan. I'm not okay," she said, sitting back up and sighing. "I just spent the entire night in bed with you and nothing happened!" She then realized what she'd just said and her face flushed a deep red once more.

Oh crap. She was getting mad again. He had to think of something quick. He was still in a precarious position from waking her up. Maybe if he asked more about it, she would think he was at least interested in whatever bedtime rituals she was referring to.

"Why? Should something have happened?" he asked, doing his best to sound interested. "I've never slept with anyone before, so I wasn't aware that I was supposed to do something."

Sarah buried her face in her hands and shook it back and forth.

"Why is this happening to me?" she groaned.

Aaron Oster

"Why is what happening to you?" Morgan asked, now very confused as to what was going on.

Sarah let out a long, exasperated breath before straightening in her seat and brushing a loose strand of hair out of her eyes.

"Nothing," she said tiredly, rising from her chair and heading to the door. "I'm going to go take a bath and get some breakfast. I'll be back soon."

And with that, she walked out, leaving a very confused Morgan staring after her.

After a few moments, he shrugged to himself.

Who knew why Sarah did the things she did?

He stared up at the ceiling for a few moments, feeling his eyes beginning to close. Then he abruptly forced them to open as a thought popped into his mind.

He'd been meaning to rank up.

Morgan quickly manipulated his reiki and opened his status.

Name: Morgan
Supermage: Rank - 10
Energy to next rank - 5,889/20,000
Ability - Divine Gravity & Air
RP - 610/610 (Regen - 6.0 per second)
Strength - 57
Agility - 68
Constitution - 60
Intelligence - 61
Wisdom - 60
Skills - Enhanced flight, Heavy impact, Gale force,
Condensed wind blade
Traits - Gravity field, Recovery
Extra - Gravity storm

Morgan nodded to himself, then reached down to his pants pocket to retrieve a core. He winced as his fingers brushed over the swollen lumps of flesh. He tried, unsuccessfully, to get the core out for the next few minutes, but to no avail.

He debated tearing the pants even further, but as soon as he began tugging on the material, he was forced to stop, as pain shot through his ruined legs once more. Finally, Morgan gave up. He closed his status and leaned back against the backrest.

Being injured sucked. Big time.

6

Morgan's eyes opened as he heard a soft knock at the door.

"Come in," he called out, yawning widely and sitting up in bed.

He'd fallen back asleep shortly after Sarah had left. Apparently, being horribly injured was exhausting.

He could no longer feel his legs, which was quite alarming- to say the least. He really hoped his recovery trait would fix them. If it didn't, he'd likely be crippled for life, which was something that he didn't even want to consider at the moment.

The door opened slowly to reveal Sarah, dressed in a clean uniform and carrying a tray laden with food. Her long red hair hung loosely down her back and her canvas uniform clung tightly to her body in several areas, meaning she'd just recently finished bathing.

Morgan breathed a sigh of relief when he noticed these particular details.

If she was bringing him breakfast so soon after taking a bath, it meant that she was no longer angry with him for waking her.

Sure enough, she flashed him a brilliant smile as she walked in, bumping the door closed with her hip as she did so.

He smiled back as she walked over and placed the tray on the bed near him.

"How are you feeling?" she asked, sitting down in the chair next to the bed.

Morgan shrugged, eyeing the food hungrily.

"Oh, go ahead," she said with a light laugh.

She could hardly blame him for being hungry after all that had happened.

Morgan nodded his thanks, then picked up a large sausage, placed it between two thick slices of bread and dug in.

Sarah watched him, frowning a bit, as he tore into the food, wondering at his odd personality.

On the one hand, he was hardened from his life on the streets and had likely seen more violence than most would see in their entire lives. He could make snap decisions, like he had last night, and could keep a cool head even in the direst of situations.

On the other hand, he was completely ignorant of the social aspects of everyday life. The whole sleeping in bed with her thing was a prime example of that. At first, she'd just thought that his hard life had stunted his growth, but she'd been trying everything she knew for the last couple of years, and nothing had worked.

She'd thought that once they spent more time alone, she could crack through his shell, and get some sort of response from him. Suffice it to say, she hadn't succeeded. At this point, she was beginning to wonder if there might be something seriously wrong with him…

"What? I'm hungry."

Sarah jerked in surprise, snapped from her thoughts, and found that she'd been staring at him the entire time.

"Sorry," she said with a grin. "Just got lost in thought and didn't realize I was staring."

Morgan nodded, taking another bite of the sausage she'd brought and washing it down with a mug of juice.

"So what do we do now?" he asked, mouth still half full of food.

"I don't know," Sarah said, slumping a bit in her chair. "Clearly, we won't be able to make it into the East Kingdom. What happened last night just proves how willing they are to kill people who try and sneak in."

Morgan nodded, chewing thoughtfully as he digested this.

He was impressed with whatever had been done to the wall. He hadn't even been aware that there was a way to suppress someone's abilities. He was just thankful that it had only partially worked on him, otherwise both he and Sarah would be dead right now. Supermage or not, he didn't like his chances of surviving a sixty-foot fall without the use of his abilities.

"I also don't think we should stick around here for too much longer," Sarah continued. "I heard a rumor that the North is sending soldiers here to try and flank Herald."

"So what do you think our best option would be?" he asked, popping the last bit of sausage into his mouth and chewing slowly.

"I think that our best option would be to head to the South. From what I've heard, they're allowing refugees through, but only if they have the correct paperwork. Still, I'm sure getting the papers shouldn't be too difficult and if we can't get them legally, we can always bribe someone."

"Yeah, you're probably right," Morgan said, leaning back in bed with a sigh. "I just wish we could have made it in. It'll be hard to find Gold if we're not where he's expecting us to be."

He yawned then, suddenly feeling very tired and his eyes began drooping.

Sarah noticed this and stood from her chair, picking up the tray and giving him a concerned look.

"You're tired. I'm guessing that it has something to do with the skill that's healing you. Go back to sleep. I'll try and gather more information in the meantime."

Morgan nodded gratefully to her, then slumped down under the covers and promptly fell back asleep.

She watched him for a few moments, noting the rise and fall of his chest and the way his long brown hair framed his face. She sighed, reaching out to smooth some of it away.

He really needed to get it cut. Maybe she would offer to do it for him once he woke up.

She smiled to herself at the thought and left the room, closing it lightly behind her and leaving Morgan to his rest.

***

Six years ago…

"Where are we going first?" she asked, as they crossed the courtyard and began walking to the mouth of a narrow alley at a leisurely pace.

"I thought the main market would be a good place to start. There are lots of people, good food, and plenty of clothing shops around," he said, winking at her conspiratorially and lowering his voice.

"I even heard that there might be a puppet show."

Sarah's eyes went wide when she heard that.

She'd heard of puppet shows. They were supposed to be very funny and full of colorful characters. She really hoped that she'd get to see it.

Starbreak

As they walked down the alley, Sarah became aware of a low buzzing sound that was growing louder by the second.

"What's that noise?" she asked, as the end of the alley came into sight.

"That, Lady Sarah, is the sound of a crowd," Hint replied.

When they emerged from the narrow alley, Sarah stared around in amazement.

There were people everywhere she looked.

Walking down the busy street, stopping by stalls to purchase goods, or just chatting amicably by the side of the road. Children ran around their parents' feet, laughing as they played their games, and merchants shouted their wares for all the world to hear.

It was loud, filthy and one of the most chaotic scenes Sarah had ever seen, and she loved it!

She dashed forward, crossing the busy street, forcing Hint to rush after her. She stopped in front of the first vendor she saw; a woman selling apples.

"Can I get you anything dear?" she asked, giving Sarah a smile.

Sarah wasn't especially hungry, but the idea of buying something at a market was so exciting that she asked Hint to buy her an apple.

He obliged, and a few moments later, the two of them set off down the busy street once more, a shiny apple clutched between Sarah's fingers.

They stopped at several more stalls, Sarah insisting on buying something at each. Soon Hint was carrying an assortment of goods, ranging from a loaf of bread to a carrot.

"Sarah, don't you think we've bought quite enough food?" Hint asked, in a slightly exasperated tone as they stopped at yet another food stall.

The vendor glared at him as Sarah turned away from his assortment of beets and turnips, but Hint ignored the man.

"We really should move on from the marketplace," he said, shifting the load in his arms. "There are quite a few shops filled with *useful* items we can buy, just down the street."

Sarah looked forlornly back at the assortment of stalls but nodded. She could always come back later.

Aaron Oster

As they left the marketplace, Sarah became aware of a commotion coming from further down the street. There were several people gathered together up ahead, and all of them were cheering for something.

Sarah, predictably, was intrigued and dashed ahead of Hint to see what the commotion was all about.

"Sarah, wait up! It could be dangerous!" Hint called after her, but she ignored him.

They were in the city. What could possibly happen to her here?

She reached the ring of people and began squeezing her way to the front of the crowd. They grumbled as she moved past them but otherwise ignored her, keeping their eyes locked ahead. Finally managing to reach the front of the crowd, Sarah looked on in confusion.

Was this what all the people were excited for?

Three boys stood in the center of the gathered crowd, two of them facing the third. All the boys were covered in shallow cuts and bruises, and one of them seemed to be favoring his left leg.

Sarah wrinkled her nose in distaste. The boys were all filthy and unkempt, and she could smell them from where she was standing. She was about to turn away when the two boys ran at the third one and the crowd began cheering again.

It was only once the first punch was thrown that Sarah realized that this was a fight. She stared as the larger two boys began attacking the smaller one, each throwing punches into his scrawny body. Sarah winced as she heard the slap of flesh on flesh, and was sure the smaller boy would go down but to her utter shock, the boy began laughing.

Then, he struck back and Sarah held her breath as the laughing boy began to execute the most amazing display of fighting skill she'd ever seen. True, she hadn't seen much fighting, but she knew enough to know that this boy was something else.

He deftly dodged a wild swing from the taller of the two boys. His knee came up and caught the boy between his legs. The crowd collectively winced as the bigger boy fell to the ground, groaning in pain, though Sarah couldn't figure out why.

The shorter of the pair- yet still significantly taller than the shortest boy- ran toward him, yelling at the top of his lungs. He began throwing a flurry of punches, all of which the small boy dodged. She heard him laughing again, as the large boy began to tire, then with his eyes flashing almost manically, began to hit back. His small fist cracked into the boy's nose, making him cry out and stagger backward, clutching at his face. Then he spun in place, bringing his leg up, kicking him hard in the stomach. The boy went sprawling and landed on his back. The smallest boy landed on him and pummeled him until he stopped moving.

Sarah's eyes went wide, as she thought the boy had killed him, but when he stepped away, she could see the prone boy's chest rising and falling. Then, a flicker of movement caught Sarah's eye, and she turned to see the first boy, getting slowly to his feet. He was clutching something in his hand and ran at the smaller boy.

"Look out!" Sarah cried, as the object the boy was holding glinted in the sunlight.

The boy turned, and Sarah got her first good look at his features. He was young, probably around her age. His face was pale and thin, his cheeks were sunken and his body was quite scrawny, but that wasn't what held her attention.

It was his eyes. Two burning pools of brilliant silver. They were so intense and so full of life! Sarah felt her heart skip a beat, as those eyes landed on her for a second, before turning back to the fight at hand.

The other boy lunged forward, the small knife stabbing out in a clumsy thrust. The silver-eyed boy stepped into the attack, smiling madly, and both of his hands came up at once. One, neatly blocking the knife, and the other catching the boy in the nose.

It wasn't a hard blow, but it was enough to momentarily stun him. The silver-eyed boy then dropped both his arms onto the other boy; one hugging the knife arm to his side, and the other landing on his shoulder. Then he yanked the other boy in, and the crowd winced again, as his knee snapped up between the large boy's legs, but this time, he didn't go down, as the other boy was still holding him tight.

The silver-eyed boy then took a half-step back and tucked his elbow against his chest. He then brought it hard across the bigger boy's face. There was a loud crack as the boy's head whipped to the side, but apparently, he still wasn't finished with him yet.

He then stepped past the boy, still keeping ahold of him, and pulled him completely off balance. Then, his leg shot forward and

Aaron Oster

swept back in a scything motion, and he leaned forward, throwing all his weight against the already off balanced boy.

With a yell, the boy was thrown bodily backward, with the silver-eyed boy landing on top of him. The crowd gave one final, collective wince as the boy pulled his fist back, and finished the other boy off with a hard blow to the side of the head.

The entire scene took less than ten seconds to play out, but to Sarah, it had felt like an eternity. She let out a cheer when the silver-eyed boy stood up and realized she'd been holding her breath. The crowd, seeing that the fight was over, began to disperse, leaving Sarah to stare at the lone boy.

***

Arnold came to a stop as he reached a crossroad where the road split off in three directions. He shaded his eyes against the late afternoon sun, as he tried to figure out which one would take him to his objective.

They were close. He was only a day away from the border, which meant that this inn couldn't be more than six hours away.

One of his men walked up behind him and tapped him on the shoulder.

"What is it?" he asked, turning to face the man and his five companions.

"We're tired, Sir," the man said, "we've been going for over thirty hours straight. You might have the *constitution* to keep going, but none of us can keep it up for too much longer."

Arnold was about to give a sharp retort when he noticed the state his men were in.

They were visibly flagging and if they didn't get some rest soon, they would likely begin to drop. They would keep marching if he ordered them to, but their pace would be drastically slowed.

He contemplated for a moment as to what the best course of action could be. Finally, he made his decision.

"Very well. You men rest for an hour while I go on ahead. There's an inn about six hours march from here. I expect you there no more than an hour after I arrive. Is that understood?"

The men saluted smartly and Arnold turned away. He took another moment to locate the correct road, then headed off at a swift trot.

He could hardly wait for this damn mission to be over and done with.

It took exactly five and a half hours for the inn to come into view. By then, the moon had already risen high into the sky, casting long shadows over the road before him. The inn was a small wooden structure that couldn't have been more than two stories high.

Arnold came to a stop outside the inn and looked up at the line of windows dotting the second floor. He yawned widely, beginning to feel the effects of his forced march and lack of sleep.

They were here. He was sure of it. Once he'd gotten what he came for, he could get some sleep.

Arnold took a step toward the inn door when he got a sudden chill down his spine. He knew that feeling well and it could only mean one thing. Danger.

Not even taking the time to turn, he dove to his left, tucking into a tight roll as he did so. He heard a light whoosh, as something flew over his head and then he was back on his feet. His eyes quickly shifted around, counting eight men standing the road where none had previously stood.

They were all dressed in a similar fashion, with hoods pulled over their heads and masks across the faces.

Assassins! He knew he had a lot of enemies, but there were very few who could afford to hire the Guild. Of those people, there was only one likely culprit.

Arnold's eyes flicked towards the inn and sure enough, three black-clad figures were climbing up to the second floor.

Simon. Of course, that bastard would be the one to send them after him.

Arnold grinned, reaching behind his back and feeling for his sword. His hand closed on empty air and he grimaced.

He'd left the sword back at the academy, as it would have been too conspicuous. *Oh well,* he thought, *guess I'll be doing this the old fashioned way.*

***

Morgan let out a contented sigh as he hopped out of bed and walked around the room.

"Looks like it worked then," Sarah said, looking up from a book she'd been reading.

"Yup," he said with a grin, jumping up and down a few times just to be sure.

His recovery trait was unbelievable. Just a minute ago, he'd been lying in bed with two useless, swollen lumps for legs. Now he was on his feet, good as new.

Sarah closed her book then and stowed it away in the small spatial bag she kept tucked inside her shirt.

"Great. Now that you can walk; go take a bath and change. You're filthy and those clothes are completely destroyed."

Morgan looked down sadly at his shredded uniform.

He'd really been hoping that they wouldn't be too bad, but he hadn't been able to get a proper look since he'd been in bed all day. Now he could see that they were so torn and tattered, that it was a wonder they hadn't already fallen off.

He looked up as Sarah handed him a new uniform and a small key.

"The bath is down the hall. I've already had them fill it, so you won't have to wait."

Morgan took the clothes and the key and placed a hand on her shoulder, meeting her eyes. "Thank you for taking care of me today."

Sarah looked down, tucking her hair behind one ear and going slightly pink. She could feel her heart rate increase as she became more flustered.

"Oh, it was no problem…" The sound of a door closing made Sarah look up in surprise and stare at a now empty room.

Of course.

7

It was nearly a half hour later by the time Morgan finished bathing and returned to the room. Opening the door, he saw Sarah sitting at a small table laden with food. It hadn't been there when he'd left, so Morgan had to assume that she'd had it brought up while he was bathing. He also noticed that there was a small basin filled with steaming water and a small bar of soap sitting on the floor next to it.

"Good, you're back," Sarah said, snapping her book shut and putting it away.

He'd never noticed how much she read before now. *How interesting could staring at some pages with words on them be?* Morgan wondered, closing the door behind him.

She stood from her seat and pointed to a chair. "Sit."

"Why?" Morgan asked.

Sarah rolled her eyes. "Just do it.

Morgan shrugged and did as she asked, walking over to the chair and taking a seat.

Sarah came up behind him and began running her fingers through his still slightly damp hair.

"What are you doing?" Morgan asked, trying to turn his head to look back at her.

"Keep your head straight," she said, grabbing his head and turning it back. "Your hair is getting out of hand, so I'm giving you a haircut."

"But I can cut it myself."

Sarah let out a long sigh, before trying a different approach.

"Have you ever had someone else cut your hair for you?"

"No; why? Is that something people do?"

"Yes. Most people have someone else cut their hair," Sarah said, running her fingers through the tangle of knots and gently working them out.

"You wouldn't know this, because you've never had anyone do it for you, but having someone else cut your hair can be a very relaxing experience."

"But I don't need to relax. I've been lying in bed all day."

He felt her yank his hair then and winced as his head was pulled roughly to the side. A gleaming knife appeared at his throat and he stared into Sarah's angry eyes.

"Is this a good enough reason for you?" she hissed.

Morgan swallowed hard as he felt the knife press into his skin. He nodded fractionally and Sarah's scowl instantly vanished, replaced instead by a bright smile.

"Great! Now I don't want to hear any more complaints until I'm finished," she said in a cheery voice.

Morgan winced, feeling at his sore scalp as she walked over to fetch the bowl of water and soap.

Why was she being so mean? Hadn't he already been injured enough for one day?!

Sarah walked back over to him and pushed his head back until it was resting on the edge of the chair.

"Now stay still until I tell you that you can move."

Morgan let out a sigh but did as he was told. He heard the light sloshing of water from behind him, then felt a trickle of warm water run over his scalp as Sarah began running her fingers through his hair, making sure to get it nice and wet.

Morgan inwardly lamented when he felt this.

He'd only just finished drying it.

With his hair now soaking wet, Morgan expected her to begin cutting it, but what she did next surprised him. He heard the sound of sloshing water again, then Sarah's fingers were back in his hair, but something was different this time. It took him a moment to figure out before he finally recognized the sensation.

Soap? Why was she putting soap into his hair? He'd washed it not ten minutes ago! Did she think he didn't know how clean himself?

His thoughts came to a screaming halt when she began to slowly massage the soap into his hair. Strong fingers ran over his scalp, digging into it and pressing in all the right places.

Morgan hadn't even been aware that something could feel this good. His eyes closed and his body slumped into the chair, relaxing in a way he hadn't even know to be possible.

It felt so... nice. He'd never felt anything like it before.

Sarah's smooth fingers began pressing into his scalp, pushing down in one spot and gliding lightly over another. She worked slowly, using the tips of her fingers, her nails and even her knuckles in a few areas. Her nails then began lightly scratching over his scalp, sending shivers down his spine and making him slump even further into the chair.

He actually let out a disappointed sigh when she stopped the massage and began snipping away at his hair with the knife. After a few more minutes of snipping, he felt Sarah's smooth fingers running through his hair again. She teased his hair first one way, then the other. He heard the snip of the knife a few more times, then felt a warm sensation as the last of the soap was washed away. He then felt a towel land on his head, and Sarah began roughly drying it, digging her fingernails in all the while.

At last, the towel was removed and Sarah began running her fingers through his hair, arranging it in the way she liked.

"Alright, stand up and turn around so I can get a good look at you."

Morgan opened his eyes when he heard this and stood from his chair with a groan. He turned to see Sarah, drying her hands with the towel; a small smirk twisting her lips as she looked him over.

"Can I assume you enjoyed that?"

Morgan nodded, his eyes still half lidded in relaxation.

He didn't know why, but he felt extremely tired. All he wanted to do right now was curl up in bed and go to sleep.

A flat sheet of ice materialized in front of his face, and he was able to get a good look at Sarah's work. His hair had been cut in a way as to frame his face, and somehow enhance his features. He moved his head from side to side, noting that while his hair was still long enough to sway with the movement, it would never obscure his vision.

"It looks good," Morgan admitted as the mirror vanished.

Sarah's smirk grew even more self-satisfied as she reached up and brushed an errant lock of hair into place.

"Then I'll just assume that the next time I ask you to do something, you won't ask a thousand stupid questions."

Morgan was about to agree wholeheartedly when he caught a slight movement from the window behind her. Looking over Sarah's shoulder, his eyes widened a touch as three men dressed in black slipped into the room.

He could have kicked himself for being so careless. Both he and Sarah had been facing away from the window for over half an hour. If any of these men had slipped in before now, they would both have been finished. As it was, they were outnumbered and completely off guard.

All these thoughts passed through Morgan's mind in an instant; then he acted. Grabbing Sarah by the arm, he pulled her forward, dropping onto his back as well. It was good that he reacted when he did, as something flashed over the area they'd just occupied.

Sarah, caught completely off guard, went flying across the room and landed on the bed. Morgan dodged to the side as one of the men motioned at him and he heard a loud thunk as something buried itself in the wall behind him.

His eyes darted around the room, swiftly assessing the situation as he decided on the best course of action.

Two of the men were moving for Sarah, who seemed to be a bit dazed by his throw.

Oops.

The other man was reaching for something at his belt and staring straight at him, so he was the biggest threat at the moment.

Morgan gritted his teeth in annoyance.

This was not good. The room was too small and fighting in these cramped confines, he and Sarah wouldn't be able to use their skills for fear of hitting one another. They had to take this fight outside.

His eyes flicked to the table laden with food and he sighed with regret.

He hoped the innkeeper wouldn't be too mad for what he was about to do.

Morgan rolled to the side as the man sent a spray of projectiles flying his way. Coming out of the roll near the table, Morgan activated *heavy impact* and *gale force*, then spun on the spot, lashing out with a powerful kick. The table went flying across the room and impacted against the man's chest with a loud splintering crack. The man was hurled back, smashing into the wall with a bone-shattering thud.

Both of the men who had been moving to Sarah turned at the sudden crashing sound. This gave Sarah all the time that she needed to recover. Face twisted in rage, she used her *condense water* skill, sending both men into the back wall near their friend and freezing them in place.

"Who the hell are these people?!" Sarah demanded, turning to Morgan.

"No idea," Morgan said with a shrug.

They both whirled back around when a loud crack echoed through the room. All three men were struggling against the ice and Morgan could see that they would be free within a few seconds.

They all seemed to be completely uninjured, which meant that his attack on the man earlier likely hadn't been nearly as devastating as he'd thought. This could only mean one thing- these men were highly ranked and very dangerous. They needed to get out and they needed to do it now.

"Stay behind me!" he yelled, then sprinted forward, hoping Sarah would do as he said.

With his *gale-force* skill activated, Morgan covered the distance between him and their attackers in just over a second, but in that short amount of time, one of them had managed to free themselves.

He grinned, then used his *flight* skill and launched into the air. Using the momentum of his forward charge, as well as his increased *strength* from his *heavy impact*, Morgan spun and lashed out with a spinning side kick.

What transpired next seemed to happen in slow motion. Morgan's leg connected with the assassin's nose with a sickening crunch, but Morgan's momentum kept him moving forward even as his attack landed. The assassin's head impacted with the wall and Morgan's foot crushed it to a bloody pulp just a second later.

Then time abruptly sped up again. Morgan stuck his other leg out and landed on the wall feet first. His knees flexed as they absorbed the impact, then he pushed back with a grunt of effort, deactivating his *flight* skill in the process.

If his calculations were correct, that should do it.

Just a moment later, there was a loud splintering crack and a massive portion of the wall was completely blown out. Morgan performed a perfect backflip as the wall was sent careening outward, and landed lightly on his feet.

He turned back to Sarah with a wide grin, expecting some kind of praise, but all he saw was a look of horror.

"What is it?" he asked, instantly on guard.

Sarah didn't answer, instead pointing a shaky finger behind him, face white with fear.

Morgan whirled on the spot, raising his arms in preparation for a fight. But no one was there. He was confused for a few seconds, before a loud sound from the street below caught his attention. Looking down, Morgan felt his blood run cold.

A very familiar and unwelcome guest was standing on the road below.

Just what the hell was Arnold doing here, and why were those black-clad men attacking him as well!?

***

Six years ago…

"Sarah! You shouldn't run off like that!" Hint admonished when he was finally able to reach her.

Sarah looked up, face flushed with excitement.

"Did you see that?" she asked in a hushed tone, as the silver-eyed boy bent to retrieve something from one of the boy's pockets.

"Yes, I saw," Hint replied, "fights happen sometimes. People don't always agree."

"But where are those boy's parents? Shouldn't they have stopped their fighting? And why didn't anyone in the crowd try and stop them?"

Hint's face clouded in sadness.

"They're orphans, Sarah. They have no family and no one was going to stop them when they provide such great entertainment."

Sarah was horrified and saddened at the same time.

The boys had no family? It must be so… lonely.

The boy straightened then, and Sarah could finally see what he'd been searching for. He was clutching a half molded piece of bread. She wrinkled her nose in disgust, but the boy seemed quite pleased with it.

Pocketing the bread, he turned to go, but Sarah called out after him.

"Wait! Don't go!"

The boy flinched, then slowly turned as Sarah ran over to him. His shoulders were hunched inward, as if afraid of another attack, but when he saw who it was, he relaxed just a bit.

"What do you want?" he asked as Sarah skidded to a halt just feet away from him.

Sarah was slightly taken aback by his tone of voice. It was flat and lacked any sort of emotion whatsoever. His eyes were different now as well. Gone was the burning exuberance, and the joy of being alive. Now, his eyes were dull and lifeless, and she imagined that she could feel an immense sense of loss in them.

She wasn't about to be put off, however.

"My name is Sarah. What's yours?" she asked, plastering a smile on her face.

"Why do you care?" he asked, eyes flicking upward as Hint came to stand behind her.

She was surprised by his answer, not expecting that sort of response.

"Because," Sarah said, placing her hands on her hips. "I want to know!"

Sarah didn't really know what had prompted her to come to speak with the boy. Maybe it was because of how he fought, or because of the way he looked while doing so; or maybe, because he was all alone, and she could relate to that feeling. Regardless of why, she decided that he was going to become her friend, no matter what she had to do to convince him.

The boy blinked in surprise, then let out a snort and turned to walk away.

"Hey!" Sarah yelled, "don't walk away from me!" But the boy ignored her.

Sarah was about to give chase, when she felt Hint's hand land on her shoulder. She looked up to him, and he just shook his head.

"Let him be, Sarah."

Sarah watched him disappear into the crowd and felt tears pricking at the corners of her eyes. She was sure the boy would want to be her friend if she just talked to him. She felt a sharp pain in her chest as he disappeared, and she wrapped her arms around Hint's waist, burying her face in his shirt.

Hint patted the top on her head consolingly as she began to cry. It seemed an odd thing; to cry over something so small, but he could see the answer clear as day.

Sarah had just her first crush, and her first heartbreak.

8

Arnold dodged to the side as one of the assassins launched their signature poisoned needles at him.

He was confident that his skin could block them, but it never hurt to be careful, especially when dealing with trained killers.

He heard a small whisper of cloth from behind him and ducked, watching the needles, reflected by the moonlight, fly overhead. He lunged forward but was forced to roll to the side as another assassin attacked.

Arnold clenched his teeth in annoyance as he was continually thwarted by the assassins.

Every time he tried to attack one of them, another one would attack from his blind spot. He didn't even have the time to use any skills, as he needed at least a few seconds of concentration to activate one.

He jumped back to avoid another set of needles, when something slammed into his back, hard enough to stagger him. Whirling on the spot, he saw one of the assassins flipping back away from him. He took a step toward that one, when he felt another impact on his back, this one much stronger than the last.

This wasn't good. If they kept up like this, they would slowly pick him apart. He could, of course, try to drag this fight out until his men arrived, but that could take another hour and he didn't think he'd be able to hold out that long. As it was right now, his only option would be a headlong charge against one of them, regardless of any attack that came his way. It was a horribly risky move, but it was either do this or die.

Arnold danced back from another attack and prepared himself for an all-out charge. Then the inn wall behind him exploded outward, sending a shower of debris down on them. One of the assassins flinched and Arnold saw his opening.

He moved forward in a blur and caught the man by his neck. He spun on the spot, crushing the assassin's throat and hurling him at the next closest man. The flying body took the assassin completely off guard, leaving him unable to react in time. The two bodies collided with a loud crunch and they both went down in a sprawling heap.

Aaron Oster

As soon as he sent the man flying, Arnold let his eyes flash momentarily up to the gap in the inn wall. He felt a grin touch his lips as he saw both Morgan and Sarah standing there, looking completely unhurt.

Now all he had to do was finish off the assassins.

By now, the others had gathered their wits and moved to try and surround him as they had before, but Arnold was having none of that. He stomped down hard on the ground, using his *eruption* skill. The ground trembled and shook, then a fountain of molten lava exploded upward, catching two of the assassins and cooking them to a crisp. The other four managed to avoid his attack and Arnold grinned as he turned to face them.

***

"What do we do?" Sarah asked, watching the fight unfolding below.

Morgan was torn.

On the one hand, he knew that Arnold was an enemy. He'd clearly been following them, likely intending to capture them both and have him killed. On the other hand, he was being attacked by the same men who'd come after them.

His mind worked furiously at the problem until a solution presented itself to him. He turned to Sarah, flashing her a wide grin and motioning her back from the opening.

"I now have access to my new extra skill. Let's see what it can do."

"Do you really think it'll work?" she asked, fear still tingling her voice.

"Only one way to find out," Morgan replied, then turned back to the fight below.

He still wasn't entirely sure what the skill would do, but it did say that it would target a thirty-foot radius. That would catch everyone below in the area of effect and hopefully put an end to them all.

Concentrating for a moment, Morgan activated his *gravity storm*, visualizing where he wanted the attack to land. Both of his arms rose before him and he felt his *RP* drop to nearly zero. His body then floated out of the opening in the wall, but Morgan knew that it had nothing to do with his *flight* skill. This was all the doing of his extra skill.

Purple lightning began to crackle over his body as his arms spread out to the sides, palms facing up toward the sky above. Then, with a howling sound so loud it nearly deafened him, a massive funnel of spinning air came crashing down. His arms snapped out at the same time and sent a streak of purple lighting into the howling tornado.

He saw Arnold's eyes widen for just a second, then the massive *gravity storm* crashed down onto him, hiding both him and the assassins from view. Morgan slowly floated down to the ground, where his skill released its hold on him. He looked on, watching the spinning vortex of wind and purple lighting in awe. He could feel the intense wave of gravity, emanating from the storm from where he was standing; and was shocked that he could unleash this sort of power.

Sarah walked up next to him and Morgan started in surprise. How had she gotten down?

Turning away from the storm for a second, he saw a long ramp made of ice sloping down from the opening he'd created in the inn wall. He flashed her a grin as she turned to look at him. Her eyes widened when they met his and she tried to say something, but the howling of the storm drowned out any attempt at verbal communication.

Finally giving up, she tapped at her eyes then pointed to him. Morgan shrugged, having no idea what she wanted to tell him. A look of annoyance crossed her face, then she gestured and a sheet of ice formed in the air over her hand. The sheet floated up and Morgan could see himself reflected in its surface.

Did Sarah want him to admire her haircut now of all times?

Then the sheet of ice floated up to eye level and Morgan froze. Staring back at him were his usual features; all except for one very noticeable change.

What the hell had happened to his eyes?!

Instead of the usual bright silver, his eyes were a bright violet with only streaks of silver showing through. The whites of his eyes had now gone completely black, making his eyes seem to glow. *No*; he realized, *they were glowing, it wasn't just a trick of the light.* The purple in his eyes also seemed to be shifting and swirling in a mesmerizing pattern, letting flashes of silver through from underneath.

Then a sudden and deafening silence overtook the area as his storm died. The moment it did, Morgan's eyes returned to their previous color, the purple and black bleeding away until only silver remained.

"You can move the mirror now," Morgan said, his voice sounding oddly muffled in the sudden stillness.

The ice mirror dropped to the ground and shattered with a loud tinkling noise. Sarah looked into his eyes once again and sagged in relief.

"Good, they've returned to normal. I was afraid that they'd stay like that forever."

Morgan nodded his agreement.

While he did look far more intimidating with his eyes glowing the way they had, it would be far too conspicuous for him to go unnoticed. He was pretty sure that his gravity storm had triggered it, as Sarah had never noticed his eyes changing color before; but he wondered at the odd color shift.

"Do you think that finished them all off?"

Morgan's train of thought came to a halt as Sarah began moving toward the ten-foot crater he'd left in the ground.

One hell of a skill indeed, even if he could only use it once every eight hours.

Morgan jogged up next to her, and together, they approached the lip of the crater. Staring down, he could make out a few bodies, but couldn't be sure if any of them were Arnold. The bodies had a slew of nasty looking injuries, from crushed bones to massive rents in their flesh. One of them was even charred to a crisp, with small streams of smoke wafting up from the corpse.

"That is one nasty skill. Glad I got out of there in time. I'm not sure that even I would have survived that."

They both whirled on the spot to see Arnold standing in the center of the road with his arms folded over his chest.

Morgan felt his heart sink even as he took up a fighting stance and prepared to go down fighting. His supermage shield flared to life around him, but he didn't yet have enough *RP* to summon a *wind blade*.

Arnold clocked an eyebrow when the purple glow surrounded him.

"Looks like the Princess was right. You are a supermage."

"What the hell do you want, Arnold?" Sarah stepped forward, her mage shield flaring a bright blue as she did.

"From you? Nothing," Arnold said, pulling a small glowing pendant from under his armor.

Sarah stumbled in surprise as he said this.

"Wait, what? Aren't you here on my father's orders?"

Arnold ignored her, fiddling with the pendant for a moment before he seemed satisfied with it. Then he raised it to his lips.

"I found him," he said, then tucked the pendant back into his shirt.

Sarah gave Morgan a confused look, but he just shrugged in reply.

He was every bit as confused as she was. It was clear, though, that they were in no immediate danger. Otherwise, he would already have attacked.

"If you're not here for Sarah, then why are you here? And who were those men dressed in black?" Morgan asked, allowing his shield to die down and relaxing his posture.

"Those men were from the assassin's guild, likely sent for the little princess over there. Simon probably got tired of waiting, so he sent them after us. As for why I'm here, well, that would be for you," he answered.

"Why me?" Morgan asked. "What possible interest could you have?"

"Oh, it's not me who's interested," Arnold said with a snort.

"If not you, then who?" Sarah asked.

As if in answer to her question, a spatial tear opened up in the air not five feet away.

Morgan blinked in surprise.

Was that a portal?

"Well, after you," Arnold said, motioning to the open portal.

"No way!" Sarah said, folding her arms over her chest. "There is no way the two of us are walking through some unknown portal."

Morgan had to agree with her.

Aaron Oster

Who knew where this portal would transport them, let alone who was waiting on the other side.

"You can either step through on your own, or I'll drag you through," Arnold said with a shrug. "Your choice."

Sarah looked as though she were about to object, but Morgan placed a hand on her shoulder. She gave him a questioning look, but he just shook his head.

There was no point in trying to fight. Arnold was much stronger than them and with his gravity storm on an eight-hour cooldown, there wasn't much that could be done.

"Fine," Morgan said, stepping in front of Sarah and walking up to the portal.

He stopped just a few inches from it, staring into the inky blackness beyond.

He really hoped this wasn't an elaborate ruse by Arnold to get them back to Simon without a struggle. Oh well. It was too late to back out now.

Taking a deep breath, Morgan stepped forward, into the open portal.

9

The slight sense of vertigo that often accompanied portal travel, hit Morgan just as he was stepping out of it. It took him a moment to get his bearings and when he finally did, he stared at his new surroundings, mouth going slightly agape.

He was standing in what looked like a bedroom, but he had a hard time believing that anyone's room could be this lavish. The floor under his feet was a blue and gray marble, flecked through with black and gold. The walls were richly decorated with an assortment of paintings, tapestries, and etchings, all depicting scenes of nature. A massive four poster bed was set against one wall and a large, furry carpet lay under it. There was a bookshelf against one wall, with a small mahogany desk and a plush looking chair sitting next to it.

The room was also dotted with several sofas and chairs, one of which contained a woman, who was lounging on her side and staring at him with a piercing gaze. Long, flowing golden hair hung in waves down her back, framing a perfect heart-shaped face with flawless, lightly tanned skin, and pouting red lips.

She was wearing a long, sleeveless blue gown that showed off her toned arms and clung to her every curve. She shifted slightly, sitting up from her lounging position, revealing a plunging neckline that showed more than a bit of her impressive cleavage.

Morgan noticed none of this, his eyes latching onto the only thing that really stood out to him.

Her eyes. They were a bright violet, just like his had been when he'd used his gravity storm. Could this be another supermage?

The woman rose gracefully from her sitting position and Morgan noticed for the first time that she was quite tall.

Nearly six feet if he wasn't mistaken.

She approached him slowly, her hips swaying from side to side and when she eventually smiled at him; revealed a perfect set of gleaming white teeth. She continued walking forward until she was standing uncomfortably close to Morgan.

He was about to take a step back when her hand shot out, latching onto his shoulder and preventing him from moving back.

The strength of her grip alone convinced him that this woman could crush him like an insect if she so wished.

Aaron Oster

"It's nice to finally meet you, Morgan."

Her voice was rich and sultry, with a slightly playful undertone.

"Who are you, and why would you want to meet me?" he asked, trying to play for time.

Why wasn't Sarah here yet? She should have come out right after him.

"My name is Katherine, Crown Princess of the North Kingdom. As to why I've wanted to meet you…" She trailed off here and flashed her perfect smile once more. "I'm sure you already know why."

Morgan went stiff as a board.

He was standing before the Princess of the North Kingdom? If that were true and she already knew what he was, he was about to die. Sarah had told him of what she'd done and how powerful she was. He really didn't stand a chance. Why did he have to keep running into people this strong?

"Are you going to kill me?" he asked, looking up into her eyes.

He now knew that she wasn't a supermage. Sarah had said she was just a super. Albeit, one of the most powerful ones in all of the five kingdoms.

Katherine's smile wavered a bit as he asked this.

This wasn't going at all as she'd imagined. Most men would have been reduced to nervous, red-faced stammering by now. Either that or openly staring at her chest and drooling. Morgan wasn't doing either, and he even seemed to be perfectly calm and composed. Even when he was asking if she was about to end his life, he appeared completely unbothered by the situation.

"There's no need to worry," she said, releasing his shoulder and allowing him to take a few steps back. "I didn't have Arnold bring you to me just so I could kill you." She placed a hand on her hip and leaned it to one side.

This was a move she'd used many times in the past. It usually both distracted and enticed at the same time. It should give her a pretty good idea of what she was dealing with. She didn't know much about him, other than what Arnold had told her, and that wasn't much.

Morgan folded his arms, keeping his eyes locked on hers.

Now that he knew she wasn't going to kill him, he needed to get some answers out of her.

"Why hasn't Sarah come through the portal yet?"

Katherine pouted a bit when he mentioned Sarah's name, but her perfect smile was back in place after just a moment.

"I set that portal on a bit of delay. Your friend and my subordinate should be arriving sometime in the next hour or so. I wanted some time alone with you before they did."

Morgan frowned when he heard this.

She was much more powerful than he'd thought. If she could not only control distance, but also the time in which it took to arrive; then he had a feeling that the power she'd shown at the academy was only a hint of what she could really do.

"So, if you're not going to kill me, then why did you want to meet me?"

Katherine moved her hand from her hip and moved it up to a small gold pendant around her neck in the pretext of fixing it.

Morgan's eyes had flickered, if only for a fraction of a second, down to her hips, but that wasn't enough to tell her if he was interested, or if his eyes only followed the movement out of reflex.

"There are many reasons why I wanted to meet you, but foremost among them is that you are a supermage. Believe it or not, this is my first time meeting one of your kind."

"How did you find out?" he asked.

He was feeling at a distinct disadvantage dealing with someone so powerful and of such a high station without Sarah here. She was a noble after all, and much better with people than he was.

Katherine slid her hand down to rest at her side, her smile slipping just a bit as she did so.

While his eyes had flickered to her chest, she still couldn't detect anything from him. No change in his heart rate, breathing, or posture to indicate as to whether he was attracted to her or not.

This was all new territory to Katherine, as she'd never dealt with anyone that wasn't susceptible to her charms. This aggravated her immensely, but, oddly enough, she felt something else as well.

Could she possibly be intrigued? She'd never garnered much respect from anyone, despite her high station. Anyone she'd ever met eyed her with either desire or envy. That was why she'd spent so much time growing her ability and increasing in power. If she wasn't

Aaron Oster

given the respect she was due, she could simply destroy the offenders and be done with them.

Now here was someone who seemed completely uninterested in her looks. Someone that she'd admittedly been hoping to be able to seduce and turn into a weapon. But now it seemed that she would need to persuade him with something other than her looks.

"Why don't you have a seat on the couch." She motioned to the sofa she'd just been seated in. Her shoulders relaxed slightly and a much more natural smile played across her features.

"Your friend should be along in the next hour or so. Then we can discuss why I've brought you here. In the meantime, can I offer you something to eat?"

Morgan was a bit surprised at the sudden shift in attitude.

He'd been expecting her to force whatever agenda she had onto him, under pain of death; but here she was, offering him food and agreeing to wait upon Sarah's arrival. He still didn't trust her, but he hadn't had the opportunity to eat dinner as those assassins had come in before he'd gotten the opportunity.

He nodded slowly, walking over to the indicated spot and taking a seat.

"Some food would be nice," he said once he'd taken his seat.

"Is there anything, in particular, you'd like? I can have the chefs make just about anything."

Chefs? Of course, they would have chefs here, as he had no doubt that this was the royal palace in City One.

"Meat," Morgan said, not sure what else to ask for.

"Just meat?" Katherine asked with a light laugh. "I offered you any meal and you just said meat, without specifying what type, what cut or how you would like it prepared. One would almost think that you grew up on the streets with such a request."

"But I did grow up on the streets," he said, brows knitting together in confusion.

For the first time since meeting her, he saw genuine surprise cross the Princess' face. It was quickly replaced by a thoughtful expression as her mind raced to process this new information.

If what he said was true, and she didn't doubt that he was telling the truth, then it would explain a lot. If he grew up on the streets, then he was most likely an orphan. Orphans had it harder than anyone and most didn't survive for very long on their own. It still didn't explain his complete lack of interest though. She needed to get to the bottom of this and only knew of one way how.

"That's quite unexpected," she finally said, walking over to a small rope hanging near an open slot in the wall. "You'll have to tell me how an orphan child managed to befriend a city lord's daughter, and manage to earn his ire; to the point where he'd try and have you killed."

Morgan gave no visible reaction when she said this, but inside, his mind was racing.

How could she possibly have all this information on him? Arnold clearly didn't know much about him, as she hadn't known he'd grown up on the streets. So if she didn't find out from him, then who?

Katherine could see that he was momentarily distracted, so she quickly raised a hand to her ear, and reached out to the only person who could give her real answers.

Vivian, I'm in my room with Morgan, but something's wrong with him. I need you to do an examination. The back door is open, just slip in when you have a free moment. We'll talk once he's gone.

She only had to wait for a few seconds before a response came through.

Of course, Princess. I'll be there shortly.

She dropped her hand from her ear, just as a light chiming sound came from the dumbwaiter and a small flat board appeared in the open slot. On it, was a piece of paper and a pen, along with an inkwell. There was also a small pamphlet, held together by a piece of spiraling wire.

Katherine reached in and took both, then walked back to the couch and seated herself near him.

Now that he was a bit more relaxed, Morgan could smell something strange coming off the Princess.

It wasn't unpleasant, though. In fact, he found that he quite enjoyed it. It reminded him of something, though he couldn't quite place it.

Katherine shifted just a bit closer to him, bumping her hips into his and leaning over him. This afforded him a great view down her dress, but Morgan didn't even take notice of this. His eyes were glued to the small pamphlet covered in writing.

"What is that?" he asked, seeing all sorts of names he didn't recognize covering the first page.

"This is a menu sent up from the kitchens," Katherine answered, flipping the menu open and leafing through a few pages.

"Since you don't know what you want, I hope you don't mind if I order for you," she said, turning to look at him.

Despite her distracted appearance, she'd been keeping a careful eye on him as she'd leaned over. It looked as though her earlier hypothesis had been correct.

Morgan hadn't even taken the slightest interest in her, his attention being grabbed by a freaking menu, instead of the scantily clad woman pressing herself into him. She hoped Vivian would arrive soon, as she was dying to get to the bottom of this.

Morgan nodded his acceptance, thinking that if anyone knew good food, it would have to be a princess.

After a few more minutes of rifling through the menu, she closed it with a satisfied click. Then she picked up the pen, dipped it in the inkwell and began to write.

As the pen scratched over the paper, Morgan's eyes began to wander around the room.

The portal was still standing open a few feet away, but according to the princess, Sarah wouldn't be arriving for a least another hour, if not more.

His attention shifted back to her as she stood and walked back over to the opening in the wall. She placed both the menu and sheet of paper inside, then pulled the rope once again. After a few seconds, they both disappeared and Morgan could now make out a thin rope attached to it.

How strange. An entire mechanism just for ferrying food up from the kitchens? The wealthy sure had it good.

Katherine turned from the dumbwaiter and sauntered back over to him, sitting down on the couch and sliding up near him once more; the barely perceptible sound of a door opening, reaching her as she settled into the couch.

Good, Vivian had arrived. Now she would get to the bottom of this mystery.

Morgan frowned as Katherine pressed against his side.

Why was she so touchy? Sarah always did the same thing though, so maybe all women acted this way.

"The food should be ready in about twenty minutes. Your friend should be here in about forty-five, so that should give us plenty of time for our first date," she said, flashing him a grin.

At least he now had a time frame for when Sarah would be arriving.

"What's a date?" he asked, wondering just what kind of food she'd ordered.

It would undoubtedly be the best he'd ever eaten if he was right, and this was indeed the palace.

"Oh, well I suppose you wouldn't know what one was," she put a finger to her lips, thinking for a moment how best to explain it.

"A date is when two people get to know one another better," she finally said, "we can talk here until the food comes up, then we can continue over at the table. Does that sound agreeable to you?"

Morgan shrugged.

Why not? It wasn't like he had anything to hide. She already knew his biggest secret. What more could she really want to know?

Katherine flashed him another one of her brilliant smiles, dropping her hand to cover one of his.

"Excellent!"

***

Six years ago…

Morgan wove his way through the busy streets, hunching his shoulders and keeping his head down. He took a quick peek over his shoulder to make sure the strange girl wasn't following him, then ducked down an alley and made his way to his most recent hiding spot. Squeezing between two buildings, he emerged into a small square with a few tattered rags bunched in one corner and a wooden crate sitting against a wall.

He slumped down into it, fishing the moldy crust from his pocket and biting into it. It tasted disgusting, but he forced himself to finish every last bit; even going so far as to lick up the crumbs from his palm. He leaned back against the wall and stared up at the sky above.

His mind then wandered over the last hour or so. The fight had been amazing, though even the memory of the feeling had

Aaron Oster

already faded. He blew out a long breath and leaned further back against the wall.

He felt nothing.

It had been this way for the last three months; ever since he woke up in an alley with no memory of the last two and some odd years.

He'd tried everything he could think of just to feel something, but the only thing that gave him joy was fighting. When he was fighting, the numbing cold would fade and he would *feel*. This led him to seek out fights wherever he could. It was like a drug, an addiction; and who could really blame him? It wasn't that he just fought either; he would go looking for fights and try to drag them out for as long as possible, to prolong the feeling.

The fight with the two boys had been a good example of this. He could have beaten them both fairly quickly, but he had purposely prolonged it, just to feel something other than the nothingness that haunted his every waking moment and even chased him into his dreams.

He rolled off the crate and landed on the concrete floor, staring listlessly up at the sky. His mind then wandered to the strange girl who'd warned him of a sneak attack during his fight; then, for some inexplicable reason, had demanded to know his name. He snorted to himself, remembering the angry look on her face when he'd ignored her. He turned onto his side and tried to go to sleep, but the girl's face kept popping into his mind for some reason.

Finally giving up, he got to his feet and began running through the stances that were ingrained into him. He had no idea where he'd learned to fight the way he did, but assumed that someone must have taught him in the past few years, as he couldn't remember knowing it before the memory lapse.

He took up a stance and began running through the motions. Left... right... hook... uppercut... His fists flashed out in rapid succession, his body twisting and pivoting at the crucial moments, to lend extra power to the strikes.

Once he was sufficiently warmed up, he began practicing more in-depth. Throwing a combination of punches, kicks, knees, and elbows, all while moving around; bobbing and weaving to dodge imaginary attacks.

Morgan began to fall into a rhythm, leaving his mind free to wander once again. The girl's face flashed through his mind immediately, her cheeks flushed as deep a red as her hair; the angry pouting expression on her face, the way she'd carried herself. As though she were the most important person in the world.

What a strange girl, he thought, feeling something bubbling up inside him.

Morgan snorted out a laugh; then froze midway through his most recent form. *He had... laughed? The only time he laughed was when he was...*

He froze. Would training give him the same joy as actually fighting?

He mulled that thought over for a few seconds, but eventually dismissed it. He'd trained plenty of times before, and it had never made him feel anything.

He sat down then, folding his legs up and beginning a few deep breathing exercises. His mind was always calm, even in the middle of a fight, but doing this always seemed to center him. It helped him think; helped him process all the information he'd collected that day, and sort them into the correct places. Now, however, he was using it to try and figure out the odd slip in his behavior.

He took in a deep, slow breath, feeling the air fill his lungs to capacity, before slowly releasing it. His mind whirled through the myriad of possibilities until it finally landed on the only logical conclusion.

As far as he could tell, there was only one thing that was different between today and any other day. The girl. She'd done something to him, something to make him laugh.

His eyes snapped open then, and he rose from his position on the ground.

He needed to find her.

10

Morgan told Katherine all about growing up on the streets of City Four. About how he'd met Sarah by chance one day while she was out in the city.

That was one of his fondest memories, the day he'd first met Sarah; though she often told him that it was both the best and worst day of her life.

Katherine in turn, told him of her life, growing up as the Crown Princess, and how she'd worked hard to improve her abilities and fighting skills.

He was shocked to learn, that despite her ridiculously high *rank* of *48*, Katherine was only twenty-four years old.

When he'd asked her how she'd gotten to such a high level of power when it took most people hundreds of years to get there, she'd laughed and gestured to the room around them.

"It's really not that hard to *rank up* when you have enough money to purchase all the cores you'll need. The hard part was resisting the temptation to *max out* my *rank* right way."

Morgan nodded at that, agreeing wholeheartedly with her.

Despite their differences in rank and social standing, he was really beginning to warm to the princess. She appeared to have a lot of the same interests as him, including an almost manic love of fighting.

Their food came up at a certain point and they moved over to the table to eat. Katherine carried two silver domed trays over to the table, setting one down before him. She then walked back to the dumbwaiter and came back with a clear bottle of amber colored liquid, as well as two glasses.

Morgan had already pulled the top off the tray by the time she arrived back and was looking down at the savory dish before him, practically drooling at the heavenly aroma wafting up from it.

Katherine hid a smile as she sat down across from him and set the bottle and glasses down.

At least I'd found something that he would drool over, she thought as she watched him.

"What kind of meat it this?" Morgan asked, reluctantly tearing his eyes away from the food.

"It's bison; a delicacy normally only found in the West Kingdom. I won't go into the details on how it was prepared, but I'm sure you'll enjoy it."

She unstopped the bottle of amber liquid and poured each of them a glass. Morgan stared as the liquid frothed and bubbled as it was poured.

He'd never seen a drink do that before.

Katherine noticed him staring and slid one of the glasses over to him.

"Go on then. Don't wait on my account."

She didn't have to tell him twice.

Morgan picked up the fork and knife, cutting off a huge chunk of the bison, and stuffing it into his mouth. The explosion of flavor that assaulted his senses when the soft and juicy meat entered his mouth, was almost enough to bring tears to his eyes.

He'd never once imagined that food could taste so good. It was both soft and tender, and the meat seemed to almost be falling apart in his mouth.

Morgan finally swallowed his first bite and flashed Katherine a wide smile.

"You were right! I've never tasted meat this good in my entire life!"

"I'm glad you're enjoying it, but you should try the sparkling cider as well. It pairs very nicely with the bison," she said, returning the smile.

Morgan nodded, reaching for the glass and wrapping his fist around the stem.

Katherine laughed when she saw this and was quick to correct him on the proper way to hold a glass.

Morgan nodded his thanks, then took a sip of the cider. His eyes widened a touch when the liquid hit his tongue. It tasted of apples and honey, and the feeling of the bubbles popping in his mouth was wonderful.

The meal continued on in silence, something which Morgan was more than grateful for.

Sarah always tried to talk to him while he was eating and it was very distracting.

It only took him a few minutes to polish off his entire plate and he sat back with a sigh of contentment.

Aaron Oster

That was the best meal he'd had in his entire life. It easily outstripped anything else he'd ever eaten.

There was a sudden loud buzzing sound and Katherine let out a sigh of regret.

"It looks like your friend will be arriving momentarily."

Morgan's head turned to the portal, which had suddenly begun glowing a bright red and a few seconds later, Sarah stepped through.

***

Sarah stumbled as she stepped out of the portal, feeling that awful sense of vertigo she so detested. It took her a few seconds to orient herself and once she did, she wasn't entirely sure if she were dreaming or not.

Morgan was sitting at a table not ten feet away. Sitting across from him was Princess Katherine, dressed in a gown that made her feel both inadequate and envious at the same time.

Just what the hell was going on here?

She blinked a few times, rubbing her eyes to make sure she wasn't dreaming.

Nope, they were still there.

"Hey Sarah, glad to see you're finally here," Morgan said, waving at her from the table.

The sight was so outrageous, so completely unexpected, that Sarah just blurted out the first thing that came into her mind.

"What the hell is going on here, Morgan?!" she yelled.

Then her face went pale, as she processed who she was standing before.

The Princess of the North Kingdom, and one of the most dangerous people alive. She still had nightmares from the way she'd destroyed that group of guards back at the academy.

"The Princess wanted to meet me. She put the portal on an hour long delay so we could have a date," Morgan replied, smiling at her. "The food was amazing!"

"Please, call me Katherine. Princess sounds so formal," Katherine said, reaching over the table and taking one of his hands in hers.

Sarah gaped, not understanding a thing Morgan had just said.

She'd been gone for an entire hour? Morgan and the Princess were having a date? What?!

Sarah's face went from a stark white to a deep red in a matter of seconds.

"You mean that after all the time we spent together, you agreed to a date with the first woman who comes along other than me?" she yelled, practically exploding.

Morgan blanched at her sudden outburst, wondering what he possibly could have done to upset her this time.

Katherine however, was quick to come to his rescue.

"Do calm down, dear, and have a seat. We have a lot to discuss and not a whole lot of time in which to do it."

She turned to face Sarah, releasing Morgan's hand in the process.

"Let me be perfectly clear. I plan on marrying Morgan. He is vital to my plans and in the short amount of time we've spent together, I've found that I quite enjoy his company."

Sarah felt the fight go out of her then and her shoulders slumped in defeat.

If the Princess of the North Kingdom wanted Morgan, then there was absolutely nothing she could do about it.

"No need to look so glum."

Sarah looked up to see Katherine smiling at her.

"I can tell that you've got it bad for our young supermage here. While I may be the Crown Princess, I don't mind sharing, if you don't," she said with a wink.

Sarah flushed a deep crimson at the insinuation and quickly looked to Morgan, who looked more confused than she'd ever seen before.

He had no idea what was going on right now. He probably didn't even know what a date was, let alone the significance of having one with a bloodthirsty monster like her.

She took a deep, calming breath, then walked over to the proffered chair and took a seat. Taking a moment to collect herself, she parsed out exactly what she wanted to ask.

"Why the sudden interest in Morgan, and how did you even find out he was a supermage?"

They'd worked very hard to keep that piece of information a secret. No one other than Gold should have known about it.

"That, believe it or not, was pure dumb luck. We found a boy after the battle to take the academy. He was barely alive and seemed to hate Morgan more than death itself. He gave us an account of the battle, but what gave him away, were his eyes," Katherine said, her gown shifting as she crossed one leg over the other.

"I thought my eyes only changed when I used a specific skill," Morgan cut in.

There was only one person she could be talking about and he was troubled at the fact that Grub was still alive.

"So you've seen it," Katherine said, turning back to him.

Sarah noticed that she subtly leaned forward as she did, revealing more of her plunging neckline to him. Her fists clenched at her sides when she saw this and she had to make an extreme effort not to punch the Princess right in her perfect face.

She would likely just break her hand on the Princess' tough skin, and who knew how she would react if she dared to strike at her.

"The eye color shift is caused when a massive amount of your reiki is used all at once," Katherine continued. "I studied up a bit on supermages during my time at the academy."

This got Sarah's attention.

"Wait. If you spent time at the academy, why attack it? In fact, what is the point of this entire war?"

Katherine turned back to her, her expression unreadable.

"I never wanted this war," she said simply. "This was all my father's idea. The glorious descendant of the Tyrant King, finally taking his rightful place as the ruler of all."

"You're descended from the Tyrant King?"

They both turned as Morgan cut into their conversation.

"You know of my ancestor?" Katherine asked, leaning toward him once again.

"Yes. I learned about him during my first lesson at the academy," Morgan said, looking thoughtful. "But I thought he was destroyed during the war."

"Oh he was, but he didn't die without leaving a line of succession."

Morgan nodded at that, then went silent once again, his mind processing all the new information.

"If you didn't want this war, then why did you attack the academy, and why kill all those guards in such a horrible fashion?"

She didn't want to ask this question. She was actually afraid to, but she had to know.

"Before we go any further," Katherine said, "I'll have you swear an oath of secrecy. I trust Morgan. As my future husband, he will be privy to all my secrets. You however, I do not; at least not yet."

Sarah colored slightly at the blatant insult, but she agreed to keep her silence.

"I have long wanted to overthrow my father. He has been sitting on his throne for hundreds of years and in all that time, has not improved the kingdom one bit. This ridiculous war is just the latest example of his stupidity and vanity. I have been secretly working for years to undermine him, but up until now, I haven't had the backing needed for a coup.

"I've been forced to bide my time, following all of his orders and playing the faithful daughter. Killing those academy guards, and in brutal fashion, fits perfectly with the persona I've crafted for myself over the years. Just a simple minded and bloodthirsty princess who will do whatever she's told. If it makes you feel any better, those academy guards were the only ones I personally killed.

"After the attack, I began desperately looking for an angle. I had contacted King Herald in secret before the attack took place, but he didn't make it back in time to stop it. Now a war rages on between the two kingdoms. It has completely wrecked the Central Kingdom, and is becoming a massive drain on our resources here. I was nearly ready to act, despite my position being so tenuous, when I heard about Morgan."

She smiled here and glanced over to him.

"I could barely dare to hope that the ramblings of an angry boy could be true, but I had to know. So I coerced Arnold into tracking him down. The moment he stepped though the portal, I knew that I'd been right. With Morgan by my side, my brothers will undoubtedly back me in overthrowing our father. With him out of the way, we can pull our forces from the Central Kingdom and try to salvage what we can. Though I do think my father's reckless actions will have greatly damaged the balance that the Central Kingdom provided."

Sarah listened to the princess' story in rapt attention.

No matter how badly she wanted to believe that she was lying, she just couldn't. Katherine was so open and sincere that she must be telling the truth, which just made Sarah hate her all the more for it. Of course the perfect princess would have to be even more perfect.

"How will marrying Morgan help you, though? If anyone found out what he was, they would have him killed," Sarah said.

"I can protect him," Katherine replied. "No one would dare attack the Queen's husband. Not even the Assassins Guild would take on such a mission."

"Assassins Guild?" Morgan cut in. "You mean like those people that Sarah's father sent after us?"

Katherine's head whipped around when he said this, her expression morphing into one of anger.

"Of course that sniveling bastard would go to the Guild. He's likely sent men after Arnold as well for not returning Sarah in a timely enough fashion."

"Can you ask him to stop?" Morgan asked. "It's really been getting annoying, having to kill all the people he sends after me."

Katherine let out a long sigh here and shook her head.

"Unfortunately, I can't. If I ask him to stop, he'll begin wondering what interest I could have in you. If anything, it would just make him all the more persistent in hunting you down. I also can't just kill him, as he's managed to worm his way into my father's good graces."

"Oh, okay," Morgan said, slumping down in his seat.

He'd really been hoping that Katherine could deal with Simon once and for all. He was really growing sick of the arrogant noble's constant harassment.

"Back to the topic at hand," Sarah said, "you still haven't answered how Morgan could help you. While he is high ranked for his age, he isn't exactly all powerful."

"I didn't say that it would happen overnight," Katherine replied. "Overthrowing a country takes a lot of work. As it is, it'll take me at least six months to get everything I need into place. By then, Morgan will be a whole lot stronger, and will be able to make all the difference."

Sarah folded her arms and glared at the princess.

"And how do you propose that he becomes powerful enough to be an actual threat to an entire kingdom in only six months? It's taken him nearly that long just to get where he is now, and the cost to increase in *rank* will just keep going up."

"That's simple. I will provide him with all the cores he needs. I can't have my future husband be unable to defend himself."

"And what will we be doing while you plan this coup? Will you keep us here as your guests until then?" she asked, placing heavy emphasis on the word *guests*.

"Not at all. The palace would be much too dangerous a place for him. As you saw earlier, I can *literally* transport you anywhere you'd like to go. Just name the place and I'll send you there."

Sarah bit her lower lip.

This wasn't going at all how she'd imagined. The damned woman had a ready answer for every question she threw at her. She did say she'd be willing to share, though, and Morgan would be a whole lot safer with her protection…

No. She couldn't think like that. If the princess could send them anywhere, then Sarah would ask her to transport them somewhere far away, then she and Morgan would make a run for it.

"Fine," she said with a sigh, feigning resignation and folding her arms over her chest.

"Excellent!" Katherine said, turning back to Morgan with a smile. "Looks like your friend approves. So what do you say Morgan? Will you marry me?"

11

Morgan blinked as Katherine leaned back toward him. He hadn't heard her last question, as his mind had been elsewhere.

He'd heard Katherine say that she would provide him with all the cores he'd need. He'd completely tuned the conversation out after that, imagining all the amazing skills he could acquire, and how powerful he could become.

"What did you say?" he asked, looking up at the smiling Princess.

"I asked if you would marry me," she repeated, smile not faltering for even a second.

"No," Morgan answered.

In truth, he wasn't one hundred percent sure what marriage was. All he knew was that people did it to have children and he wasn't interested in that.

Katherine looked both surprised and hurt at his reply. Sarah couldn't have looked happier.

"Well, you heard him. Better just send us back to the inn," she said, already rising halfway out of her seat.

But Katherine wasn't so easily dissuaded.

"Morgan, do you even know what marriage is?"

"Yes, people get married to have children. I don't want children, and if we get married I'll have to take care of them," he replied.

Katherine laughed lightly at his response.

"People don't automatically have children if they get married. In fact, all it would really take to have children would be for us to sleep together."

Morgan's mind came to a screaming halt when Katherine said those words. His blood ran cold and his heart rate rapidly increased. His mind went immediately back to the previous night he'd spent sleeping with Sarah.

He remembered how angry she'd been when she'd woken up in bed with him that morning. At the time, he'd thought it was because he'd woken her, but this was so much worse than he ever could have imagined. Was Sarah going to have a baby now that they'd slept together?

Thankfully for Morgan, Sarah noticed his look of horror and was quick to put two and two together.

"You can calm down, Morgan. She means something different. I'm not going to have a baby."

Morgan looked at her, hope now filling his eyes.

"Are you sure?"

"Yes, I'm quite sure," Sarah deadpanned.

"Would one of you mind explaining what you're talking about?" Katherine cut in to their conversation.

"No!" Sarah immediately answered, face going red in embarrassment.

Morgan however, had no such qualms and was quick to explain what he thought might have happened. By the time he was done with his story, Katherine was laughing so hard that she could hardly seem to breathe.

Sarah was hiding her face in her hands, neck flushed red and groaning to herself. Morgan on the other hand, was looking between the two of them, not understanding what could possibly be so funny.

If anything, they should be happy that he'd avoided a potential disaster. He was too young to have children and he didn't think Sarah wanted any right now either.

Finally managing to calm down, Katherine gave him a warm smile.

"Thanks for that. I can't remember the last time someone made me laugh so hard!"

"Please don't encourage him," Sarah begged, finally looking up.

Her face was a deep red, the kind of red that Morgan associated with anger, but it looked as though Katherine's presence was stopping her from lashing out at him.

"Alright, Morgan. How about I explain what a marriage to me would entail, what expectations I will have of you, and what benefits you will gain as a result. Then you can decide if you're interested or not. Does that sound agreeable to you?"

"Sure," Morgan answered with a shrug.

In truth, if marriage didn't automatically produce children, then he wasn't really sure why people would do it in the first place. It all just seemed kind of pointless to him.

Katherine lightly cleared her throat, then began.

Aaron Oster

"Marriage is a special sort of partnership between two people, that is sealed by a binding contract. In the case of a royal marriage, the contract is bound using very powerful magic. This is done to ensure that both parties can be completely honest with one another, without fear of one divulging the other's secrets. Any questions so far?"

Morgan shook his head.

It all sounded pretty straightforward to him, and he could definitely see the appeal of having someone he could completely rely on.

"Now, I'll first tell you what I'll be expecting from you, and then I'll tell you what you can expect from me."

She waited for him to nod, then continued.

"As my husband, you will be expected to support me, both in public and private; in any decisions I make, provided they are reasonable. You will have to make appearances with me as my husband in social gatherings, and eventually, provide me with children. You will also have to stand with me against my father and make a public demonstration of your power.

"As for the benefits," she continued. "Your marriage to me will protect you from anyone looking to harm you, including Simon, and I will provide for all of your needs. You will live here in the palace with me; food, money, cores, access to beast zones and anything else your heart may desire will be at your fingertips. So, what do you say?" she asked once again.

Morgan was silent for a long while as his mind turned over all the pros and cons.

On the one hand, he would be forced to reveal his identity and make a very public stand against the king. If Katherine was to be believed, however, she stood a very good chance of overthrowing her father. From his point of view, she was asking for very little and offering a lot; but then again, he didn't feel like tying his life to someone he'd just met...

"Sorry, not interested," he answered after a few seconds.

"Great!" Sarah replied. "Now can we leave?"

Katherine looked hurt.

"Come on, Morgan. Why not?" she asked, pouting a bit. "Haven't I offered you a good deal?"

"You have," Morgan replied. "But I don't know you all that well. Besides, I have things to do, and can't spend all my time here."

"Aww, don't be like that!" Katherine said, leaning forward and taking one of his hands in her's. "Just say you'll marry me. I promise you won't regret it."

"Nope."

"Please?"

"Nope."

"Pretty please?"

"Still no."

Katherine leaned back, pouting at him, but still not ready to give up.

"How about a compromise. You say you'll help me overthrow my father and that you'll think about the marriage proposal, and I'll give you everything I promised."

Morgan had opened his mouth to shut her down again, but stopped as he heard her new deal.

All he had to do was help her kill her father and say he'd think about it? Why not, then?

He nodded.

"You have a deal."

Katherine let out an excited squeak and hugged him tightly.

"You won't regret this!" she said excitedly.

It took Morgan a few seconds, but he eventually managed to extricate himself from her embrace.

"So what happens now? And where is Arnold, by the way? Shouldn't he have arrived by now?" Morgan asked, noticing the mercenary's absence for the first time.

Katherine's smile turned predatory when he asked this and she released her grip on his hands.

"I trapped him on the way here. I didn't want him to overhear my plans, and I also have an image to maintain. Can't have him thinking that I'm soft. As for what happens now... well, that would be up to you. You can't stay here as it wouldn't be safe. I can send you anywhere you would like to go, though. Just name the place and I'll open a portal."

"We want to go to the East Kingdom," Morgan immediately replied. "We were supposed to go there, but the border was closed

Aaron Oster

due to the war. I tried getting over it and the two of us almost died because of it."

"Where in the East would you like to go?" she asked.

Before Morgan could give his answer, Sarah cut in.

"Just over the border."

Morgan turned to give her a questioning look, but her expression gave nothing away.

"Are you sure that's where you want to go?" Katherine asked him.

He wasn't sure why Sarah had asked to only be transported over the border, but he trusted in her judgment enough not to question her.

"Yeah. Just over the border would be fine," he answered.

"Very well," Katherine said, rising from her seat.

Then she thrust her arm out to the side. A small whirling portal appeared and her arm sank in up to the elbow.

Before Morgan could ask what she was doing, her arm came out holding a bundle of clothing. She placed those on the table and stuck her arm back in, coming out this time with a small leather bag.

He watched in fascination as she pulled one item after another from the portal and set each on a growing pile on the table. After another minute or so, the portal closed and Katherine turned her attention back to him.

"I had a few new outfits made for you. I can't very well let my future husband run around in those rags."

"I only said I'd think about it," he immediately replied. "What's wrong with my uniform?"

He was a bit offended that she would call his very expensive combat uniform 'rags.'

"While those might have served you well in the academy, they'll hardly do in the real world. Especially if you're planning on going into a *high ranked beast zone.*"

Morgan was about to object, when he remembered how easily a *rank 6* frost-fox had penetrated the uniform just a few months ago.

"I see your point."

Katherine patted his hand once more, making Sarah grit her teeth in annoyance.

Had they completely forgotten she was here?

"The new clothes are made of the same canvas material, but with a few alterations," she continued.

Picking up a shirt, Morgan could see that this was indeed different. It was the same dark blue as the one he was wearing now, but there was some metal plating on the chest and forearms, as well as the back. Additionally, there were no straps whatsoever, leaving him to wonder how it would adjust.

"I've had it enchanted just for you," she continued, handing him the shirt so he could feel it. "There's no need for straps, as the entire uniform will size itself to fit you. Additionally, it will not have to be cleaned or maintained, and it will even repair itself, should it be damaged."

Morgan's eyes went wide as she said this. The material was indeed soft and pliable and had the same light feeling like the one he was wearing now.

A uniform like this must have cost a fortune. But she was a Princess, so it probably wasn't a big deal to her.

Next, she handed him a pair of pants. These were black, and had metal plating over the shins; and just like the shirt, did not have a single strap or buckle.

"The uniforms are woven through with adamant as well. It's a much stronger metal than steel, and will take a lot more punishment than what you're wearing now."

Morgan had never felt like hugging anyone before, but right now, he could understand why people did it. He didn't really know what to say to her, but he then noticed that Sarah was standing off to the side, glaring at them sullenly.

"Did you make any for Sarah? I'd feel bad if she wasn't as well protected as I was."

"Of course," Katherine said, reaching into the pile and coming out with a set for her. "I figured you'd ask, so I had a few made for her as well."

"A few?" Morgan asked, his eyebrows going up. "How many did you have made?"

"Five sets for each of you," she replied, shaking the bundle at Sarah until she came over and took it from her.

"I don't really know what to say," Morgan said, staring down at the new clothes.

Five sets? The cost must have been astronomical.

Aaron Oster

"You can thank me by putting them on," she said with a laugh. "I want to see how you look in them."

Morgan nodded eagerly and began pulling at the straps holding his uniform shirt in place.

"You're going to change right here?" Katherine asked with a smirk.

"Yeah, why not?" Morgan asked, loosening the last straps.

"You can't just change in front of people!" Sarah exclaimed, glaring at him.

"Why not? I've changed in front of you plenty of times," Morgan said, pulling his arms through the sleeves.

"Don't listen to her, Morgan. You go right ahead and change. I don't mind," Katherine said, "And apparently, neither does Sarah." She gave Sarah a knowing look, which predictably, made her blush.

Katherine watched as Morgan's shirt came off, taking note of his lean and muscled body. A few noticeable scars traced across his chest and stomach, but that was to be expected. Life on the streets was hard, after all.

She had to admit that he was really quite pleasing to look at, though a bit too scrawny for her tastes. She was sure that a few months of good food would fix that right up, though.

She watched Sarah out of the corner of her eye and saw that she had her eyes glued to him as he loosened the straps on his pants.

That girl really did have it bad for him.

Morgan's pants came off next, leaving him in only his underwear.

If all I have to do to get him to strip was buy him new clothes, maybe getting him into bed wouldn't be so difficult after all, Katherine mused.

She debated asking him to take those off as well, if only to tease Sarah, but decided that she may very well have a heart attack, so just let it be.

Besides, his total willingness to just strip in front of two women of nobility spoke of a serious underlying issue. She really hoped Vivian would have some answers for her once they left.

Morgan pulled the new uniform on and was thrilled when it conformed perfectly to his body. The material felt both sturdy and flexible, far more so than his previous uniform had been.

"It feels amazing!" he exclaimed, finally turning his attention back to the two women, one of which was smirking and the other, red-faced.

Did he make her angry by not listening to her again? He might have to apologize once they left. Sarah didn't seem to be too fond of Katherine for some reason. He wasn't really sure why. He thought Katherine was wonderful.

"I'm glad you like it," she said, a smirk still playing around the corners of her mouth.

"Sarah, you have to put yours on!" Morgan said excitedly.

Sarah let out a long sigh.

"Fine, but I'm not changing here," she said, daring either of them to argue with her.

"You can change back there," Katherine said, gesturing to a door set into the far wall near her bed.

Sarah shot her one last glare, then marched off to the room, opening the door and closing it behind her, with what Morgan thought was a little more force than necessary. As soon as the door was closed, Katherine turned her attention back to him.

"There are a few items other items I'd like to give you as well," she said, leading him back to the table.

"More stuff?" Morgan excitedly asked.

"Yes, more stuff," she replied with a light chuckle.

She picked up a small leather bag and pulled four gleaming cores from inside.

"These cores are packed full of energy and should be helpful in boosting you at least a few *ranks*." She placed the cores back in and handed him the bag.

He gleefully took it and was about to tie it to his belt when he remembered that he no longer had one.

"Here, let me help with that," Katherine said, bending down and wrapping a belt around his waist. She pulled it tight, then buckled the two ends together for him.

"There," she said, straightening up, her face just a few inches from his own. "How is that?"

Morgan had been temporarily taken off guard by what Katherine had done, but when he felt the belt tighten itself snugly to his side, any discomfort he had vanished.

Aaron Oster

"Much better," he said with a smile, taking a step back and fastening the pouch to his new belt.

"Now, one last thing. It is traditional for a man to buy his wife to be a ring. I'm guessing that you don't really have any money for one, though."

"You're not my wife to be." Morgan shot her down once again.

"The sort of ring people would expect you to get would cost somewhere in the three to five thousand platinum range," Katherine continued, completely ignoring his comment.

To say that Morgan was dumbfounded would have been the understatement of the century.

A ring would cost him three to five million gold? Who in the world even had that kind of money? And why the hell would anyone spend that much on something so insignificant as a shiny rock?

"I can see that you understand, so I'll make you a deal. I'll buy myself a ring and say it was from you, but in exchange, I would like a keepsake from you."

"I only said I'd think about it," he said for what felt like the hundredth time.

"Don't be like that, Morgan," she said with a pout. "Haven't I given you a bunch of nice things?"

Morgan blew out a breath but nodded, trying to think of something to give her.

She did give him a bunch of expensive presents, so the least he could do was give her something in return.

His mind finally alighted on something and he walked to where he'd discarded his old uniform pants. He quickly dug out the contents, making sure to pocket his coin purse before holding up a glittering blue and red core.

"I took this from a *rank 9* ice-bristle wolf. I fought it when I was only *rank 7* and nearly died in the process. Would this be okay?" he asked.

"Yes. It most certainly would," she said, taking the proffered core and placing it on the table.

She'd have a jeweler set it into a necklace for her.

"Now I have something for you." She picked up a small pendant from the table, then walked over to him, and slipped it over his neck.

"This is a very special piece of jewelry," she said, taking the end of it and tucking it under his shirt.

"If you ever need me, simply press the small button on the right side and I will open a portal in your location. Or, we can use it for long-distance communication. Just press the button on the left side and call out to me with your mind. But you have to promise to keep this a secret. If the wrong person got ahold of it, they could use it against me."

Morgan nodded seriously, very aware of what kind of danger she was referring to.

"What about Sarah? Can I tell her?"

"Tell me what?" Sarah asked.

Morgan looked past Katherine to see Sarah emerging from the room. She was wearing a similar uniform to his, but with a few key differences. For one, her top was sleeveless, leaving her arms completely bare and unprotected. Another difference was in the tightness of the cut. While Morgan's uniform had fitted itself to be snug, Sarah's clung to her like a second skin, accentuating every curve of her lithe body.

"I gave him a way to contact me should he ever need to," Katherine said, turning to her. "But I'll have you keep that bit of information to yourself."

"I have to ask," Morgan said, eyeing Sarah's uniform. "Why is hers sleeveless? Doesn't that sort of defeat the purpose of armor?"

"I made it that way because Sarah is a mage. Anything that could punch through her shield wouldn't be stopped by the armor. The other kingdoms tend to be on the hotter side as well, so I figured it would be more comfortable."

"But I have a shield too. Why didn't you make mine sleeveless as well?"

"I had no idea you had a shield of your own," Katherine said, feigning surprise. "But what do you think of her uniform? Doesn't she look good in it?"

Sarah flushed a deep red as she said this.

She was well aware of how the uniform clung to her body. Normally, she wouldn't suffer the indignity, but the enchanted material was too valuable to pass up. She was also sick and tired of Princess Perfect flaunting her body. She had a nice figure as well and she wouldn't be outdone, not even by Katherine.

Aaron Oster

"Sure, I guess," Morgan said with a shrug, remembering just a moment too late about his resolution to ask her what she wanted him to say.

Oh, well. Maybe next time.

"Just open the portal and let us go," Sarah said, folding her arms under her chest. "It's late and I'm tired."

"Oh, alright," Katherine said, waving her hand in the air.

A portal came into existence just a foot away from her face, making her jump.

"Come on Morgan, we're leaving!" Sarah said, marching straight through the portal.

Morgan took a step toward the portal, but he was stopped by a hand on his shoulder. Turning back to Katherine, he gave her a questioning look.

"Be careful out there, and don't hesitate to call me if you need my help."

She pressed a small bag of coins into his hand, then did something that caught him completely off guard. Leaning down, she kissed him softly on the cheek, leaving a strange tingling sensation in its wake.

"Something to remember me by," she said in a soft voice, then gave him a light shove on the chest, sending him into the portal.

***

As soon as it closed, the portal that had been standing open for the last hour suddenly flared to life and Arnold walked through, looking very disoriented and more than a little angry.

"How long did you plan on keeping me trapped in there?" he asked, folding his arms over his chest and glaring at her.

Katherine's mask had snapped into place as soon as Morgan was gone, and when she turned to face the mercenary, she was once again the ruthless and bloodthirsty princess of the North.

"As long as felt like it. Now I have another mission for you."

Arnold glowered at her, but his grimace vanished when a heavy coin purse thudded into his chest. Opening the top, he could see a pile of glittering platinum coins shining back at him.

"That was for you last mission," Katherine said.

When he gave her a look of surprise, she smirked at him.

"What? Did you think I wouldn't pay you? How could I expect to keep your loyalty if I didn't?"

Arnold nodded slowly, tucking the heavy purse into his pocket.

He still wasn't on board with serving this backstabbing witch, but as long as she continued paying him this well, he wouldn't complain... Much.

"Your next job will be a bit more complicated. I want you to tail Morgan and Sarah for the next six months. I know that the Assassins Guild is still after them and I can't very well have my future husband die on me."

"So he's agreed?"

"Of course he has!" Katherine said with a snicker. "Who could resist me?"

Arnold had to agree with her on that.

Despite knowing what a psychotic bitch she was, even he couldn't help but admire her figure. Especially now, with that ridiculously revealing dress she was wearing.

"When do I leave?" he asked, face not betraying so much as a hint of what he was thinking.

"Right now. I'll be opening a portal a few miles away from their location. I've left a tracker in your coin purse so you don't lose them again. Just make sure they don't spot you," she said, narrowing her eyes and letting a threatening tone enter her voice.

"Can't have them thinking that I don't trust them."

Arnold nodded once as a portal opened before him. He took one last look at the princess, then stepped through.

***

As soon as Arnold vanished, Katherine let the mask slip once more and walked back to the table where Morgan's core still sat. Lifting it to eye level she examined it for a few moments, as a small smile played around her lips.

She could hardly believe it, but she was actually interested in Morgan. A commoner orphan from the streets of City Four. Who would have thought?

She heard a light shuffling from behind her, and Vivian emerged from the secret door placed near the back of her room.

Aaron Oster

"So, did you get a good look at him?" she asked, turning to examine the woman.

Vivian was as plain looking as a person could be, brown eyes, brown hair and a very nondescript face. Her figure was average at best, and she walked with a slightly slumped posture. She was as forgettable as a person could be, which was the whole point.

Vivian's real talent came from her ability, an ability so unique that Katherine had never found anything like it anywhere else in the five kingdoms. Vivian was a healer, but her ability extended much further than that. Her ability was so potent, that she could read the brainwaves of her targets, and interpret their thoughts from them. In essence, she was a mind reader; but one that could diagnose any problem; whether physical or mental.

"Yes," she replied, waiting for Katherine to take a seat, before taking one of her own.

"So what's wrong with him?" Katherine asked, draping one leg over the other, and reclining back into the sofa.

Vivian was silent for a few moments, as she tried to find the right words to explain what she'd found.

"His mind is - for lack of a better term – strange," she began.

"How so?"

"Well for one, he seems to be missing a large chunk of memory; about two year's worth I'd say. But that isn't even the strangest part." Vivian's brow furrowed as she continued.

"Whoever messed with his memory did something else. They've modified his pituitary gland and in a way I've never seen before."

"I'm not a healer, so you'll have to explain what this pituitary gland does," Katherine said.

"The pituitary gland is a small gland located at the base of the brain. Without getting too technical, it's basically the master gland which produces hormones in the human body. Whoever messed with his mind did something to that gland, which caused a lot of changes to his brain chemistry; and the way he thinks and acts."

Katherine was both intrigued and disgusted.

Just who would go through all this trouble? Blocking out some memories was one thing, but modifying his mind was truly something else.

"What kinds of changes are we talking about?"

"Well, for one, the complete lack of a desire for any activity of an intimate nature and even the ability to comprehend it as well."

"Is that even possible?" Katherine exclaimed, her eyes going wide. "And what about his ability to have children. Was it taken away as well?"

Vivian shook her head, a small smile playing at the corners of her lips.

"No, I double checked to make sure. Everything will function as it should."

Katherine's brows furrowed at that.

Just who would take the time to suppress desire towards the opposite sex, and even the ability to comprehend what sex was; but leave his ability to have children untouched? More importantly, who had that kind of power, and how was it even possible?

"You still haven't explained how it's possible to erase the ability to *comprehend* what sex is," Katherine said.

"The same way that some people cannot comprehend mathematics or why killing an innocent is wrong. In theory, it's possible, though I never thought I'd see a case like this." Vivian shook her head in disgust.

"What else did this person change?"

"They permanently altered his levels of serotonin, the chemical that controls moods such as happiness, or anger. It's being kept at an extremely neutral level, meaning that unless his mind is placed under an immense amount of stress, he'll never fly into a rage or panic. He'll never be overly expressive in anything he does, either. Any normal person would probably turn into a psychopath if subjected to the constant numb feeling, but they compensated by making the release of adrenaline from a fight give him the same feeling as joy or happiness. They also made food be a source of pleasure, and he'll feel a rush of endorphins whenever he eats something especially good."

"Did they change anything else?" Katherine asked, mind whirling as she pieced together a theory from everything she'd heard so far.

"Yes. His fear response has been tempered, his ability to feel pain dulled, and his capacity to ignore it heightened to the point of insanity."

Aaron Oster

Vivian went quiet here, as Katherine slowly pieced all this together until an answer presented itself to her.

"From everything you've just told me, I can only draw one conclusion. Someone who knew what Morgan would become decided to try and turn him into the perfect killing machine, then erased his memories of the incident. They left his ability to have children untouched - so he could reproduce, and potentially have supermage children - but blocked him from feeling desire, to remove a potential weakness."

Katherine's face grew paler and paler the longer she spoke.

"The real question is, when will they be back to collect their prize, and will we be able to stop them when they do?"

She looked up to Vivian, who had the same look of horror she imagined she did.

"Can you fix him?"

Vivian bit her lip for a moment, before finally shaking her head.

"Tampering with someone's brain is a very dangerous thing," she answered in a quiet voice. "I don't want to take that risk."

Katherine let out a long sigh but accepted her answer all the same.

Vivian was her most trusted aide and she valued her advice over any other.

Katherine gave her a smile then and dismissed her. She waited for the door to close behind the woman, then slumped back in her chair, a feeling of dread overtaking her.

It looked like she had some competition where Morgan was involved. Her answer as to why he didn't seem attracted to her was answered, but now that she had it, she almost wished she hadn't asked. There had to be a way to fix him. No one should be subjected to the kind of experimentation that had been done on him. The question was whether she should tell him or not.

She slowly massaged her temples as she felt a headache coming on.

For now, she had a new threat to worry about. One that was potentially even more powerful than her. Perhaps even another supermage.

12

Morgan stumbled as he stepped through the portal and into a small forest clearing. He felt confused and disoriented for a few moments, then the vertigo from the portal travel wore off and his mind began racing.

Katherine's kiss had left him feeling strange. There was no better word for it. There was only one other time he could recall feeling the same way, and that was when Sarah had done the same thing. He still distinctly remembered the feeling of her soft lips on his cheek.

The feeling faded and Morgan began to assess their new surroundings, putting the strange feeling to the back of his mind. Trees surrounded him on all sides, climbing high into the night sky. He could feel slight dampness in the air and the ground underfoot was much softer than he was used to.

Sarah walked over to him a slight frown creasing her brow.

"Do you know where we are?" she asked.

"Somewhere in the East Kingdom, I'd assume," Morgan said with a shrug.

"Would you mind flying us up so we can get a better vantage point?"

That was actually a good idea and Morgan inwardly berated himself for not thinking of it first.

"Yeah. Hop on," he said, turning his back to her.

He felt her clamber on and he got a good grip under her thighs before using his *enhanced flight*. They rose quickly; the damp night air clinging to them as it blew past.

"We can't trust her, you know," Sarah said as they rose.

"Why not?" Morgan asked as they neared the tops of the trees.

He already knew that he couldn't entirely trust the Princess, but he wanted to hear Sarah's thoughts.

"She clearly has an ulterior motive for wanting to marry you," Sarah said, "Trust me, the best thing to do is to get as far away from her as we can and hope she never finds us."

Morgan wasn't sure if he entirely agreed with her.

Aaron Oster

It was clear to him that Katherine did have an ulterior motive for wanting his help. She wanted the throne and she was going to use him to achieve her goal, but the marriage part seemed - to him at least - entirely genuine. That was not to say that he was interested though, which was why he'd turned down her proposal.

"If you say so," he said, feeling her relax a bit in his arms.

Apparently, he'd said the right thing for once. Maybe he was finally getting the hang of this social thing.

They cleared the tops of the trees and Sarah let out a light gasp, which Morgan wholeheartedly agreed with.

The bright moonlight revealed a dense forest, bordered on one side by a massive river and on the other by a large open plain; filled with tall swaying grass. As they rose higher, Morgan could just make out the outline of the border wall to the west, meaning they were well inside the East Kingdom.

He finally stopped when he reached the maximum height his skill would allow and just hovered up there. The wind blew gently around him, bringing with it the smell of salt and damp. The full moon cast a pale blue light over everything, giving it an otherworldly appearance; and the damp breeze carried with it the sound of breaking waves.

"It's beautiful up here," Sarah said, leaning in closer to him, but Morgan wasn't really listening.

"I've spotted a settlement further east. I think that will be our best chance to find this Duchy that Gold mentioned."

Sarah let out a long sigh, then turned her attention in the direction Morgan mentioned. She could indeed see a large settlement some way off, though it would take them a good few days to reach it.

They stayed up in the air for another minute, then Morgan dropped back down to the ground. Sarah hopped off his back and stretched mightily, covering a yawn with the back of her hand.

"It's probably well past midnight by now," he said, rubbing at his eyes. "Best to get some sleep and head out in the morning."

As Sarah watched him settle down with his back to a tree, she had the sudden urge to go and cuddle up next to him. Giving herself a shake, she dismissed the idea and walked to a spot a few feet away.

Katherine had gotten into her head and she wasn't thinking clearly right now. She was exhausted, both physically and emotionally. At least Morgan had agreed with her about avoiding the Princess. Soon enough, things would go back to the way they were; just the two of them against the world.

With that thought in mind, she curled up on the ground, a small smile on her lips as she drifted off.

***

Despite the late hour, Lord Simon was still very much awake. It had been nearly a week since he'd hired the Assassins Guild but had yet to hear any news from them, good or otherwise. There had been some good news that week, though. Edmund's forces were slowly but surely pushing Herald's back. They were gaining more ground by the day and would soon push him out of the capital altogether.

A knock at the door snapped him from his wandering thoughts.

He wasn't expecting anyone this late at night. This could only mean one thing.

"Enter," he said, interlacing his fingers on his desk and composing his face into a neutral expression.

The door opened, revealing a man dressed in the uniform of the Assassins Guild. The man swept in without so much as a sound and closed the door behind him.

"Well?" Simon asked as soon as the door was closed.

"We encountered the targets and our men engaged. They were all killed and the targets escaped."

Simon was a little surprised to hear a woman's voice from under the black mask but didn't show it.

Damn uniforms made them all look the same.

"So you failed, then," he said flatly.

"Not at all. The standard procedure for any job is to send the newest recruits out first. This is both to test our newest members, as well as gauge the threat level of our target."

Simon frowned at that.

That seemed a bit careless for a guild of professional killers. Wouldn't the targets be more alert if they tried and failed on the first attempt?

"I can guess at what you're thinking and I can assure you that we will succeed. We have gauged their power and have sent the appropriate teams after them. We lost track of them for a few hours after the initial attack, but have since located them inside the East Kingdom."

"How long will it take? My patience is already wearing quite thin," Simon said.

"We should have them in our custody within the next forty-eight hours, and have them back here in no more than two after that."

"And Arnold?"

"As good as dead."

Simon folded his arms and stared into the slits where the assassin's eyes would be.

"I expect you won't fail this time," He said, allowing a scornful tone to enter his voice.

"You can be rest assured that the mission will be carried out," the woman said, then turned on her heel and walked out of the office.

Simon waited until the assassin was gone before allowing the roiling anger he'd been suppressing, rise to the surface.

He slammed a fist down, splitting his desk in two and sending bits of wood flying in all directions.

How hard could it be to capture two damn teenagers?!

***

Arnold stepped out of the portal right near the border wall and was forced to make an undignified dash to the tree line to avoid being seen.

Damn that woman and her twisted sense of humor!

Thankfully, the guards seemed intent on watching the other side of the wall and he made it to the cover of the trees without incident.

Once there, he pulled the coin pouch Katherine had given him and after a moment of fishing around, came out with a small circular device that looked like a compass. The only difference was that there were no reference points marked on it and when he held the object flat on his palm, the needle pointed in one direction without wavering.

This must be the object that would help him track Morgan. He only wished it would tell him how close he was, as he didn't want to accidentally bump into him.

Arnold snorted to himself, then began walking in the indicated direction.

This would not be an easy job. Those damned assassins weren't done with them yet, and it would be difficult to protect Sarah and Morgan without being seen. He had no doubt that they would also be sending people with the power to put him down, so he would need to be alert at all times.

Arnold's foot sank into the ground before him and he let out a loud curse as he was suddenly up to his waist in mud.

He hated the East Kingdom. Damn bogs and marshes everywhere.

It took him a good few minutes to work himself free and once he finally did, he was covered in stinking mud. Arnold let out a long sigh as he tried to wipe off the worst of the gunk.

He could already tell that this mission was going to suck.

***

Six years ago...

Sarah was almost inconsolable for the next few minutes and Hint desperately searched for something to take her mind off the strange boy. He bent down next to her and wiped her eyes gently.

"Forget about that boy, Sarah. He's only a street urchin. Don't forget who you are. You are the Lady of City Four and, one day, you may even rule here."

Sarah sniffed a few times, her bottom lip still quivering slightly.

"Besides," Hint continued, finally remembering something. "That puppet show is supposed to be starting about now."

Sarah's sadness lasted all of two seconds after that. Once Hint mentioned the puppet show, she perked right up again and became her usual, happy self. They headed down the main street and took a few turns until the street opened up into a small courtyard.

Aaron Oster

Wooden benches lined the area and a small stage stood against one wall. There were already several children seated before the stage and Sarah eagerly went to join them.

As soon as she sat down, though, the other children stood up and moved to sit somewhere else.

Hint watched from his position at the back of the square, letting out a long sigh as a hurt expression crossed Sarah's face. He imagined that she wouldn't be making many trips to the city in the future. He only wished she could make just one friend her age, but her stature and her father's overbearing manor would make that almost impossible.

He was about to walk over to sit down next to her, when he caught a flash of movement off to his right. Turning his head, he was surprised to see the dirty orphan from before weaving his way through the crowd.

What could he be doing here, he wondered.

The boy stopped in the middle of the quickly filling square and looked around for a moment, then headed directly for Sarah.

Hint's first instinct was to rush in and stop the boy before he reached her. After all, it was his job to protect Sarah, but after a moment, he forced himself to stay where he was. Sarah wouldn't be a child forever and he wouldn't be around for too much longer. If there was any chance she could make a friend, even this unknown street urchin, then maybe she would be alright.

Hint subtly readjusted the small crossbow with a poison-tipped bolt that he had hidden up his sleeve. Just because he was willing to give the boy a chance, didn't mean he would risk Sarah's life. He would keep a close eye on them, and at the first sign that she was in any trouble, he would act.

Sarah felt a pang of sadness as all the other children stood and left. She felt tears pricking at the corners of her eyes again, and tried to hold them back.

This was the worst birthday of her life. She would never come back to this horrible place after today.

If she wasn't so curious about the puppet show, she may already have stood and asked Hint to leave. She had actually begun to consider it when someone sat down on the bench next to her.

She turned, expecting to see Hint, but was surprised to see the same silver-eyed boy from before. She felt her tears vanish instantly, and her heart fluttered in her chest for a moment.

Why had he decided to come back?

"What did you do to me?" the boy asked in a flat tone.

Sarah stared at him for a few seconds, then her face began to go red in anger.

She had saved his life, then he'd ignored her. Now he showed up out of the blue and demanded to know what she'd done to him?! What did that even mean?

Sarah turned her nose up at him and let out a huff.

"I don't know what you're talking about, but you have a lot of nerve just sitting down next to me and making demands!"

The boy shrugged.

"Okay." Then he stood and went to walk away.

Sarah stared after him in shock.

What was wrong with him?!

"Where do you think you're going?" she called out after him.

This time, the boy actually turned back instead of ignoring her.

"You couldn't help me and the baker normally throws her old bread out now. If I'm fast enough, I might actually get some bread without any mold on it."

Sarah blinked, then a sly grin spread across her face as an idea took shape in her mind.

"Would you stay if I gave you food? Fresh food, bought only an hour ago," she clarified.

The boy nodded, then walked back to sit down next to her.

Sarah turned in her seat and motioned Hint to her side.

"Is something the matter?" he asked, eyes boring into the boy.

"No, nothing's wrong. I just wanted some of the food we bought earlier," she said with a grin.

Hint looked between her happy face and the boy's expressionless one and nodded. He removed a loaf of bread, an apple, and a small square of cheese from the small sack he'd been forced to purchase. The boy reached for it, but Sarah held out her hand to stop him. The boy gave her a confused look, but her grin only grew wider.

"Before you can eat, you have to tell me your name."

The boy shrugged again.

"It's Morgan."

What an odd name, Sarah thought as Hint handed him the food. She'd never heard it before. It didn't even sound remotely like a Northern name. Maybe he was from another kingdom.

Sarah watched him as he took the food, almost reverently and took a huge bite out of the fresh bread. She heard the crunch of the crusty loaf, but she also heard something else. A groan of satisfaction came from Morgan as he bit in and his eyes widened a bit as he tore the first chunk free and began chewing.

She saw his lips turn ever so slightly upward, the first sign of emotion she'd seen since his earlier fight.

"So, Morgan..." Sarah began, not really sure what to talk about.

She'd never had friends before. What did friends talk about? Wait... was he even her friend? He hadn't mentioned it.

"Do you wanna be friends?" she blurted out, face going pink with embarrassment.

Morgan took a moment to swallow before replying.

"No," he said, then bit into the apple, face lighting up as he did.

"Wait, what?" Sarah exclaimed. "Why not?"

Morgan shrugged.

"Why would I need friends?"

"Well..." Sarah began again, mind racing as she tried to figure something out.

Morgan continued tearing into the bread, cheese, and apple while she thought; completely ignoring her, in favor of the first good meal he could ever remember eating.

"Friends look out for each other," she finally said.

"I can look out for myself," he replied through a mouthful of food.

"It's rude to talk when your mouth is full!" Sarah snapped at him.

She was quickly becoming frustrated with Morgan and his complete lack of decorum.

She had been nothing but nice and he continued to be rude. She had even given him food.

Her thoughts came to a screeching halt at that and her annoyance melted away.

"Friends give each other good food," Sarah said.

She had to smother a grin as Morgan's head snapped up at that, and she settled back against the backrest of the bench as the first puppets came onto the stage.

She now knew how to get him to stay.

13

Morgan awoke to a low hissing sound off to his side. Opening his eyes, he looked blearily around the clearing until his eyes alighted on some sort of scaly creature. He squinted until it came into focus, and saw that it had its back to them and was eating something on the ground in the center of the clearing. He was about to dismiss it and go back to sleep, when a tan blur flew into his vision and sank its teeth into the lizard's neck.

Morgan was on his feet in a flash. He whipped his head frantically around until his eyes settled on Sarah's sleeping form. Not even taking the time to wake her, he dove forward and scooped her into his arms, then took to the air; the sound of the two animals fighting following him the entire way.

Sarah woke with a start and began thrashing so violently that Morgan actually began to fear dropping her.

"Calm down! It's me!" he said, narrowly avoiding a fist to the face.

"What the hell is going on?" Sarah yelled, eyes coming into focus and glaring up at him.

"If you'll just calm down and look at the ground, you'll understand what's happening," Morgan replied in an even tone.

He'd found that the best way to deal with Sarah when she was angry was to stay calm. Her anger always passed quickly, so it wouldn't do him any good to yell back.

Sarah glared at him, then looked down to the ground twenty feet below, where a pack of jungle cats were tearing into a giant lizard.

"Oh," Sarah said, feeling a bit guilty for the way she'd reacted.

"No worries," Morgan distractedly answered.

Sarah let out a long sigh.

"We should have learned our lesson about falling asleep in hostile territory without taking some precautions."

Morgan shrugged, still looking down at the fight below.

"Next time," Sarah continued, "we should set a watch or sleep off the ground."

"Uh-huh," Morgan replied, not even listening to her at all now.

His eyes were glued on the four creatures below as they tore the lizard limb from limb.

"Do you think those are beasts?"

Sarah glared at him, realizing he'd been completely ignoring her. She let out another sigh, already knowing where this conversation was heading.

"Yes, Morgan; they're probably beasts," she said, rolling her eyes.

"You think we can take them all?"

Yup, there was that note of excitement she'd become used to hearing.

"I don't know, Morgan, but I honestly don't feel like fighting right after I just woke up," She turned her head and tried to bury it in his chest, but it just bumped against the metal plating of his new armor, making her wince.

Damn that Katherine and her damn armor, she thought, crossly.

"Alright, how about I just leave you up in a tree then," Morgan asked, already floating over to one.

"You are not leaving me up a tree!" she yelled, wrapping her arms around his neck.

"So you'll fight them with me?" he asked with a grin.

Sarah glared at him for a full ten seconds, before finally relenting.

"Fine," she said, "but you'll owe me!"

"Deal!" Morgan said excitedly and drifted down to the ground.

He set Sarah down and assessed the situation, trying to decide how best to take these beasts on.

The cats were much larger than they'd appeared to be from the air. Each was at least four feet at the shoulder and over eight feet long- and that was without including the tail.

Their coats were light tan, with small black and brown spots along the sides. A line of bristling black fur stretched from the base of their necks, down their spines and to the tips of their tails.

"You have any clue what these things are?" Morgan asked in a lowered tone.

Aaron Oster

Sarah shook her head in the negative.

"Do you think it's wise to attack a pack of beasts of unknown *rank?*" she asked, making one final effort to try and dissuade him from a fight.

"We'll never know if we don't try," he said, flashing her a grin.

"Damn it all to hell!" she hissed. "You're going to get us killed one day. You know that, don't you?"

It wasn't a real question, but Morgan answered anyway.

"Probably," he replied, his grin widening.

Sarah just rolled her eyes, then turned her gaze back to the feasting cats.

"So, what's the plan?" she asked.

"Simple. I'll go in and hit them and you support from the rear."

"That's not a plan!" she exclaimed, but it was already too late.

With a whoop of excitement, Morgan sprinted toward the group of cats, glowing with purple light as his shield flared around him.

"Why me?" Sarah asked, taking up a fighting stance and preparing for the fight ahead.

Morgan dashed toward the still distracted group of cats, angling himself to attack the one on the far left. His fists clenched in anticipation of the fight and a wild grin was plastered across his face. The cats must have had good hearing, because they all turned to face him as he approached, just not fast enough.

Morgan's fist crashed into the side of the first one's head with a satisfying crunch. The cat let out an angry yowl as it staggered back from him, but still managed to retain its footing. Morgan ducked, narrowly avoiding a lunging cat from his right, then spun in place and caught the next one around the throat.

He used *heavy impact,* locking his arm tight around the cat's neck, then violently twisted his hips. There was a loud crack as the cat's spine was severed and it fell limp in his arms.

One down.

A loud whoosh escaped his lungs as another one of the cats bowled into him, driving him to the ground and landing on top of him. He grunted as the heavy weight settled onto his chest and the cat's razor-sharp claws began raking at his shield.

He twisted his body violently to the right, but the cat went along with the movement, pressing more of its weight down on him. He tried twisting again, but without any success. The cat brought its clawed paw down on him once again and his shield buckled, shattering under the force of the blow.

The cat let out a victorious roar, then was promptly killed by a barrage of icy spears that slammed into it from the side.

"Thanks!" Morgan called out, shoving the heavy weight off himself and getting back to his feet.

That had been way too close for comfort. He would definitely need to be more careful when fighting multiple opponents in the future.

As he regained his footing, it became apparent as to why it had taken Sarah so long to get the cat off him. A third cat lay dead, punctured by *icicle spears* and coated in frost.

That left just one more; the one he'd staggered right at the beginning of the fight.

Looking around the clearing, the injured cat was nowhere to be seen. He straightened from his fighting stance, eyeing the three cat corpses and turning to look at Sarah.

"Did you see where the last one went?"

"No. I was too busy saving your sorry ass," she replied, pulling a core retrieval rod from the spatial bag.

"Here," she said, tossing him the rod. "This was your idea, so you'll be the one getting your hands dirty."

Morgan caught the rod and shrugged.

He didn't mind retrieving the cores.   In fact, he enjoyed it.

Bending down near the first cat, he plunged the rod into it and retrieved the core. He quickly opened its status and examined it.

Name: Soot-spine leopard core
Rank - 12
Total available energy - 2,106/2,106

This core was taken from a soot-spine leopard and has no special properties.

Aaron Oster

Morgan heard a loud crunching sound and closed the core's status to see Sarah pulling a core free. The next second, it crumbled to powder in her hand and she went to retrieve the third one.

Morgan felt annoyed for a second, then shrugged. She had killed two of them, after all. Concentrating on the core, he quickly absorbed the energy, then checked his status.

Name: Morgan
Supermage: Rank - 10
Energy to next rank - 10,328/20,000
Ability - Divine Gravity & Air
RP - 610/610 (Regen - 6.0 per second)
Strength - 57
Agility - 68
Constitution - 60
Intelligence - 61
Wisdom - 60
Skills - Enhanced flight, Heavy impact, Gale force, Condensed wind blade
Traits - Gravity field, Recovery
Extra - Gravity storm

Morgan closed his status.

He was more than halfway to the next rank, which confused him for a few moments. Hadn't he had just about 6,000 energy the last time he checked?

Then it came to him and he felt like smacking himself.

Of course. The assassins he'd killed last night! It had been so long since he'd killed any actual people, that he'd completely forgotten about getting energy from them.

He chuckled to himself, glad that he hadn't asked Sarah.

She probably would have berated him for being so forgetful.

His mind then turned back to the task at hand.

He was getting closer to ranking up again. In fact, he could probably do so right now, since that fall two nights ago had probably ensured he would receive the maximum number of attributes when he did.

Morgan was reaching to retrieve another core, when a low, rumbling growl shook the entire clearing; and he cursed to himself.

It felt like every time he was about to rank up, something would prevent him from doing so.

He debated ignoring the beast, and *ranking up* anyway, when the growl sounded again; much more menacing this time. Morgan felt the hair on the back of his neck prickle, as he slowly rose from his crouch. His eyes darted around the surrounding trees as he tried to place where the growl had come from. He felt Sarah's shoulder bump his and was quick to put his back to hers.

The growl came again, this time from a different direction and Morgan felt his heart rate increase as adrenaline began pumping through his body.

He still found it odd that the mass of reiki acting as his heart would function in the exact same way as his old one. If he couldn't sense the core of power there, he wouldn't have even known the difference.

"What do you think it is?" Sarah asked in a low voice.

Her voice was tense and her body rigid as they slowly turned in place, trying to spot the beast that was stalking them.

"If I had to guess, I'd say that the cat we couldn't find went to get some backup," Morgan answered.

He could feel the beast's eyes on him, glaring with malicious intent, but he couldn't actually see it.

"You just had to pick a fight, didn't you?" Sarah hissed as the growl came again, this time from the opposite direction.

"We can always try to escape," Morgan replied as he felt a grin work itself onto his face.

Despite the undoubtedly fearsome beast they were about to face, he couldn't help but be excited.

A flicker of movement caught Morgan's attention and his head snapped in that direction. He gave Sarah a sharp nudge in the ribs, eliciting a curse.

"What was that for? I- " she began, turning to glare at him. She stopped mid-sentence when her eyes fell on the beast stalking out from between the trees.

"Oh. Shit. We are so screwed!"

14

Despite the elegant way in which Sarah had voiced it, Morgan was forced to admit that she was probably right.

He'd never even imagined a beast could look so terrifying.

The cat that was slowly emerging from the trees resembled the ones they'd been fighting, in the same way a housecat resembled a tiger. To begin with, it was nearly twice as long and nearly two feet taller at the shoulder; not to mention that it looked to outweigh the others by at least a ton.

The difference in appearance was also quite noticeable. The cat was a darker brown in color and the spotted pattern on its sides extended over its entire body, making it difficult to track against the background of the trees. A line of bristling black quills stretched down its back, to the tip of its tail. The quills also covered its shoulders and a section of its underbelly, proving a layer of protection.

A pair of canines curved downward from its upper jaws, extending down past its chin, and a pair of slitted pupils stared back at them inside gleaming golden eyes. Its paws didn't make so much as a sound as it padded towards them and a set of wicked looking claws extended from each one, tearing up the soft loam underfoot.

Morgan's eyes followed the massive cat as it began to slowly circle them, lunging in every few seconds before pulling back. Every time it did, it would move in a little closer, quills rattling in anticipation.

This beast was intelligent. Or at least intelligent enough to realize the two of them posed a threat. Despite its terrifying appearance, he was still fairly confident they could win, but it wouldn't be an easy fight.

"Any idea what that thing is?" Morgan asked out of the corner of his mouth.

"If I did, don't you think I'd have said something?" Sarah growled.

Morgan shrugged.

It was worth a try.

"I'll try and get its attention. I won't use any skills until I know what type of beast we're up against."

"Don't be stupid!" Sarah hissed back. "If you try and hit that thing bare-handed, you'll skewer yourself!"

"I'm not planning on hitting it," Morgan replied, taking a step away from her and readying himself. "I just have to figure out if its skills are mage or super based. Then I'll know what type of *wind blade* to use. I have a feeling that choosing correctly will make all the difference."

Sarah nodded, only now remembering that the type of *wind blade* he used would determine how much damage he could dish out. And since his new *condensed wind blade* skill was so expensive to use, he'd only be able to use it once before needing to wait for his *RP* to regenerate. In a fight like this he would need every point he had.

Morgan crouched low as the cat feinted again, carefully analyzing its movements and committing them to memory.

This opponent was extremely dangerous. He and Sarah could always try using their powerful new skills, but if they missed they would both be left defenseless. There was also the possibility that Morgan's extremely flashy gravity storm would attract unwanted attention.

He would still use it, but only as a last resort. His shield was still down and would be so for at least another hour. He'd discovered that if a mage shield was broken, it would take some time until it was usable again.

He did have another line of defense. His supermage trait, *gravity field*, would decrease all incoming damage by ten percent. He also had the new set of enchanted armor from Katherine. If all else failed, he could always go for an all-out attack and hope he survived long enough for his recovery trait to heal him; but that, like using his gravity storm, would only be a last resort.

"Hope you're ready for this," he said, flashing Sarah a grin. "Try and slow it down, and if you get a clear shot, take it."

Sarah nodded, her blue shield coming up around her as she did.

That, apparently, was a mistake. The second the shield flared to life, the cat's eyes locked onto her and it let out an earth-shaking roar, then pounced right at her.

Morgan winced at the sheer volume of it, then used *gale force* and dashed to intercept it.

Aaron Oster

He needed its attention on him. Sarah couldn't soak up damage the way he could and if she got injured, she wouldn't be able to heal herself.

Morgan launched himself at the cat and lashed out with a powerful kick. Catching it mid-leap, the force of the kick was just enough to send the cat off course, but just barely. With an angry yowl, it flew past Sarah, claws missing her by a hair.

"Holy shit!" Sarah exclaimed, nearly falling over in shock.

The cat had attacked with such speed that she hadn't even had time to react!

"Stay on your toes!" Morgan yelled, dashing past her and engaging with the cat.

Just from that one kick, he was able to feel that he'd underestimated the beast's weight. The only reason he could think of was that the quills were heavier than he'd originally thought.

The cat had landed on its feet and turned to glare at him.

Well, he'd gotten its attention. Now to see what it was made of.

It let out a mighty roar and pounced, claws extending a good eight inches as it attempted to disembowel him. Morgan dodged back and to the side, narrowly avoiding its glittering claws. Aiming for the unprotected head, he used *heavy impact* and punched a closed fist toward one of its eyes. The cat dodged back, turning what would have been a crippling blow into a glancing one. Morgan's fist connected with the bone of its brow instead of the actual eye, splitting the skin and opening a shallow cut.

Hissing in pain, the cat whirled on the spot and slammed its spiked tail into his side. Morgan winced as multiple barbs punched through his armor and pierced his side. He was thrown back under the force of the attack, but managed to catch himself with his *flight* skill and landed back on the ground. He felt at his side as he landed and his hand came away slick with blood. The wounds weren't too deep and nothing felt broken, so the armor had done its job; for the most part anyway.

The cat turned to him, blood streaming down one side of its face from where his fist had injured it. It roared again, then an icy haze settled over it as Sarah used her improved *frostbite* skill. This new skill was called *bitter frost* and it slowed targets by thirty percent. It also had the additional effect of lowering the target's resistance to damage by five percent.

The cat visibly slowed, as the haze settled over it. Then Sarah's *icicle barrage* hit it full force, sending ten icy spears into its unprotected side. Four of the spears sunk into the cat's flesh, but the rest were deflected as the spines along its back rose with a rattle.

From the looks of it, Sarah's attacks hadn't been much more than flesh wounds. The cat was still relatively unharmed and all they'd really managed to do was enrage it.

The cat whipped its head back and forth, trying to decide who to attack, eventually coming to rest on Sarah. It let out a low rumbling growl, then all the spines along its back rose at once, making it appear to double in size. The spines began glowing a brilliant blue and the cat crouched low as if in preparation to pounce.

Morgan had begun dashing to intercept the cat, when he realized it wasn't attacking. Rather, it was slowly crouching lower and lower, as the blue glow intensified. An *icicle barrage* slammed into the crouching cat, but this time they simply bounced off the glowing spines.

"Shit! What the hell is that thing made of?" Sarah exclaimed, then started throwing one barrage after the next at it, as if hoping to get in a lucky shot

Morgan kept a close eye on the cat.

Something was definitely wrong here. It had demonstrated that it had a mage ability, but it wasn't attacking at all, even as Sarah pelted it with one attack after the next.

The spines began rattling as the cat's head came close to touching the ground, and Morgan finally understood what was about to happen. He dashed toward Sarah with all the speed he could muster, even as the cat rose from its crouch, head pointed to the sky in a mighty roar.

Morgan dove forward, catching Sarah around her waist as the massive cat let its attack loose. The glowing blue spines shot from its back in a massive area of effect attack, the spines buzzing through the air like a swarm of angry hornets.

Morgan bore Sarah to the ground just as the attack went off, but he wasn't fast enough to completely avoid injury. He winced as one spine tore a furrow across his cheek, and another pierced right through his shoulder and into Sarah's arm. She let out a cry of pain, as the glowing spine punched through her mage shield like it wasn't even there.

Morgan shielded her as best he could, and after a few seconds, it grew quiet. He rose cautiously to his feet, turning to survey the damage that had been done. The cat stood in the center of a forest of bristling spines. They were everywhere; protruding from the ground, the trees, and even from a few rocks. The spines had gone through them all.

The cat stared at him, as new spines slowly regrew from its back. Morgan grimaced as he gripped the spine lodged is his shoulder and ripped it free. He could feel his uniform start to soak up the blood, but did his best to ignore it. He was surprised at the cold feeling coming from the spine clutched between his fingers. He briefly examined it, noting with interest that it was some kind of metal he'd never seen before.

He had no time to examine it now. The cat was vulnerable after that attack. Now would likely be his best chance to strike.

Moving his arm to the side, he used *condensed wind blade*, watching as a swirling lance of air formed over his arm. The lance glowed a rich purple color, as the reiki in his core strengthened it.

He now knew that the cat had a mage ability, which meant that his piercing weapon would deal double damage. He just hoped that the cat didn't have any resistances against reiki, though he thought it was unlikely.

He heard a loud curse as Sarah rose to her feet behind him. She was clutching at her bleeding arm and didn't look at all pleased. Morgan himself could feel the burning pain in his shoulder, but he ignored it for now.

He could be in pain once the beast was dead. For now, he needed to concentrate on finishing it.

"Sarah, now's our best chance! Quick, while it's recovering!" he yelled.

Hoping she would back him up, he used *gale force* and flew at the angry cat, dashing over the ground at more than twice his normal speed. The cat roared its challenge, then bounded towards him as well, muzzle bunched up in a snarl.

Morgan dodged a swipe from its massive paw, then stuck out with the lance of air. The cat yowled in pain as the whirling blade punched into its shoulder, but it twisted its body out of the way and avoided further injury.

Morgan clenched his teeth as the cat danced back and he dashed after it, determined to end it before its spines regrew completely. The cat abruptly changed direction as he moved in and this time, he wasn't fast enough to dodge. Its claws made a horrible shrieking sound as they scraped over the chest plate and Morgan was now very glad for the improved armor. He then spun in place, landing a heavy kick to the side of the cat's head and snapping one of its fangs. The cat staggered back under the force of the attack, as blood sprayed from where the tooth had been knocked loose.

It shook its head and roared in pain, sending a shower of blood spraying across him. Darting forward, it attempted to take a chunk out of his arm in retaliation for its lost tooth. Morgan put all his weight on one foot, then pivoted to the side and slashed the blade across its ribs. The piercing weapon wasn't as effective at slashing attacks, but the blade still cut a bloody furrow across its side.

The cat spun and attempted to batter him with its tail, but since the spines had yet to regrow, the damage was minimal. Morgan grinned when the attack merely bounced off his armor, then lunged forward once more. The cat attempted to dodge back, and a ball of ice the size of a small boulder slammed into its head.

The cat staggered under the force of that blow, momentarily stunned and Morgan saw his chance. Activating both *gale force* and *heavy impact*, he darted forward in a blur of motion.

He'd found that using the two skills in bursts, rather than keeping them active, saved him a lot of RP. The rapid shift in both strength and speed would also throw his opponents off and allow him to strike a decisive blow.

Morgan dodged a clumsy swipe of its paw and, with a cry of triumph, sunk the whirling purple blade deep into the cat's skull. The beast shuddered a few times as the blade tore its brain to pieces, then crashed to the ground in a heap; blood pooling underneath it from the massive hole left in its head.

15

Morgan dismissed his wind blade and winced as the pain in his shoulder hit him. He turned back to Sarah, who was clutching at her bleeding arm with a pained expression on her face.

"Are you alright?" he asked, clutching at his own wound and walking over to her.

"I don't know," she said with a grimace, her hand clamped tightly over the injury.

"Let me see," he said, crouching down next to her.

He gently pried her fingers away from the wound and examined it closely. Then he pulled the damaged uniform shirt over his head and tore a strip from the bottom.

"It doesn't look too bad. It may hurt for a few days, but it should heal just fine."

He then asked her to wash the wound out, before tightly binding it with the strip of the shirt. Sarah watched him as he worked and it was only then that she noticed the line of blood running from his shoulder.

She'd been too busy with her own, comparatively minor, injury to even notice.

"Your shoulder looks horrible!" Sarah exclaimed, as soon as Morgan moved back and she got a better look at it.

"It's not as bad as it looks," he said with a shrug.

"Don't give me that!" she said, feeling guilty for not tending to his obviously more severe injury before he dealt with hers. Getting to her feet, she started washing away the blood, then tore another strip from the shirt and cleaned away the rest. Sarah was shocked by the sight of the gruesome injury.

The quill had gone clean through, tearing muscle and even scraping the bone. How could he just stand there and not even show an ounce of discomfort? Was he even human?

Morgan stood still as she finished cleaning, and then bandaging, the wound.

He would heal fully in twenty-four hours, but blood loss was still a big risk. This would hopefully do the job until then.

He examined the binding once she was done and nodded his thanks. Sarah then fished a new armored shirt from her bag and handed it to him.

"I know the uniforms are supposed to be self-healing, but I'm not sure how long it'll take," she said, taking the torn one and placing it in the bag.

Her injury had been on her arm and since her uniform was sleeveless, she didn't need to worry about changing. Morgan's, on the other hand, had been thoroughly shredded and covered in blood.

Morgan nodded his thanks once again, then pulled the shirt over his head, feeling it tighten and conform perfectly to his body.

"Well, let's go check out what kind of beast we just fought," he said, a grin now spreading across his face.

Sarah just let out a long sigh and slumped down to sit on the ground. "You go check it out. I'm too tired," she said, waving him on.

"Suit yourself," he said with a shrug, then ran toward the now dead body of the massive cat.

He stopped before it, crouching down and pulling the core retrieval rod from his belt. He had a bit of a hard time getting it, but after a few minutes of effort, he removed a glowing red and blue core. Excitedly, he pulled up the core's status so he could see what kind of beast they'd just fought.

Name: Magesteel-spine leopard core
Rank - 10
Total available energy - 7,106/7,106

This core was taken from a magesteel-spine leopard. As this core is from an intermediate beast, the amount of available energy has been greatly increased.

To say that Morgan was shocked would have been an understatement.

With the level of difficulty, as well as the damage output on that thing, he'd expected it to be at least rank 16. This fight raised even more questions about beasts and how their power was measured. Sarah had told him that all beasts evolved, but the soot-spine leopards were rank 12, and they were just regular beasts.

He turned to look at Sarah, who was now lying flat on her back and appeared to be sound asleep. Morgan shook his head in amazement.

He was way too amped up to sleep right now. He also needed answers and he thought he knew someone who might be able to supply him with some.

Fishing Katherine's pendant from under his uniform shirt, he closely examined it. It was a small piece of flat metal with two small protrusions on either side. Other than that, it just looked like a regular silver coin. Pressing the small protrusion on the left, he spoke into it, feeling just a bit foolish talking to an inanimate object.

"Katherine?" he asked questioningly.

"Morgan!" Katherine's sultry voice sounded in his mind after a few seconds. "It's good to hear from you so soon. Did you decide to call and arrange our marriage, after all?"

"No."

There were a few seconds of silence and Morgan could almost see her pouting on the other side of their connection.

"So, what do you need?" she asked, after a few more seconds of silence.

Yup, he could definitely detect a pout in her voice.

"I actually had a question and was wondering if you could answer it for me. We just took down a beast and when I examined the core, it said that it was an intermediate beast. I've seen a few different types of cores and the amount of energy seems to wildly fluctuate between them. I just can't seem to get a sense of how power is measured when it comes to beasts. The beast we fought was the same *rank* as I was, but the fight was a lot more difficult than it should have been."

"No one at the academy explained it to you?" Katherine asked, seeming to perk up a bit.

"No, and it's really starting to bug me," he replied.

"Alright, I'll do my best to explain. Beasts are lumped into five categories. Ranked from weakest to most dangerous, they are: basic, evolved, intermediate, advanced, and pinnacle. Basic beasts are the most common and the ones that you'll run into the most. They are the easiest to defeat and greatly resemble their animal counterparts. Their intelligence is also quite lacking and they're no smarter than your average animal."

"Evolved beasts are a bit rarer, but still quite common. You will not find an evolved beast under *rank 9*, as they only exist when a basic beast breaks through into *rank 9*. This doesn't happen with all beasts, however. That is a common misconception. They tend to be more intelligent and powerful than the basic beasts, but are still quite manageable to defeat on your own."

"Intermediate beasts are where the real danger begins. They are a lot more intelligent than an evolved beast and tend to be a whole lot more powerful. They still resemble their animal counterparts, but always have a distinct characteristic that makes them stand out. Most supers or mages would be extremely hard pressed to take one of equal *rank* out alone. Because of their power, the amount of energy available is always significantly higher than that of an evolved beast. If I may ask, what kind of beast did you just fight?"

"A magesteel-spine leopard," Morgan replied. "And you're right. It wasn't an easy fight."

"Really?!" Katherine sounded quite excited.

"Yeah, why?"

"Did it fire off its area of effect attack?"

"You mean where glowing blue spines flew in all directions and almost killed us?" Morgan asked.

"Is there anyone in the area?" Katherine asked.

"No, why?" Morgan asked, wondering why she sounded so excited.

His head whipped to the side as a swirling portal suddenly opened, not five feet away, and Katherine stepped through, dressed in a uniform cut in a style similar to Sarah's. There were a few key differences though. For one, hers was red and white in the fashion of the North Kingdom's military. For another, it was a whole lot more revealing. The pants had a line of open slits running up the outside of both her legs and the shirt had a deep neckline that revealed quite a bit of cleavage.

Morgan noted all of this as she stepped through. For a moment he wondered what the purpose of wearing armor would be if so much was uncovered, then he remembered Katherine's *rank*.

If something was powerful enough to actually harm her, then a layer of armor wouldn't make any difference. There was also the East Kingdom's heat to contend with. It was still quite early, but the heat was already beginning to hit him, so he could understand why her uniform had so many gaps.

When her eyes landed on him, Katherine flashed him a warm smile, then came over and gave him a tight hug. Morgan felt the air rush out of him as she did and his ribs creaked ominously under the immense pressure.

"Can't breathe!" he wheezed.

"Oh no! I'm so sorry!" she said, quickly releasing him and looking him over.

"It's alright," he said, rubbing at his ribs.

Holy crap, she was strong. If she'd squeezed just a little tighter, his ribs may very well have snapped.

"I'll have to be more careful in the future," she said sheepishly. "Now, where is that leopard?"

Morgan pointed over her shoulder and her eyes lit up when she saw all the spines littering the ground.

"Would you mind telling me why you want these?" Morgan asked as she began collecting them.

"Magesteel is a very rare metal and isn't a naturally occurring resource," she said, as she worked. "It's extremely hard to find, as it only grows on certain beasts and will only be potent if the beast infuses it with mana before it dies."

"What can it be used for? And what would have happened if it didn't infuse it with mana?" he asked curiously.

Katherine was a literal fountain of knowledge. He'd learned more in the few minutes he'd spent speaking with her than he had over the last few weeks. Then again, he had been on the run for most of that time,

"Magesteel is used in all kinds of things, but mostly for enchanted weapons and armor," she said, walking over to a new spot and stooping down once more.

"If the beast had died before using its attack, the spines would have turned soft and eventually disintegrated, so you can imagine why I'm so excited."

Morgan nodded, watching as she bent down to pick up another bundle, then open a small portal and deposit them there.

"You were explaining about beasts before you came over," he said. "Would you mind continuing?"

She looked up at him and flashed her perfect smile. "For you, anything. Now, where was I... Oh yes, advanced beasts."

She stood up and headed to the tree line where more spines were located and Morgan followed after her.

"Advanced beasts are extremely dangerous and far rarer than the intermediate ones. They are both powerful and intelligent, and an advanced beast of equal *rank* would not be able to be bested by a single person. Advanced beasts don't much resemble any animal found in the wild. Rather, they are a mix of several different ones that are blended together to create an extremely dangerous opponent. Even you should be wary about tackling one alone and, even with Sarah, don't go up against one that is even a single *rank* above you."

"Are they really that dangerous?" Morgan asked, mind going to the azure-crystal wyvern core in his pocket.

"Yes. Even I wouldn't take one on alone unless it was at least *5 ranks* under my own."

They must be truly dangerous if Katherine was this serious about it. Who could have killed the two rank 39 advanced beasts, whose cores were set as prizes in a tournament?

"The most powerful of all the beasts are pinnacle beasts," she continued.

"I thought pinnacle beasts were just a name given to beasts who had reached the maximum *rank*," Morgan said, brows coming together in confusion.

"Another common misconception," she replied, waving her hand as she pulled up the last of the spines.

"Pinnacle beasts are in a class all their own. They are each one of a kind and have actual names. They are so rarely found that entire expeditions are sent after them when we get wind of one. They have intelligence comparable to that of a human and power that far exceeds even the strongest supers and mages."

"How strong are we talking?" Morgan asked.

"Strong enough that I would be loathed to take on a *rank 19* alone."

Morgan's eyes widened when she said this and she nodded her head in agreement.

"I've only ever seen one pinnacle beast and that was over ten years ago. My father got wind of one and sent his most powerful soldiers out after it. I insisted on going along, as I was extremely curious. It didn't take long for us to find it. All we had to do was follow the path of destruction in its wake. When we first came upon it, I didn't think much of it. It resembled a human in size and shape. The only differences were skin color and facial features. But when the soldiers launched their first attack, it transformed."

She shuddered slightly at the memory and continued with her tale.

"It was horrible. There were forty soldiers *ranked* from *34* to *42*. Not even half of them survived. I was presented with the core afterward and found out that the beast was only *rank 27*. The amount of available energy was staggering. I had only awakened my ability a few months before, so I was still at a relatively low *rank*. That core had enough energy to push me up into the *30's*."

"Seriously?!" Morgan asked, now both excited and a little afraid at the same time.

He wanted to fight one. These pinnacle beasts sounded like the ultimate challenge and if he could defeat one on his own.

"I know what you're thinking," Katherine said with a grin. "And don't worry, if I ever find one, I'll be taking you along with me. I expect you'll do the same for me. We will be getting married, after all."

"Never agreed to that," Morgan said as Katherine opened a portal.

"I really should get going," she said, placing a hand on one of her shapely hips and looking around the clearing. "It's risky for me to be here, though it was definitely worth coming over."

"For the magesteel," Morgan said with a nod.

If it was as valuable as she said, then it must be a risk worth taking.

"That. And to see you, of course," she said, flicking him on the nose and laughing lightly.

"Oh, okay," Morgan said, "I have one more question before you go. I've actually been wondering about this for a while. If supers and mages have such long lives, why aren't there more people at the maximum *rank*?"

"Let me answer your question with one of my own," she said after thinking for a few seconds. "How many people actually awaken an ability? Of those people, how many actively try and improve?"

Morgan shrugged.

He had absolutely no idea.

"About eighty percent of the population will awaken an ability," Katherine said, answering her own question. "Of that eighty percent, not even ten percent will make any real effort to increase in *rank*. Of those that do, not even one percent will reach the *rank* where their lifespan will be increased."

"I thought all supers and mages automatically had an increased lifespan," Morgan said.

This bit of information was quite troubling. It meant that he only had a limited amount of time to reach the required rank. Otherwise, he'd just die of old age.

"Most do and that's why so few even try. You will have to reach *rank 19* for your first big jump in life expectancy. Once you break through, your life expectancy will go up by around a hundred years. After you break through *29* it'll further increase by another two hundred. I'm not entirely sure what a supermage can expect, though, as your *rank* won't stop progressing at *50*."

Morgan nodded at that and Katherine gave him a grin.

"Any other questions before I go?" she asked in a playful tone.

"None for now, but thanks," he said, returning the smile.

It was good to know that he had someone he could count on for information any time he needed it. Sarah knew a lot, but this experience had just shown him that there were many things she didn't know.

"I'll be going then," she said.

Then she leaned in and kissed him on the cheek. She pulled back, noting that his demeanor nor expression hadn't changed in the slightest.

She would have to tell him soon of the damage that had been inflicted on him, but she didn't want to say anything yet. Not until she'd found some way of fixing it.

"Thanks again for all this amazing magesteel. I'll send you something nice as a thank you."

She winked at him, then stepped through the portal.

16

Morgan felt at the place where she'd kissed him, wondering at the strange feeling he was once again experiencing.

What was it? Maybe this was how all people felt when receiving a kiss. He really wished he had something to compare it to, as the feeling was beginning to nag at him.

He shook himself once more, as the odd feeling faded, and concentrated instead on something he'd been trying to do for a while, checking how much energy he had in total and finally move up to *rank 11.*

He pulled all his cores from his pockets and taking a few seconds to look at each, he quickly did some math in his head. By the time he was finished, he was astonished at the amount of energy available to him.

He had a total of seven cores, including the ones Katherine had given him. Altogether, they netted him just over 150,000 energy. That was enough to boost him at least ten ranks, if not more. The only thing he didn't know was how much breaking into rank 19 would cost. For now, he would just move up one rank, as he didn't want a potential loss of attribute points.

He pulled the azure-crystal wyvern core from the pile and put the rest away. Pulling up its status, he looked at the available energy.

Name: Azure-crystal wyvern core
Rank - 39
Total available energy - 68,376/68,376

This core was taken from an azure-crystal wyvern. As this core is from an advanced beast, the amount of available energy has been massively increased.

The amount of energy never ceased to amaze him. He thought about absorbing only part of the energy and another screen popped into view showing how much he'd need to move to the next rank.

Energy to next rank - 10,328/20,000

Morgan concentrated on the amount of energy he wanted to use and a message popped up in the core's status.

Would you like to absorb 11,500 energy from the azure-crystal wyvern core?

Yes/No

Mentally selecting *yes*, Morgan felt a shudder run through him as he *ranked* up. Along with that feeling came the familiar sharpening of his mind and reflexes, as well as the feeling of strength, coursing through him. He examined the core one last time, noting the available energy had dropped to *56,876/68,376*. Tucking the core away, he excitedly opened his own status to see the changes.

Name: Morgan
Supermage: Rank - 11
Energy to next rank - 1,828/22,000
Ability - Divine Gravity & Air
RP - 650/650 (Regen - 6.4 per second)
Strength - 60
Agility - 72
Constitution - 63
Intelligence - 65
Wisdom - 64
Skills - Enhanced flight, Heavy impact, Gale force,
Condensed wind blade
Traits - Gravity field, Recovery
Extra - Gravity storm

He did a quick run through of his skills next, but there were no increases in power.

There was one change, though. His condensed wind blade had gone from a cost of 350 RP to 340 RP. This wasn't a huge decrease, but if it kept going down as he ranked up, the cost might eventually become manageable.

Morgan closed his status and looked over to where Sarah was still passed out on the ground.

Aaron Oster

He really should wake her, but she looked quite comfortable and he was loathe to incur her wrath.

He was about to walk over to rest against a nearby tree, when he stumbled, as a flash of memory slammed into him.

Cold. Dark. Pain. A woman with black hair. The sound of shouting men. A cool hand over his eyes. Nothingness.

Morgan came to himself as the memories faded, leaving him with nothing but a dull throbbing pain in his head and a profound sense of loss.

He already had a feeling that those were memories from the missing years of his life, but what could have triggered them? Was it something he saw, or did the increase in rank boost his wisdom enough for him to remember?

The headache began wearing off as he slowly got back to his feet.

Whatever was happening, he needed to remember more. That meant that he now had another reason to rank up as quickly as possible. For now, all he had were more questions. Foremost among them, who was the woman with the black hair?

He couldn't remember distinct features, but there was a feeling he didn't recognize attached to her. He knew whoever this woman was would have answers to all his questions. He needed to remember more, if only to figure out who she was.

He shook himself once more to get rid of the feeling of loss, then walked over to wake Sarah.

It was already past nine and they really should be going.

He tried, unsuccessfully, to wake Sarah up, finally just slinging her onto his back and heading deeper into the forest.

There was some sort of settlement just a few days away. There, they could get directions and restock on supplies.

He wanted to get there faster, but decided against running, because the motion would likely wake Sarah. In the end, he floated a few inches off the ground and sped off through the woods, heading in the direction of the settlement.

***

Arnold peeked out from between the trees and let out a sigh of relief.

This morning had been one of the most stressful of his life. First, Sarah and Morgan had faced a pack of jungle cats. Then an intermediate beast. He'd been afraid that he would have to jump in at one point but had been relieved when they'd defeated it. His relief had been short-lived, as Katherine had shown up just minutes later.

His fear had abated when all she'd done was collect the cat's spines, but it had spiked again when she'd shot him a warning glare right before stepping into her portal. The warning was clear. If he failed and Morgan was hurt, she would hunt him down and kill him.

Arnold took a moment to look around the clearing, then took off at a brisk jog, glancing down at his tracking device to make sure he was on course.

If he wasn't mistaken, they were headed for the trade town of Garr, which was about four days away. He would need to be wary, seeing as he hadn't spotted any assassins since their first encounter back in the Central Kingdom. He'd be an idiot if he thought that they'd lost them. If anything, it made him more nervous that they hadn't attacked yet, which could only mean one thing: they were setting a trap.

This thought alone was enough for Arnold to pick up his pace a bit.

He couldn't let Morgan out of his sight for even a moment. It would be a lot more difficult once they reached the town, but for now, it wasn't too hard to keep close without being spotted.

He reached up, wiping the condensation from his brow and grimacing in annoyance.

It wasn't actual sweat. It would take a lot more than a brisk jog to make him sweat at his rank. It was the damned climate of the East Kingdom. It was always hot and muggy here, and the condensation kept collecting on his skin. He wiped his forehead once again, reminding himself what was at stake. He would either get a bag stuffed full of platinum or lose his head. If he had to choose, he'd take the platinum.

He slowed as he heard the telltale swish of air from up ahead, meaning that Morgan was flying not too high off the ground.

Smart of him to do that. He'd avoid all the mud and wouldn't risk being seen by anyone by flying over the trees.

Aaron Oster

He grimaced as his boot sank into the soft ground with an audible squelch for what felt like the hundredth time that morning and ripped it free with a grunt of annoyance.

He was so caked in mud that he likely resembled it more than himself at the moment. That bag of platinum better be a heavy one.

***

Sarah woke up just after noon. She was confused at first, but after the fog of sleep cleared from her mind, she was quite pleased to find that Morgan had let her sleep.

"How long have I been out?" she asked, yawning widely.

"About four hours," he replied, as he wove in between the trees.

"I'm sorry," she said, feeling a bit guilty.

"You don't have to be. It was no trouble. In fact, I've found that it's easier to travel through the air than on foot. The ground is soft and muddy. Since the air is so damp, any physical exertion would have left me drenched in sweat. Flying doesn't require any, so long as I don't go over the weight limit and the constant breeze keeps me cool and dry."

Sarah blinked, noticing for the first time how damp the air truly was.

If they had been on foot, it really would be a lot more difficult. She could feel how the breeze, even damp as it was, worked to keep her skin mostly dry and cool. She also had to grudgingly admit that the new armor the princess had provided was doing an excellent job in regulating her body temperature.

"How much further can you go before your *RP* runs out?" she asked, trying to get her mind away from the touchy subject.

"I'll have to land in about fifty seconds to regenerate my *RP*," he said.

She could detect a slightly bitter tone in his voice when he said this.

"What's wrong?"

He let out a sigh, speeding up slightly as the trees started becoming a bit more spaced out.

"The new *enhanced flight* skill is great. The only problem with it is, I can only stay in the air for around 160 seconds at a time before being forced to land."

"I realize that it can be annoying, but I'm sure the cost will become more manageable once you rank up a few more times."

Morgan nodded, then drifted slowly down to the ground.

"We may as well eat while my *RP* regenerates. I haven't had a chance since we fought those beasts earlier."

"What kind of beast was it?" she asked, hopping off his back and reaching into her uniform shirt for the small leather bag.

She fished out some dried meat and hard bread from the bag, before tucking it back down her shirt. Morgan began speaking as soon as they sat down and she listened in rapt attention as he explained all that had happened.

"You told me that you wouldn't call Katherine!" she exclaimed once he was finished.

Morgan shrugged in reply, biting into the tough jerky and tearing off a piece.

She glowered at him, but his expression didn't change.

Why did he have to be so infuriating?!

"Don't you have anything to say for yourself?" she demanded.

"Not really. I needed help and you were asleep. Besides, the information she provided was excellent."

He popped the last piece of meat into his mouth and stood up.

"We should get going. We still have a lot of ground to cover."

Sarah blew out a long breath, but climbed onto his back all the same. They flew on in silence for a time, landing every few minutes and walking so that Morgan could replenish his reiki. Finally, the silence was just too much to bear.

"Why do you trust her more than me?" Sarah asked.

"I don't," Morgan replied.

Sarah was a bit taken aback by the abrupt answer, but she wasn't about to be dissuaded.

"Really?" she asked, putting as much sarcasm as she could into her words. "Then why is it that the moment I'm asleep you call her?"

"You looked tired and I didn't want to wake you up," he replied.

Sarah clenched her jaw in frustration.

She wasn't getting anywhere with this line of questioning. She had to try something else. Maybe she could guilt him into giving her a straight answer?

"I feel as though you don't value my opinion since your meeting with her. She's more powerful and more knowledgeable than I am. So be honest, do you like her more than me?" She bit her lip when she asked this question, feeling her heart rate increase as she awaited his reply.

Morgan was about to reply but forced himself to stop.

He wasn't the best when it came to dealing with emotions, but he'd known Sarah for long enough to tell that she was upset and not just a little bit.

He ran over his entire experience over the last day, from his meeting with Katherine to the way Sarah had reacted.

When he looked at it from her point of view, it made a lot more sense to him. He wouldn't be too happy if a stranger came in and Sarah started listening to them over him. He just had to find the right words to convey it to her and hope she understood what he meant.

"Katherine is more knowledgeable and more powerful than you," he began, feeling her body stiffen up against his.

"But I've only known her for a day. She's different than you are and I can understand her better than I can understand you, but I've known you for years. You took care of me when I was hungry and you were the only friend I ever had. I like Katherine, but I *like* you. Do you understand what I'm saying?"

He didn't really know how to describe it any better than that.

Sarah was very quiet as she took it all in, a small smile curling her lips as the light breeze of their flight tickled over her skin.

She understood what he'd just said and most likely, even better than he himself did. She still didn't trust Katherine, but she did trust Morgan enough that her presence would no longer bother her.

She pressed her cheek against his back and sighed in contentment.

"Yes, Morgan. I understand."

17

They went on like this for the next three days, traveling through the air in bursts and waiting for Morgan's reiki to regenerate. They'd tried walking in between, but the soft ground and patches of mud soon dissuaded them from doing so.

Sarah had moved up to *rank 11* during this time. Her injury was already beginning to heal and Morgan was glad for it.

He felt a little bad when his shoulder had just stitched itself back together the next day, but Sarah had assured him that she felt fine. Things seemed to be back to normal after their talk a few days ago. In fact, Sarah seemed to be in an unusually good mood, though he couldn't fathom why.

Katherine had contacted him the day before and had come through a portal to deliver on her promise to bring him something for the magesteel spines she'd collected. He'd been a bit scared that Sarah would go back to being angry, but surprisingly enough, she didn't seem to mind at all.

Katherine had given both of them a wrapped package, then had promptly hopped back through the portal, blowing him a kiss as she did so. Sarah had become a bit aggravated when she saw that, but it didn't last very long.

Morgan glanced down to his hands.

He couldn't see them, as they were currently tucked under Sarah's legs, but he could feel the comfortable leather of the gloves that Katherine had given him. They were fingerless, just like the training gloves he'd had back at the academy, but these were interwoven with magesteel, giving them far more durability. There were also four rounded metal studs protruding from each knuckle.

He smiled to himself as he remembered slamming his fist into a tree and leaving four indents without feeling so much as a twinge of discomfort.

Katherine already seemed to know him well and had supplied him with the perfect weapon to enhance his hand-to-hand fighting. She hadn't forgotten about Sarah and had given her a combat knife. She would find this useful if she ever had to face an opponent up close.

Aaron Oster

Morgan felt his reiki running low and drifted down to the ground, landing softly and feeling Sarah slide off his back.

She groaned lightly, stretching her arms over her head, then dropped them and twisted from side to side.

"You really aren't that comfortable," she complained, sticking her knuckles into her lower back and arching her back. There was a series of loud pops and she sighed in relief, straightening and flashing him a grin.

"I'm sorry I'm not more comfortable," Morgan said in a flat tone, to which Sarah responded by sticking her tongue out at him.

"I think we should set up here for the evening," he said, tugging the gloves from his fingers and tucking them into a special seam on the inside of his uniform shirt.

Apparently, this was where Sarah had been keeping the spatial bag Gold had provided. He hadn't even known about it but felt a lot more secure now that his money and cores were hidden there. The best part about it was that the compartment was between the metal chest plate and the fabric of the uniform, so there was no discomfort or any visible sign that he was hiding anything.

Sarah looked around as well, nodding in agreement.

"Guess this as good as we're gonna get in this damned marsh," she said with a sigh.

"We'll reach the town tomorrow, then we can sleep somewhere cool and dry," Morgan said, scanning the surrounding area.

Something shiny on the ground caught his eye and he bent down to retrieve it.

Rising from his crouch, he examined it closely.

It was just a piece of flint, but it was shiny. Maybe he could get something for it in the town.

He tucked it away in the hidden compartment, then began scanning the surrounding trees for wildlife.

They hadn't run into anything as dangerous as the magesteel-spine leopard, but they had come across several of the smaller jungle cats, so they had to be wary of their surroundings.

"I can hardly wait to have a hot bath and a dry bed to sleep on," Sarah said, pulling one arm behind her head and leaning to the side.

It was only because he was paying such close attention to their surroundings that Morgan realized that something was wrong. He held up a hand and Sarah was instantly alert, eyes scanning the surrounding trees for any sign of movement.

Morgan's eyes were flicking around quickly as he made his way over to Sarah.

Whatever was out there, it would be better if he was close to her when it attacked.

There was a light whistling noise and Morgan ducked as a trio of needles flew over his head. He whirled to face three black-clad figures that had seemingly appeared from thin air.

"How the hell did they find us?" Sarah exclaimed.

Taking a quick peek over his shoulder, Morgan confirmed his suspicions.

They were surrounded and he had no doubt that these assassins would not go down as easily as the ones they'd fought previously. In a situation like this, there really was only one thing to do. Retreat.

He spun around and grabbed Sarah around the waist, then activated his *enhanced flight* skill. He got a foot off the ground before he felt the skill slip away from him and they dropped back down.

He landed on his feet and released Sarah, feeling his heart rate redouble.

They'd somehow blocked him from accessing his skills.

Sarah also seemed to realize that, as she tried unsuccessfully to use her own skills. Four more black-clad figures appeared, increasing their number to ten.

There was only one option left. Though he hated to do it, he would need to call Katherine.

He quickly moved his hand up to his neck, then felt something hit the back of his head. He stumbled forward, vision going blurry from the force of the impact. He shook his head and turned to see who had attacked him. One of the assassins was staring at him with a slightly wide-eyed expression.

Sarah was lying on the ground and he could see a small red mark on her temple.

He gritted his teeth, feeling strength surge through his body.

Aaron Oster

"I'll tear your heart from your chest and feed it to your corpse!" he growled, feeling his power returning.

Whatever they were using to dampen his power, it was apparently wearing off.

"How are you still conscious?" the assassin asked, sounding more curious than afraid.

"I'm tougher than I look," Morgan said, then launched himself at the man, pulling his fist back to crush his skull.

Something heavy slammed into the side of his head then, sending him reeling. He staggered, trying to regain his balance. Then something slammed into him from behind. He fell to one knee, grimacing as he fought against unconsciousness. A blurry figure came into view, stopping just a few inches from him.

He had to fight. Had to survive.

Morgan tried to get up and force his uncooperative legs to straighten. He felt a sharp prick in his neck and blackness overtook him.

***

Six years ago…

Morgan chewed on the bread, feeling the most wonderful sensations running through him. Even more surprising than the wonderful taste of something fresh was the warm feeling spreading throughout his body.

It wasn't quite the wild joy he felt while fighting, but rather, a warm, pleasant feeling that made him want to sigh in contentment.

He stopped eating for a moment as Sarah burst out laughing when the weird looking things on stage did something. The warm feeling began to slowly melt away, so he quickly took another bite and felt it return.

If what Sarah said was true, then he could be feeling like this all the time. All he had to do was be her friend, not that he really knew what that would entail. He understood the concept, but what he didn't understand was why people did it.

Sarah suddenly laughed uproariously again and Morgan turned to study her. She was leaning forward in her seat, cheeks flushed and a wide grin on her face. The stupid yarn and cloth constructs on stage said something and she roared with laughter again, clutching at her sides as she did so.

Morgan found - for some reason - that the longer he watched her, the better he could understand the friendship thing. He took another bite of the bread and chewed slowly.

He was already stuffed to the brim. He'd never eaten so much in his life. Or at least, he was pretty sure he hadn't.

Sarah laughed again, then turned to see him staring at her. She grinned widely; her sparkling green eyes flashing with mirth and Morgan found his lips twitching upward as well. Sarah didn't see it, as she'd already turned back to the stage, but Morgan was stunned.

He sat back in his seat, feeling a warmth flood through him that had nothing to do with the food he'd been eating.

He felt… happy? Was this was happiness felt like?

Morgan pondered this while the show continued, but no matter how much time passed, the feeling didn't recede. Every time Sarah laughed, he found that the feeling grew just a bit stronger.

Just who was this girl? Was she using some type of magic on him?

Morgan immediately dismissed the idea. Though he wasn't very good at telling age, he was pretty sure that Sarah was around the same as him. According to everything he'd overheard, the earliest one could expect an ability was at the age of twelve.

He really hoped he'd get his then.

The show finally came to an end and Sarah clapped and cheered along with all of the other children gathered there, as the creepy yarn constructs bowed and bobbed off the stage.

As the people began clearing out Sarah turned to him, her wide grin still fixed in place.

"So, what did you think of the show?"

Morgan shrugged. "I was too busy eating."

Sarah pouted at him, blowing out her cheeks and sticking out her bottom lip.

"You're no fun, you know that?"

"I thought about what you asked me earlier," he said, feeling the odd urge to smile again, but forcing it down. "I think that I do want to be your friend."

Sarah's pout vanished in an instant and she barreled into him, wrapping her arms around him in a tight hug.

Aaron Oster

Morgan staggered back under the force and immediately began trying to get her off.

Thankfully, she let go after only a few seconds and practically beamed at him.

"Oh, I'm so excited! We're going to have so much fun together!" she squeaked, jumping up and down.

Morgan watched her with an odd mixture of confusion and amusement.

He didn't know what it was about her that allowed him to feel, even if only for a little bit; but so long as he could, he would be sticking around.

"I take it you enjoyed the show?"

They both turned as a man came out from behind the stage. He was dressed in a flamboyantly colored shirt, wide billowy pants, and shoes that were far too large to be practical. Morgan immediately distrusted him, but Sarah seemed to have no such qualms.

"Yes! It was very funny," she said, giggling at the memory. "Were you the one controlling them?"

"Why, yes, my dear lady. I was!" the man replied with a grin of his own.

Morgan felt then that something was off. He cast his eyes around the square and noticed that the only one still there aside from them was Sarah's... father? Uncle? Older brother?

Morgan actually wasn't sure, as she'd never mentioned who he was, but judging by his appearance and the way Sarah acted around him, he would assume he was her father.

The man noticed his look and his eyes began darting around the empty square as well.

The man was clearly perceptive and he appeared to notice their situation.

He pushed himself off the wall and quickly strode over to the two of them.

"...definitely my favorite part!" Morgan caught the end of what Sarah was saying, as he turned back to the oddly dressed man.

"I'm so glad to hear that the daughter of our esteemed city lord was so pleased with our performance!" the man said with a flourish.

The entire thing seemed to go right over Sarah's head, but Morgan didn't miss a thing. He was a bit surprised to learn that she was the daughter of the city lord, though he supposed it would explain why she was so bossy; but how would this man know who she was? Sarah had never mentioned it.

Her... *bodyguard?* Morgan nodded to himself. Her bodyguard apparently hadn't missed it either, as he placed a hand on Sarah's shoulder, eyes flicking around the abandoned square.

"Hint! Did you see..." Sarah faltered when she saw the serious expression on his face.

"What's wrong?" she asked, looking between him and the strangely dressed man.

"We're leaving. Now," he said, turning her quickly and making for the square exit.

Morgan was right on his heels when the oddly dressed man spoke up again.

"Leaving so soon? The party is only getting started!"

Hint ignored the man and continued on toward the exit at a fast pace.

"Hint, what's going on?" Sarah asked again.

"Nothing is going on, Lady Sarah. We just need to leave," he replied.

Morgan could hear the strain in his voice and knew they were probably in a great deal of danger right now. Though he still couldn't see anything out of the ordinary, his senses were practically screaming at him that he was in imminent danger.

They had nearly reached the exit when there was a loud explosion from right above their heads and a mountain of rubble rained down on top of them. Morgan leaped back, his reflexes sharp as a cat's, and managed to avoid the worst of the falling debris.

Hint reacted even faster, which Morgan found quite impressive for someone his age. He grabbed Sarah by the shoulder and flung her back where she collided with him. They both went sprawling as a choking cloud of dust filled the square.

Morgan could hear someone laughing from behind them, a high pitched cackling sound that made his skin prickle; not in fear, but in anticipation. He could already sense a fight coming, though he was pretty sure it wasn't one he could win.

"What's happening?" Sarah asked as she untangled herself from him.

She staggered slowly to her feet, rubbing at her eyes and coughing as the choking dust invaded her lungs. Morgan had gotten to his feet as well and had pulled his shirt up over his mouth and nose. His eyes darted around the square, picking out wavering forms in the choking dust.

He was pretty sure that the collapsing wall had gotten Sarah's guard, which meant that right now, they were on their own.

Morgan debated for a few seconds as to what his next course of action should be. These people, whoever they were, were clearly only interested in Sarah. If he hid before the dust cleared, they would likely not bother looking for him once they had her.

Then again, he'd actually been able to feel something through the numbing cold that had pervaded his every waking moment for the last few months.

She had also promised good food, Morgan thought.

That was what decided it for him. If this had happened just a few hours earlier, he wouldn't have thought twice about abandoning her, but now…

"We have to go. Come with me," Morgan said, then grabbed her hand and pulled her toward the small sewer grate near the far wall of the square.

***

Morgan came to with a blinding headache. His mouth felt very dry and his eyes were crusted shut. He tried to move his arms but found that they were bound behind his back. He groaned lightly, cracking his eyes open and squinting into the surrounding gloom.

It was already night and the only illumination came from a small fire burning off to his left. He blinked a few times, trying to take stock of his situation.

The last thing he remembered was the attack by the assassins. Then their abilities had been blocked and he assumed he'd been knocked out.

He tried testing his bonds, wondering if his increased *strength* could help him break them, but had no luck. Craning his head around, he found that he was tied to a long stake driven deep into the ground. He could also see Sarah and was relieved to find her already awake.

A relived look crossed her features when she saw he was finally awake.

"We need to get out of here," she said in an urgent whisper.

Morgan was about to agree when a shadow fell over them, blocking out the flickering light of the fire. Turning his head, he saw one of the assassins staring down at him.

"You can try to escape, but I think you'll find that you just don't have the strength to break those ropes."

The man had a dry, raspy voice that put Morgan's nerves on edge.

"And don't even bother trying to use your abilities. So long as we have our blocker here, you won't be getting access to them."

He chuckled then and walked back to the fire, sitting down across another assassin.

Morgan's eyes quickly flicked around the camp. It hadn't escaped his notice that there were only two of them.

Where had the rest gone?

"Can you see any more other than the two at the fire?" he asked in a low voice.

He felt Sarah shifting around a bit and after a moment, she replied.

"No, just the two. But how are we going to get out of here? I've already tried using my skills, but none of them are working!" she said in a slightly panicked tone.

"Don't worry about that. I have a plan," he replied in as calming a voice as he could manage.

The assassins wouldn't know this, but they were only partially suppressing his ability. Even now he could feel his strength returning bit by bit. He guessed that his supermage status protected him from whatever they were using.

He gave one of his hands a quick jerk while activating *heavy impact*. The ropes didn't snap, but they came just loose enough for him to slip his hand free.

"How are you planning on getting us out?" she asked.

He picked his hand up and wiggled his fingers near her face.

"You're free?!" she exclaimed.

"Not entirely, but all I needed was a hand," he replied, already reaching into his armor for Katherine's pendant.

He could, of course, free them both and try to fight, but he didn't know if there were others waiting nearby and he didn't want to take that kind of risk. They would only get one chance to escape and if he messed it up there wouldn't be another.

Pulling the pendant from under his shirt, he pressed both buttons at once.

"Katherine, we need you!" he whispered, hoping that the assassins near the fire wouldn't hear him.

He held his breath, waiting for her to reply or for a portal to open near him. As the seconds ticked by, he felt his hope dwindling.

Whatever they were doing to block their abilities must be interfering with the pendant's enchantment as well.

Morgan frantically tried to come up with another plan, but ultimately decided that their best option now would be to make a run for it. He tensed his arm in preparation to break the rope when four more assassins walked into the camp.

"Shit!"

Morgan craned his neck back and saw what had caused Sarah's outburst.

He could now see that there weren't only six assassins, but over twenty. There was no way they would make it away from this many.

Morgan's mind whirled as he tried to come up with a solution.

"Morgan, if you have a plan, I'd like to hear it!" Sarah hissed.

"I've already tried to contact Katherine, but the pendant isn't working. Do you have any ideas?" His voice had a bit of an edge to it.

He didn't like being cornered with no way out.

"Actually, I do," Sarah replied after a few seconds.

Morgan, who had been prepared to give an angry retort, stopped himself just in time.

"You do?" he asked in a hopeful voice.

"Yes, but we'll have to hurry, so listen closely."

He felt her shift around behind him for a few seconds.

"Can you reach back with your free hand and touch me?" she asked.

It was an odd question, but Morgan did as she asked. Keeping an eye on the assassins milling about, he slowly slid his free hand back until he felt his fingers brush over her.

"Good. They didn't search us when we were captured, so the bag is still inside the compartment in my armor. I need you to pull it out and fetch one of the *Beast Zone* keys."

"Sarah, you're a genius!" Morgan said, grinning widely.

He never would have thought to escape through a Beast Zone.

"I know. Now hurry up before they come back over here!" she hissed.

Morgan kept his eyes on the assassins as he slowly inched his hand up Sarah's side. The angle was very awkward and he had to lean to one side and hunch over when his arm wouldn't go any further. Finally, he felt the bare skin of her arm and moved his hand to the opening on the side.

"Hurry up," she said, shivering lightly as his fingers traced over her bare skin.

"Just a second," he said, pulling the fabric away near her shoulder and sliding his hands into the secret compartment.

Sarah froze when he did this and his hand scrabbled around for a few seconds, trying to find the small leather pouch. The cloth separating Sarah's chest from the compartment was thin, and Morgan could clearly feel Sarah's heart pounding through the material. That alone made him try to work even faster.

He hadn't realized she was so afraid.

His hand brushed against something soft and Sarah let out a light gasp, then his fingers curled around the hard leather of the bag.

"I've got it," he whispered, removing the bag from her armor and bringing it back around.

"Good," Sarah replied, sounding a little breathless. "Now get a key out and open the portal underneath us. We should both fall in without any risk of being stopped."

"Alright," he replied, sticking his arm into the bag and fishing around until he found the small pouch with the keys.

Did it matter which one he used? He didn't really think so, as he would call Katherine as soon as they were inside. She would find the area where they'd left, then clear it of assassins and contact him when it was safe to emerge.

"Hey, what are you doing?"

Morgan's head whipped up as one of the assassins seemingly noticed him.

"How did you get free?!"

"Shit!" Sarah yelled, and he plunged his hand into the bag and removed the first key his fingers closed on.

Plunging the key into the ground, Morgan twisted and with a loud humming noise, a portal opened right beneath them.

He started falling through, then cried out in pain as something impacted against his hand, hard enough to break bones. Then he was tumbling through the portal, emerging a few seconds later on the other side. He groaned as the vertigo hit him, then shivered as an icy blast of wind blew across his body.

He was still tied to the log and presumably Sarah was as well. He blinked, shaking his head to clear the nausea and looking around the icy landscape of the *Beast Zone*. Sharp pain from his hand made him look down and he felt an icy chill run through him that had nothing to do with the cold.

He turned around, getting to his knees and using his *heavy impact* to free his other hand. Then he stood and moved around the log to Sarah.

Her eyes flicked up to meet his as he came around and a small smile came to her lips. Her face was all flushed, but she didn't appear to be angry.

"You did a good job getting us out of there so fast," she said, her voice still sounding oddly breathless. "Now hurry up and untie me. We'll need our winter gear if we're going to survive in here for a day or two."

Morgan quickly bent at the waist and with two quick tugs freed her from the ropes. She got to her feet, then took him by surprise by leaning in and kissing him lightly on the cheek.

"Guess I owe you again," she said with a smile. Her eyes flicked down to his hand and look of concern crossed her features.

"What happened to your hand?" she asked, taking the mangled limb between her fingers and raising it gently.

Morgan winced as she did this and took a moment before replying.

"I was attacked right before we fell through."

He stopped for a moment, to make sure he had her full attention.

"Sarah, the key was in that hand."

Her eyes widened a bit as the true horror of their situation hit her.

"Will they be coming in after us?" she asked, already taking up a fighting stance.

"No," Morgan replied. "The key was definitely broken by the attack that did *this* to my hand."

He raised the hand in question.

Sarah's expression began to relax at this.

"We have a bigger problem, though. Without the key, there's no way out."

18

Arnold cursed to himself as his leg got stuck in another muddy hole. He cursed at his bad luck as he slowly pulled his foot from the sucking mud.

This was the fourth time in the last hour that he'd gotten stuck in one of these. He was already at least two miles behind Morgan and Sarah, and the light was beginning to fade. It would soon be night and he'd never manage to navigate this bog in the dark.

Finally working his foot free, he took off at a jog, lifting the small device to make sure he was still heading in the right direction. There was a light squelching sound from up ahead and he instinctively threw himself to the side. A loud crack rang through the forest as one of the trees behind him splintered and cracked. Quickly regaining his feet, Arnold looked around, spotting three figures dressed in black.

"I see you've finally made your move," he said, pulling a metal rod from his belt and giving it a flick. A loud clicking sound filled the air as the rod extended to its full length of two feet.

It wasn't a sword, but it was better than nothing.

"I'm surprised you spotted us," the figure before him said.

A woman, by the sound of her voice.

"This terrain is a bitch, but at least she seems to be on my side this time," he replied with a wicked grin.

If they were here for him, they'd likely set a trap for Sarah and Morgan as well. He couldn't afford to take too long with them.

"We had a very hard time finding people of sufficient *rank* to take you down, mercenary. Feel honored that you will die by our hands!"

Arnold snorted, then allowed his *crimson coating* skill to cover the two foot pole.

It was one of his most powerful skills and would only last for sixty seconds, after which he wouldn't be able to use it for the next 48 hours.

All of the assassins converged on him at once and he crouched low, pulling his rod back and swinging it out in a wide arc. Two of the assassins dodged the blast of red energy, but one wasn't so lucky. Arnold grinned as he was cleaved into two, both halves burning to ash within seconds by roaring crimson flames.

He ducked a kick from one of the assassins but felt a sharp pain in his lower back as the other opened a wide gash there. He spun, bringing the glowing rod around, but the assassin had already backed off. He tried to turn back as he realized his mistake, then felt his arm go limp as the woman slashed into the tendons near his shoulder.

The glowing rod dropped from nerveless fingers and he clenched his teeth against the pain.

They were good. He'd give them that.

He quickly ducked, feeling the whoosh of air as something passed by overhead. He stuck his leg straight out and spun, scything the assassin's legs from under him. He then dropped his knee into the assassin's chest and blew his head off using his *concave* skill. Blood sprayed out of the man's body, showering him in gore, but Arnold grinned as he beheld his handy work.

They were good, but they were also way too predictable.

He quickly rolled to the side, hearing the wet squelching sound of something hitting the dead assassin's corpse. He sprang back up to his feet, retrieving the rod in his left hand and faced the remaining assassin.

"Looks like it's just you and me, sweetheart," he said with a bloody grin, allowing the *crimson coating* to cover the rod once more.

"Don't get too cocky, mercenary. I've killed more men than you can imagine and they were in far better shape than you!" she hissed, lunging at him with lightning speed.

Two glowing green knives materialized in her hands and Arnold could detect the strong odor of poison.

That was no ordinary poison. It was the sort of poison that only an ability could produce. He would have to be careful to avoid so much as a scratch from those knives. Otherwise, he would likely end up a corpse himself.

He dodged back as the assassin rushed in, her daggers flashing in a flurry of attacks. Arnold grinned as the assassin seemed to grow more and more frustrated with her inability to hit him.

She was so obvious that it was almost laughable.

Aaron Oster

"Do you really think I'd fall for such a cheap trick?" he asked, ducking another slash and sweeping the glowing rod in a sweeping arc.

She nimbly dodged out of the way and the glowing red energy sheared a few nearby trees in half.

"Oh, saw through my ruse, did you?" she asked, cocking her head to the side.

"If pretending to grow frustrated to make me overconfident is a ruse, then it's a pretty weak one," he said, "a good ruse always has a grain of truth to it."

His eyes flicked to a spot behind her and a plan quickly formed in his mind. Pulling the rod back, he quickly lashed out at her again, but just as he brought it around, the crimson energy disappeared as his timer ran out.

But his own ruse had the intended effect. The assassin took an involuntary step back into the sinkhole he'd spotted. With a cry of alarm, she fell backward as her foot was engulfed by the sucking mud. A shadow fell over her and she looked up to see Arnold grinning down at her.

"Always make a ruse convincing," he said, bringing the metal rod crashing down on her head.

He felt the bone give way under the blow and he felt an odd sense of satisfaction, as blood and brain matter flew in all directions.

Popping the skull was his favorite way to kill. It always felt so satisfying.

He quickly straightened, flicking the rod to get rid of the worst of the filth. He slammed it into a tree point first, shortening the weapon before clipping it to his belt. He then felt at his other arm to try and guess at the extent of the damage.

The tendons were completely severed and it would be next to useless until he found a healer.

Grimacing to himself, he pulled the tracking device from his pocket and checked the needle. He felt his heart sink. The needle was spinning crazily, stopping every few seconds to point in a random direction.

What the hell was going on?

He gritted his teeth, shoving the device into his pocket and setting off at a dead run in the direction it had last been pointing.

Whatever had happened couldn't be good.

It was dark by the time he found the assassin's camp. Barreling in, he didn't bother asking any questions or being subtle. He was in no mood. Instead, he went on a rampage, slaughtering anyone in his path. These assassins were far weaker than him and fell easily to his attacks, injured or not. At one point the assassins actually began to flee, but he managed to catch one before he escaped.

"You're going to tell me what happened to the two people you were sent after," he growled.

The assassin was terrified but tried to put on a brave face.

"I will not betr... Ahhh!"

The assassin's noble speech turned into a pained screech as Arnold promptly snapped his left forearm.

"You can tell me what I want to know or I can torture you for the information," Arnold said in a calm voice. "Personally, I'd prefer torture."

He slid his hand further up the assassin's broken arm and tightened his grip.

The assassin couldn't give the information fast enough after that.

Arnold listened as the assassin spoke, nodding along with him.

"Is that all?" he asked when the assassin finally went silent.

He nodded his head vigorously and Arnold promptly bashed in his head. The feeling of the man's skull caving in didn't even give him the slightest amount of pleasure.

"Damn it!" he yelled, kicking the corpse and sending it flying into the surrounding trees.

Katherine would be furious. If they were in a Beast Zone and the key really had been destroyed, he was a dead man.

Arnold growled and began pacing back and forth, trying to think a way out to get out of this.

No. He couldn't think like that. First, he needed to examine the area where they'd been kept. Perhaps there was some sort of clue as to where they ended up.

Walking over to the circle of bare earth, his eyes immediately caught the glint of metal. Bending down, he picked up the small and mangled *Beast Zone* key. Carefully brushing away the dirt so as not to damage it further, he brought it closer to his face, squinting as he

Aaron Oster

tried to make out what it said. After another moment, he breathed a huge sigh of relief.

It was a staged zone key. That meant that there were others out there. More importantly, it meant that Katherine wouldn't kill him.

Quickly fishing her pendant from his pocket, he pressed the button on the side.

"Open a portal. Something happened."

Just half a minute later, the air next to him warped and a portal winked into existence. Arnold took a deep breath to mentally prepare himself for what was ahead.

Katherine might not kill him, but she would definitely still be angry that he'd lost them.

He took one last deep breath, then stepped through the portal.

***

The man sat high up in the trees above the clearing where Arnold had just left. He'd watched the entire show from start to finish. How the assassins had captured Morgan and dragged him back here. Morgan and Sarah's daring escape into the *beast zone* and even the fight between Arnold and the rest of the assassins.

No one had seen him, of course. He was too well hidden to be spotted. Even if they'd looked directly at him, they would have seen only a tree. He stared down at the empty clearing, arms folded over his chest and feeling distinctly uneasy.

He really wasn't sure why the goddess had allowed something like this to happen. He couldn't follow them into the *beast zone*, which meant that Morgan would have no protection at all. She was taking a big risk and he couldn't fathom why. Sure, if he survived it would be all well and good, but the *zone* he'd entered was far above his ability to handle and getting out would be nearly impossible.

Then again, the mercenary had left through a portal, so maybe he had help. He wasn't really sure who the man was, but the goddess had assured him that he was there to watch over Morgan and that he shouldn't interfere.

The man shifted on the tree branch he was perched on, wondering what he should do next. His mission over the last few months had been to follow Morgan. Now that he was gone for an indeterminate amount of time, what would he do? Should he be looking for a key to get them out?

A light whooshing sound off to his right announced the arrival of the goddess.

"Did I miss the party?" she asked, her light girly tone not at all matching her current features.

She looked the same as last time, with the exception of the heavy cloak now gone.

"I'm sure you know what happened here and probably had some hand in it as well," the man replied, not bothering to move from his seated position.

"No fooling you, is there?" she giggled, walking lightly down the branch without so much as a wobble.

"Why did you send him in there? Doesn't this defeat the whole purpose?"

"Not at all. I need him in there. Otherwise, he'll never progress in time," she replied, stopping only a foot away and grinning down at him.

"From what I can see, he's actually progressing pretty quickly. Normal ability users take months in between *ranks* at this point."

"That they do, but *ranks* aren't what I'm referring to. If he'd kept going at his current rate, he would never have-shall we say-found the true power he needs."

The man cocked an eyebrow.

"Care to elaborate?"

"Nope," she replied with another giggle, twirling on the spot and beginning to hum to herself.

The man sat in silence as the crazy goddess danced around on the branch, wondering just what kind of power she could be referring to. After all, wasn't increasing in *rank* the only way to increase power?

He was rudely snapped from his thoughts when a warm hand suddenly clamped down on his arm.

He looked up to see the goddess' face not five inches from his. He jumped in surprise and her red painted lips quirked up in a mischievous grin.

Aaron Oster

"Don't go overthinking what I said. Mortals are delicate creatures and I wouldn't want to break your poor mind."

She tapped her lips for a few seconds, making him squirm uncomfortably in her steel grip. Her smirk widened a bit, but she mercifully continued speaking.

"Right now, though, I have another job for you."

"And what would that be?" he asked, feeling his heart rate increase, despite his best effort to control it.

Her proximity was unnerving and her looks definitely weren't helping the situation.

"Oh, just a little job in the South Kingdom. I'll fill you in once you get there," she then stepped back, simultaneously winking at him and blowing a kiss, then vanished into thin air.

The man sat there for a few moments feeling his racing heart slow to a manageable level. Then he rose from his seated position and hopped down to the ground, fifty feet below. Landing lightly on the balls of his feet, he surreptitiously readjusted his pants, telling himself that any man would have reacted the same in his situation.

He took one last look around the clearing, wondering just what the goddess could have planned for all of them next.

Whatever it was, he just hoped he would live through it. After all, it would suck to die after all the time he'd spent on Morgan without seeing what the goddess had planned for him.

19

Sarah watched as Morgan hacked the large log they'd been tied to into smaller pieces with his wind blade. Small chips flew with each slash and he'd stop every few minutes to collect them. She watched him as he worked and her mind began to wander.

They'd been trapped in here for about three hours so far. Morgan had already tried to contact Katherine, but the amulet wouldn't work. He thought that it might have something to do with the magic of the *zone* and she tended to agree. She'd fished their winter gear out of their packs while Morgan was wracking his mind on how they might escape or even survive.

The *beast zone* they'd landed in was freezing and even with their winter gear, they wouldn't last more than a few hours. Morgan had remembered something Gold had told them about *staged beast zones*. He'd said that there was an exit portal that could take them anywhere, but the problem with that was it was on the top *stage*.

There were a total of nine *stages* in this zone, the last of which was *rank 31*. Neither of them was stupid enough to believe that they were strong enough to even survive on that stage, let alone beat it.

So they'd come up with a plan, both for survival and escape. They knew that this *stage* was only *rank 6*, so they could easily kill off anything here. They also knew that it would be impossible for them to survive if they stayed down here. Their plan was simple. They'd fight their way up the mountain, absorbing cores and growing stronger. Morgan also had a theory that they would be able to get out of the wind and snow once they got higher up.

She had wanted to set out immediately, but he had insisted on chopping up the wood, as there was no way of knowing if they would find any at all. When she'd asked how he planned to start a fire, he'd actually grinned; reaching into his armor and pulling out the piece of flint he'd found earlier.

So now she stood here, watching out for beasts while he cut up the huge log. She'd already killed off three packs of frost-foxes and six ice-clawed wolverines, but no other beasts had shown up in the last hour.

Her eyes turned back to Morgan, who had been forced to work with only one hand. His other had been too horribly mangled and would only heal in another twenty or so hours. As she watched him chopping the wood, her mind couldn't help but wander back to when they'd been tied up together.

She felt her heart skip a beat at the memory and her cheeks flushed a bright red. She knew they'd been in a tight spot, but Morgan had practically groped her when he'd been rooting around inside the compartment in her armor. To her great shame, she had to admit that she'd been excited by it; almost hoping that he'd do more, but he was clueless as ever.

She shuddered violently as a freezing gust of wind tore at her hair and clothes. For once, she was actually grateful for it.

Morgan would have no idea of the implications of what she'd asked him to do by fetching the pouch, which just solidified the idea in her mind that something must be wrong with him. The only thing on his mind right now would be how to survive and get them out of here alive.

She let out a long sigh, feeling her tension ease up a bit.

If there was one bright side to being stuck in here, it was that she would have him all to herself, even if he wasn't attracted to her in the way she wanted.

"That's the last of it."

She looked up, surprised to see that Morgan was finished with his wood chopping.

"Do you think it'll all fit in the bag?" he asked, nodding to the large pile of logs, chips and small twigs.

"I hope so," she replied, looking up to the sky.

Time seemed to run differently here than it did in the Five Kingdoms. She could tell it was nighttime, but it wasn't quite dark outside. The nights here, it would seem, were more like a perpetual twilight.

She pulled the leather bag from inside her coat and together they began piling the logs inside. This took them a good ten minutes, after which Morgan leaned back, yawning widely and rubbing at his eyes.

"We need to find somewhere we can rest for the night. Tomorrow morning we'll head for the *Matriarch* and move up to the second stage."

Sarah nodded in agreement.

It was at least a few hours to the Matriarch's territory from here and she was way too worn out to trek all the way. There was just one problem, though.

"Where can we find shelter and how will we stay warm?"

Morgan looked around for a few seconds, before pointing over to a large, ice-covered boulder about half a mile away.

"We can set our backs to that. I'll explain the rest as we walk."

Sarah just sighed but followed all the same.

If she stood still for too much longer, she'd likely freeze to death.

"The boulder will give us some cover from the wind," Morgan began as they walked. "You'll use your skill and build us the other walls and a ceiling, then we'll clear out a small area where we can build a fire."

Sarah felt her spirits rise a bit at this.

She'd had no idea that Morgan knew so much about survival in the cold. Then again, the North Kingdom did have bitterly cold winters, so it made sense that he knew how to make it in terrain like this. They still had a problem.

"What are we going to do about food?" she asked, lifting her arm to shield her face from the wind. "Water isn't an issue, but we'll starve to death if we don't eat."

"Last I checked, there was no shortage of beasts around here," he replied with a shrug.

Sarah grimaced at that.

She'd never eaten beast meat before and didn't think that fox or wolverine would be particularly tasty.

They finally made it to the large boulder and Morgan began stamping down the snow underfoot, while she built thick walls of ice around them. She made sure to leave a small hole in the ceiling for air and for the smoke to escape, but other than that, didn't leave an opening.

She didn't want to take the risk of beasts getting in.

Morgan had been right, though. Once they were out of the wind and enclosed in a small area, it became noticeably warmer, though she still didn't think she'd be able to sleep here.

Aaron Oster

"Get some wood out and we'll start a fire," Morgan said, blowing on his hands and wincing.

Sarah was quick to follow his instructions and pulled two logs, some twigs, and woodchips from the bag. She didn't know how to start a fire, but she'd seen it done before.

Morgan reached into his uniform, getting out the small piece of flint, then directed her on lighting the fire. After only a few minutes, a small fire sat burning in the middle of their impromptu shelter.

"What are you doing?" Sarah asked, as Morgan pulled off his coat and then his uniform shirt.

"You do realize that the fire won't keep burning all night. We'll have to huddle together for warmth. You can leave the pants on, but you'll need to take your shirt off. The metal on there will only leach the little warmth we have."

Sarah's eyes widened and she felt her cheeks flush a deep crimson.

"There is no way I'm going to do that!" she exclaimed as Morgan set his coat on the ground near the fire.

"Sarah, this is no time for you to be getting upset," he replied in a calm tone. "I know we're in a tough spot, but if you want to survive, you'll need to keep a level head."

Sarah gawked at him.

He thought she was angry? Didn't it even occur to him that there might be another reason she was loath to strip in front of him?

She let out a long breath, then began working herself out of her coat.

In truth, it really wasn't a big deal. She was still wearing a bra under the uniform and Morgan seemed to be completely uninterested in her. It was like getting undressed in front of a child, really.

She shrugged out of her coat and reached down to the hem of her armored shirt, then closed her eyes. She felt her heart pounding as she slowly drew the uniform up, revealing her bare abdomen, then stopped, shivering in the cold.

Not a big deal, just pull it off quickly. He won't even care, she told herself.

No matter how much she tried to convince herself, she was still having a hard time going through with it. Shaking slightly, she tugged the shirt over her head in one smooth motion, leaving her in only a bra. Heart racing, she cracked an eye to see what Morgan would think, then felt her cheeks flush. Not in embarrassment, but in anger.

He wasn't even looking at her.

Morgan was facing the other way, pulling small logs from the bag and piling them against the wall, completely oblivious to the trauma she'd just gone through.

He finally looked up at her and his brow furrowed in concern.

"You really shouldn't stand there for too long. You'll get frostbite. Grab your coat and come over here so we can get some sleep." He pat the coat he'd spread out on the ground.

Sarah felt her anger evaporate in an instant.

Here she was angry that he wasn't ogling her, while he was busy being concerned for her health.

Cracking a smile at her own hypocrisy, she leaned down and grabbed her coat. Making her way over to Morgan, she sank down onto the coat he'd spread out with a sigh. Taking her coat from her, he draped it around both their shoulders and snuggled up close to her.

"As far as I can tell, we have about six hours until it becomes fully light outside, though I could be wrong," he said, leaning a bit closer to the fire.

She nodded, still feeling a bit subconscious about sitting practically topless next to him.

"Best if we get some sleep then," he said, yawning widely.

"Yeah. Um, how exactly will this work?" she asked, gesturing vaguely to the makeshift sleep roll.

"Just lay down with your back to me and our combined body heat, along with the fire, should keep us relatively warm. I've also stacked some logs so we can easily get one going in the morning as well."

She nodded again, then slowly lay down on the coat, feeling her heart begin to race. Then she felt him press up against her back and her coat was pulled more snugly over them. She expected him to drape an arm over her, but he didn't, keeping it at his side instead.

She could feel the warmth of his body pressed up against her back and feel the hard muscles of his chest and abdomen, and the

Aaron Oster

steady beating of his heart. She smiled to herself, despite her nerves and their dire situation.

If only Katherine could see her now.

***

Katherine watched as Arnold stepped through the portal. He looked quite the worse for wear, which didn't bode well for Morgan.

"What happened?" she asked, allowing just a hint of her displeasure to show through.

When it came to dealing with Arnold, she had to be every bit as intimidating as she could. People like him only responded to one thing- fear.

"I was attacked by the Assassins Guild," he said with a grimace, reaching over to clutch at his dangling right arm.

"Obviously. Why else would you be here, dripping blood all over my floor?" she said with a sneer.

"By your presence here, I can assume that Morgan is still alive." She leaned forward in her seat and steepled her fingers. "So, where is he?"

Arnold shivered lightly at the icy tone in her voice and she felt a small hint of satisfaction at that. She'd worked long and hard to perfect every aspect of her personality and even though she was extremely worried, not even a hint of that showed through.

Arnold licked his lips a few times, then began to recount the events of the last few hours.

"Don't worry, though" he quickly said when her expression hardened. "The *beast zone* they went into was *staged*, so there's at least one more key. If my guess is right, it's back at the academy."

Katherine felt a huge sense of relief at those words, though she didn't let it show.

Beast zones were the only places where her ability to open portals wouldn't work. Even the pendant she'd handed Morgan wouldn't function there. She'd been afraid that they'd actually be trapped in there forever, but even if they didn't find a key, they could technically still get out.

"You're going to fix this for me," she said, rising from her seat and smoothing the front of her uniform.

"I won't have my plans ruined just because you were lax in your duties. Do I make myself clear?" She made sure not to raise her voice even once.

The effect would be far more terrifying this way.

"Of course, Princess," he quickly replied.

"Good, now go get yourself fixed up. I expect you back here in an hour." She turned her back on him, waving a dismissive hand.

She heard the quick pattering of footsteps on the marble floor, then the sound of her door closing. As soon as the door closed, her shoulders sagged and she sank into one of the many couches in her room.

This wasn't good. Morgan was trapped in a staged beast zone and his only way out was to either beat the most powerful beast in the zone or for them to rescue him. Knowing Morgan, he would likely attempt to battle his way out.

Sarah seemed less battle-crazy, but she would likely go along with what he said if she thought there was no other way out.

She lightly drummed her fingers on the armrest of the sofa as she tried to figure out her next move. The war was going well for her father, with King Herald being pushed back further and further each day. At this rate, she might be forced to accelerate her plans, but with Morgan trapped, that wasn't an option.

And those damned assassins.

She grimaced as she thought of the pompous and self-important Simon. The man had come by the palace the other night for dinner and she had been forced to attend.

A man after her father's heart.

He'd spent most of the night talking about his daughter, Sarah, and how Edmund's oldest son, Daniel - her younger brother - would make an excellent husband for her.

The worst part about it was that her father had actually seemed to be swayed by him and was likely considering the marriage.

She stood from the couch and began pacing, trying to figure out her next move. She couldn't act until Morgan was safe. She also couldn't move against Simon directly. She stopped in her tracks as an idea suddenly came to her and she smiled for the first time that night.

Aaron Oster

It was about time that she had someone visit those damned assassins and discouraged them from pursuing her future husband.

20

Morgan opened his eyes, blinking slowly as sunlight streamed down overhead. He was warm under the thick coat and felt Sarah shift slightly in her sleep. He was loath to get out from under the warm coat, but he knew that they would have to get moving soon and it was best to get these things over with quickly.

He extracted himself from under the coat, shivering as his bare chest was exposed to the freezing air outside. He quickly pulled one of the old canvas uniform shits from the bag and tugged it over his head. He tightened the straps at his sides, then pulled out the new enchanted uniform shirt and tugged that over his head as well.

It shrank and conformed to his body, and he was glad to feel that his mobility had been only slightly hampered by the extra layer he was wearing. He examined his still mangled hand. It had swollen to more than twice its original size and was an ugly mix of yellows and blues. He quickly tucked it into a pocket, wincing slightly in discomfort, then set about getting a fire going.

He glanced back to Sarah's sleeping form, wondering at her odd behavior. She'd kissed him again when they'd come through the portal and he'd gotten that same weird feeling again, though it was quickly tempered by their situation. She'd also acted really strange last night when he'd told her to get undressed so they could stay warm through the night.

He held his hands out to the fire, feeling warmth flooding back into him after he'd been exposed to the cold. He had to wonder once again if there was a secret *luck* attribute that no one knew about. After all, what were the chances that he would pick up a random piece of flint or that they would come through into this freezing wasteland with enough firewood to last a month?

Morgan snorted to himself, then turned his attention back to the problem at hand. It was cold inside but would be much worse once he went out. He would need to do so soon though, as they were completely out of food. They'd thought they would be in a town by now and hadn't bothered to conserve their rations the previous few days. He looked at Sarah's sleeping form once more, debating whether to wake her up or not, but ultimately decided against it.

She would need all the rest she could get. He was used to living hard, though he may have gone a bit soft since entering the academy. He rose from his crouched position near the fire, then removed two uniform shirts for Sarah and laid them near the fire to warm.

Then he floated up to the ceiling of their makeshift shelter and flew out into the open air. The wind hit him like a punch to the face, instantly dashing any lingering sleep from his mind and making him feel more alive than he had in weeks. He floated up higher, wind buffeting him from all sides as he took in their surrounding landscape.

It was white as far as the eye could see with only the looming shadow of the mountain to break it up. The sun sparkled off the snow, making it extremely bright and difficult to see. He floated up there for a few seconds more, then dove out of the air, corkscrewing as he did so. He pulled out of his dive when he was just feet away from the ground, letting out a loud whoop as he gained altitude once more.

A flicker of movement from the corner of his eye caught his attention and he turned in the air, spotting an ice-clawed wolverine eyeing him hungrily.

It looked like he'd just found breakfast.

***

Six years ago...

"We can't leave!" Sarah yelled, trying to free herself from Morgan's grip. "Hint was near the wall when it collapsed. He needs our help!"

"He's dead," Morgan replied, still dragging her to the grate. "There's nothing we can do to help him. If you don't leave him, then he'll have died for nothing."

He heard a loud sob when he said this, but Sarah stopped resisting, allowing him to drag her to the grate.

"Oh Lady Saaarahhh!" Morgan heard the man call out in a sing-song voice. "Where did you go? We just want to talk to you. No need to be afraid!"

Starbreak

Sarah shuddered when she heard that voice and quickly squatted down near Morgan to help him remove the grate. Tears streamed freely down her cheeks, but she pulled with all the meager strength her body had to offer.

Finally, they managed to get the grate off and Morgan quickly peeked over his shoulder. He could see shadows looming through the dust and gave Sarah a shove, forcing her into the hole. She let out an indignant shriek as she fell through, landing in two feet of stinking garbage below.

She glared up as Morgan's face appeared above and despite her tears, she felt a small surge of hope.

Maybe Morgan would be able to get her home. Then the guards would come to kill these bad men and save Hint.

Her heart seized in her throat as a big, meaty hand appeared, latching onto Morgan and dragging him away from the sewer entrance. She quickly pressed herself up against a wall, glad that her colorful dress was now so stained with the muck that she blended in with her surroundings.

A face peered over the edge a moment later. It was painted with bright colors, but the man's face beneath the colorful mask was anything but friendly. Sarah quivered in terror, doing her best to stifle her sobs as the man looked around.

Thankfully, the dimness of the sewer, along with Sarah's muck-smeared clothes, created an effective camouflage and the man removed his head a moment later.

"I don't see 'er!" She heard a rough sounding voice call out.

"Well, go down and have a look, you dumb shit!" Another voice called.

Sarah had to stifle a gasp at the foul-mouthed men and resisted the urge to cover her ears as they continued arguing.

"I'm not going down into that mess! It smells like your mother's ass!"

"Oy don't go pokin' fun of my mother!" A third voice called out.

"I'll do as I please!" The second voice answered.

"Shut up, both of you!"

Sarah shivered as she recognized the voice of the colorfully dressed man who had approached them.

Aaron Oster

"We don't know where the girl is, but we've got this little street rat right here. He'll tell us where she ran off to. All we have to do is beat it out of him."

Sarah then heard Morgan's wild laugh and a whole lot of cursing. Finally, there was a meaty *thwack* and the cursing subsided.

"Little shit damn near took my ear off," one of the men said.

"I'm kinda sorry he didn't. It would have improved that ugly mug!"

There was a chorus of laughter following that remark, followed by more cursing and meaty thwacks.

"Enough already!" the voice of the brightly dressed man called out. "You can kill him when we're done questioning the little brat. Until then, I don't want to hear any more whining."

There was a chorus of mumbled yesses and the voices began to fade.

Sarah kept herself pressed up against the wall until she could no longer hear the voices, then she cautiously approached a small ladder near the grate and clambered up the slippery rungs. Peeking over the edge, she could no longer spot the men, so she climbed out and hurriedly made her way over to where the large pile of rubble still blocked the exit.

What was she going to do? Morgan had been captured by the men who were after her and according to him, Hint was probably dead.

She felt the tears start running down her face again as she approached the pile of rubble and didn't spot any movement.

Was Hint down there, trapped under all that stone?

Sarah shuddered and was about to break down crying again, when she heard a shout come from one of the rooftops.

"Hey you, girl!" Sarah looked up, startled by the sudden noise, but was relieved to see two men in guard uniforms.

"Oh, thank goodness!" Sarah called out, looking up with new hope in her eyes.

The guards would help her. They would dig Hint out of the rubble and help her save Morgan.

She watched as the guards clambered from the roof onto the rubble and made their way down to street level.

"What happened here, girl?" One of them asked, looking down at her with a mixture of disgust and pity.

"A bunch of men tried to kidnap me!" Sarah exclaimed, feeling her tears coming once more. "They buried Hint under all that rubble and took Morgan! You have to help me!"

The guard snorted at her and turned to his partner.

"You hear that, Hicks? We'd better report this right away," he said.

For some reason that Sarah couldn't figure out, the man was speaking in a very odd tone of voice that didn't match the seriousness of the situation at all.

"You're right. We should definitely report this," the man, who Sarah assumed to be Hicks, said.

"Good! I want you to gather up some guards and clear all this rubble away, too. Hint is trapped under there and we need to get him out!"

"Oh, right away, my lady!" Hicks replied, giving the other guard a wink. "I'll just go do that right now," he said, turning his back on her and walking away.

"I think I better help him," the other guard replied, then turned to leave as well.

"Wait!" Sarah called after him. "You can't leave. I need you to track down Morgan for me!"

The guard turned around, his amusement now turning to annoyance.

"Listen, girl, it was funny before, but don't go thinking that you can order around city guards. Now, why don't you scamper off before we decide to lock you up for the night?"

Sarah was incensed.

Didn't these guards know who she was?!

"I order you to stop!" she yelled, feeling her anger overcome her grief, if only for a moment. "I am Lady Sarah, daughter of Lord Simon, and you will obey my orders!"

The guard froze, his foot already propped up on a stone block. The other guard had already made it to the top, and called down to the man.

"You coming, Leroy?"

"No, you go on ahead. This girl might have some answers after all," he called back, waving the other guard on.

"If you say so," he called back, then he disappeared from view.

Sarah glared as the other guard turned back to her.

"Why did you dismiss him? I needed him to get more guards!"

"We were worried that we'd lost you, Lady Sarah," the guard said, reaching out and grabbing her by the arm. "Kook will be so happy to hear that I've found you."

Sarah winced in pain as the guard's grip on her arm tightened and he began dragging her across the open square.

"Ow! Let go of me! What do you think you're doing?" Sarah yelled, struggling against the much stronger guard.

A ringing slap caught her across the face, and she cried out as she felt her vision fuzz over for a second.

"Shut up, you little bitch, or you'll get another!" the guard said, dragging her more forcefully to what looked like a blank wall.

Sarah staggered after him, tears streaming from her eyes, as she realized that this man was clearly working with the others from before. He was likely taking her to them now, and who knew what they would do once they had her?

The guard approached the wall and pushed against it in a few places, then, amazingly, the wall swung inward, revealing a long downward sloping tunnel. Sarah swallowed hard as she was dragged inside, her last glimpse of daylight vanishing as the door swung shut behind her.

***

Sarah was just waking up as Morgan drifted down through the opening in the roof with a dead wolverine slung over his shoulder.

"Sleep well?" he asked, placing the beast down near the fire and fishing her combat knife from the pack.

"Yes, actually," she said, sitting up and shrugging off the coat.

She began shivering as soon as she did, and quickly reached for the uniforms he'd laid out for her.

He had to wonder why women seemed to have something against going bare-chested the way men did. He knew that they didn't like it for some reason, though he couldn't really fathom as to why.

Sarah noticed him staring, and flushed, quickly turning her back to him and pulling the canvas shirt over her head. Morgan shrugged to himself, and set to skinning the wolverine. It was awkward at first, as he was forced to work with only one hand, but after a few minutes, he'd gotten the hang of it.

"Why are you skinning that thing?" Sarah asked, laying her coat on the ground and sitting down next to him. "Don't you just want the meat?"

Morgan looked up at her, giving her an odd look.

"We're in an icy wasteland and you're asking me why I'm skinning an animal that's perfectly suited to this climate?"

"No need to be snarky," she said, swatting him on the shoulder. "Is there anything I can do to help?"

"Yes, actually," he said, then quickly cut several thick slabs of meat from its ribs, legs, and hindquarters.

"Cut the rump meat into strips and place them on that rock I put near the fire."

Sarah looked over to the flat stone he'd shoved in there, the action now making a lot more sense to her.

Using her *condense water* skill, she soon had a sharp-edged knife made of ice. She then began to inexpertly attempt to cut the meat, making small sounds of frustration when they came out all mangled and ragged.

Morgan finished skinning the beast, then looked over to where Sarah was destroying their breakfast.

"You know what? How about I cut those up, and I'll leave you to watch them while they cook."

Sarah gave him a grateful look as he bent down, and began expertly slicing the meat into thin, even strips.

"Where did you learn to do this?" she asked.

As far as she knew, he'd survived on the streets by scavenging. He'd never told her anything about hunting or how to cook. In fact, back at the academy, he'd specifically told her he didn't know how.

"I told you about the two years that I'm missing from my memory?" he asked, finishing to slice the meat and placing it on the hot stone.

"Yes."

Aaron Oster

He'd told her the day after they'd emerged from their first trip into the beast zone with Gold. She'd found it very strange, but she hadn't known him yet back then, so she couldn't help him remember anything.

"My memories have slowly been returning over the last few days," he continued as he prodded at the meat, flipping it over on the hot stone and hearing the fat sizzle.

"Just bits and pieces, nothing concrete. I honestly didn't even know I could skin and butcher an animal until just now, but the moment I started, it just felt natural to me, as though I'd done it a thousand times before."

He turned to look at her, and Sarah could see something she'd never seen in his eyes before. Doubt. As long as she'd known him, he'd never once questioned who he was, or where he came from, but now, with the resurfacing of lost memories, he'd begun to have them.

She placed her hand over his and gave him her brightest smile.

"Don't worry about it. You'll regain your memories in time, but you are who you are, and none of your lost memories will change that. I'll always be here for you, no matter what."

She leaned in then and wrapped her arms around him, and for the first time ever, Morgan didn't mind it at all.

***

Morgan ducked as the ice-clawed wolverine alpha took a massive swipe at him, then jumped back as Sarah's *icicle barrage* slammed into its side, turning it into a pincushion. The *zone Matriarch* dropped to the ground in a lifeless heap as blood pooled around it.

"That fight was much easier than I thought it would be," Sarah said, walking over to the beast and removing the core retrieval rod from her belt.

"Yeah, it really was an easy fight," Morgan mused, looking to the other side of the icy cave, where a tunnel led to the next *stage*.

It had only taken them three hours to get here, and none of the beasts had really put up much of a fight. The *stage* was so easy, it was almost laughable.

Starbreak

He couldn't forget that the next one might be a whole lot more challenging. Best not to become too overconfident, lest it cost them their lives.

Sarah straightened, clutching the core in her hand.

"Do you wanna take a look at it?" she asked, extending her arm out to him.

Morgan just shook his head.

"Absorb it. You killed the beast, so it's yours."

They'd decided not to divide the cores up, rather, whoever did the brunt of the fighting would get to keep it.

Sarah shrugged, then the core disintegrated in her hand and fell to the floor.

"You ready to go up to the next *stage*?" he asked.

"Not yet. I want to check my status before we do."

Morgan nodded, deciding to check his own while she was at it.

Name: Morgan
Supermage: Rank - 11
Energy to next rank - 6,771/22,000
Ability - Divine Gravity & Air
RP - 650/650 (Regen - 6.4 per second)
Strength - 60
Agility - 72
Constitution - 63
Intelligence - 65
Wisdom - 64
Skills - Enhanced flight, Heavy impact, Gale force, Condensed wind blade
Traits - Gravity field, Recovery
Extra - Gravity storm

He closed his status with a sigh, and waited for Sarah to close hers as well. He'd decided against using the cores he had, rather using only those of the beasts he killed here, as it would be more beneficial to his growth.

"Alright, I'm ready to head up," Sarah said as she closed her status.

Morgan nodded, and they headed into the icy tunnel.

21

They emerged from the opposite end of the tunnel about twenty minutes later, and Morgan took a few moments to examine their new surroundings. The area before them was wide open and had a definite upward slope to it. Large, icy rocks protruded in some areas, and he could see other places where the ground sloped sharply downward.

"What *rank* do you think this *stage* is?" Sarah asked, her breath steaming in the frigid mountain air.

"No idea. We'll only know once we run into the first beasts," he replied.

"Any idea which way we should go?"

"Nope."

Sarah let out a long sigh.

"Guess we just walk straight and hope we find the *Matriarch* or *Patriarch*."

Morgan grimaced when she said this.

"What?" she asked. "Plan not good enough for you?"

"That's not it. We have no idea if it's a *Matriarch* or *Patriarch*, and it's such a mouthful to say every time. From now on, I'm calling them *Arc's*."

"Really?! We're stuck in a frozen wasteland full of monsters that want to kill us, and the thing that bothers you is the terminology used to define a *zone* boss?"

"Yes," Morgan replied, then walked past her and began trekking through the snow.

Sarah just shook her head but was quick to follow.

It didn't take long for them to come across their first beasts, and the two of them stopped as a pack of what looked like frost-foxes padded down the mountain towards them. Except, they were slightly too large to be frost-foxes, and their fur was a shade lighter as well.

"No idea what those are, but I call dibs," Morgan yelled, using *enhanced flight* and rocketing toward them.

"Hey!" Sarah indignantly called out, but he ignored her.

He covered the distance quickly, and dropped out of the air, free-falling ten feet to land in the middle of the pack. The foxes all turned to him in surprise, and that momentary distraction was all he needed. His uninjured hand flashed out in a rapid series of blows, and within seconds all of them lay dead.

"Aww, they died so easily," Morgan complained as Sarah caught up with him.

"Serves you right for rushing off without me!" she exclaimed, throwing a rod at him. "Since you killed them, feel free to pull the cores out yourself.

"Oh, alright," Morgan said, then stooped to collect the cores.

He was a bit surprised at the size of the first one, so he was quick to examine it.

Name: Snow-fox core
Rank - 7
Total available energy - 654/654

This core was taken from a snow-fox and has no special properties.

Morgan was surprised at the amount of energy they provided, seeing as they were so weak. Then again, he had a feeling that anything under *rank 9* wouldn't really pose much of a threat.

"It's called a snow-fox," Morgan said as he absorbed the energy and moved on to the next. "It's not an evolved beast though, so maybe it's just a bigger species of the frost-fox."

He absorbed the rest of the cores and dusted off his palms, now feeling quite a bit better about the easy fight. He had gained over *2,500 energy* from only a few seconds of work.

"They were all *rank 7*, so this *stage* likely won't have anything over *rank 8*, except for the *Arc*," he said.

Sarah nodded, and the two of them began walking again. The going began to get much tougher the higher up they went. The snow tended to collect in drifts, leaving them to wade through snow that was waist deep at times. At a certain point, Morgan had been forced to fly them over a bank that was in their path, leaving him to wonder as to what kind of moron had designed this *zone*.

There was no way that anyone would be able to get through here in any sort of timely fashion.

Aaron Oster

They went on like this for the next two hours, periodically fighting off packs of snow foxes. They stopped at a certain point, and Morgan built a small fire, removing some of the wolverine meat and sticking it directly into it. While they were waiting for it to cook, they suddenly heard a loud snuffling sound from behind them and turned to see a massive wolverine coming over a rise to their right.

"Dibs!" Sarah called, even as Morgan was rising to his feet.

"Hey, no fair!"

"Someone needs to watch our lunch, and you got to kill the last pack, so it's my turn," Sarah said with a grin.

"But this is a new type of beast!" Morgan complained, eyeing the approaching wolverine with longing.

"Nope. Fair's fair!" Sarah replied, then dashed off to face the oncoming threat.

Morgan watched as she quickly and efficiently took the beast down, using her *icicle barrage* and *condense water* skills to utterly destroy it. She then returned to him with a bounce in her step, plopping down next to him and grinning widely.

"What kind of beast was it?" Morgan asked, almost sulkily, as he pulled the meat from the fire and allowed it a few seconds to cool.

"It was a steel-clawed wolverine," Sarah replied, taking one of the juicy pieces of meat and popping it in her mouth.

She hadn't been sure she'd enjoy it, but the wolverine was oddly tasty despite the lack of seasoning.

"It wasn't an evolved beast, so it's likely another variant."

Morgan nodded as he took a large bite from his meat. The food seemed to help him get over the missed fight pretty quickly, and soon he was back to his normal self. Morgan kicked some snow over the fire and winced as he jostled his hand.

"How much longer until it heals?" Sarah asked, noticing his discomfort.

Morgan looked up at the sky, and judged it to be around four in the afternoon, though it could have been later. The day and night cycles seemed to be completely screwed up in here.

"About four more hours," he said, tucking his injured hand into his pocket with a grimace. "I just really hope we won't have an issue with the *Arc* once we reach it," he said, as they started their march through the snow once more.

The wind began to pick up just a few minutes after the resumed their hike up the mountain, making their climb a thoroughly miserable one. They came across two more of the steel-clawed wolverines, and Morgan cheered up a bit as he got to fight one, but the longer the two of them walked, the more miserable they became.

Sarah was beginning to lose the feeling in her toes, when Morgan called out to her.

"I think I found the *Arc's* territory!"

She looked up, and could just make out a grayish shape up ahead.

A cave, maybe? That would definitely be welcome after hours of bitter cold.

They sped up their pace, stomping their feet hard to get their blood pumping and avoid frostbite. The distance was quite deceiving and it took them nearly twenty minutes to reach the mouth of the cave, but as soon as they walked in, there was an immediate difference in temperature.

"It must be a good thirty degrees warmer in here!" Sarah exclaimed, as she clapped her hands together and jumped up and down.

"At least," Morgan agreed, doing the same, but keeping a lookout for the *Arc*.

When they'd warmed themselves as best they could, they began walking down the stone tunnel. As the light behind them receded, they became aware of a different source of light up ahead.

"You think that's where our *Arc* is hiding?" Sarah asked.

"Only one way to find out," Morgan replied with a grin.

"You're hopeless. You know that, right?" she said, shaking her head.

"So you keep telling me."

They reached the end of the tunnel and Morgan held out an arm to prevent Sarah from going any further. The cavern before them looked oddly similar to the one on the previous *stage*. The only difference being that this cavern was made of stone.

A massive gray and white fox lay in the center of the cavern, appearing to be fast asleep, but both of them knew better than to rush in. The moment they would leave the tunnel, the beast would rise from its supposed slumber.

Aaron Oster

Morgan had to once again wonder at the idiot who had designed this place. Come to think of it, Gold never had explained how these places came into being and he resolved himself to ask when they next met.

"So how do you wanna do this?" Sarah asked, looking over the massive fox and biting her lip nervously.

"Same as always, I guess," Morgan replied with a shrug. "Though it might be a bit more difficult with my hand still being injured and all."

"How much longer?" Sarah asked. "It might be worth it just to wait, so you can fight at full strength."

"At least another hour, but by then it'll likely be a lot colder and we'll want to have hunkered down for the night. Though, if we can manage to stay in here, it would make things a lot easier."

Sarah let out a long sigh. "Alright, let's get this over with."

Morgan nodded, and both their shields flashed as they were activated. Morgan then used *gale force* and leaped forward, activating *enhanced flight* and speeding across the open cavern.

The fox rose from the ground as soon as he left the tunnel exit, its icy blue eyes locked onto him. It suddenly glowed a bright red, then let out a loud bark and the room was engulfed in a howling blizzard of stinging snow and ice.

Morgan hesitated as the fox vanished from view, landing on the ground and squinting around for any hint of the beast.

This was not good.

He began running in the direction where the fox had last been, only to be forced to roll to the side as a gray and white shape blurred into view, not three feet from him. He felt the wind of its passage ruffle his hair as it passed by overhead, then it was lost from sight, swallowed up by the swirling snow.

"Morgan! Can you hear me?" Sarah's worried voice cut through the howling wind.

"Yes! I'm coming to you. Don't move!" he yelled back, then took off in her direction.

He was forced to dodge the lunging fox two more times before her glowing blue shield came into sight.

"Glad to see you're alright," she said, looking him over.

"I'm not really sure how dangerous this fox is, but I can't see more than five feet in any direction and with its coloration, it's practically invisible!" Morgan replied, eyes flicking around frantically for any hint of movement.

"Maybe we limit the direction from which it can attack," Sarah replied.

Morgan was about to ask how, when she began building walls of ice using her *condense water* skill.

"Good thinking," Morgan replied as she built up walls on either side of them, then turned and placed her back to his.

"Stay sharp. I'm not really sure if it'll be able to break through the walls. They were a bit of a rush job."

Morgan just grunted in reply, keeping his eyes locked straight ahead.

Sarah had built a sort of funnel, with the ice wall extending about five feet in both directions in front and behind them. They waited in silence and as the seconds ticked by, Morgan began to wonder if the fox was smart enough to realize the trap and was just going to wait them out. Then a pair of glowing blue eyes emerged from the swirling snow, followed by a narrow face and gleaming white teeth.

"It's on my side!" Morgan yelled, using his *condensed wind blade* as the massive fox leapt at him.

The swirling wind condensed into a two foot saber, and Morgan slashed out with it as the fox's claws made contact with his shield. With a sickening squelch, the blade sank into the *Arc's* neck, sending up a fountain of blood.

The bladed form of his *wind blade* worked a bit differently than the lance. While the lance whirled in a rapid circle, the wind on the bladed weapon was oscillated along the edges, making the cutting power that much stronger.

The blade howled as the fox collided with him, and tore clean through its neck, neatly separating its head from its shoulders. He staggered back under the fox's weight, but was thankfully able to retain his balance.

The fox hit the ground in two separate pieces, and the blizzard around them petered out, leaving a tangible silence in its wake.

"Whew! Glad that's over!" Sarah said from behind him.

Morgan turned and saw her arching her back as she stretched, pressing her knuckles into her lower back.

Aaron Oster

"Yeah. It was definitely an interesting fight," he replied, bending down by the beast and retrieving its core.

Name: Blizzard-fox Patriarch core
Rank - 10
Total available energy - 4,017/4,017

This core was taken from a blizzard-fox. As this core was taken from a zone Patriarch, and an evolved beast, the amount of available energy has been slightly increased.

"Looks like this was an evolved beast," Morgan said, absorbing the energy from the core. "No wonder its ability was so dangerous."

"Guess we're moving on to the next *stage* now?" she asked, coming up next to him and looking around the now snow covered cave.

"Maybe…" he replied slowly, eyeing the tunnel exit with an idea forming in his mind. "Let's check out the tunnel first. I think I have an idea on how to stay warm tonight."

22

Just twenty minutes later, the two of them were sitting by a warm fire while pieces of wolverine meat sizzled on a flat rock. Morgan came up with the idea to stay in the tunnel for the night and have Sarah block up both sides, leaving just a small gap near the top to let air in and allow the smoke to escape.

Sarah leaned back against the wall with a content sigh. She'd bunched her coat up beneath her, as it was already quite warm inside and she'd wanted something between her behind and the cold stone floor.

"Some hot water would really be nice right now. Any ideas on how we might be able to boil some?" Morgan asked, prodding at the slices of juicy meat with her knife.

They were eating meat from the wolverine's belly for supper, and she could see the streaks of fat practically melting as the thin slices became crispy.

"I do, but I'm not exactly sure if it'll work or not," she replied, tugging the enchanted armor over her head, leaving her in her canvas uniform.

"Go for it. We've got nothing to lose," he said, pulling the meat from the stone and adding more.

Sarah nodded, then stood from her seated position on the ground and began to cast around for small stones. When she'd gathered enough, she placed them directly in the fire to heat up.

"I'll need your help for this next part," she told Morgan, as he pulled the last of the meat off the fire.

"I need you to cut a hole in the stone using your *wind blade*. If my plan works out, we may even have some hot water to wash ourselves," she said with a smile.

Morgan nodded excitedly, then formed a *wind blade*. He chose the lance, as he knew it would easily tear up the surrounding stone. Walking over to the far corner of their shelter, he plunged it into the ground.

Sarah watched in fascination as the whirling blade of air sank into the stone as easily as a hot knife through butter.

"How big do you want the hole?" Morgan asked.

Aaron Oster

"That size should be good for drinking," she replied, seeing it was about eight inches deep and five across. "Now make another one, wide enough to sit in and about a foot and a half deep."

Morgan nodded and after only a few short minutes, had the hole dug to her specifications. Sarah examined both, then nodded her satisfaction. Concentrating for a moment, she quickly filled both holes with water. Then, walking back to the fire, she used her knife to roll some of the hot stones out.

"Oh, that *is* a good idea!" Morgan said with a grin, dismissing his wind blade and walking over to help.

"Gee, thanks," Sarah sarcastically replied.

The rocks landed in the water with a hiss, setting off an explosion of steam that temporarily blinded them.

"It'll probably take a few minutes for the water to heat up for our baths, so we may as well eat in the meantime," Morgan said.

He started walking back to the fire, when he suddenly stopped. Sarah was concerned for a moment, then saw the look of relief on his face. He pulled his hand from his pocket and she watched in amazement as the swollen mess began to heal. First, the swelling went down, then the broken bones reset themselves. Finally, the cuts scabbed over and disappeared, leaving his hand whole and unblemished.

She watched as he flexed his fingers a few times and noticed that his shoulders had slumped, as the tension she hadn't even realized was there left him.

He must have been in a lot more pain than he was letting on, she thought as Morgan made his way over to the fire and sat down.

"You coming?" he asked, looking back at her as he reached for one of the crispy pieces of meat.

"Yeah, just a second," she replied, walking back to the smaller hole and dipping her finger in to check the temperature.

She quickly pulled it back with a hiss and stuck it in her mouth to cool.

Yup. Definitely hot enough, she thought.

She then used her *condense water* skill, forming two mugs made of ice. It wasn't the best plan and the water wouldn't stay hot for long, but it was the best she could come up with. She quickly dunked the two mugs in and made her way quickly back to Morgan.

"Drink it quickly, because it's already cooling," she said, handing him one of the mugs.

He nodded his thanks and took it from her, taking a sip and letting out a content sigh as the steaming liquid warmed his insides.

Sarah helped herself to some of the meat, taking a large sip from her mug and sighing as well.

Who knew a cup of hot water could be so satisfying?!

They finished their meal in silence, listening to the crackle of the fire as they enjoyed being truly warm for the first time since they were trapped here.

Sarah kept eyeing the makeshift bath, already imagining how good it would feel to sit in there for a few minutes. Morgan bit into a piece of meat with a crunch, and it was only then that she realized her dilemma.

Morgan! How was she going to be able to take a bath with him here?! She could make an ice wall, but they were quite see-through and she didn't want to risk lowering the temperature in here by using more ice.

She bit her bottom lip as she tried to solve the problem, but no matter how she thought of it, she could only come up with one solution.

"You'll have to leave while I take my bath," Sarah said.

Morgan looked up from his meal at her words and raised an eyebrow.

"And where would I go?" he asked, crunching another piece of meat and taking a sip from his mug, which had already begun melting.

"Why don't you go explore some of the third *stage*?" she asked, trying to appeal to his love of fighting. "I'm sure you'll run into some strong beasts and when you're done fighting, you can come back and have a nice warm bath."

Morgan thought that over while he finished eating. It was obvious that Sarah was trying to get him out by using one of his greatest weaknesses, his love of fighting. Then again, he didn't really care. Exploring on his own would give him a good opportunity to gather more energy and *rank up*.

"Alright," he said, finishing his meal and rising to his feet. "I'll be back in an hour. Make sure you keep the fire going and have a hot bath ready for me when I get back."

"I'm not your damn maid!" Sarah exclaimed as he walked over to the far ice wall.

"Then don't," Morgan said with a shrug.

He crouched and leaped up, catching the top of the ice wall with his fingertips. Then, in one smooth motion, he pulled himself up and over the wall. He landed gracefully on the other side and waved at her one last time before turning and jogging further down the tunnel.

Sarah glared at his retreating back, but when he didn't turn around, she sighed and began stripping out of her remaining clothes. It was only once she'd completely undressed that she noticed that Morgan had forgotten both his coat and his armor.

Shaking her head at her friend's carelessness, she quickly padded over to the shallow impression and sank in with a sigh of contentment. The water rose up around her as she sat and she could feel her tense muscles relaxing as steam rose around her. She undid her braid, letting her long red hair run free. She leaned back, placing her head on the lip of the impression and closing her eyes.

Morgan could take care of himself. Right now, she had more important things to focus on.

***

Morgan jogged swiftly down the tunnel, feeling the air growing cooler by the second as he approached the exit. He silently berated himself for forgetting his coat in his excitement, but decided against going back, as Sarah would likely be angry if he did- not that he'd understand why.

He shook his head as he neared the exit to clear his wandering mind.

Who cared why she acted so odd sometimes? Right now, he had a new stage to explore!

He came to the end of the tunnel and emerged onto another snowy landscape, but this one was vastly different than the last two. The ground was still set in an upward slope, but the temperature was a lot milder. That was not to say it wasn't cold, but the massive wooded forest sprawling before him was likely the reason.

The abundance of trees would shelter him from the worst of the wind, making it effectively twenty degrees warmer. Morgan let his eyes flick around the wooded area, trying to catch any movement that would indicate life. After a moment, he relaxed and began jogging forward once more. He made sure to tear chunks out of the tree bark as he ran, to make sure he could find his way back.

He stumbled as another memory struck him.

"Always leave a visible trail. This way, you don't get lost; and if you're injured, it will be a visible sign to anyone who comes looking for you."

He stopped, clutching at his head as the memory faded. The voice was vaguely recognizable, but he still couldn't place it. Perhaps it belonged to the mysterious woman he'd seen in his first memory.

A light crunching sound brought him to full alert and he quickly turned in the direction of the noise.

"Oh crap. That's not good," he said aloud to himself, as three ice-bristle wolves padded out from behind the cover of the trees.

They were huge, every bit as large as the one that had nearly killed him all those months ago, back in the academy. Morgan could feel his heart begin to race as they padded towards him, blue eyes seeming to glow in the fading light. He was taking a step back when one of them suddenly pounced right at him without any warning, muzzle bunched up in a snarl.

Morgan, who remembered his last fight with these beasts well, was a bit surprised at how slowly it seemed to move. The last time he'd fought one, he could barely keep up, even with his *tailwind* skill active.

It hit him as he moved neatly out of the way, avoiding the attack altogether.

These beasts were likely rank 9, which meant that they were a full two ranks under him. He had nothing to be afraid of.

He let out a laugh, then dodged back from another wolf and rolled to the side to avoid a third.

Now, what would be the best way to kill them all? he mused, as he casually moved aside from each one. A wild grin stretched from ear to ear as he decided on his course of action. It was kind of overkill, but he owed these bastards for what their buddy had done to him last time.

"You're all about to experience some nasty weather!" Morgan said, practically cackling with glee. He crouched, then

Aaron Oster

launched himself a good ten feet into the air, simultaneously activating his most powerful skill, *gravity storm,* as he did.

He felt the skill take effect, leaving him hanging up in the air as purple lightning crackled over his arms. Looking down, he could see that the three wolves had conveniently crowded together, all looking up at him with snarls of rage. Their fur was glowing a bright blue and standing on end, just like the last one he'd fought."

"Say goodnight!" he yelled.

Then the massive black funnel cloud slammed down on them. His arms shot out and the purple lightning arched into the *gravity storm.* He floated back down to the ground and watched in satisfaction as his skill tore the wolves, as well as a thirty-foot chunk of forest, to pieces.

He waited for the storm to wear off, a gigantic, shit-eating grin plastered across his face.

He'd likely have to run once the skill had run out, as every beast on the stage had probably seen it, but it had definitely been worth it.

The skill ran out and the storm dissipated, leaving a thirty-foot patch of clear ground in its wake. Walking forward, he could make out the charred and crushed remains of the three wolves.

Yup. Definitely worth it!

He tore their cores free and examined each, noting that they were all *rank 10*, not *9* as he'd originally thought. He quickly added up the energy they provided and came up with around *6,200* energy. He quickly absorbed the energy and examined his status, discovering that he had roughly *3,000* energy until his next *rank*.

"What the hell?" he said with a shrug, then dug out the azure-crystal wyvern core and absorbed *4,000* energy, leaving the core with *52,876/68,376*.

He shuddered lightly as the *rank up* took effect and he felt himself grow stronger. He waited for a few seconds for more memories to invade his mind, but thankfully, nothing happened.

It would be bad to be incapacitated now, when he was out here alone.

Breathing a sigh of relief, he tucked the core away and opened his status.

Name: Morgan

Starbreak

Supermage: Rank - 12
Energy to next rank - 956/24,000
Ability - Divine Gravity & Air
RP - 680/680 (Regen - 6.7 per second)
Strength - 63
Agility - 76
Constitution - 67
Intelligence - 68
Wisdom - 67
Skills - Enhanced flight, Heavy impact, Gale force,
Condensed wind blade
Traits - Gravity field, Recovery
Extra - Gravity storm

He decided to check his skills next to see if the *rank up* had lowered any of his skill costs.

Enhanced flight - Manipulate gravity and air to reduce your weight and move quickly through the air.
Cost - 9 RP per second
Max. height - 60 Ft
Max. speed - 40 Ft per second
Max. carry weight - 200 pounds (Adding any more weight will reduce speed by 1 foot per second for each additional pound).

Heavy impact - Manipulate gravity and air to make your blows land significantly harder (Currently X2.25).
Cost - 12.5 RP per second

Condensed wind blade - Manipulate gravity and air to create a dense whirling blade in the shape of your choice. The type of weapon you create will determine additional effects.
Piercing weapon - Double damage is dealt to mages or beasts with mage abilities.
Slashing weapon - Double damage is dealt to supers or beasts with super abilities.
Cost - 325 RP
Duration - Until dismissed

Gale force - Manipulate gravity and air to significantly increase your speed (Currently X2.25).
Cost - 12.5 RP per second

That was great. While the power of his skills hadn't increased, the cost had gone down by a significant amount. Next he checked up on his traits.

Traits:

Gravity field - Your body is surrounded by a dense field of gravity, making all attacks, both physical and magical, 10% less damaging.

Recovery - The spirits of the air have blessed you with the power of healing. If you can survive for 24 hours after being wounded, no matter the injury, your body will be completely healed.

He sighed. No changes there, though he'd really been hoping that the timer on his recovery trait would have been shortened. Oh well.

Next, he checked up on his extra skill.

Extra:

Gravity storm - Create a storm of intense gravity, damaging winds and lightning in a targeted area.
Cost - 600 RP
AOE - 30 Ft
Duration - 30 seconds
Cooldown - 8 hours

No changes there either.

Morgan closed his status and examined his surroundings sheepishly. It hadn't been very smart to start checking his status after the attack he'd just used. He looked up at the sky and judged it to be night already, though the absence of true darkness still unnerved him a bit.

He turned his back on the bare patch of earth his skill had left, and made a mad dash back the way he'd come.

He only hoped that nothing would follow.

23

Arnold stepped out of the portal and into a half-destroyed building, in what was now the main battleground of the war between the North and Central Kingdoms.

Good to be back, he thought sarcastically as the portal slammed shut behind him, effectively cutting off his only escape route.

Katherine had given him forty-eight hours to get the correct key, after which she'd threatened severe bodily harm. It was always fun working for an insanely powerful psychopath.

He quickly scanned his surroundings, noting that he'd come out in an area that seemed to be abandoned. Stepping through a gap in the wall, he emerged out into a destroyed plaza. A massive destroyed fountain occupied the center, and he could see the bodies of several North Kingdom soldiers lying on the border of the square. The bodies were rotting and the stench alone was enough to make him gag.

Katherine really had a sick sense of humor dropping him here.

His eyes roamed around the rubble-strewn plaza, noting the large brown spot where Morgan had stabbed Grub and left him to die. Oddly enough, the body of the other boy was nowhere to be seen.

Maybe Grub had come back for it before fleeing.

He started down one of the nearby alleyways, weaving in between half-demolished buildings and avoiding rotting corpses.

This place really was a mess.

He stopped for a moment, as the sound of distant fighting reached his ears.

Likely another battle in this ridiculous war, he thought to himself.

He continued on, heading deeper into the academy grounds, staying low and weaving in between more half-destroyed buildings.

As he wove his way deeper in, he began seeing small groups of soldiers either running to a distant skirmish or fighting in small groups in the narrow streets. He was forced to stop whenever a clash like this occurred and watch as one group killed off the other.

The battles were short and brutal, with neither side escaping uninjured. Arnold was a hardened veteran and had killed thousands in his lifetime, but even he had to suppress a shudder at some of the injuries inflicted by these skirmishes.

After nearly an hour of hiding and running between different sources of cover, he finally made it to the *Beast Zone* commission office, or what was left of it, at least.

The building had a massive chunk missing out of one side and the roof had partially caved in on another. Small holes riddled the walls and he could spot more than a few dead bodies buried in the rubble.

They really were all over the place here, he thought as he entered the building.

He quickly made his way to the back room and found that it was, thankfully, mostly intact. He quickly began his search, rifling through drawers, breaking through hidden compartments, and even tearing up the flooring.

He found the places where the keys had been kept, but every single one of them was empty. Arnold growled under his breath and kicked out at one of the desks, sending it crashing into the far wall.

If he couldn't find that damn key, Katherine would have his head.

"My, my. Aren't we in a bad mood today?"

Arnold whirled around at the sound of that voice and felt his stomach drop out from under him.

Just a few extra toppings on the shit sandwich that was becoming his life.

"I have to say that I'm surprised to see you here. After all, you're the one who started this all," Gold said, leaning against the doorframe and giving him a bright smile.

***

Morgan stamped out the fire as he and Sarah prepared to take on the third *stage* of the *zone*. He'd had a pretty good night of sleep last night, as had Sarah, though she'd seemed to be upset when he'd told her that they wouldn't need to huddle together for warmth.

"You about ready to go?" he asked, pulling the magesteel gloves over his hands and cinching his coat shut.

"Yeah, just give me a minute to finish," she replied, going back to braiding her hair.

She'd left it loose after her bath the previous evening and for some reason was only putting back into a braid now. He'd gotten to take a bath once he'd come back and it had been extremely enjoyable, though Sarah had insisted on leaving until he was done.

He knew that she didn't like getting undressed in front of him, but he really didn't care one way or the other, so he found it strange that she had.

Maybe he should stop trying to figure her out and just accept that that was the way she was.

"I'm ready now," she said, tossing her braid over her shoulder and tucking their spatial bag inside her armor, before closing up her coat.

"Great. Let's go then!" Morgan excitedly said, kicking out at the ice wall and shattering it into a thousand tiny pieces.

He'd already briefed her on what the third *stage* looked like and the kind of beasts they'd most likely be facing. She'd been a bit annoyed when he'd told her about reaching *rank 12*, but she seemed to get annoyed at most everything he did, so that wasn't out of character for her.

"What other types of beasts do you think we'll have to face?" Sarah asked as they emerged from the tunnel.

"No idea, but I bet it'll be fun!" he replied with a grin. "Now come on, we're burning daylight! If we move fast enough, we might even be able to clear the fourth *stage* today."

He picked up the pace and began jogging through the calf-high snow, making Sarah cry out in protest.

"I can't run in this!" she exclaimed, forcing Morgan to stop and turn back around.

"Do you want me to carry you?" he asked, half expecting an angry retort.

"Yes," she replied with a smug grin. "Now bend down so you can carry me like a proper Lady should be carried."

Morgan just shrugged to himself. He had offered, after all.

As soon as she was settled in behind him, he took off at a jog once more. Feeling Sarah's arms tighten around him, he couldn't help but remember their first day at the academy when he'd been forced to carry her so they would make it in time for orientation.

He'd only been running for about five minutes when he spotted a pack of ice-bristle wolves.

"Looks like we've got company," Morgan said, dropping Sarah to the ground and taking up a fighting stance.

The four wolves growled in unison, then ran at them, teeth bared in hatred.

What's with these things? Morgan wondered as he used *wind blade* and ran at them.

A barrage of ice spears flew past him, taking one of the wolves down and crippling a second. The other two swerved out of the way just in time, but their change in direction slowed their momentum. Morgan crashed into one, burying his *wind blade* into its skull and killing it instantly. He spun in place, as he sensed the other coming up behind him.

Before the wolf could pounce, however, a ball of ice slammed into its side, cracking ribs and sending it to the ground with a pained yelp. Morgan's blade put it out of its misery.

"Well, that was much easier than last time," Sarah said with a grin.

Morgan was a bit surprised as well. He'd taken them down easily enough last night, but he'd used his most powerful skill to do so. He hadn't been expecting such an easy fight once they went hand to hand.

Or hand to paw, he supposed.

Sarah collected the cores, keeping three and handing him one. She had killed three of them, so it was only fair. Once they'd absorbed the cores, Sarah climbed on his back, and this time Morgan used his *flight* skill.

The going was much easier after that. They ran into several more packs of the ice-bristle wolves, but none of them really put up much of a challenge. Their first real fight came when they ran into a massive blue and white bear. It was larger than the dire-flame bear had been, with a temper to match, but in the end, the two of them prevailed,

"I think I see a cave up ahead," Sarah said from her position on his back.

Morgan had spotted it as well and angled towards it.

"Do you think this is where the *Arc* lives?" he asked, landing on the snow-covered ground.

"Like you always say, only one way to find out," she answered, flashing him a grin.

As soon as they entered the cave, the temperature noticeably dropped. The forest had been cold, but this cave was *freezing*!

"Holy shit!" Sarah exclaimed, rubbing her arms and shivering. "What the hell just happened? Aren't these caves supposed to be warmer than the outside?"

Morgan frowned.

Caves normally were warmer, which could only mean one thing: the Arc must be the one causing it.

They came to the end of the tunnel and stopped.

"What. The. Hell. Is. That?!" Sarah asked.

Morgan had to agree with Sarah's assessment. The monster bear that lay at the center of the cavern was nothing like he'd ever seen before. It was massive, at least half as big again as the dire-flame bear, and nearly twice as broad.

Its fur was an icy blue color, streaked throughout with white and gray. Its fur also seemed to be coated in frost, and it generated a cold so intense that he was sure it would burn to the touch.

"You think we can take that thing?" Morgan asked.

He wasn't entirely sure the two of them could, at least not now. If he wasn't mistaken, the bear was most likely an evolved beast, and probably around *rank 15*. At their current *ranks*, this would be an extremely dangerous fight.

Sarah bit her lip for a minute, before eventually shaking her head.

"No. I don't think this is a fight we can win right now."

"What about if we used our most powerful skills?"

"Mine probably won't do much to a beast like that," she answered. "And I don't think unleashing your *gravity storm* in a cave is a very good idea."

"Good point," he replied.

He could imagine bringing the entire mountain down on their heads if he wasn't careful.

"Suggestions?"

"We go back and fight until we've gathered enough energy," she replied. "We can always use the cores Katherine gave you, but we could have a potential loss of attribute points if we do that."

Morgan nodded his agreement and the two of them turned away from the sleeping bear.

However he looked at it, this was going to be a tough fight. He could hardly imagine what the Arc on the ninth stage would look like.

They spent the rest of the day fighting the beasts of the third *stage*, and collected enough energy for Morgan to move up to *rank 13*, and Sarah to *12*. It was nearing nightfall by the time they reached their new *ranks*, but despite their exhaustion, decided to take on the *Arc*.

They could see clouds rolling in and the temperature had taken a significant dip, meaning that they were in for some truly nasty weather. If they killed the *Arc*, however, they would be able to camp in the tunnel and not have to worry about the intense cold the beast radiated.

They headed into the tunnel once more, noticing the intense cold as they drew closer to the sleeping monster.

"Let's go over the plan one more time," Sarah said.

"Why? We've already discussed it at length. It seems pointless to rehash it," Morgan said.

He already had two *condensed wind blades* active, one bladed and one piercing. They weren't sure if the beast had a mage or a super ability, and draining half his *RP* to find out he'd picked the wrong blade would not be ideal. By now, his *RP* had fully regenerated, so he was ready to go.

"Because," Sarah said, glaring at him. "It never hurts to double-check! Or have you forgotten that we're going to fight a giant monster bear that's probably much higher *ranked* than us?"

"How could I forget?" he asked with a grin. He'd been looking forward to this all day.

Sarah just rolled her eyes and continued on.

"My job in this fight will be to hamper the bear's movement as much as possible, while you will be the main damage dealer. I won't waste my mana on attack skills, so you'd better not screw up!"

Morgan's grin only widened.

"You don't have to tell me twice!"

They came to the end of the tunnel then and the massive bear came into view. If anything, it looked even bigger than it had before, and if he squinted, Morgan thought he could see the gleam of metal coming from the bear's claws.

"You ready?" Sarah asked, already beginning to shiver from the extreme cold radiating from the massive *Arc*.

Morgan nodded.

This fight would have to be quick. If they took their time, the cold alone would be enough to kill them. They were also tired from the day's fighting, but if they wanted to survive the night, they needed this cave and the only thing standing in their way was that giant bear.

***

Six years ago…

Pain was the first thing that greeted Morgan as he slowly came out of unconsciousness. He blinked a few times, waiting for his eyes to become accustomed to the dim lighting of the room. He was sitting on a hard wooden chair and his hands were firmly bound behind his back. His throat was parched from the stale air, and his head pounded terribly.

Those men had really did a number on me, he thought, running his tongue across his teeth. At least they were all still there, though his jaw felt tender enough that something was probably broken.

"Looks like the little shit is finally up," a gruff sounding voice called out.

A moment later, a filthy and morbidly obese man came into view. His right ear was heavily bandaged with a dirty rag and Morgan felt a small sense of satisfaction at having inflicted the wound.

The man must not have liked the look in his eye, because he snarled, then backhanded him across his face, rocking his head to the side. Morgan winced as he felt his tender jaw flare up in pain, but otherwise didn't react.

He knew men like this all too well. Men who had never awakened an ability. Weaklings and cowards who only felt safe picking on someone who couldn't possibly fight back. Someone like him. He knew how to deal with these types and wasn't about to be cowed by a coward.

Morgan turned his face back to the man and casually spat out a wad of bloody spittle.

"That all you got… bitch?" Morgan asked, raising an eyebrow at him.

He wasn't sure why this insult worked so well against these types, but it almost always got a reaction.

The man's face twisted up in rage and he pulled his hand back to strike Morgan again, but something in his eyes made the man stop.

Morgan could almost see what was going on behind those piggy eyes of his.

Here he was, a big and strong man, but this little boy just sat there, staring him down as though he were completely unconcerned with him.

The man shook his head and brought his arm back again.

He would teach this smug little shit who was really in charge here. He would make him beg for mercy and only then would he kill him.

"Go on then," Morgan said, eyes burning with an almost manic intensity. "Hit me you, little bitch. Hit the tied up ten year old and show all your friends what a man you are."

The man hesitated, turning to see that the other members of his gang had indeed walked into the room and were staring at him with expressions of disgust.

"What?" he asked, dropping his hand and turning his ire on the others of his gang. "The little shit was asking for it!"

"We need him alive, Scruff. Kook specifically said to leave him alone until he got back," one of them said.

"I wasn't going to kill him," the man that Morgan now knew to be named Scruff said, "I was just gonna teach him a lesson, is all."

"Yeah, real lesson you've taught him," another man responded with a sneer. "You hit a tied up kid and he still made you look like the little bitch you are!"

This comment was followed by guffaws from the gathered men, which just made Scruff that much angrier.

He whirled on Morgan, pulling a rusty looking knife from his belt.

Aaron Oster

"I'll teach you to disrespect me, you little turd! We'll see who's the bitch when I slit your throat!"

He let out a roar and launched himself at the seemingly defenseless Morgan before any of the others could intervene.

Morgan, however, just grinned at the man, feeling the familiar rush of battle overtake him. He waited until the man was practically on top of him before executing his move. He'd assumed that the man actually had no knife skills, and his assumption was proven to be correct when he came in with a clumsy slash, instead of a thrust, as anyone with even a modicum of skill would do.

Morgan suddenly threw his weight to the side, and the man's knife neatly cut into the ropes binding his hands to the chair. As the chair came back down on all four legs, Morgan twisted in his seat, slamming a cupped palm into the man's good ear. This move was designed to stun him while Morgan freed himself.

Scruff staggered back, off balance, and howling in pain from his burst eardrum. Morgan quickly leaned down, undoing the clumsy knots in a matter of seconds. He then hopped off the chair and kicked out sideways, cracking off one of the legs to form a makeshift weapon.

He quickly snatched it up, keeping his eyes on the other men to see if they'd interfere. He hadn't expected them to, but had to double check that none of them were moving in on him.

All of them were standing back, giving the two of them room to fight. This was normally how it worked in the underground. If you couldn't hold your own, then you didn't deserve to live.

He turned his attention back to the fat man, who had pulled his hand away from his bleeding ear and was glaring at Morgan with so much hatred that he imagined he could see it coming off him in waves.

"Die!" he yelled, making a clumsy lunge at him, which Morgan was careful to avoid.

The man might be slow and have no idea how to fight, but he was still a fully grown man. If he got ahold of him, Morgan didn't doubt for a second that he would win.

The man stumbled past and Morgan swung out with his improvised club, cracking the man painfully across his knife hand. He howled in pain and predictably dropped the knife. If Morgan was a novice, then he might have been tempted to stoop for the knife, but he knew that would be a mistake. Instead, he placed a foot on the knife and kicked it away, sending it skittering across the floor.

Scruff turned to glare at him, shaking out his hand and grimacing in pain. He knew that he was embarrassing himself and if he didn't subdue Morgan in the next few seconds, one of the others here was liable to put a knife in his back.

He turned his little piggy eyes on Morgan once again and this time slowly shuffled in, arms spread wide to prevent him from escaping. Morgan danced back from him, swiping out with his club whenever he got too close, but the man would not be deterred. Morgan took another step back and stumbled as his foot landed on a loose bit of stone.

"Ha!" Scruff yelled, using the momentary distraction to lunge at him.

To Morgan's credit, he did manage to land a solid blow on the side of the man's head, but his momentum still carried him forward. He crashed into Morgan, sending him to the ground with his larger frame and superior strength.

The air whooshed out of Morgan's lungs as the three hundred and fifty pound man landed on his skinny frame, and he felt his ribs creak ominously under the strain. Then, a heavy blow landed on the side of his head and his vision swam as stars danced before his eyes.

"There! That'll teach you!" Scruff shouted.

He was panting heavily and his eyes roamed around the room until they alighted on his knife. He rose off the prone boy and waddled over to it, bending down to retrieve his rusty dagger.

Morgan felt precious air flood his lungs as the man got off of him and he rolled quickly on his side to avoid an expected blow. When it didn't come, he turned his still fuzzy vision towards the lumbering figure, which was now crouched down a few feet away. It took Morgan a few seconds to figure out what the man was doing and when he did, he almost laughed.

He quickly sprang to his feet, snatching up the wooden club and dashing towards the stupid man.

His idiocy would cost him dearly.

Scruff heard a light scuffing sound and half turned on the spot to see what it was. The last thing he saw was a flash of silver and a large brown object approaching at great speed.

Aaron Oster

Morgan stood straight, watching as Scruff's body slumped to the ground, the wooden chair leg protruding from one of his eyes.

"That was quite impressive." Morgan's head, as well as those of the gathered thugs, all whipped around at the sound of the new voice.

A flamboyantly dressed man emerged from behind what had appeared to be a solid brick wall. His smile was anything but friendly though, and the gleam in his eye was almost a predatory one.

Morgan didn't answer, keeping his eyes on the man and tensing his muscles in preparation to either fight, or flee.

"You're quite the rare talent," the man said, approaching at a casual walk. "We could use someone like you in our organization." He stopped a few feet away and extended a gloved hand.

"All you have to do is tell us where the girl is and you can join us. Just think about it. Food, clothes, protection, a place to sleep, and a future in our organization. It can all be yours. So… what do you say?" the man asked.

Morgan stared the man down.

Truth be told, it was a tempting offer and had he not been so curious about the strange effect Sarah had on him, he likely would have given her up. As it was, he still wanted to figure out if she could help him feel something aside from the numbing emptiness that constantly plagued him, and that was worth more than any amount of food this man could offer.

He relaxed his posture as though he were considering the man's offer, but he was slowly inching towards the small exit off to his right.

The colorful man, whose name he was pretty sure was Kook, wasn't stupid and his smile vanished in an instant.

"I was hoping that you'd see sense, but I can see that we'll need to use more… persuasive measures to get our answers."

The men behind him began inching forward when the brick wall behind the man suddenly swung open and Sarah, of all people, came running out, screaming loudly and clutching a dagger tightly in her small fist.

Kook half turned to see what the commotion was all about, then cried out in pain as Sarah sank the dagger into his side, still screaming incoherently. Everyone stared at her in disbelief;

everyone but Morgan. He knew how to capitalize on a moment of weakness and he took his chance.

Dashing forward, he snatched Sarah's hand in his and dragged her toward the still open brick wall, hearing the sound of Kook's agonized cries following a moment later.

24

"I've already told you that I'm here under Princess Katherine's orders! She needs the key to get Morgan and Sarah out of that *Beast Zone*," Arnold said, for what felt like the hundredth time.

"So you have," Gold replied dryly, giving him a good shove in the back to keep him moving.

Arnold grimaced as he stumbled forward under the force of the shove, but managed to catch himself in time to avoid another face plant. It didn't hurt, as his *constitution* was high enough that falling didn't really cause pain, but it was annoying. Gold always seemed to shove him hard enough that dirt would end up in his mouth.

They were well outside the destroyed academy grounds by now and he had no idea where they were going. Gold had used some sort of skill to bind his hands and no matter how hard he strained, he couldn't break free. He'd also found that he couldn't use his skills, which was what really alarmed him.

No one had been strong enough to cut him off for years now and he hadn't even been aware that Gold had the ability to do so.

"Please! You have to believe me!" Arnold exclaimed.

He hated begging, but if Katherine showed up, she wouldn't take being captured as a reason for leniency.

"No. I don't think I do," Gold replied, giving him another shove.

This one did send him sprawling. He flew forward, landing face first and tearing a five foot furrow in the ground. His mouth had been open when he fell, so the amount of dirt that entered was far greater than the last few times.

"You piece of shit!" Arnold yelled, spitting out clumps of dirt and glaring at him.

"I'll take that as a compliment," Gold said, then grabbed him by the hair and began dragging him as he kept walking.

Arnold stumbled awkwardly after him, half bent over, but being forced to keep up all the same.

"We should arrive by King Herald's camp in a day or so, so best get comfortable," Gold said cheerily, continuing to drag the cursing mercenary behind him.

***

Morgan took one last deep breath, activating his supermage shield as he did so, then dashed headlong into the open cavern. He used *gale force*, feeling the wind instantly pick up as he got his massive speed boost.

The bear was on its feet in an instant and the temperature dropped by a further ten degrees. The bear snorted once, then roared, sending an icy blast out over the entire chamber.

"Holy shit! It's freezing!" Sarah exclaimed from behind him.

A second later, two sheets of ice blurred past him and slammed into the floor on either side of the bear.

The bear shook itself, then began glowing a bright blue, signifying a mage ability. It rose to its hind legs just as Morgan reached it and slammed his piercing *wind blade* into the monster's hide.

Morgan cursed as the blade bounced off and he was forced to leap back as the bear took a swipe at him with a glowing blue paw. The bear tried to take a step forward, when two blocks of ice encased its feet. A second later, an icy haze settled around it, signifying Sarah's *bitter frost* skill.

The bear landed back on all fours, then let out an angry roar that shook the entire cavern. Morgan launched himself at the beast, despite the spark of fear that had struck him. He used *heavy impact* and *gale force* this time, making sure that he could deliver a blow at maximum power, but he never got a chance to deliver the attack.

The bear's icy blue eyes seemed to glow, then it stomped its front paw and a wave of cold spread throughout the room. Morgan felt himself considerably slow down as the wave hit him and the bear's massive paw slammed into him, shattering his shield and sending him flying into the opposite wall.

The breath was knocked out of his lungs as his back impacted with the wall and he heard several loud cracks, signaling that something had definitely just broken. He landed on the ground in a heap, but forced himself to focus through the pain and used *enhanced flight.* He flew up off the ground and saw that the massive thing was already charging at him.

Morgan guessed it had decided that he was the softer target.

Sarah attempted to slow it down by throwing ice walls in its path, but the massive *Arc* just crashed right through them.

"Bring it on!" Morgan yelled, feeling a warm liquid in his mouth, followed by the coppery taste of blood.

He flew toward the oncoming bear, but felt very sluggish moving through the air. The bear swiped at him and he could see that he wouldn't be able to get out the way. So instead, he threw both his *wind blades* up in an *X* and caught the massive paw. He was knocked backwards by the force of the attack, but since he was in the air, he managed to avoid crashing into anything.

The bear roared in fury, then barreled towards him and began glowing blue once more.

Again? Morgan couldn't afford to be slowed down even more.

"Morgan! Keep it in place!" Sarah yelled from across the cavern.

"I'll try!" he yelled back, then deactivated his *flight* and landed painfully on his feet.

He wasn't sure what had broken when he'd hit the wall, but at least his legs seemed to be working.

He grimaced as the bear reared up on its hind legs again, towering over him and roaring so loudly that the entire cavern seemed to shake. He took the opportunity to attack the bear, dismissing his slashing *wind blade* and summoning another piercing one. Then he darted forward, using *heavy impact* and slammed five hard blows into the bear's midriff. Three of the blows were turned away by the beast's frost covered fur, but the fourth and fifth punctured deep holes into it. He jumped back as it roared in pain and attempted to take his head off with its massive teeth.

It landed on all fours again, blood pooling under it from the open wounds. He quickly darted in again, wincing as his back twinged painfully.

That wasn't good. Injuries to the spine were very dangerous and his body could give out at any second if the damage was too severe.

Starbreak

The bear met his charge with an attack of its own. It swiped out at him with one of its massive paws, and Morgan attempted to block the attack again. He caught the paw between his two blades with a grunt of effort, then the bear lunged forward and clamped its jaws into his left shoulder.

Pain like he'd never felt before lanced throughout Morgan's body. It wasn't only the searing pain from the beast's razor sharp teeth, but the wave of cold that seemed to be spreading from the point of contact.

He literally felt as though his blood were freezing in his veins.

The pain made him lose control of one of his *wind blades,* but Morgan still forced himself to act. Screaming in pain, he brought his right arm up in a vicious uppercut, connecting with the bear's neck. He still had his *heavy impact* active when he did so, and felt the bear's throat cave under the powerful blow.

Its jaws went slack and it staggered back from him, trying to take a breath through its crushed windpipe. Then its entire body was encased in a block of ice nearly two feet thick, all the way up to its shoulders. Morgan looked past the bear to see Sarah slumped on the ground and panting hard.

That was incredible, he thought, eyes widening a bit in amazement.

Morgan turned his attention back to the bear, who still had its head and shoulders free of the ice block. It was still trying to pull a breath of air into its starving lungs when Morgan buried a whirling *wind blade* into its skull.

Morgan winced as soon as he dismissed his *wind blade,* and began pulling his armor over his head.

"What are you doing?! The bear might be dead, but it's still freezing in here!" Sarah exclaimed, rushing over to him.

"Bear bit me," he replied as his teeth began to chatter. "My left shoulder is stiffening up quickly and the cold is spreading to the rest of my body. Get a fire going quickly, otherwise I don't think I'll be alive for too much longer," he said, pulling his canvas shirt over his head as well and staring to jump up and down.

The movement caused him a tremendous amount of pain, but he knew it would keep his body warm until Sarah got a fire going.

Aaron Oster

Her face went a bit pale, but she nodded her understanding and quickly retrieved the small leather bag from inside her armor. She pulled some kindling out, getting it lit quickly with the flint and her combat knife. She then began piling on logs and soon had a roaring fire going.

Morgan nodded his thanks, then stepped right up to the fire and leaned his shoulder toward it. He gritted his teeth against the pain, as feeling began to return to his frozen shoulder. He felt first a horrible prickling feeling, like he was being poked with a thousand pins and needles, then the duller, but more intense pain of the bite.

A few seconds later, the puncture marks in his shoulder began to bleed and he let out a sigh of relief.

Sarah was at his side in an instant. She'd torn strips from his damaged uniform with her combat knife and now used them to bind his shoulder.

"Thanks," he said, trying to crack a smile and failing miserably.

"You know, this wouldn't keep happening if you were just a little more careful when fighting," she admonished, tying off the bandage and moving around him to check for other wounds.

He felt her prodding at his back and couldn't help but flinch as her fingers prodded against the bruised skin.

"You've cracked a few ribs, but it feels like your spine is still intact," she said after a few moments. "It looks as though we'll be taking the next twenty-four hours off. There's no way you can fight in this condition."

Morgan let out a long groan as she said this, but knew she was right.

With the way he felt right now, he would only get himself killed.

"Alright, but let's at least take a peek at the fourth stage before we make camp for the night."

Sarah rolled her eyes.

"How about you go and check it out, but I don't want you walking. You'll only make the injury worse," she warned. "I'll collect the bear's core for you and meet you in the exit tunnel."

"Deal," Morgan said with a tired grin.

He grabbed his coat and slung it over his shoulders, then floated up off the ground and headed into the exit tunnel.

Starbreak

As he flew down the tunnel, Morgan began to notice a definite increase in temperature. The tunnels were all fairly well lit, which he found to be quite odd.

Shouldn't they be pitch black?

He shrugged inwardly, deciding that it likely had something to do with the magic of the *zone*. As he approached the tunnel exit, a blast of heat suddenly washed over him. He was so shocked that he nearly fell out of the air.

Quickly pulling the coat from his shoulders, he flew out of the tunnel and emerged into the fourth *stage*.

His mouth dropped open in amazement as he examined his new surroundings and a smile slowly crept onto his lips. He quickly spun in the air and rocketed down the tunnel, heading back to the third *stage*.

Sarah was never going to believe this!

25

"Holy crap!" Sarah exclaimed, as she emerged from the exit tunnel and took in her new surroundings.

Morgan floated out of the tunnel behind her, a wide grin plastered on his face.

"What did I tell you?" he said, sounding just a bit smug.

"I can't believe we're finally somewhere warm!" she exclaimed, quickly taking off her coat and her armored shirt.

She would have to change back into the armor she'd just stripped off, as it was much more durable and more suited to this new climate, but she would wait until she had some privacy. Then again...

She bit her lip, eyeing Morgan as he flew around the area, examining their new surroundings. She couldn't blame him for that, as they were quite breathtaking.

They were standing in a massive cavern covered in glittering crystal that seemed to stretch on for miles. Small streams of magma flowed throughout the area, reflecting off the clear crystal and lighting the entire area in an odd orange glow.

Sarah shrugged to herself, then began unbuckling the straps that held her canvas shirt in place. She kept an eye on Morgan as he flitted around the cavern ceiling, nearly forty feet above her head. She pulled the canvas shirt off of her body, then bent down and pulled the armored shirt back on. She sighed as the light material conformed to her body, then stuffed her coat and canvas shirt into the small leather bag.

She looked down at her bulky snow pants, then back up at Morgan. *No,* she decided.

She may be sort of comfortable changing her top, but she would not strip down to her underwear in front of him.

"This place really is something!" Morgan said, coming down from his inspection of the cavern ceiling.

He was clutching a piece of clear crystal in one hand and he tossed it to her as he landed.

Sarah caught the crystal and examined it. Clear in color, and shot through with red and yellow, it was one of the most beautiful things she'd ever seen. She went to hand it back to Morgan, but he just waved his arm.

"Keep it. I know girls like shiny rocks." He then walked away from her and began looking for a good place to set up camp for the night.

Despite herself, Sarah could feel her face flushing in pleasure. Morgan had given her a piece of jewelry! Well, sort of...

She grinned all the same, and carefully tucked the piece of crystal away. When they got out of this damned place, she would have something nice made out of it; maybe a necklace, or bracelet.

"Hey, I think I've found a good spot to bunk down!" Morgan called out.

She let out a long sigh, then walked over to see what he'd found.

"Check this out," he said, pointing to a crack in the cave wall.

Sarah looked at it, but didn't understand what he was seeing.

"I don't..." Then she stopped, as she realized what she was seeing.

"After you," Morgan said with an exaggerated bow.

Sarah suppressed the urge to laugh, but just barely. Turning her body sideways, she squeezed her way through the narrow gap and into the small cave set behind it. She turned around once she'd gotten in and helped Morgan squeeze through as well. She caught the momentary wince as his broken ribs were aggravated when he slid through the narrow opening, but didn't comment on it.

Once he was inside, they set about making camp. The cave was quite snug, only about ten feet across and just high enough that they wouldn't bump their heads standing upright, but it was definitely a safe place, as no beasts would be able to get in.

"Do you think this cave was built in here on purpose?" Morgan asked.

Sarah turned to see him stripping off his heavy pants and quickly turned away, face flushing red in embarrassment.

"Warn me when you're changing!" she yelled, trying to calm her suddenly racing heart.

"What? It's hot in here and I'm not going to wear these thick winter pants if I don't have to," he replied.

Aaron Oster

"It's not something you do, Morgan! People don't just strip in front of each other!"

"Katherine didn't seem to mind and she's a princess. Honestly, you're the only one who seems to care," he replied.

She whirled around in anger, thankful that he was wearing pants now, and glared at him. He just stared at her impassively and shrugged, as if to say, what do you want from me?

She let her anger melt away and she headed for the cave exit.

"I'm going to change as well. You stay here and get supper going. I'll be back in a minute."

Morgan shrugged again, catching the leather bag she tossed to him and began pulling pieces of wood from inside. She watched him work for a few seconds, marveling at how well he hid his discomfort, then headed out of the small opening and back into the open cavern beyond.

She headed away from the crack in the wall and walked for a good few minutes, until she was sure that he wouldn't catch her changing if he decided to come out. She looked around for a moment, before spotting a large rock protruding from the cavern floor.

Perfect!

She walked around the rock and laid the armored pants on the ground next to it. She began pulling at the straps holding the heavy winter pants, looking furtively around to make sure Morgan hadn't followed her.

She crouched down once the buckles were loose and undid her boot laces, sliding them off her feet, along with her pants. She grabbed the armored pair from where it was lying on the ground and was about to pull them on, when a loud menacing growl made the hair on the back of her neck stand on end.

She froze, turning slowly until her eyes alighted on a massive furry beast standing not ten feet from her. The beast was around the same size as the *Arc* they'd just fought, but there were some very distinct differences. For one, the beast appeared to be some sort of badger-like creature, except its fur was striped with red and gold, instead of black and white.

Its claws were well over a foot long. They curved into wicked points and seemed to glow in the soft lighting of the cavern. Her eyes traveled slowly up the massive beast's body until their eyes met. Sarah felt her heart rate quicken, as she met the two black glittering pools that gave the beast an almost demonic appearance.

Its muzzle bunched up, revealing a mouth filled with several rows of razor-sharp teeth.

Holy shit! This stage was no joke.

Sarah got to her feet very slowly, not even daring to break eye contact with the massive badger. She was in a bad situation, to say the least. She was far enough away from their camp that she couldn't count on Morgan for backup, not to mention that the bottom half of her body was clad only in a pair of underwear.

As she straightened, she noticed the badger's muscles beginning to bunch up.

"Oh, screw it!" she yelled, activating her mage shield and using *icicle barrage*.

The beast roared, shaking the cavern with its rage as ten icy spears slammed into it in quick succession. Sarah jumped back, trying to create as much distance between her and the beast as possible and crossed her fingers that her attack would work.

Her *icicle spears* connected with the badger in a hiss of steam and her eyes widened as not a single one of her attacks made it through.

What was it with this damn Zone? Was it built specifically to kill mages with her ability?

The badger lumbered towards her, its fur rippling as waves of heat poured off it. Sarah gulped as the areas where the badger's feet connected with the ground melted into pools of magma, giving her a pretty good idea of what would happen to her, should that beast land a hit.

"Damn pest!" she yelled, using *bitter frost* in an attempt to slow the lumbering monstrosity. Of course, it had no effect at all.

"Shit!" she yelled, dodging a swipe from its glittering claws.

She winced as a blast of heat hit her and she quickly back-peddled, wincing as sharp stones dug into her bare feet.

Sarah grimaced as the badger spun in place, determined not to let her escape. She wasn't cut out for this up close fighting.

She quickly used *condense water*, but instead of solidifying it into ice, she collected a sphere of water around three feet in diameter. She hoped it would work, as it had her cost nearly half her *MP*.

Aaron Oster

As the badger spun to face her again, she launched the sphere of freezing water right into its face. There was a massive explosion of steam as her attack landed, but Sarah didn't wait to see what had happened. Instead, she turned her back and ran as fast as she could.

She ignored the multitude of rocks digging into her feet, instead leaning forward and putting on more speed. She heard a loud roar and chanced a peek over her shoulder.

"Shit! Shit! Shit!" she yelled, watching wide-eyed as two tons of angry badger erupted from the steam cloud.

It was soaking wet but otherwise looked to be unhurt. But boy, did it look mad.

"Why me?!" she yelled, pumping her aching legs even faster.

She was now glad that Gold had made her do all that running back at the academy. Otherwise, she'd likely already be that badger's dinner. It was gaining on her and would be on top of her in a matter of seconds if she didn't do something quick.

Only one thing left to do.

She skidded to a sudden halt, then spun around to face the oncoming monster.

This better work, she thought, then slammed both hands onto the ground and used her most powerful skill, *icy wave.*

There was a loud crackling sound, then a wave of icy spikes spread in a conical shape before her, shooting up from the ground with astonishing speed. The badger, seeing the danger it was heading towards, tried to veer away at the last moment, but the momentum of its charge was too great. With a pained yowl, it crashed headlong into the field of razor-sharp icicles.

Sarah watched in fascinated horror as the massive beast plowed through the field of knives, the icicles tearing massive bloody furrows and punching deep into it. The beast thrashed around for another minute, trying desperately to reach her, but the wounds inflicted by her *icy wave* were too much. Finally, bleeding from numerous gashes and massive rents in its hide, the beast collapsed in a pool of blood.

Sarah stood stock still for a moment, body shaking with adrenaline and fear, then she let out a loud whoop.

"Yeah! Take that you furry bastard! Mess with me and you'll end up a corpse!" she hopped up and down, completely forgetting where she was and reveling in the joy of vanquishing a tough enemy.

Starbreak

"Um, Sarah?"

Sarah froze as she heard that voice and slowly turned to see Morgan giving her a concerned look.

"Why aren't you wearing any pants?"

26

"Alright, I think this is a good spot to camp for the night. What do you think?" Gold asked Arnold cheerily as they stopped just outside the city limits.

Arnold let out a snort.

"Does it even matter what my opinion is? You'll just do what you want anyway."

"Right you are, my dear psychopath," he said, patting him none too gently on the cheek. "But what fun is a road trip without conversation?"

Arnold just scowled. Gold had marched them on for the last ten hours and had only stopped now that they'd finally made it out of the last city in the Central Kingdom, which left him to wonder as to where they were headed.

He felt a boot connect with the side of his knee and grunted as he hit the ground in a heap. He was really starting to hate this man.

"Oh, don't give me that look," Gold said, pouting a bit. "It makes me feel like you don't like me."

Arnold's eyes widened a hair, wondering at Gold's stability.

Gold let out a low laugh and turned to examine their campsite for the evening. It wasn't much, just a small clearing a few feet from the road, but it would conceal them from any passing soldiers. Not that Gold would need to worry about the likes of mere men.

Gold turned back to him with a grin.

"Well, aren't you the popular mass murderer? So tell me, Arny. Who are your friends?"

"Arny?" Arnold exclaimed, face going red with anger. "No one gets away with insulting me like that!"

Then the rest of Gold's statement sunk in.

"Wait, what friends?"

"Why, that group of people all dressed in black standing behind you," Gold casually said, gesturing to the seemingly empty forest.

Then six figures seemed to appear, as though from thin air. Arnold stumbled back in surprise.

"We're no friends of his," said the lead figure, in a gruff voice. "Just leave him to us. We have no quarrel with you."

Arnold grimaced at that. So the Guild had found him already and judging by what he'd seen so far, or rather, what he hadn't seen, he could be pretty sure that they were out of his league.

"I'm sorry, but I'm afraid I can't do that," Gold replied, in the same cheery voice. "You see, that man killed thousands of civilians on the day his kingdom attacked ours. I believe King Herald has more of a claim on him than anyone else. Don't you agree?"

"Get out of our way!" another one of them said, shoving her way to the front. "Do you know who we are, peasant? We are the elites of the Assassins Guild. Now leave or die!"

"You're not very good assassins, if you go around announcing yourselves like that," Gold said, placing his hand over his mouth to cover a yawn. "Now if you don't mind, kindly leave. We have a big day ahead of us tomorrow and I'd like at least an hour of sleep before we continue."

The assassin let out a low growl, then a mage shield suddenly covered her body.

"No one insults the Guild and lives to tell the tale!"

A boulder the size of a house fell from the sky and squished her flat. There was a loud crunch of bones and an explosion of gore as the assassin's body popped like an overripe tomato, coating the others liberally in her blood and internal organs.

"What the shit?" Arnold yelled, leaping backward at the sudden attack.

When the hell had Gold moved that boulder into the sky?

The other assassins stared at the bloody smear that was once their comrade, in utter disbelief.

Gold was right, Arnold thought, *they really are horrible assassins. What kind of trained killers were so ineffective at doing their one job?*

Finally, the group seemed to collect themselves.

"You will pay in blood for attacking one of our members!" one of them said, taking a step forward.

"No, I won't," Gold said in a sing-song voice, and another boulder fell from the sky, squashing him flat.

The rest of them broke, scattering into the surrounding trees and hurling threats back at him as they fled.

"Bunch of cowards."

Arnold turned to see Gold staring after them with a look of disgust on his face. He turned back to Arnold with an appraising look.

"Guess you weren't lying," he said, waving his hand in the air.

Arnold sighed in relief as the stone cuffs holding his arms behind his back fell to the ground with a muffled thump.

"No shit!" he replied, rubbing at his aching wrists. "Now can you give me that damn key so I can get your students out of that *Beast Zone?*"

"Nope," Gold replied, another grin coming to his face. "If the Princess is as innocent as you say, then I'll be meeting her in person before handing over any key."

***

Morgan watched Sarah as she angrily pulled on a pair of pants. He then looked over to where the massive beast lay dead in a field of icy spikes and had to wonder at just how powerful it had been, for her to be forced to use her most powerful skill.

He turned back to Sarah, who had just gotten the pants over her shapely hips and was closing the snap at the front. The pants then tightened as they conformed to her legs and she looked up to see him watching her.

"Creep!" she yelled, then stalked towards the dead beast, her face red with anger.

Morgan blinked. He had to admit that it had been an odd sight. He'd heard some shouting coming from outside the cave and he'd come out to investigate, only to see Sarah, clad only in a pair of silky underwear and her shirt, fighting a massive badger.

The sight had been so strange, that he hadn't even been interested in the beast, but rather why Sarah was fighting it half naked. He had to admit that the thought of challenging a beast with only his skin as protection was exciting in a sort of primal way, but in their current situation, it was hardly appropriate. What if she'd been injured?

And why'd she called me a creep? he wondered.

He shrugged to himself, then headed back towards the small cave. He squeezed his way back in, wincing as his broken ribs scraped against the stone, then made his way over to the fire. The last of the wolverine meat was cooking there, but wasn't quite ready yet. He sat down, balling up his coat and placing it against the wall, then carefully leaned back to test his weight against it.

He felt a slight twinge of discomfort, but it wasn't too bad. He looked around for the core he'd been about to examine before he'd left to investigate the noise he'd heard, and spotted it lying on the ground just a few feet away. He grabbed it excitedly, settling back into the coat and opening the core's status.

> *Name: Dire-frost bear Matriarch core*
> *Rank - 14*
> *Total available energy - 7,217/7,217*

> *This core was taken from a dire-frost bear. As this core was taken from a zone Matriarch, and an evolved beast, the amount of available energy has been slightly increased.*

Wow, Morgan thought, *the amount of available energy was incredible!* It had even more energy than the steelwool-ram they'd fought a few weeks ago and it had been rank 15. Then again, this beast was a hell of a lot tougher to take down.

Morgan quickly assigned the energy and checked his status.

> *Name: Morgan*
> *Supermage: Rank - 13*
> *Energy to next rank - 18,117/26,000*
> *Ability - Divine Gravity & Air*
> *RP - 720/720 (Regen - 7.1 per second)*
> *Strength - 67*
> *Agility - 80*
> *Constitution - 71*
> *Intelligence - 72*
> *Wisdom - 71*
> *Skills - Enhanced flight, Heavy impact, Gale force,*
> *Condensed wind blade*

Aaron Oster

Traits - Gravity field, Recovery
Extra - Gravity storm

He was getting pretty close to the next *rank* and wondered if he would lose any attribute points if he just *ranked up* now. Before he could decide, he heard the scrape of metal over stone and Sarah came into view, squeezing through the crack and coming into the cave.

"So what kind of beast was it?" Morgan asked, leaning forward and turning the meat over.

Sarah still seemed to be angry at him from before, but she answered all the same.

"It's called a fire-fur badger, and it was *rank 16*," she replied, slumping to the ground with a groan.

"That's not good," he replied, pulling their supper from the fire. "The *Arc* on the previous *stage* was only *rank 14*. If the first beast we run into is that strong, it can't bode well for our chances here."

Sarah nodded in agreement, the last of her anger fading away as he handed her a piece of meat.

"So what do we do?" she asked, taking a careful bite of the steaming meat, before chewing slowly. "Will we have to go back to the previous *stage* to train some more? Because even with all the energy I just got, I'm only *rank 13*."

"Same here," he replied, tearing off a chunk of his meat and chewing heartily.

After a long day of fighting and all the injuries he'd sustained, he was in desperate need of some nourishment.

"I'm pretty close to the next *rank*, but if the first *beast* was *rank 16*, then the *Arc* may very well be over *18*, which means that we won't be able to progress until we're at least *rank 19*."

"Oh, I can assure you that the *Arc* – excellent name, by the way- on this *stage* is only *rank 18*. Although, you are correct in assuming that you'll need to be stronger in order to defeat it."

Sarah and Morgan both jumped at the sound of an unexpected voice and both whirled to see a man squeezing his way into their small cave.

Morgan was getting ready for a fight, when he caught sight of the man's face and froze on the spot.

The man squeezed his way through and stood to examine the two shocked teenagers before him.

"I know we don't exactly know each other that well, but I was expecting something a bit different than shocked expressions. Then again, you wouldn't really expect anyone to be here, so I understand your surprise."

The man nodded, then seated himself near the fire and reached out for a piece of meat. Morgan and Sarah both just stared as the man dug in, tearing off a massive hunk and barely chewing before swallowing.

He looked up to see them both staring and raised an eyebrow.

"Well, don't stop eating on my account! Go on," he said, gesturing with the piece of meat.

When neither of them continued, he let out a long sigh and set his food down.

"Fine; let's get to the reason I'm here, shall we." he said, licking his fingers. "I figured it's about time the two of us had a chat, don't you agree?" Samuel asked.

27

Katherine was pacing back and forth in her room, waiting restlessly for Arnold to contact her. It had been nearly thirty hours since he'd left, and she'd yet to hear anything from him.

If that sack of shit had run off on her, she would hunt him down and feed him his own testicles,

She stopped her pacing and forced herself to take a deep breath. She was a princess; she had to remain calm at all times in order to make well thought out decisions. Slowly, she allowed her clenched fists to uncurl and made her way slowly over to a plush sofa.

She sank into it with a sigh and felt at the small core resting on a chain around her neck. True to her word, she'd had the core Morgan gave her made into a necklace. All cores looked beautiful, with their swirling red and blue pattern, but most people would just absorb the energy and be done with it.

She'd seen thousands of cores in her years as a fighter, but this one held a special significance to her. It wasn't just who had given it to her, but what it represented as well; a way for her to end the war and overthrow her idiot of a father.

She suddenly felt a slight tingle run down her spine and quickly pressed a hand to her ear. Arnold's voice came through after a moment and she breathed a sigh of relief.

"I think I found the key, but we have a bit of a situation."

Katherine scowled when she heard that. Of course, things were never easy. Ever!

"I have a guest that insists on meeting you before handing it over. It's Gold, the mage from the academy."

Katherine sat up straight.

Gold? What possible interest could he have with Morgan? Then again, he had stalled her back at the academy to cover their escape…

"I'm opening a portal. Tell him to come through." She concentrated then, closing her eyes and allowing her ability to seek out her targets.

It only took a few seconds to locate them and with a minor effort of will, a portal popped into existence, connecting the two areas.

A moment later, she felt them enter. She sat up straighter in her seat, quickly fixing her long golden hair and readjusting her armored top. She considered delaying them so she could put on a new layer of makeup, but dismissed the idea in the end. Morgan needed her now. She wouldn't jeopardize him and her entire kingdom, just for vanity.

A few seconds later, Arnold stepped through, looking quite the worse for wear. Then Gold stepped through, looking as unconcerned as a man taking a stroll on the beach.

"You look like you took a hundred-foot fall and decided to land on your face," Katherine commented as Arnold stepped up to her.

"An apt description, I assure you," Gold said with a grin.

Arnold merely scowled and folded his arms.

"Oh, don't look so glum. You're lucky I didn't kill you. Be grateful."

His scowl deepened and Katherine was forced to intervene before it came to blows.

"May I ask as to why you insisted on accompanying Arnold here?" she asked him, making sure to keep a neutral tone.

She wasn't exactly sure how strong Gold was, but she knew from her time at the academy that his *rank* was at least in the *40's*.

"You may," he replied cheekily, then walked over and plopped down in one of her sofas.

Arnold let out a growl and his fingers twitched as though suppressing the urge to attack the man.

"You can go, Arnold," Katherine said with a dismissive wave. "I'll call you when I require your assistance."

Arnold threw Gold one last glare, then walked stiffly out of the room. She waited until the door closed behind him before turning back to Gold.

"Why did you insist on coming with? And more importantly, do you have the key to the *Beast Zone*?"

Gold interlaced his fingers and examined her for a few long moments, his eyes stopping on the glittering core before moving up to meet her eyes.

"I had to see for myself if that murdering toad was telling the truth, but I can see now that he was. You're not at all what you pretend to be, are you Princess?" he asked, his mouth turning up in a slight smirk.

Katherine folded her arms and stared at him levelly.

"You still haven't answered my second question. Do you have the key?"

Gold shrugged.

"I have *a* key, though if I'll hand it over to you, is yet to be seen."

Katherine let out a long sigh and allowed her shoulders to slump.

"Out with it then. What do you want?"

"A simple test," he replied. "Pass it, and I'll hand you the key. Fail, and you get nothing."

"I can always take the key by force," she said, allowing a ripple of power to flow out from her.

Gold didn't even flinch.

"You can try," he said with a shrug. "You may even succeed, but you won't do so without a considerable amount of effort on your part, and I'm willing to bet that this city wouldn't survive the battle."

Katherine inwardly winced when he said that. He had her dead to rights. She could attack him, but a fight between the two of them could very well level the city, costing hundreds of thousands of lives.

"Fine," she agreed. "What exactly do you have in mind?"

Gold leaned forward, a wicked grin spreading across his face.

"Have you ever heard of the infernal-bane lyvern?"

Katherine's eyes widened when she heard that name and she felt her pulse quicken in fear, as Gold's grin widened.

"Good. I thought you would've."

***

Morgan stared, heart racing with adrenaline, as the most powerful being in the world set down his half eaten meal, licked his fingers clean and turned to look at him.

"Talk to me?" he dumbly asked.

Why would the most powerful being he knew of - a being that Dabu, an omniscient supermage, had described to be as old as time itself - want to speak with him!?

"Yes," he said with a smile, then opened his mouth to continue, but was rudely cut off by Sarah.

"Samuel?! What the hell are you doing here? How did you get in? Can you get us out?"

The questions came one after another in rapid succession and Samuel held up a hand as if to ward her off.

"Whoa there, one question at a time!" he said, chuckling lightly.

"Fine," Sarah said, leaning forward with a huge grin on her face. "How did you get in? More importantly, can you get us out?"

"To answer your first question, I got in by walking. To answer your second, I can't take you out of here."

Sarah's excited expression vanished, replaced by one of anger instead.

"What the hell kind of cryptic shit answer is that? Why can't you take us out?"

"That would be against the rules," he simply replied.

"What rules?"

"Well, telling you would be against the rules as well," Samuel said with shrug.

Morgan decided that it was best to cut in before Sarah tried to attack the all-powerful being.

"If you can't get us out, then why come here?" he asked, surprised at how calm he suddenly felt.

"To speak with you, of course. Haven't you been listening?"

Sarah let out a huff of anger and folded her arms, glaring at Samuel.

At least her anger's directed at someone else for a change, Morgan thought.

"Alright, out with it then. Why is a god interested in speaking with me?" he asked, being as blunt as possible.

Just where was this confidence coming from?

"Figured me out, have you?" Samuel said with a raised eyebrow. "Now I wonder who could have... Ah, you had that visit with Dabu."

"How did you...?"

"Know? Who do you think sent you there?" he asked, picking up his meat and taking another chunk out of it.

"Wait, what?"

Morgan was now very confused. If he was understanding Samuel correctly, then he had been the one to send him to see Dabu, but Dabu had said that he'd brought him there, so who had done it?

"Yes, yes, I know it's a lot to process, but let's get to why I'm here and you can ask me questions when I'm done."

Morgan reluctantly nodded and Samuel turned to Sarah.

"Will you be joining us?" he asked.

Sarah glared at him, but rose to her feet and sat down near Morgan, wrapping both of her arms around one of his and pulling it tightly to her chest.

Morgan didn't even bother trying to fight her. First of all, he was in too much pain and secondly, it felt oddly pleasant.

Samuel cleared his throat a few times before starting to speak.

"The reason I'm here is simple. I have a task for you, Morgan. One that I believe only you can accomplish."

"Really? What would a god need me for? Can't you just do it yourself?" he asked in a dry tone, feeling Sarah squeeze his arm even tighter.

He could feel her heart pounding rapidly from the contact and just then realized that he hadn't told Sarah what Samuel was. She had been extremely rude to him and was probably afraid of what he might do to her.

"That's an easy enough answer. It's against the rules."

"What rules?" Morgan asked with a raised eyebrow. "You keep mentioning them, then say you can't tell us, as that would be breaking them. Just what kind of god are you, anyway?"

"Sorry, can't answer that," he said with a wave of his hand.

Morgan opened his mouth to argue, but Samuel held his hand up to forestall him.

"Just hear me out. I promise my offer is worth your while," he said with a mysterious grin.

Morgan snapped his mouth shut and looked to Sarah. She met his gaze with her frightened one, but after a moment, gave a nod.

"Go on. I'm listening," he finally answered.

"Great! Now as you know, there is currently a war raging between the North and Central Kingdoms. This, of course, is not good, as I worked very hard to keep the balance all these years. Your task is simple. Kill Edmund and help his daughter Katherine take the throne, before the Pinnacle Kings awake."

"Katherine already contacted me about this issue with her father. She asked me to help her overthrow him, so I was going to do it anyway. She gave me a pretty good deal too," he replied with a grin.

"But what exactly is a Pinnacle King?" he asked.

"Oh, you've already agreed? Wonderful! As for the Pinnacle Kings… When the Tyrant King's war was stopped and the kingdoms were forbidden from fighting, I set up an… insurance policy. Five massively powerful beasts were created, one for each kingdom, so if they ever went to war again, the Pinnacle Kings would destroy them all."

Sarah gaped at him and Moran quirked a brow.

"Isn't destroying the world kind of extreme?"

"In retrospect, it was a bit extreme," Samuel said with an embarrassed laugh. "But once they were placed, I could no longer remove them."

"Let me guess," Morgan said, "that would be against the rules."

"Exactly! Glad to see you're catching on!"

Morgan let out a sigh, wincing as his broken ribs scraped against one another.

"How long do we have?"

"Four weeks from when the war started," Samuel replied.

"What?" both Sarah and Morgan exclaimed at once.

"That would only give us…" Sarah stopped and began counting in her head.

"Four days," Samuel replied. "And yes, I know it's not a lot of time."

"No shit!" Sarah exclaimed.

"How do you propose we stop this war in four days when we're still stuck in here?" Morgan asked.

"Sorry, can't help you there," Samuel replied with a shrug.

"If the war isn't over by then, the first of the Pinnacle Kings will awaken in the North. After that, a new one will awaken every

Aaron Oster

month until they all rise. So long as the last one doesn't wake, you still have a chance, but once he does…" Samuel shrugged again.

"End of the world," Morgan said, rubbing at his temples.

Why him? Sure, he liked fighting powerful foes, but he wasn't nearly strong enough to kill Edmund and the time frame was ludicrous.

"You said it's possible to kill them. How difficult would killing one be?" he asked.

"Well, the Pinnacle Kings are infused with the energy of the world. Each is at the maximum *rank* of *50* with their abilities, it'll be extremely difficult to take even a single one down."

Morgan winced at those numbers.

If a regular pinnacle beast was dangerous enough that Katherine would only take one on if it was a full 30 ranks below her, then he didn't even want to imagine what a rank 50 pinnacle beast infused with reiki could do.

"I see the situation is sinking in," Samuel said solemnly. "Not to worry, though. Just kill Edmund in less than four days and all will be right in the world."

"You failed to mention what I get out of this," Morgan said, looking up at him. "If I'm to undertake this ridiculously difficult task, then the reward better be worth it."

"Oh, it is," Samuel said with a grin. "If you kill Edmund, I'll fix you."

"Fix me?" Morgan asked, confused.

"Yes. You may have noticed a gap in your memory. I'd say about two years' worth," Samuel said, "What you may not be aware of is that the person who messed with your memories, did some… shall we say, alterations to your body and mind."

To say that Morgan was shocked would have been the understatement of the century.

Someone had messed not only with his mind, but with his body as well?

"Who did this to me and why did they do it? What did they change?" Morgan finally asked.

"Well, to put it simply, they made some very significant changes to your body and those changes are affecting your behavior, mood, and the way you interact with just about anyone."

Starbreak

Morgan felt Sarah's arms tighten painfully around his and she let out a small gasp.

"Wait, how exactly did they change him?" Sarah cut in, leaning forward and staring at Samuel intensely, all signs of her earlier fear now gone.

"I'm sure you've noticed that he has no sense of propriety. He also doesn't seem even remotely attracted to you, despite you obviously being a beautiful young woman. You may also have noticed his complete inability to understand anything in the, shall we say, romantic department."

Sarah flushed at this, but the entire thing had gone entirely over Morgan's head.

Just what on earth were they talking about?

"As you can see from the baffled expression on his face, he has no idea what I'm talking about," Samuel said a second later as if he'd read his mind.

"And you can fix him?!" Sarah excitedly asked.

"Of course. I wouldn't offer if I couldn't."

Morgan decided that enough was enough.

"Alright, I have no idea what you're talking about, but I'm guessing it's something important. The real question is who did this to me, and why?"

"Well, I can't give you an exact name, as it would be against the rules. Let's just say that they're the competition. As to why, they wanted the perfect warrior and things like emotions or attraction to the opposite sex, are unnecessary distractions," he said with a shrug, rising from his seated position with a light groan.

"Wait, what? Who wants to use me?" Morgan exclaimed, feeling his heart rate quicken.

"So, will you accept the mission?" Samuel asked, completely ignoring his question.

Morgan was about to reply, but Sarah cut him off.

"He will!" she excitedly said, squeezing his arm tightly.

Morgan winced as she did this. He was beginning to go numb with how hard she'd been squeezing.

"Excellent. Just what I wanted to hear. Now, one last thing before I go." He waved his hand and an invisible force slammed into Morgan.

He gasped as a massive pain wracked his body, then he passed out.

***

Sarah felt Morgan slump against her and turned to see that he'd fallen unconscious.

"What did you do to him?" she demanded, turning to glare at the smiling god.

"Do calm down, Sarah. I just helped him. My competition cheated by messing with Morgan, so figured I could cheat a little too. So long as you are in this *beast zone,* you will no longer need to train to gain the maximum attributes per *rank.* Now you can *rank up* to your heart's content. Oh, and I also healed him," he added.

"Just keep in mind that you'd better get out of here quickly. You only have four days, so you'd better hop to it. He's also been slowly regaining his memories. I've stopped that for now, as it would only be a hindrance rather than a boon." He turned as if to go, then stopped as he seemed to remember something important.

"Oh. One more thing," he said, looking her straight in the eye; bright silver eyes piercing into her very soul.

"The path to true power does not lie in merely *ranking up.* Make sure to keep that in mind when doing so."

With that he nodded and abruptly disappeared, leaving a very confused Sarah to lower her unconscious friend to the ground.

***

Six years ago…

Sarah struggled and fought against the guard as he dragged her further down the long corridor, sloping ever downward.

"If you keep struggling, I'll hit you again!" the guard yelled at her, causing Sarah to immediately stop, as her face still hurt from when the guard had slapped her earlier.

"Finally using our heads, are we?" the guard said, sneering back at her. "Don't worry your pretty little head. Once your father pays your ransom, we'll be more than happy to let you go. Can't say the same for your little friend, though." The guard chuckled, taking a right turn down a corridor.

Sarah felt her heart sink when she heard that.

They would let her go, but kill Morgan? That wasn't fair! All he'd been doing was helping her escape and he didn't deserve to die for that.

As they took another turn, Sarah's eyes were inexorably drawn to the dagger sheathed at the man's belt. She bit her lip as they took yet another turn, debating whether she had the courage to grab the knife and go after Morgan.

There was also still the issue of her not knowing where they were keeping him, though she had a feeling she'd be finding out soon enough.

"Ah, looks like we're almost there," the guard said, pointing to another door disguised as a section of wall.

Now that she knew what to look for, Sarah could spot the irregular deep pattern in the brick that outlined the door.

If Morgan was through that door, then this was her chance to act.

She waited for the man to stop by the door, before she lunged forward, twisting out of his grip and tearing the dagger from its sheath.

"Hey, what are you…" the guard began, as he turned to glare at her.

Then he spotted the dagger in Sarah's hand and she grinned as she waived it before him.

"Get out of my way or I'll stab you!" Sarah said, clutching the knife in a shaky hand.

To her horror, the man just laughed at her instead of running for his life as she'd expected.

"I mean it!" Sarah yelled, feeling an edge of panic creeping into her voice.

"Why don't you hand me the knife before you hurt yourself?" the guard said, reaching for her with a sneer on his face.

Sarah screamed, then closed her eyes and ran forward, thrusting the dagger out before her and felt it sink into something soft. She heard a loud scream and cracked an eye open.

The guard was doubled over, clutching at the dagger which was protruding from between his legs. Sarah stared, wide-eyed as the guard staggered over to her, face twisted in pain and red with rage. He shuffled awkwardly forward as blood began to drench the front of his pants.

"You... Little... Bitch!" he gasped out, reaching out for her with a clawed hand.

Sarah staggered back, terror written on her face as the man continued shuffling towards her. The man let out a pained groan and slumped onto the ground, clutching at the dagger embedded in his crotch.

Sarah saw this as an opportunity and ran forward, kicking out at the man's hand and accidentally driving the dagger in deeper. The guard let out a high pitched scream that didn't sound at all right coming from a grown man, then he passed out.

Sarah reached down with shaky hands, wrapping both of them around the dagger hilt, and pulled with all her might. After a few seconds, the dagger came free, along with a fountain of blood. She screamed as she was covered in the stuff and she staggered over to the still closed door, half panicking and half disgusted.

She fumbled with the latch, feeling on the verge of panic and tried her best not to think about what she'd just done. Finally finding the hidden latch, she flipped it up and the door opened with a loud creak. The first thing she saw when she came in was the back of the man who had started all of this, the man named Kook.

Sarah felt her fear melt away as her eyes landed on Hint's killer, and she let out a scream of rage; barreling into the room and charging straight at the man. He turned in surprise and she sank the dagger deep into his side, screaming all the while. The man dropped to one knee, clutching at the dagger in his side and staring at her in incomprehension.

Then something snatched her arm and dragged her out of the room. She immediately began to struggle but stopped when she heard Morgan's familiar voice.

"You need to calm down."

Sarah almost stopped running, but Morgan was stronger than he looked and he tugged her along behind him.

"Morgan, how did you..."

"No time," he said, stopping by the first intersection. "Which way to get out of here?"

Sarah stared at him for a few moments of incomprehension, then her mind abruptly caught up with what was happening and she almost lost it right there. She would have if Morgan hadn't been there with her. Taking a few deep breaths to calm her racing heart, she pointed a shaky hand towards the corridor that led up to the surface.

"Good. Come on." He grabbed her hand and pulled her down the corridor she'd indicated.

Sarah felt the strong grip on her wrist and used that feeling to ground herself.

Only she knew how to get out of here. Morgan was counting on her to lead them and she wouldn't let him down.

She took a few more shaky breaths, then surprising found that she felt calm despite her surroundings. They came to another intersection and she immediately pointed him in the right direction. Morgan took the turn quickly, dragging her along in his wake. She did her best to keep up with him, but she was wearing a dress and shoes that were not suited for running. Add to that, that she normally didn't need to run like this and that all combined to have her panting for breath after only thirty seconds.

"Need… Break…!" she panted as they took another turn and the ground began sloping upward.

"No time," Morgan answered.

Sarah was about to retort, but the sound of crashing footsteps, followed by angry shouting, convinced her otherwise.

Her breathing became more and more labored as they continued running uphill, but she didn't dare stop. The voices behind them were growing louder by the second and she no longer had any delusions that they would treat her well if they caught her.

"Exit… Ahead!" she wheezed, stumbling slightly as Morgan somehow increased his speed even more.

They skidded to a halt by the exit and Morgan began searching for the switch that would release the door. After a few desperate seconds of fumbling around, he finally found it and the door slid open with a loud grinding noise.

Sarah wanted to take a few seconds to catch her breath, but Morgan was dragging her through the door into the now dark square and she was stumbling along behind him, her vision going fuzzy as she gasped for air.

Aaron Oster

"We're almost there," Morgan said, looking back at her and noticing her condition worsening.

"Where?" she asked, only managing the one word.

"Sewer. Too risky climbing the rubble," he answered.

Sarah let out an involuntary groan, but didn't make any further sound of a complaint as Morgan dragged her towards the still open sewer grate.

They had almost made it when a group of men burst from the hidden door and immediately spotted them.

"There they are! After them!"

Sarah chanced a glance over her shoulder and saw no less than ten dirty men running at them, all brandishing an assortment of weapons.

"Down we go!" Morgan called out.

And that was all the warning she got as the two of them plunged, once again, into the filthy sewer.

28

Katherine stared as Gold pulled a gleaming black key, embossed with the number *49* in red lettering, from his robe pockets.

An advanced Beast Zone key.

"Are you insane?" she said, practically exploding. "You're willing to risk the lives of your students, just to have me fight the most powerful *Beast Zone Patriarch* known in the Five Kingdoms?"

"Yup! I can't defeat it on my own, so you're going to help me," he replied, getting up from his seat and beginning to stretch.

"What's wrong with you?!" she yelled. "Even if we go full out, with no stops for food or sleep, it'll take at least thirty-six hours to get through to the end! Not to mention how long it'll take to defeat that monster once we get there!"

"Yup," he responded again, completely nonplussed. "Now, would you like to change before we go?"

Katherine was wearing her enchanted armor, the same type she'd had made for Morgan, but with a few alterations. Hers was a dark red in color and showed a lot more skin than either of theirs. Her top was sleeveless, with a neckline that dipped quite a bit, completely defeating the purpose of wearing the armor other than as a fashion statement. There were also long slashes along the outsides of her legs, revealing the lightly tanned skin beneath.

The only metal plating on the outfit was over her shins, and that was just for decoration.

She let out a snort of derision as she rose from her seat.

"No armor will protect me from the beasts in there, as you well know."

Gold shrugged, then stuck the key into the air and twisted. A swirling portal appeared right in the center of the room and he gestured for her to enter first.

"If this is some sort of ploy to trap me in there, I'll make sure to find a way out. And when I do, I'll tear you a new one. Are we understood?" she hissed.

"Perfectly. Now, ladies first."

Katherine huffed, then with a toss of her golden hair, walked through the portal.

***

Arnold watched from a crack in the door, as both Katherine and Gold entered the portal and felt his heart rate quicken.

He'd been wanting to get away from the psychotic bitch for weeks and she'd given him the perfect opportunity. She'd be gone for at least four days, which would give him plenty of time to get away.

In the beginning, he'd been afraid that she could track him anywhere, due to her ability, but after careful study, he was fairly certain he'd figured out her limits.

He'd begun suspecting that she wasn't all powerful when she'd dropped him in the middle of a swamp in the East Kingdom. She could get a general location in an area, but she could only track specific people if they contacted her first.

He took off down the large corridor at a swift walk, hearing his footsteps echoing down the lavish hallway.

The real question was where he should go. King Edmund hadn't kept his promise, and the Assassins Guild was still after him, so who would take him in and offer him protection?

His mind whirled as he made his way into the main hall of the palace. Here, there were more people; nobles, servants and citizens, all waiting for a meeting with the King's oldest son. He was in charge since his father was off fighting a war and his sister was supposedly helping with the effort.

Arnold snorted to himself as he made his way out of the massive double doors and out into the beautiful palace gardens.

He had a lot of valuable information about the princess, as well as the status of the war in the Central Kingdom.

Now, who would be interested in something like that? he mused to himself as he walked down the beautifully cobbled path toward the front gates.

The answer came to him as he passed under the massive archway and a smile slowly crept onto his face.

He knew exactly where to go.

***

Morgan yawned as he blinked the sleep away from his eyes and sat up slowly. His head felt a bit fuzzy, but otherwise he felt fine. He rubbed at his eyes, trying to figure out what was wrong with that when his brain finally kicked in.

He'd been pretty badly injured the previous day. Had he been sleeping for twenty-four hours?

"Good, I see you're awake."

Morgan turned, surprised to see Sarah already awake and kindling a small fire in the center of the cave. The events of the previous evening began coming back to him bit by bit.

"What happened?" he asked, rubbing at his head and wincing slightly.

Something definitely felt off, though he couldn't place his finger on it.

"Samuel did something to you and then you passed out," she said, standing from the fire and walking over to him.

Morgan's eyes followed her as she walked to the small crack in the wall and pulled in a leg from the badger she'd killed the previous day. She was wearing her armored pants, but all she had on besides that was a bra. Her hair was damp as well, meaning that she'd just washed herself and was likely still in the process of drying.

Something wasn't right about that.

"Shouldn't you be worried about walking around like that in front of me?" he asked, as she came back into the cave.

Sarah froze when she said this, looking at him wide-eyed.

"You never mentioned it before," she carefully said as she set the leg down. "Why mention it now?"

Since Samuel had said that Morgan couldn't even comprehend anything remotely sexual, she hadn't bothered putting her shirt on when she'd finished bathing. She wasn't about to go naked in front of him, but she'd felt comfortable wearing only this in front of him until he'd said something about it.

Morgan blinked.

She was right, of course. He never had mentioned it before. In fact, he'd often wondered why she was so obsessed with propriety when it came to clothes, bathing or anything else for that matter.

He looked up to Sarah, who was staring at him with a mixture of hope and fear.

Aaron Oster

"Tell me something, Morgan. Can you tell me why it would be considered embarrassing for me to walk around like this in front of you?"

Morgan thought about that for a few seconds as Sarah pulled her armored top over her head.

"From what I've gathered, a woman would only undress in front of a man if they felt comfortable doing so and from previous experience, I gathered that you felt uncomfortable doing so around me..." he trailed off, as his eyes widened.

Did he understand? His mind whirled through all his previous actions, the way he'd behaved in front of Sarah, and everything he'd seen and heard back in City Four. It was now so obvious to him, that he had no idea how he'd missed it all.

"Can you tell me something else?" Morgan looked back to Sarah, who was now blushing madly.

He now knew she wasn't angry, but rather, embarrassed about something. This was incredible.

"How do you feel, now that you understand?" she asked, biting her lip and looking down.

"I don't feel anything," he replied, thinking that it was quite odd that he didn't. "That isn't right though... I should be feeling something. You are well proportioned and you are pleasing to the eye, so why don't I feel anything?"

He put his hand up to his chin as he tried to figure it out.

Samuel had said the previous night that he would fix him, then he'd said that someone had messed up his ability to feel, or comprehend anything remotely sexual.

"But I do understand!" he exclaimed, looking up at Sarah, who now looked quite crestfallen.

"Why are you so upset?" he asked, reaching out and grabbing the badger leg.

He needed to do something with his hands while all this new information settled into his mind.

"You do *understand*, but you don't *feel* anything. It looks like Samuel decided to give you a taste, just to prove that he really could fix you. Damn that bastard!" she yelled, slamming her fist against the cave wall.

"Calm down," Morgan said as he began skinning the leg with Sarah's knife. "Samuel said that if we depose Edmund and place Katherine on the throne, he'll fix me completely, right?"

Sarah looked a bit sheepish at that and nodded, sitting down on the ground next to him.

"What will you do about Katherine, now that you know?" she asked in a quiet voice. "Will you take her up on her offer of marriage?"

Morgan's mind traveled back over his interactions with the Princess. With his new understanding, he knew that she'd been acting extremely provocative towards him the entire time and had to wonder if she had any real interest in him, or only in his power.

Then again, he'd only made the deal to gain power, so he really wasn't sure where it would go.

"I'm not sure," he replied, slicing the meat into strips and handing them to her to begin cooking. "For now, we need to focus on getting out of here. Then we have to worry about the world ending."

He gave her a weary grin as she set the meat to cook.

"Ask me again once the world isn't in jeopardy of being destroyed."

Sarah nodded, content with his answer for now.

"So, did anything else happen after I passed out?" he asked, leaning back against the wall.

A wide smile worked itself onto her face and she nodded emphatically.

"Samuel did something incredible! He made it so that we don't need to work hard to gain the maximum attributes in between *ranks*! While we're in here, anyway."

Morgan sat bolt upright at this.

"Are you sure?" he excitedly asked.

She nodded, her grin growing even wider.

"I tried it out as soon as he left and got the maximum attributes per *rank*!"

"Where are you holding now?" he asked, pulling all his cores from his pockets as well.

Sarah gave him a smirk.

"*Rank 17.*"

Morgan was utterly stunned.

The god who had been going on and on about rules and the end of the world actually did something to help.

"How much do you have until you reach *18*?"

"About *1,300*," she replied with a shrug. "I've never gone up this many *ranks* at once. The feeling is indescribable!"

Morgan quickly began opening all his cores stats and adding up the energy in his mind.

He had nearly 200,000 energy to use, so if he absorbed it all, he should get a good way into rank 18. He wanted to know exactly how much it would be from 18 to 19, though.

"Here," he said, holding out a core to Sarah. "Absorb the energy you need to get to *rank 18* and tell me how much it'll cost to get to *19*."

Sarah nodded excitedly and took the core from him. After a few seconds, a shudder ran through her body and she let out a light sigh. Then her eyes focused on the air in front of her, as she looked over her status.

"It looks like it will cost *114,000* energy to the next *rank*," she said, closing out her status and handing the core back to him.

Morgan inwardly winced at that number, but Sarah was quick to reassure him.

"That badger I killed gave me over *10,000* energy and it was just a basic beast. Can you imagine what the *Arc* will give us, or what we can expect to get on the next *stage*?" she excitedly asked.

Morgan thought that through before nodding.

"I see your point. This won't be nearly as difficult as I believed."

He then looked at the cores with both excitement and apprehension.

"What's wrong?" Sarah asked, seeing his hesitation.

"I've been slowly regaining my memories as I *ranked up*, but I've never moved up this fast before. I'm afraid that the new influx of information will incapacitate me, but at the same time, maybe I'll be able to remember exactly who screwed with my brain."

"Samuel said that he's stopped the memories from returning for now," Sarah said, trying to break the news as gently as she could.

"What? Why?" Morgan asked.

He hadn't been looking forward to the pain of regaining them, but he did want some answers.

Starbreak

"He said that the information would only hinder you for now."

Morgan gritted his teeth in annoyance, now seeing why the god had given him the capacity to understand.

The crafty bastard hadn't done him any favors. He'd just replaced one thing with another.

He let out a long sigh, then shrugged.

There was nothing he could do about it, so there was no point in getting upset.

"It's fine. At least I won't have to worry about the splitting headache," he said, then turned his attention to the cores and began absorbing them one by one.

29

Morgan shuddered as each new *rank* hit him, feeling his muscles strengthening and his mind expanding with each newly acquired *rank*.

At last, he was completely out of cores and he took a deep breath, opening his status.

Name: Morgan
Supermage: Rank - 18
Energy to next rank - 1,592/380,000
Ability - Divine Gravity & Air
RP - 920/920 (Regen - 9.1 per second)
Strength - 87
Agility - 100
Constitution - 91
Intelligence - 92
Wisdom - 91
Skills - Enhanced flight, Heavy impact, Gale force, Condensed wind blade
Traits - Gravity field, Recovery
Extra - Gravity storm

"What the hell?" Morgan exclaimed as he saw the amount of energy it would cost to get him to the next *rank*.

"What?" Sarah asked, looking up from her place by the fire.

"The energy cost to my next *rank* is *380,000!*"

"Holy shit! Why is it so high?"

Morgan let out a long breath and shrugged.

"No idea. Maybe it's a supermage thing."

He went back to looking through his status to see if his skills had improved, now quailing at the amount of energy he would need for his breakthrough *rank*.

Enhanced flight - Manipulate gravity and air to reduce your weight and move quickly through the air.
Cost - 7.5 RP per second
Max. height - 60 Ft

Max. speed - 40 Ft per second

Max. carry weight - 200 pounds (Adding any more weight will reduce speed by 1 foot per second for each additional pound).

Heavy impact - Manipulate gravity and air to make your blows land significantly harder (Currently X2.25).

Cost - 10 RP per second

Condensed wind blade - Manipulate gravity and air to create a dense whirling blade in the shape of your choice. The type of weapon you create will determine additional effects.

Piercing weapon - Double damage is dealt to mages, or beasts with mage abilities.

Slashing weapon - Double damage is dealt to supers, or beasts with super abilities.

Cost - 300 RP

Duration - Until dismissed

Gale force - Manipulate gravity and air to significantly increase your speed (Currently X2.25).

Cost - 10 RP per second

So the cost of all his skills had gone down to a manageable level, and along with his massive *RP* increase, he would be able to use his skills a lot more than he had been. His traits and extra skill hadn't changed at all, so he decided that they would probably only change once he reached *rank 19.*

"We'll need to test the way we move before we head into any sort of fight," Morgan said, taking a seat as Sarah removed the meat from the fire.

She nodded as he took a bite from the meat and grimaced. Apparently, badger wasn't all that tasty.

"Are you worried?" she asked as he forced another chunk of meat down his throat.

"About what?"

"About everything! The whole Pinnacle Kings, world ending thing. The fact that someone out there messed with your brain and is likely coming for you. Or the fact that we're still stuck in a damn

Beast Zone, with our only escape being defeating the *Arc* on the final *stage!*"

By the time she finished her tirade, she was panting and out of breath. Morgan gave her an odd look.

"No time to be worried about things that are out of our control. Right now, we just need to focus on one thing: getting out of here. After that, we can focus on something else."

Sarah glared at him as if she were indignant at his calm demeanor.

"Think about it this way," he continued. "As long as we're in here, no one can get to us, so there's no need to worry."

"Did you already forget about the other keys into this place?" she asked with a raised eyebrow.

"No. But the likelihood of one of our enemies getting their hands on one is slim to none. And if they do get in here..." He shrugged, swallowing the last of the meat, "we'll worry about it then."

Sarah blew out a long breath and allowed her anger to slip away. Morgan was right, she needed to remain calm and focus on one thing at a time. Right now, that was getting to the next *stage*.

Morgan stood from his seated position by the fire and stretched, feeling his tight muscles relaxing as he prepared himself for the day's fighting.

"I say we aim for *stage 6* today," he said, pulling his magesteel gloves over his fingers and flexing them as the gloves conformed around his hands.

"Do you really think we can make it?" Sarah asked, kicking out the fire and sticking the remaining badger meat in their bag.

"If the *Arc* is *rank 18*, then we can probably make it through without too much trouble. The next *stage* is a risk, as the *Arc* may be over *rank 19*. The chances are actually pretty high, but you've got a pretty good chance of hitting *rank 19* today, so I'm not too worried."

Sarah bit her lip as Morgan walked to the crack in the wall and squeezed out of it.

She really hoped he was right.

***

As Morgan had predicted, the *stage* went by fairly quickly. After their massive increase in their attributes, it was barely a challenge. They breezed through the stage, having only a little trouble against the *Arc*, a *rank 18* inferno-badger.

Sarah was the one to take it down and since it was an evolved beast, she got about *13,000* energy from it.

They then took a break for lunch, after which they moved up to the fifth *stage*. Sarah looked around with wide eyes as they walked into another crystal cavern, this one filled with sparkling blue quartz and lit by small perforations in the walls.

The light bounced off the crystal, lighting the entire area in brilliant blue light beams. She soon discovered, that while pretty, the uncertain lighting wouldn't help them in a fight. If anything, it made fighting the wolf-sized lizards all the more difficult.

The beasts on this *stage* so far had been *ranked* between *17* and *18*, making Sarah wonder if they could actually defeat the *Arc* at the end of the *stage*.

They took a quick break after their latest fight against a black and blue lizard and she took a peek at her status, to see that she only needed about *10,000* energy until she reached the next *rank*.

"I'm nearly there," she said, wiping the sweat from her brow and taking a sip of water from the makeshift mug she'd created.

"That's great! I'm nowhere close, though, even after all those beasts. I still need over *270,000* energy."

Sarah just shook her head, marveling at the amount they'd managed to collect in a single day, and it wasn't even half over yet. As far as she could tell, this stage was quite a bit larger than the last and the beast attacks were far more frequent than they had been on previous *stages*.

In addition, they were running into evolved beasts every once in a while and they proved to be difficult fights, even with their massive increase in power.

She handed Morgan the mug, which he took from her with a grateful nod and downed in one gulp. This *stage* may have been cooler than the last one, but it was at least eighty degrees right now. With no breeze, it felt even hotter.

There was a loud skittering noise from off to their left and a massive red and black lizard emerged from one of the many side tunnels on the stage.

"Looks like an evolved beast, if I'm not wrong," Morgan said, dropping the cup and taking a running leap at the beast.

She watched as he used his *condensed wind blade* to punch a massive hole through the beast's chest. He then reached in and ripped the core free. She gagged, watching his arm emerge, dripping with blood and covered in gore.

"Why didn't you use the rod?" she exclaimed as he absorbed the energy.

"Seemed like a waste of time," he replied with a shrug. "Besides, the armor is self-cleaning and I have four more pairs I can change into."

Sarah just blew out a breath and shot a freezing cone of water at him, completely drenching his right side. Morgan sputtered and cursed as he was soaked, and glared at her as she walked past him with a smug grin.

"One of these days, you'll be on the other end of a soaking," he muttered, and she had to suppress the urge to giggle.

It took them the better part of the afternoon to find the *Arc's* territory, as the increased beast population and the confusing mess of tunnels led them to make one wrong turn after the next.

"Finally!" Sarah said with a groan, as they spotted the large tunnel leading into the final room of the *stage.*

She was just about ready to drop. They'd been fighting non-stop for the last six hours, a feat which she was quite impressed with. She was absolutely certain that they would not have been able to manage, had they still been at their earlier ranks.

"I'm going to go out on a limb here and guess that we'll be facing some sort of lizard," she said as they entered the tunnel.

"Really? And what gave you that idea?" Morgan asked.

He was in a very good mood, having gotten to fight more that day than he had in a while. Sarah still hadn't reached *rank 19,* as Morgan had insisted on doing the bulk of the fighting.

"Don't you think we should at least try to get to the next *rank* before taking on an *Arc* that is likely much more than we can handle?"

"Stop worrying," Morgan said with a wave of his hand. "Nothing bad will happen."

"Famous last words," she muttered as they came to the end of the tunnel.

The room was a large open cavern and Sarah had to wonder at the laziness of whoever had created this place. Couldn't they have mixed it up a bit? Why did every *Arc* room need to be a damn cavern?

Then her eyes fell on the monstrosity lying in the center of the room. It was a lizard, as she had guessed, but it bared only a passing resemblance to the ones they'd been fighting all day. It was a light red in color, with a smattering of gray and white scales across its belly and back.

Its body was compact like that of a bear's, instead of the long sinuous bodies they'd become used to during the day. Its legs were short and powerful looking, tipped by four steps of wickedly sharp claws. It had a long, sinewy tail that twitched around behind it and after getting a good look at its face, she saw that it resembled a cat's more than a lizard's.

The most notable feature, however, was the long line of black and red spines running down its back. They were currently lying flat and she had to wonder what purpose they served.

Probably nothing good, she thought as she turned to see Morgan's reaction.

He predictably looked excited at the prospect of fighting, but there was no way she would let him fight that thing yet.

"Morgan, judging by how that thing looks, I'd say it's an intermediate beast. I don't think we can win against it if it's over *rank 18*. I suggest we leave now and come back once we break through into the next tier."

For a moment, she actually thought he might see sense, but then he shook his head and used his *wind blade*.

"You use your *icy wave* and I'll charge it head on. With our new power, we should have no problems taking it down. With my *heavy impact* skill and the correct *wind blade*, I'll have an effective *strength* of around *390*. There's no way the lizard could stand up to an attack like that, even if it is over *rank 19!*"

Sarah let out a long breath. She recognized that look in his eyes. The gleaming, almost predatory, hunger for battle. The need to go out and pit himself against the strongest of foes, despite the odds. Up until last night, she'd wondered just where this lust for battle came from, but now she was only concerned.

He didn't think straight when he got like this. Sure, he kept his cool and didn't rush in blindly without a plan, but he'd ignored some huge dangers that had almost gotten him killed in the past, and she had a feeling that they couldn't take this beast on as they were now. She had to put her foot down.

"I won't fight that thing with you," she said, folding her arms and staring him down.

"We can't win and I won't help you get yourself killed. Now use your head. You can't win this fight alone, so if you go in now, you'll lose."

Morgan paused for the briefest of moments, his battle haze breaking for that moment, then a violent shiver ran through his body and he grinned at her.

"I guess we'll just have to see!" And with the sound of rushing wind, he dashed from the tunnel exit and into the cavern.

30

Katherine ducked the swiping claws of an eight ton steel-mane jaguar, then brought her massive mace around in a powerful swing, caving in the beast's side with a clang of metal on metal. She felt the reverberation run through her hand, and her lips quirked upward as the cat slammed into the opposite wall, black blood oozing from the massive rent in its side.

"That's the spirit!" Gold exclaimed, as his diamond golem tore through another one of the beasts.

They'd been fighting through the *Zone* for the last ten or so hours and despite the desperate need to help Morgan, Katherine had to admit that she was enjoying herself.

When was the last time she'd gotten to do some actual training, or face any real sort of challenge? The beasts they'd been fighting so far were around rank 42, so they didn't pose a serious threat to her, but they were slowly growing stronger.

Gold walked up next to her and gestured at the dead monster lying in a pool of spreading blood.

"You gonna get the core?"

"Of course," she replied with a snort, flipping her still perfect hair and holding out a hand. A second later, the core tore itself from the beast's chest and flew to land neatly on her palm. She then opened a spatial tear and unceremoniously threw it in.

"I do have to wonder how you're still spotless after the killing spree we've had so far," Gold commented as they walked down the stone corridor.

"You look to be just as clean as I am," she replied.

"Ah, but that's because I'm a mage. I don't attack head-on. You, on the other hand, should be covered in gore, but you're spotless. What's your secret?"

"Practice," she said, speeding up and walking ahead of the annoying man.

Gold was insistent, however.

"Oh, come on, you can tell me. I won't tell anyone else." He held up a hand, pinky extending outward.

"Pinky promise!"

"Screw you, asshole," she replied, just as another group of beasts came into view.

Thank God for small favors, she thought as she charged into battle.

***

Morgan sprinted into the room, watching as the lizard-cat thing rose from its prone position on the ground and issued a roar in challenge. He heard Sarah cursing away at him from the mouth of the tunnel, but ignored her.

He could take this beast on his own.

He grinned as his body tingled with pleasure and anticipation. He collided with the lizard with astounding force, activating his shield as he did so. His *wind blade* shrieked as it skittered over the monster's tough hide and Morgan spun in place, lashing out with a powerful kick that sent the lizard into the opposite wall.

He stopped for a moment as the lizard tore itself free and violently shook itself to get rid of all the rubble sticking to its hide.

Morgan frowned as the beast let out a rattling hiss. It began to glow a bright red and its long red and black spines rose from its back, crackling with black colored lightning.

The beast didn't have a scratch on it. All he'd managed to do was piss it off.

A wild grin spread across his face as the lizard launched itself at him with blinding speed. It wasn't nearly as large as some of the beasts he'd faced, but it was a whole lot faster. Morgan used *condensed wind blade*, then crossed both of them to catch the oncoming blur of teeth, claws and black lightning.

He narrowly avoided being hit by the beast's claws, retaliating with four quick strikes of his *wind blades* into the creature's skull. Every blow bounced off and Morgan cursed as he was forced to jump back.

He used *gale force* and *heavy impact*, rolling to avoid another flurry of wild slashes from the beast, then sprang to his feet and dashed in to attack its unprotected side. That was when everything went horribly wrong.

The beast let out a rattling roar that shook the entire cavern, then a nimbus of crackling lightning spread outward in an ever expanding dome. Morgan tried to move out of the way, but he was going too fast. He leaped into the air, using his *flight* in a desperate attempt to avoid the crackling energy, but to no avail.

Morgan felt his body go numb as the lightning struck, completely shattering his shield and sending him crashing to the ground in a twitching, writhing heap. He vaguely heard Sarah screaming in the distance and tried to get up, but his body refused to respond to his commands.

He gritted his teeth against the pain. His entire body felt as though it had been completely fried.

He could vaguely see the lizard slowly making its way towards his prone form, but no matter how hard he tried to move, his body just refused to respond. He then desperately tried to use his skills. If he could fly, then he could get away. His skills refused to activate.

He gritted his teeth, trying to force his unresponsive body onto its side. He'd almost managed it when a sudden spasm wracked him and he was forced on his back once more, body twitching as the electricity continued coursing through him. Then, he felt a heavy weight land on his chest and he could no longer stand the pain. Morgan blacked out.

***

Sarah let out a scream of horror as she watched the nimbus of black lightning strike Morgan midair. She watched as his body contorted and twitched as the electricity crackled through him, frying his nerves and cooking his internal organs.

She stood frozen as he hit the ground, his body still twitching every few seconds from the aftershock. He didn't get up.

"No," she whispered as she watched the nightmarish lizard approaching his still form.

He couldn't be… Morgan was too strong to have…

Sarah could feel tears prickling at the corners of her eyes as she saw smoke curling up from Morgan's blackened and burned body.

Aaron Oster

"No!" she screamed, feeling the tears now pouring down her face.

Sadness and rage threatened to overtake her as the lizard stopped before Morgan and placed its leg on his chest, as though to claim his prize.

"You'll pay for that, you bastard!" she screamed, feeling her voice crack and blood coat the inside of her throat. She used *icicle barrage*, sending one volley of icy spears after the next into the beast, screaming incoherently all the while.

It staggered back under the assault, but her attacks didn't seem to be doing anything at all. She gritted her teeth, summoning a massive amount of water and feeling her *MP* plummet. In a matter of seconds, it bottomed out and she screamed again, unleashing a massive torrent of frozen water at the lizard.

As soon as it struck, she froze it solid, leaving the beast encased in a four foot block of ice.

The beast was as good as dead now.

Her eyes fell on Morgan and her rage wore off, replaced instead by vast, crushing sadness.

This was all her fault. If she'd only agreed to fight alongside him, this never would have happened.

Hot tears streamed down her face as she walked over and crouched down near him. He looked even worse up close. His face was blackened and burned, with huge patches of blistering skin showing through. His hair was almost completely gone and the stench was almost unbearable.

She felt bile come up in her throat and felt on the edge of panic. Her heart was beating so rapidly in her chest, that she felt as though it were about to come out. She began to feel lightheaded and the world started swimming in her vision.

She suddenly heard a loud ominous crack and her head whipped up, eyes widened in horror as a massive crack spread across the surface of her ice block.

How the hell was that thing still alive?

She let out a snort and looked back down at Morgan.

Did it really matter? What was the point if he wasn't around? She'd just let the beast have her and her misery could end.

Her eyes slid away from his face, roaming over the rest of his body and she felt her heart skip a beat. Despite the gruesome appearance of his face, his armor appeared to be completely undamaged. She quickly placed her ear down to his chest and after a few tense seconds, heard the slow beat of his reiki-heart.

He was alive!

Sarah felt her tears of despair change to those of joy in an instant.

But how?

She heard another crack and saw the fissure in her ice block widen.

No time for that now. She had to get him out of here.

She carefully slid her hands under him and quickly stood, cradling him in her arms. His body was a good deal bulkier than it had been the last time she'd carried him, so it was a bit awkward, but she managed it all the same.

There was a loud explosion of shattering ice, followed by the rattling roar of the lizard, and Sarah took off for the tunnel exit. She heard the sound of sharp claws hitting the ground behind her, but didn't dare look back.

She was almost there. Just a little bit more…

Sarah cried out as a sharp pain flared across her back, then she barreled into the tunnel and the sound of pursuit abruptly stopped. She kept running, moving at least halfway down the tunnel before coming to a stop.

She crouched then, placing Morgan gently on the ground and panting hard as she tried to recover her breath. She could feel a sharp, stinging pain from her back and knew that she was at the very least bleeding from a nasty gash.

She'd recovered enough *MP* by now, so she quickly erected two ice walls to either side of the tunnel, then she flattened a sheet of ice against the wall to examine her back. She could see a long, jagged tear running from her left shoulder to the center of her back. She quickly reached down and pulled her uniform over her head, wincing at the discomfort it caused.

Looking again, she let out a sigh of relief as she saw it was only a scratch.

Guess the armor was actually good for something, she thought, crouching down next to Morgan.

She gently ran her hand over the blackened armor, wondering how he could possibly have survived the attack. Her question was answered a moment later when her fingers reached his waist and didn't find even a single tear in the armor.

She carefully curled her fingers under the hem of his shirt.

She gasped as she pulled his shirt up to reveal only slightly burned skin underneath. Tugging the shirt up further, she discovered that the same held true throughout. While his face was horribly damaged, his body seemed to be almost completely unharmed.

Her eyes began to water again as she pulled his shirt back down and looked at his ruined face. He'd gotten horribly hurt, and all because she'd been a stubborn idiot. His body might be fine, but with damage like that to his head, who knew if he'd survive?

Sarah wanted to dissolve into a wailing mess of self-loathing and pity. She wanted to curl in on herself and cry until there was nothing left to give, but she couldn't. Her resolve hardened as she looked down at her best friend and the only person she loved in this entire world.

He would survive the next twenty-four hours, and once that time passed his recovery trait would heal all of the damage. He would be good as new.

She leaned down, placing her lips on his now blackened and burned ones. She'd wanted to do this for the longest time, but had never had the courage to do so. Sarah straightened up, wiping away her tears and took a deep, shaky breath.

He would survive. No matter what.

31

Morgan took a deep breath and opened his eyes. He was lying on his back and staring up at a leafy canopy above his head. Bright sunbeams came through, leaving dappled spots across his shirt. He slowly sat up and his momentary confusion melted away as his eyes took in a familiar clearing.

A small cottage stood in the center and a dark-skinned man sat before it, reading a book.

What was he doing back here?

Morgan cast his thoughts back to what he'd been doing prior to coming here, but he was drawing a blank. Shrugging to himself, he rose to his feet and headed into the clearing.

"Did you bring me here?" Morgan asked as he approached the table.

Dabu jumped in surprise and looked up at Morgan with a slightly confused expression.

"Morgan, what are you doing here?"

Just like the last time, Dabu's rich voice and powerful aura washed over him, making Morgan relax his shoulders and feel oddly at peace.

"I have no idea," he replied, walking to the other side of the table and taking a seat. "I remember being stuck in a *Beast Zone* with Sarah for the last few days, but everything else is kind of hazy."

Dabu closed his book with a snap, looking concerned for a moment. His eyes then seemed to gaze off into the distance, and after a few seconds, he relaxed.

"It looks as though you bit off more than you could chew and were nearly killed as a result," the omniscient supermage said, giving him an admonishing look.

"Why on earth would you attack a *rank 24* intermediate beast while still at *rank 18*?"

Morgan's eyes widened when he heard this.

He'd nearly died attacking a rank 24 beast?

"Is Sarah okay?" he quickly asked, and let out a sigh of relief when Dabu nodded.

They sat in silence for the next few minutes, Morgan fidgeting uncomfortably in his seat, while Dabu stared at him, unblinkingly.

He didn't know why, but he sensed that Dabu was disappointed in him somehow.

"You are lucky to be alive," Dabu finally said and Morgan winced at the harsh rebuke in his tone.

"Do you have any idea what kind of disaster you could have brought on this world, just because you wanted to fight a strong opponent?"

His voice cracked out like a whip, and Morgan looked down.

Why did this man have the power to make him feel so ashamed? He'd never felt shame before, but he was sure that this was what it felt like.

"And what about your friend? She very nearly let herself be killed when she thought you were dead!"

Morgan's head shot up when he heard this and he met Dabu's steely gaze with his own uncertain one.

"I didn't mean for it to happen," he said, feeling very strange. His chest was constricting very tightly and his heart was thumping erratically.

Dabu's tone softened slightly when he saw that he was getting through to him.

"I know what fighting does to you," he said, surprising Morgan even more with his seemingly limitless knowledge.

"How?" he asked, feeling the tightness in his chest slowly easing. He already knew the answer and it was only confirmed a moment later.

"I know what was done to you and how it had affected your mind," he said with a sigh. "I was hoping to keep it a secret until I had permission to fix you, but I can see Samuel's mark on your aura, so I can guess that he's offered you some sort of deal."

Morgan blew out a long breath and leaned forward, placing his chin on his palms.

Every time Dabu answered a question, he just had more questions.

"Can you please explain exactly what's been done to me and why? Can you tell me who did this to me and can you explain what you meant by 'Samuel's mark on my aura'?"

Dabu actually smiled and Morgan felt some of his tensions ease.

"I cannot tell you who did this to you, as there are certain rules I must adhere to. Breaking them would be bad, for you and I both."

Morgan grimaced at that.

Again with these damn rules. Whose rules?

"I can see that you've heard this before, but I cannot tell you more. All I can say is that you will understand one day. For now, I'll answer all the questions I can. We do have some time, as I'm guessing your mind fled here in order to escape the pain of your physical body. Since you are in a comatose state, there should be no damage to your mind from staying here until your body heals itself."

Morgan blew out a long breath, but nodded in agreement.

Dabu may not have answered his question about these so-called 'rules', but he had learned one thing at least. There was a being out there who could control omniscient ranked supermages that resided in other worlds. A being with the power to control even a god.

Morgan shivered despite the warmth of the clearing.

Whoever this being was, he hoped to never meet them.

"To answer your first question," Dabu said, snapping Morgan from his thoughts. "Your body was modified in a way so as to produce the perfect warrior. Feelings like desire, or passion, were repurposed to fuel your desire for battle. You feel good when you fight, alive in a way that you cannot describe. On the other hand, when there is no fighting to be done, you feel empty inside. Am I correct?"

Morgan nodded, both horrified and fascinated at the same time.

"There were several chemicals in your body that were repurposed for the task of keeping your mind clear so that even through the lust of battle, you would still be able to think tactically. There were some other small changes as well, but you get the picture," Dabu finished.

"Is there any way I can stop myself from doing it again?" Morgan asked after a few moments of silence.

Dabu smiled at that.

"Through self-control and discipline. You must be stronger than your desires if you wish to be victorious. You went into that battle on a high, without giving yourself time to cool down from the day's fighting. Your body was flush with endorphins and all you wanted to do was keep that feeling.

"You also need to remember, that should you complete whatever task Samuel has set you, you will be cured. When that happens, your body and mind will be flooded with a slew of new emotions and feelings. It is important to train your mind as well as your body. That is the only advice I can offer."

Morgan nodded, feeling as though a great weight had been lifted from his shoulders. He'd been afraid that there would be nothing he could do and until Samuel fixed him, he'd be stuck at the whims of his battle-hungry mind.

"Now, to answer your second question. Everyone who has an ability, be they human or beast, exudes an aura. When someone interacts with an especially powerful being, it leaves a very distinct mark. The mark will fade over time, but judging from what I can see, yours will stick around for at least another week."

"What exactly is an aura, and how can you see them?" Morgan asked, wondering if this would be against the rules. He really hoped it wasn't.

"Ah, now there's something I can help you with," Dabu replied. "An aura is the residual energy from your heart made manifest and those with the knowledge to see them can learn quite a bit about someone's power."

Morgan's heart skipped a beat.

"So what you're saying is that you can tell what someone's *rank* is, just by looking at them?" he excitedly asked.

"That, and a few other things," Dabu replied.

"Can you teach me?" Morgan asked, leaning forward across the table.

If he could see someone's rank before a fight, it would make everything so much easier.

Dabu thought about it for a few seconds, before slowly nodding.

"Very well. It has been a few centuries since I've taught someone, but I believe imparting this skill to you would be beneficial to your growth."

Morgan nodded excitedly, expecting him to begin instructing him. What Dabu did instead was place his hand on the table, facing palm up.

"Place your hand on mine."

Morgan gave him a slightly confused look, but did as he was instructed. Dabu's hand wrapped around his and a purple sphere of light appeared around their clasped hands. Morgan's eyes widened as a warm tingling sensation seemed to flow out of Dabu and into him. The sensation only intensified the longer it went on and he soon felt as though every cell in his body was shaking itself apart.

Just when he thought he wouldn't be able to take any more, the sensation vanished. Morgan blew out a shaky breath as Dabu removed his hand.

"What was *that*?" he asked, rubbing at his still tingling hand and finding that he was a bit out of breath.

"Open your status and see," Dabu said with a grin.

Morgan shrugged and did as he was told, streaming a flow of reiki up to his eyes and viewing his status.

Name: Morgan
Supermage: Rank - 18
Energy to next rank - 176,917/380,000
Ability - Divine Gravity & Air
RP - 920/920 (Regen - 9.1 per second)
Strength - 87
Agility - 100
Constitution - 91
Intelligence - 92
Wisdom - 91
Skills - Enhanced flight, Heavy impact, Gale force,
Condensed wind blade
Traits - Gravity field, Recovery, Aura sense (inherited)
Extra - Gravity storm

Morgan excitedly selected the new skill, as his eyes fell upon it and a new window opened.

Aura Sense (inherited) - You have been bestowed the gift of sight by an omniscient. By concentrating on a target and thinking the word 'sense,' you will be able to view the target's aura. The aura will currently reveal the target's name, rank and ability type; provided that they are no more than nine ranks above your own.

Morgan closed his status and looked to Dabu with wide eyes. "I had no idea that skills could be taught!" he exclaimed.

"They can't," he replied, instantly squashing Morgan's excitement. "If you look carefully at the skill, you will see the word 'inherited' next to the skill name. Inherited skills are a special type of skill that cannot be learned through any means. The only way to learn this skill is to have someone who has reached the *omniscient rank* teach it to you."

"That's ridiculous," Morgan deadpanned. "Why even have a skill like that if only one in a billion could ever have a chance of possibly learning to use it?"

Dabu laughed then, white teeth contrasting with his dark skin and his rich voice rolling out over the clearing. Morgan could feel that sense of peace again and his shoulders relaxed as the annoyance leaked out of him.

"Yes, it is quite ridiculous, but that is just the way of things," Dabu said, still chuckling.

A thought struck Morgan then and he felt his heart skip a beat in excitement.

"Are there any others?" he asked, leaning forward eagerly.

"There are," Dabu replied, "and before you ask, no; your *rank* isn't sufficiently high enough for me to teach you anything else."

Morgan sat back slightly disappointed, but at the same time, excited about the possibilities. He was about to ask Dabu another question, when a sharp pain shot through his head, making him wince.

"It would appear that our time together has come to an end," Dabu said.

"Wait, that's impossible! There's no way that I've been here for twenty-four hours," Morgan replied.

"Ah, but it is entirely possible. Time runs differently here than in the mortal realms. What feels like a minute here, can translate to decades in another world."

Morgan just shook his head in amazement. He winced again, suddenly feeling a light tugging at the center of his chest. He knew that he likely only had a minute or two left, and he needed some more questions answered.

"Do you have any advice for me before I go?" he asked, feeling the tugging sensation increasing.

"The difference in strength between *ranks 18* and *19* is the largest out of any of the breakthrough *ranks*. Once you *rank up*, you will have a massive increase to all your attributes. Your body will grow stronger and your life expectancy will go up. Do not fight that beast before you reach *rank 19*."

"And another thing, before you go. You'd better apologize to your friend when you get back. She looks terrible and hasn't slept a wink since she dragged you from that battle."

Morgan nodded quickly, feeling that his time was running out.

"Samuel said something about stopping King Edmund before the Pinnacle Kings wake. Can you tell me anything about them?"

For the first time ever, he saw Dabu look completely stunned.

"Dabu?" Morgan prodded, already feeling his mind fading from the clearing.

Dabu looked up at him and began to say something, then the clearing abruptly vanished.

32

Morgan's eyes opened and he blinked a few times as they adjusted to the dim lighting of the tunnel. He knew that he hadn't physically visited Dabu, so his eyes shouldn't need to adjust, but the mind was a funny thing.

Then the air was knocked from his lungs as Sarah slammed into him, wrapping him up in a crushing hug. He gasped, forcing himself into a sitting position and feeling her shaking against him with great, wracking sobs. Had this been a few weeks ago, Morgan would just have sat there and waited for her to finish. Now, however, he understood the concept of offering comfort to others in their time of need.

He brought his arms up and hugged her back, being careful not to squeeze too tightly. He hoped he was doing it right. He sat there for the next twenty minutes, holding his friend while she shook against him. Eventually, he felt her body beginning to relax as her sobs subsided and after a few more minutes heard the slow deep breathing that indicated sleep.

Dabu really hadn't been kidding about her not sleeping, Morgan thought as he gently eased her off himself and onto the ground.

Looking her over, he could see that she didn't look nearly as put together as she normally did. Her hair was disheveled, her face was smeared with dirt and there were heavy bags under her eyes.

He let out a soft sigh, knowing that he had a lot to make up for when she woke up. He pulled a shirt from their pack and rolled it up, placing it under her head. Then he pulled one of their coats from the bag and draped it over her sleeping form. Morgan froze when he was halfway through the motion, wondering what had prompted him to do it.

Shaking his head, Morgan straightened up and began checking himself. His armor was whole and undamaged, meaning it must have cleaned and mended itself while he was unconscious.

Good, he thought. He wouldn't need to change.

He looked down both sides of the tunnel before heading down the one leading back to the fifth *stage*.

He had some training to do.

***

Six years ago…

Morgan landed with a splash in the foul-smelling sewer water, hearing Sarah let out a loud scream before she landed as well. He continued running, half carrying, half dragging the girl behind him as he wove a familiar path through the dark tunnels.

A few seconds later, he heard the telltale splash as the men followed them in. He could hear their shouts echoing off the tunnel walls, but he was fairly confident he could get away from them. He came up to an intersection and took a hard right, hearing Sarah's labored breathing as he dragged her along with him.

He didn't know why, but he felt a bit guilty for pushing her so hard. They were running for their lives though, and he wasn't about to spare her the discomfort if it was a difference between life and death. He stumbled and almost fell when it finally caught up with him.

He felt bad about something.

He grinned to himself, despite their predicament and pulled a hard left, doubling back into a second sewer pipe that would lead into the city proper. He was almost beside himself with excitement, another emotion he was just feeling now.

They all seemed to be coming back at once. He could hardly believe it. It was almost worth the hell he'd been through, just to be feeling something again.

"How… Much… Further?" Sarah wheezed from behind him and Morgan snapped back to reality.

He quickly looked up as they passed another grate and he got a quick flash of the streets above.

"Almost there. Just keep going," he said.

He could still hear the echoing bangs as the men shoved their way clumsily through the sewers after them and didn't want to slow down for fear of being caught.

He was pretty sure they were already safe, but disaster often struck when one dropped their guard.

"There," Morgan said, pointing to a ladder up ahead.

Aaron Oster

He came to a skidding halt, the sewer muck sloshing around him as he began climbing up. Reaching the top he gave a mighty shove, knocking the grate free and climbing out into the open air.

He took a deep breath of the fresh night air, glad to be out of the sewers. Then he turned back and held his hand out to help Sarah up. She came out, wheezing so hard that he thought she may very well pass out. Her face was beet red and she pulled in the air with huge, heaving gasps.

Morgan took a quick look around the moonlit main street but didn't see any sign of pursuit, so he decided that they could take it a little easier on the few blocks they had left to the Lord's manor. He didn't want to think what he would do once they reached the manor and just had to hope that they would let him shelter there until they took care of Kook and his goons.

"We're almost there," he said, watching as Sarah leaned over, heaving for air.

He should probably help her. She wouldn't make it back otherwise.

He leaned down and pulled one of her arms over his shoulder.

Sarah gave him a grateful look and the two of them set off at a light jog, with Morgan taking most of her weight as they went.

Morgan took a left into the first alley he saw, heading further in and emerging on the other side. He stopped for a moment, looking around for the narrow street that connected the city to the open courtyard before the Lord's manor. He spotted it after a few seconds and dragged Sarah over in that direction.

They had nearly made it to the alley entrance when a man stepped from the deep shadows of a nearby building, thrown by the moon overhead. He heard Sarah let out a gasp of recognition, and Morgan couldn't blame her.

Kook stood in their path, the only thing standing between them and freedom. Morgan stopped, his eyes flicking down to the man's side, where his shirt was stained red from where Sarah had stabbed him. The man looked pale and unsteady on his feet, but the longsword he held clutched in one hand was steady and unwavering.

That was not a good sign.

"Thought you could get away, did you?" Kook said, chuckling darkly.

His laughter turned into a wracking cough and soon he was wheezing as blood poured from his open mouth.

He quickly stood as Morgan made to dart in, holding the sword out point first.

"Don't think you'll be getting past me that easily, boy!" he growled, teeth stained red with blood. "I may be a dead man, but I'll be damned if I don't take the two of you with me!"

Morgan stopped, eyes locked onto Kook's. Most people would make the mistake of watching the weapon, but Morgan knew that the real threat would come from the man, and if he watched him closely he could predict the weapon's path.

Kook was a man on the edge. He might not have an ability, but he was still extremely dangerous. Not to mention that he was a full grown man, albeit, a heavily injured one.

There was one thing Morgan found odd as the man slowly closed in on him- the lack of anyone else in the open square. The lack of city guards this close to the manor wasn't just troubling; it was downright alarming.

"Sarah, I'm going to try and keep his attention on me. You try to get around him and find some guards."

"I can't!" she hissed. "The guards are in on it. I don't know who to trust!"

Morgan cursed under his breath.

Well, that would explain the lack of guards. This just made things more complicated, but so long as they could get past Kook, they had a pretty good chance of getting away.

"Fine. Stay behind me. Make sure that I'm between you and Kook at all times," he said as the man closed in, sword gleaming in the moonlight.

"Why are you helping me?" Sarah felt obliged to ask.

"You came for me when you didn't have to. No one's ever done that for me before and if that's what friends do, then I want to be your friend."

Sarah felt her cheeks color slightly and a warm fuzzy feeling spread throughout her body.

Morgan really liked her!

Then Kook let out a yell and lunged forward. Morgan rolled to the side, scooping up a small pebble from the road and flinging it in a sidearm throw at the man's head.

This was meant to serve a dual purpose. It would give him a good idea of the man's reflexes and with any luck, cause him to be distracted for a second or two. He dashed in as soon as the pebble had been released, but wasn't prepared for Kook's reaction.

Instead of blocking the rock, he lunged in, taking the small projectile in his right eye and skewering Morgan through his shoulder with the icy steel. Morgan let out a hiss of pain as the sword withdrew, now coated with his blood and darted forward to skewer him again.

Morgan's reactions were fast and he nimbly dodged, feeling a smile creeping onto his face. He felt the excitement welling up inside of him, as he had his first real challenge in a while. Even though he was injured and the situation was dire, this was what made him feel most alive.

He ducked another swipe of the sword and drilled a stiff punch into the area where Sarah had stabbed the man. Kook let out a pained grunt and staggered back as a fresh wave of blood spurted from the clumsily bandaged wound.

"Little shit!" he growled, as Morgan quickly back stepped, keeping his eyes on the man the entire time.

Morgan winced as his shoulder throbbed in pain. He could feel hot blood pumping from the wound and judged how weak Kook was now compared to him. He grimaced as he realized that at this rate, Kook would kill them both before he bled out, which meant that he would need to take a stupid risk.

He chanced a glance back and saw that Sarah was listening to him, keeping him between herself and Kook. She looked afraid but determined.

Morgan turned back to the man, who was now breathing hard and blinking rapidly. He could see perspiration on Kook's brow and as he moved his hand up to wipe it away, Morgan made his move. He darted in, closing too quickly for Kook to react and formed his fingers into a blade, plunging his hand into Kook's bleeding side.

The man screamed in pain as Morgan dug his fingers in deeper, gripping whatever he could and tearing with all his might. Kook screamed and brought the pommel of his sword down on the top of Morgan's head.

Morgan heard a loud crack and his vision flashed red as he momentarily lost consciousness. He grimaced against the horrible pain lancing through his skull and dug his hand in deeper. He heard Kook yell again, but it now sounded somehow distant.

He yelled, shoving his arm as deep as he could until his hand came into contact with something soft and squishy. He didn't hesitate for a second, digging his nails into the organ and squeezing with all his might.

He heard one last scream, then felt a blinding pain from his head as Kook, presumably brought his sword pommel down on his skull once again. Morgan staggered back, his hand emerging from the man's guts drenched in blood and bile. He got a fuzzy view of the night sky as he fell backward, blacking out from the combination of pain and blood loss, a massive grin plastered across his face.

***

Sarah woke up just as Morgan made it back into their makeshift camp. She felt well rested and slowly sat up, noting the coat that slid off her as she did. Had Morgan placed that there?

She looked up at him, and saw a slightly guilty expression on his face. That was new as well. Morgan never looked guilty.

She opened her mouth to say something, but Morgan quickly cut her off.

"I'm sorry for what I did. It was reckless and I could have gotten us both killed."

The monotonous tone in which he recited it was a little off-putting, but Sarah knew that it was more sincere than any apology she'd ever received. She wasn't about to let him off the hook though.

She folded her arms and fixed a scowl on her face.

"That's not good enough," she said.

"That's why I got you these," he said.

Her eyes widened as he opened their bag and began piling up one core after the next until there were over twenty of the red and blue spheres sitting on the tunnel floor.

"I may have gone a bit overboard since you probably won't need that many and once you're at *rank 19* you won't be able to use them…" he trailed off here and offered her a shrug.

But Sarah still wasn't satisfied.

"That's still not enough for me," she said, turning her nose up at him.

Aaron Oster

"Well then, what can I do to make it up?"

She grinned as he said those words and turned her cheek to the side, placing her index finger against it.

"I want a kiss."

She felt a flood of satisfaction wash over her as Morgan's eyes went comically wide. That look alone would have been worth it, but she had gone through twenty-four hours of hell not knowing if he would survive or not, so this was the least she would get from him.

"Really? That's what you want?" Morgan sounded more confused than embarrassed, but she still didn't care.

"Yes, right here," she said, tapping her cheek again.

"I don't know how."

"It's really not that hard and you've seen people doing it, haven't you?"

He nodded reluctantly, then got down on his knees next to her.

She felt her heart begin to pound rapidly in her chest as Morgan slowly leaned in. When his lips were only an inch away, she quickly turned her head so they landed squarely on hers. She felt him stiffen in surprise and slid her arms around his head, preventing him from escaping.

Morgan had absolutely no prior experience and neither did she, so the kiss was very awkward, to say the least, but Sarah enjoyed every second of it. After a few seconds, she finally released him and sat back with a slightly dreamy expression.

Morgan just ran the back of his hand over his lips, a slightly confused look on his face. Then he shook himself and the confusion vanished in an instant.

"I take it that we're even now?" he asked, folding his arms over his chest.

Sarah just grinned goofily at him and nodded.

She knew that he hadn't felt anything at all from that kiss, but she most definitely had. Before yesterday, she never would have had the courage to do what she just did, but after Morgan had nearly died, she decided that she would no longer be meek or sit on the sidelines. She would take what she wanted and damn the consequences.

"Good. Now we should *rank up* before taking on that *Arc*. I also have a lot to tell you about the time I spent passed out.

Sarah nodded. She could still feel that big goofy grin on her face, but she didn't care. She was content.

***

"Are you ready?" Sarah asked, holding up the last core she would need to *rank up.*

Morgan had recounted his entire tale, including his new ability to discern *rank* and ability. Now the two of them were both on the cusp of *ranking up.* Sarah had insisted they do so together and he didn't care one way or the other, so here they were.

He nodded and she grinned back at him; the same grin she'd been wearing since tricking him into kissing her on the lips. He knew that a kiss on the cheek and a kiss on the lips were different, with very different connotations.

He had suspected that Sarah might have feelings for him after running through all his memories of their time together, but what she had just done proved it without a shadow of a doubt.

The kiss had been strange for him. There was once again no better way to describe it. There was a feeling that he could almost recognize, but then it slipped away before he could grasp its meaning. Now all he could remember feeling was Sarah's mouth pressed against his and the distinct feeling of being uncomfortable. He just hoped that she didn't make it a regular thing from now on. He could handle her hugging him, but if she started randomly kissing him he didn't think it would go over too well.

"Morgan?"

Morgan looked up, only now realizing that Sarah had been calling his name for the last few seconds.

"Sorry, I got distracted. What did you say?"

"Your core? Are you ready to *rank up*?"

Morgan nodded, feeling the worrying thoughts about Sarah vanish as he prepared to break through into *rank 19.*

"On three," Sarah said, her eyes focusing on the air before her as she opened the core's status.

Morgan nodded, doing the same with his.

Aaron Oster

"One...Two...Three!" Sarah shouted the last number and Morgan assigned the energy, feeling the core crumble in his hand.

For a few seconds, nothing happened, then a massive shock ran through his body. The feeling was like that of moving up from *rank 13* to *18*, multiplied by one hundred. Morgan could feel his reiki flooding through him, strengthening his muscles, nerves, and bones. He could feel his skin growing tougher and his senses sharpening.

The changes he was experiencing weren't all physical, however. Morgan could feel his mind opening up, expanding to understand concepts that had previously eluded him and ideas that he never would have thought of.

He could feel his reiki-heart pulsing with power as it used the massive amount of energy he'd collected to fuel his breakthrough. Then the reiki condensed once more, settling back into place where his heart used to be, but Morgan could feel that something was different now.

Concentrating inward, he could see that his reiki was no longer entirely purple. There was a new spot of color sitting at the very center of his heart. Tightening his concentration, Morgan's view zoomed in to the small golden sphere of crackling energy sitting at the center of his core. He examined it for a few moments, baffled at what it could possibly be. Nothing in his lessons with Gold had hinted that supermages used an energy source other than reiki.

"Holy shit!"

Sarah's voice cut through his wandering thoughts and Morgan opened his eyes, getting his first look at her since the *rank up*. Sarah was still sitting across from him, staring at him with wide eyes. Morgan was beginning to wonder what she was staring at, when his eyes began to pick out some subtle but noticeable differences in Sarah's appearance.

Her face had become slightly narrower, accentuating her cheeks more and making her appear to be slightly older than she was. Her body had slimmed down a bit and he could see that her arms now had some very noticeable definition to them. That wasn't all. If he wasn't mistaken, she was at least an inch taller than she had been before the *rank up*.

"I could say the same thing," Morgan replied once he'd finished looking her over.

Sarah just shook her head and conjured a mirror made of ice. "Look," was all she said.

Morgan stared at his reflection in dumbfounded amazement. He barely recognized the person who was staring back at him and if he hadn't been seeing it with his own eyes, he still might not have believed it.

His face, unlike Sarah's, had broadened slightly, giving him a stronger jawline than he had previously. His cheeks no longer had a sunken appearance and his complexion looked to be much healthier, but the one thing that stood out among all else, were his eyes.

Gone was the bright silver color that he was used to seeing. Instead, they had been turned a deep violet with a single brilliant golden ring around each of his pupils. They were now the same color as when he'd used his *gravity storm*. This time though, they seemed to be a permanent fixture.

He shook his head as his eyes traveled down to his shoulders. They had broadened quite a bit and he could see clearly defined muscles through the clinging fabric of his armor. He lifted his arms and could see the same definition through the tight material.

He was quick to finish his examination and shook his head in bafflement. It was clear that there had been some major changes, but no one had even hinted that this would even be possible. Dabu had said that the *rank up* would be significant, but he felt like the man would have mentioned the cosmetic changes his body had gone through.

"You done yet?" Sarah asked.

Morgan gave himself one more look, noting that he had missed a very significant detail. He had grown by a full two inches. What the hell?

"Yes," he answered, his voice cracking a bit with the nervous tension he was feeling.

The mirror vanished in an instant, leaving him to stare into Sarah's disbelieving eyes once more.

"Do you have any idea what happened to you?" she asked.

Morgan blew out a long breath but shook his head.

It seemed that every time he thought he'd figured one thing out, a dozen other mysteries arose in its place.

"Maybe looking at my status will answer some of my questions," he said, rubbing at his temples.

Sarah nodded slowly and he noticed her very obviously running her eyes over him. He felt his mood lighten a bit at that. It was good to know that Sarah would act the same towards him, despite the changes.

"Yeah, I should probably check mine too," Sarah replied after a few seconds. Her eyes abruptly unfocused as she concentrated on her status.

Chuckling lightly to himself, Morgan reached for his own power, feeling it flood into his eyes as his status appeared.

33

The first thing he noticed upon opening his status was the obvious addition of small golden flecks throughout his otherwise violet colored screen. For another, there were quite a few new additions and many changes to his skills. In fact, almost every single one of them had been altered in some way. But the one thing that stood out above all else was his ability.

Name: Morgan
Evolved Supermage: Rank - 19
Energy to next rank - 0/89,000
Ability - Divine Gravity & Air
RP - 1,280/1,280 (Regen - 12.8 per second)
DV - 10/10 (Regen - 0.1 per minute)
Strength - 121
Agility - 152
Constitution - 137
Intelligence - 128
Wisdom - 128
Skills - Advanced flight, Gravity impact, Explosive movement, Storm blade
Divine - Shock-blast
Traits - Gravity field, Recovery, Aura sense (inherited)
Extra - Gravity storm (2nd category), Starbreak

Morgan's mind reeled with the overload of information, but he quickly focused in on the first major change since his last *rank up*.

Evolved Supermage: When certain prerequisites are met, a genetic mutation will occur that will alter a supermage's body on a cellular level. The result will be a slight increase in power, as well as the ability of choice.

Morgan gaped.

What the hell was going on?! He thought that there were only three types: supers, mages, and supermages. So what was an Evolved Supermage?!

The description was horribly vague and not at all helpful.

He blew out a long breath, deciding that he would find a way to visit Dabu as soon as he could. Maybe he would have some idea of what was going on.

He only hoped that those damn rules wouldn't get in his way.

He closed that tab and moved on to the other major change since his *rank up.*

Divine: Divine skills are unique. Use your DV (Divine Points) to power your divine skills.

Morgan felt like throwing something.

What the hell kind of answer was that? First the new ability, and now a new type of skill?

Glaring at the floating words before him didn't seem to have any effect whatsoever, and Morgan gritted his teeth at the less than helpful explanation.

If he didn't know any better, he'd think that some god, possibly even Samuel, was messing with him.

He blew out a long breath, feeling his annoyance melt away.

It would do him no good to become upset. Besides, he still had a bunch of new skills to examine. Maybe they would shed some light on his slew of unanswered questions and if not, at least he'd enjoy looking at all his cool new skills.

Morgan felt a grin spreading across his face as he opened his skills and began looking through them.

Skills:

Advanced flight - Manipulate gravity and air to reduce your weight and move swiftly through the air. You can now reach half your maximum speed instantaneously.
Cost - 15 RP per second
Max. height - 80 Ft
Max. speed - 60 Ft per second

Starbreak

Max. carry weight - 400 pounds (Adding any more weight will reduce speed by 5 feet per second for each additional pound).

Gravity impact - Manipulate gravity and air to massively increase your striking power for a short burst (Currently: Strength X3).
Cost - 100 RP
Duration - 3 seconds
Cooldown - 60 seconds

Storm blade - Manipulate gravity and air to create a hardened whirling blade in the shape of your choice. You can change the shape of your blade without dismissing it. For an additional cost, you can charge your blade with electricity.
Blade Cost - 450 RP
Duration - Until dismissed
Charge cost - 75 RP
Duration - Single strike

Explosive movement - Manipulate gravity and air to massively increase your speed for a short burst (Currently: Agility X3).
Cost - 100 RP
Duration - 3 seconds
Cooldown - 60 seconds

Morgan stared open-mouthed at his new and very different skills. At first, he was almost annoyed about losing powerful skills, like *heavy impact* and *gale force*, but then he took a closer look at his attributes.

Truth be told, his *strength* and *agility* were already massive. In the beginning, he'd needed those skills to help make up the difference in strength and speed between him and more powerful opponents. Now he was quite powerful in his own right, plus his new skills would triple his *strength* and *agility* for an entire three seconds.

That might not seem like much, but when he would be moving that quickly, three seconds would be all he needed.

He was quite pleased with his *advanced flight* skill. Moving quickly in the air had been a real issue when fighting, but he could now reach half his maximum speed in an instant, which would make combat so much easier.

The biggest change was to his *condensed wind blade,* which had now become *storm blade.* His double damage bonus was now gone but had been replaced by the ability to charge his blade and deliver a powerful electric shock upon impact. He would definitely need to test it out to see how much of a punch the skill packed but had a feeling that he would not be disappointed.

He moved on to the next tab, opening his divine skill for the first time.

Divine:

Shock-blast - Send out a massive shockwave of divine power, stunning everyone within the area of effect.
Cost - 10 DV
AOE - 15 Ft
Duration - Varied

Morgan growled in annoyance. The skill sounded amazing, but the varied duration made it wholly unreliable in battle. Using this skill would likely be more of a hindrance than a help.

He exited the useless tab and moved on to his traits next.

Traits:

Gravity field - Your body is surrounded by a dense field of gravity, making all attacks, both physical and magical, 15% less damaging.

Recovery - The spirits of the air have blessed you with the power of healing. If you can survive for 20 hours after being wounded, no matter the injury, your body will be completely healed.

Aura Sense (inherited) - You have been bestowed the gift of sight by an omniscient. By concentrating on a target and thinking the word 'sense,' you will be able to view the target's aura. The aura will currently reveal the target's name, rank, and ability type, provided that they are no more than nine ranks above your own.

Morgan grinned. At least these skills didn't disappoint. It was nice to see that his resistance to damage had increased and that the timer on his *recovery* had gone down by four whole hours. His *aura sense* hadn't improved, but he guessed that it had more to do with practice than simply increasing his *rank*.

Extra:

Gravity storm (2nd category) - Create a more powerful storm of intense gravity, damaging winds and lighting in a targeted area.
    Cost - 750 RP
    AOE - 40 Ft
    Duration - 45 seconds
    Cooldown - 7 hours

Starbreak - Create a dense ball of superheated air and compressed gas, which will explode upon impact with a selected target.
    Cost - 1,200 RP
    AOE - 25 Ft
    Cooldown - 12 hours

Morgan was satisfied with the increased power of his *gravity storm*, but what really caught his attention was the final skill on the list, which he now carefully re-read. Just the cost of the skill, as well as the massive cooldown time, was enough to tell him how devastating it would likely be. He couldn't really imagine what the skill would look like, but he sure as hell couldn't wait to try.

He closed his status and rose from his seated position on the ground. He was surprised at how light he felt and how well he could move. He'd been expecting to have to adjust to his new height and proportions, but it felt as though he'd been this way his entire life.

Sarah closed her status then too, and rose gracefully to her feet, grinning as well.

"I take it your new skills are impressive?" Morgan asked, feeling his own grin spreading across his face once again.

"Hell yeah!" she excitedly exclaimed and began rapidly explaining her new skills to him.

Apparently, her old skills hadn't changed much, only receiving increases to their power, but she now had two new skills: *ice golem* and *glacial impact.*

The first was pretty self-explanatory. She could summon a golem made of ice to fight on her behalf, but the second was the truly impressive one. *Glacial impact* would summon a mass of ice and water, over twenty feet in diameter, which she could then launch at a selected target.

Morgan was quick to explain his new skills as well, and Sarah lamented along with him about the apparent uselessness of his new divine skill. What completely floored her was his new ability.

"I've never even heard of something called an evolved supermage," she said, rubbing at her chin, brow furrowed with concern.

"Do you think this has something to do with the modifications done to you?"

"I hadn't thought of that," Morgan replied, his mind beginning to race with the possibilities.

If whoever had modified him somehow knew about this new ability of his, then they were even more dangerous than he'd originally thought.

"At least we know why your appearance changed, though," Sarah said.

Morgan nodded.

It would only make sense that a new and more powerful version of the supermage ability would come with some cosmetic changes, though he still wasn't sure how it would translate over to actual combat.

"I don't know what's happening to me, but to be safe, I don't think we should tell anyone else. Even the people we trust."

Sarah nodded in agreement. It would be foolish to tell anyone about this.

It was bad enough when Morgan was a regular supermage. Now that he was an evolved supermage and had some kind of divine power to boot, all of the Five Kingdoms would band together to hunt him down.

Morgan looked toward the exit of the tunnel and his familiar wild grin spread across his face.

"You think we can take that overgrown lizard down now?" he asked, giving her a sidelong glance.

For once, Sarah actually returned his feral grin with one of her own.

"I don't doubt that for even a second."

34

"Hold on, I can see the tunnel opening up ahead," Katherine said, gesturing to the yawning tunnel mouth just a few hundred yards away.

"So it is!" Gold said, marching straight past her and continuing on to the tunnel mouth.

Kathrine clenched her jaw in aggravation, but otherwise didn't let her annoyance show. They'd been in this damned *zone* for the last thirty-five hours, and now that they were nearing the end, even she could begin to feel the slight fatigue that the near constant fighting was beginning to have on her.

Gold's attitude hadn't changed either. In fact, his flippant and lighthearted manner had grown exponentially worse since they'd first entered the *zone*. Now, the moron was walking right up to the *Patriarch's* territory without taking a moment to set up a strategy on how to tackle the beast.

"So what's your plan?" she asked, catching up to him just as he entered the tunnel.

"We go in and hit it until it's dead," Gold answered.

"What the hell kind of plan is that?" Katherine exclaimed. "You do realize that the strongest beast known to the Five Kingdoms is literally at the end of this tunnel, right?"

"Yup, it'll definitely be a fun fight."

Katherine scowled, then took a deep breath to steady her nerves. She'd never fought this particular beast before, so she didn't know much about its attack patterns or specific abilities. All she did know was what others had told her.

She had to wonder how Gold had even managed to get his hands on the key. Last she'd heard, it had been in the possession of the East Kingdom's royal family.

Her thoughts were interrupted when she saw the tunnel opening up ahead, and stopped just inside the exit. Thankfully, Gold stopped as well and she got her first good look at the infernal-bane lyvern. It lay on a raised pedestal at the center of a massive crystal cavern. Huge pillars of the crystal grew all throughout, breaking up the battleground and giving them plenty of places to hide should the beast prove to be too much for them.

The lyvern wasn't nearly as large as Katherine had first thought. It was just over twenty feet from nose to tail. She couldn't tell its exact height, as it was lying down, but she estimated that it would be about eight feet at the shoulder- almost a normal sized monster. Despite its relatively diminutive size, however, it was truly a terrifying beast to behold.

Its body was long and narrow, with the front half of a lion and the back half of a wyvern. It was a dark, blue-gray in color and the only way to distinguish between the soft fur and hard scales was the soft light reflecting off of them. The scales and fur blended seamlessly halfway down its back, but there were scales scattered over the fur as well. The scales in its fur, unlike those on its back half, were a lighter blue in color, so they stood out in sharp contrast against the darker fur.

Katherine shifted a bit and accidentally stepped into the open chamber. The lyvern was on its feet in an instant, and she swallowed hard as a pair of gleaming amber eyes stared at her from across the room. A low, rumbling growl resounded off the crystalline walls, and Katherine could see its long, scaly tail flicking back and forth.

The only thing she didn't see was its mane, the one distinguishing feature she'd been expecting to see.

"Where is the…" she began to ask Gold, when her question was preemptively answered by the beast in question.

The lyvern roared, and a mass of billowing red and black flames shot from its body. Katherine was quick to step back into the tunnel and watched wide-eyed as the flames took on a cohesive shape. After a moment, they settled into what was clearly supposed to be its mane. The black and red flames danced around its head, the scales on its body reflecting the light and giving it a truly terrifying appearance.

It crouched and two sets of gleaming claws emerged from its front paws, slicing into the stone as easily as she would a steak. She noticed that its back claws were the ones to watch out for. Over eight inches long and wickedly barbed, they looked like the perfect tools for rending flesh from bone.

"Do you really think the two of us can take that thing?" she asked Gold, who didn't look in the least bit concerned.

"Where did all your confidence go, Princess? Aren't you supposed to be one of the most powerful supers alive?" Gold quirked a brow.

"One of the most powerful, yes. One of the most stupid, I think not," she replied. "I know when I can't win a fight, and I'm getting the sense that I can't win against that thing."

"It's not that big," Gold said, once more trying to brush it off.

"If that's the case, how about you go in and fight it first," Katherine sarcastically said.

"Okay," Gold said, then waltzed right into the open chamber.

The lyvern's eyes instantly locked onto him and its flaming mane flickered as the fire intensified.

He's insane, Katherine thought as she watched him use his mage shield and conjure a couple of twenty-foot tall diamond golems.

She stood at the tunnel exit for a few seconds, before finally shrugging to herself.

They did come here to fight the lyvern, after all, and the sooner she killed this thing, the sooner she'd be able to rescue Morgan.

Katherine held her arm out to the side and a portal opened right above her hand. A massive two-handed mace fell from the open portal and she deftly caught it in a single hand. She swished it through the air a couple of times, then nodded to herself.

She heard a loud roar and turned her attention back to the beast. The lyvern had locked onto one of the golems and crouched on its pedestal, tail whipping back and forth in agitation. The golem took a step forward and Katherine watched in shock as the lyvern opened its mouth and roared again.

A beam of condensed black and red energy shot from the beast's mouth and struck the golem center mass.

"Better get in there while it's distracted!" Gold cheerily called out, as the golem began to glow white hot.

Then it actually began melting under the intense heat and Katherine grimaced as the beam of energy punched through the golem, leaving a gaping hole through the center of its chest.

This was not going to be a fun fight.

Katherine took a deep breath, then stepped into the chamber. As soon as she stepped in, the lyvern's attention fixed on her once more and its glowing amber eyes shone with intelligence.

Katherine swung her mace out behind her, conjuring a mass of crackling black energy at its tip. Just as the lyvern opened its mouth to use its energy blast again, she swung forward. The pillars of crystal around her shattered with a loud boom, as reality tore open from the force of her attack.

A rainbow-colored blast shot out in an arc, slicing through crystal and stone alike, and sucking them into itself as it passed, but the lyvern wasn't just any old beast. It roared its challenge and responded with an attack of its own. Its mane exploded outward in a massive sphere, just as her attack was about to hit.

There was a loud shrieking sound as the two energies battled one another and finally, Katherine's attack petered out. Her attack didn't leave empty-handed, though. Just as her attack was about to fade, it sucked a good portion of the flaming shield into itself, weakening the beast just enough for one of Gold's diamond golems to punch through.

The shield shattered with the sound of tinkling glass, but the lyvern leapt into the air and avoided being struck. Then it twisted its sinuous body and decapitated the golem with a swipe of its tail. The golem toppled back, but Katherine had taken the opportunity to dart forward and close some of the distance between her and the cat.

She snapped her fingers, targeting the lyvern and trying to separate the space between its body and its head. The lyvern reacted with impossible speed, contorting its body in the air, then pushing off a crystal pillar behind it, which took it out of reach of the attack.

"Shit!" Katherine yelled as the lyvern flew at her, mouth opening wide and a glowing red energy gathering in its paw.

Then one of the crystal pillars slammed into it from the side, smashing into the ground. The beast's body tore a swathe of destruction through the crystal, before coming to rest over a hundred feet away.

Katherine saw her opportunity and dashed forward, flashing across the distance in the span of a heartbeat, then brought her heavy mace down on the lyvern's head. The force of the attack forced the beast's head a good two feet into the solid stone, extinguishing its mane. Katherine pulled her mace back for another strike, then was thrown back by a blast of kinetic energy that spread from the lyvern in a massive dome.

She cursed as she flipped into the air, and landed on the ground thirty yards away, digging her heels in as her boots tore twin furrows through the crystal underfoot.

"Well, that didn't work," Gold said, as the lyvern pulled its head from the ground and shook itself violently.

"It did work, dipshit. Just not as well as I'd hoped," Katherine said, as the lyvern's mane flared back to life.

"Well, any plans?" Gold asked, as the lyvern began glowing an angry red.

That's not good, Katherine thought as the beast prepared to use what would undoubtedly be an extremely powerful skill.

Katherine dropped her mace and stood straighter. Only one thing to do in a situation like this: meet power with power.

"You might want to step back," Katherine said, as her body began to glow with a brilliant multicolored light.

This was one of her most powerful skills and she was loathe to use it, as she could only activate it once a week. Then she shrugged to herself. What good were skills if one didn't use them?

The lyvern roared a challenge and Katherine answered back, yelling out as she launched herself at the beast. The lyvern suddenly doubled in size, still glowing an angry red, and its mane turned a pitch black. The crystal around it began to glow and Katherine could feel the waves of heat emanating from the monster.

They lyvern then opened its mouth and shot a black beam of flame so intense, that the very air warped around it. Katherine grinned, then abruptly vanished, reappearing right near the beast's right side. She lashed out with a powerful kick, then vanished again and appeared near its head, slamming a fist into its front shoulder.

She watched out of the corner of her eye, as the black fire punched a twenty-foot gap in the cave wall, then she vanished again and punched the lyvern right in the jaw. The beast roared in pain as Katherine's attacks began doing some damage and it tried to retaliate, but Katherine was moving too quickly.

She teleported around, delivering powerful strikes to vulnerable areas as the skill counted down in her head. Just as the timer was about to run out, she used another skill, and a mass of chaotic energy formed itself into a massive sword around her clenched fist.

Then she appeared right before the massive beast, pulling her blade up for a devastating blow. The lyvern's eyes glinted then, and Katherine knew she'd been tricked. A massive paw slammed into her, razor claws shredding through her uniform and slicing deep into her side. She hissed in pain as she flew back from the creature, but managed to land on her feet and keep ahold of her *reality blade*.

"Now would be a good time to help, dumbass!" she yelled at her seemingly useless partner, as hot blood trickled down her side.

"Do calm down, Princess," Gold replied.

Katherine took a second to glare at him and saw him preparing to use some kind of skill.

Then her attention was drawn back to the lyvern as it let out an earth-shaking roar. It began to glow red once again, and this time its scales actually changed color to match its aura. That could only mean one thing - she and Gold were about to witness this monster's most powerful attack.

Katherine began running toward the beast when there was a loud rumbling crack from behind her. Taking a quick peek over her shoulder, she saw Gold gesture toward the lyvern. There was a massive boom as something broke the sound barrier, and a split second later, the beast was thrown clear across the chamber, leaving a stream of blood in its wake.

Katherine had no idea what kind of skill Gold had used, but this was her chance. She focused her remaining chi on her last powerful skill and activated it. A nimbus of crackling black energy began forming in her left hand, as she sprinted across the chamber. The lyvern was just regaining its feet when she reached it, and slashed out with her *reality blade*, cutting its right foreleg off at the knee.

The beast roared in pain as it buckled forward, and Katherine slammed her left hand into the beast's head. The crackling miasma of black energy expanded as it made contact, and Katherine leapt back as the lyvern's head was engulfed.

A moment later, it vanished, and the lyvern toppled lifelessly to the ground without its head.

Katherine stood there, panting as her blade faded away and hardly believed that it was finally over.

"Well done, Princess. An excellent showing," Gold said, clapping slowly as he approached.

Katherine was about to snap at the infuriating man, but decided against it. She'd just defeated a massively powerful beast and with almost no help from the idiot next to her. So, like any good sport, she decided to rub it in.

"I'm sorry that I can't say the same about you," she replied evenly, holding her hand out and fetching the beast's core. "But I guess fighting isn't for everyone."

"Indeed. Especially since I needed the distraction to fetch these," Gold said, jangling a small leather bag before her face.

Katherine snatched the bag from his outstretched hand and reached inside, feeling a bunch of small metallic discs. Quickly removing one, her suspicions were confirmed as she saw a *beast zone* key clutched between her fingers.

"You crafty bastard," Katherine said, as she began removing them one by one. "You hid the keys in a *beast zone* so no one could get at them!"

Gold shrugged, pulling the key from his pocket and opening a portal back into her room at the palace.

"I needed those keys if we were to rescue Morgan and Sarah, but I couldn't exactly take you on your word. So, I decided to kill two birds with one stone."

Katherine finally found what she was looking for; a small key with the numbers *6-31* written on top. She pocketed it and tossed the bag back to Gold. She walked past him without saying a word and stepped through the portal.

35

Morgan and Sarah came to the tunnel exit and examined the room once more. Everything looked exactly the same as it had the day before, including the massive lizard lying at its center. Morgan felt his heart rate increase at the sight of the beast that had nearly done him in but otherwise maintained a calm demeanor.

"Can you get any details on that thing?" Sarah asked.

She had insisted they both bathe before going into battle, which Morgan really couldn't understand. If they were about to fight, wouldn't it make sense to bathe after?

Sarah had been adamant, though, and they were now both dressed in fresh sets of enchanted armor. Sarah had also taken the time to comb her long red hair, and braid it carefully.

He understood that women liked to be presentable at all times, but still thought it was strange. As soon as the fight was over, they would have to bathe again, and all their time would have been wasted. But he still felt a little guilty for the ordeal he'd put her through, so he'd acquiesced without too much complaining.

Morgan nodded, then tightened his focus on the lizard and used *aura sense*. As with the last few times he used the skill, a red light flared around the beast and small letters floated up over its head. Now he was able to get a better idea of what they were facing.

Name: Electric-spine lizard Matriarch
Rank - 24
Ability type - Super

Morgan relayed this information, grateful that he'd been able to examine the beast before the fight. Now he knew what to expect. He and Sarah might be *rank 19*, but the lizard was still a full *5 ranks* above them. Not to mention that it was most likely an intermediate beast, which would mean a difficult fight at best.

"So, what's the plan?" Sarah asked, clenching and unclenching her fists in anticipation.

"I say, same as always. You try and pin it down and I'll attack head-on. We both need to test our new skills anyway, and this will be the perfect opportunity to do so."

Aaron Oster

Sarah bit her lip for a moment, loathe to allow him into danger again after such a close call, but eventuall, she nodded.

"Fine, we'll go with your plan. But the moment I see that it's too much for you, I'll be the one attacking."

Morgan nodded in agreement. He wanted to use his most powerful skill right away, but that wouldn't really give him a chance to test the others out.

"Alright then, let's go!" Morgan exclaimed, feeling the rush of excitement that always accompanied battle.

This time he was careful to keep himself in check and stepped carefully into the open chamber. The lizard rose as soon as he entered and let out its rattling hiss of warning. Morgan ignored it and activated his shield. His body flared with purple light as it was coated in his reiki in all but one spot.

He looked down in surprise, as a small circle in the center of his chest glowed gold, standing out against the deeper purple of the rest of his shield. Seeing the change made him wonder how this new *divine* energy, which didn't feel at all godly, would affect his skills.

Then again, he should probably be more worried about the ability-change thing a bit more than some shiny new skill.

The lizard let out another hiss, then its spines began rattling as it gathered its body up to pounce at him. Morgan used his *advanced flight*, then pushed off the ground, rocketing towards the beast at an astonishing speed. He closed the gap faster than he'd thought possible, and shot straight past the beast, smashing into the opposite wall.

"Ow," he said, pulling himself free of the small crater in the stone and turning to face the lizard once again.

He could hear Sarah laughing from across the cavern and scowled. Why did she always find it so funny when he hurt himself by mistake, but got all teary-eyed when something else hurt him?

He rubbed at his head, then stopped, surprised at the complete lack of pain. Looking down, he felt like smacking himself as he saw the rich purple glow of his shield. He really needed to get his head in the fight.

Morgan shook himself, then crouched and dashed toward the lizard, who had by now turned its attention to Sarah. She had her shield up and had a nearly endless barrage of massive icy spears slamming into the beast. He could see frost coating its body, and a block of ice forming on its right leg. She really was amazing.

"Hey, ugly, over here!" Morgan yelled, taking the beast's attention off Sarah.

The lizard whirled, and as though understanding what Morgan had just said, hissed in anger and began glowing a bright red.

"Oh no, you don't!" he yelled, slamming into it full force and throwing a heavy punch into its jaw.

The lizard was rocked to the side under the force of the blow and Morgan was amazed at the speed and power he'd just displayed and all without using a single skill. He danced nimbly back as the lizard tried to rake him with its claws, then darted in and punched it six times in rapid succession, aiming for vital areas like the eyes, nose, and ears.

He had a feeling that it wouldn't be nearly this easy if Sarah wasn't hindering its movement so much, but despite the heavy barrage of blows, the beast was only mildly dazed. Morgan shrugged to himself at that. It made sense, after all. This was a rank 24 beast. Regular punches wouldn't be enough to take it down at his current rank.

He leapt back as the beast broke free of the ice encasing its legs, and used *storm blade*. A whirling purple blade formed in an instant, and Morgan shaped it into the weapon he desired- a two foot cone of condensed air. As with his shield, he could spot small flickers of gold every few seconds running across the surface of the blade.

The lizard's spines rose off its back then, and a crackling field of black lightning began coating them.

Morgan grinned, then used his new *explosive movement*, as well as *gravity impact*. Time seemed to slow around him, as his senses sharpened to an almost unbelievable degree. He could feel the timer counting down in his mind, but that seemed to be moving in slow motion as well.

He saw the black lightning crackling slowly across the surface of the spines, and he knew what to do next. He ran forward, his *storm blade* changing in an instant from a lance to a saber. Then, with one massive swing, he neatly severed the row of spines from the lizard's back.

Aaron Oster

He whirled on the spot, feeling that he was nearly out of time, and lashed out with a powerful spinning side kick, right into the lizard's hind leg. Time abruptly sped up then, and the lizard screeched in pain as its back leg was crushed to a pulp. Morgan leapt back, just a little disoriented from the rapid shift, but not fast enough to dodge the incoming tail.

His shield reverberated under the force of the attack, but it held, which surprised him more than anything. He caught himself with his *advanced flight* skill and looked down to where the beast had struck him. The tail had hit him right in the chest, and he could see a fine line of cracks running across his reiki shield, in all but one place. The smooth golden disc was completely undamaged and he was forced to reevaluate the worth of this new energy.

It appeared to be much more powerful than reiki, which was strange enough, as reiki was supposed to be the truest energy source available. The lizard let out a screech of rage and he was forced back to the present. He would figure this all out later. For now, there was a fight to finish.

He shot forward through the air, watching Sarah sending massive half-moon blades made of ice at the lizard. When had she learned to do that?

The lizard was hissing in pain, as each blade bit deeply into its scaled hide, sending splatters of blood all over the cave floor. Morgan quickly reformed his *blade* into a lance and used his skill's new *charge* ability.

He heard a loud whining howl as the blade's natural oscillation increased tenfold. After only a second, a massive amount of friction began to produce lightning. He stared in awe as the purple lightning crackled and flashed across the blade, interspersed every few seconds with flashes of gold.

He grinned widely as he dropped from the air, blade first.

"Eat this!" he yelled, before his blade slammed into the lizard's scaly back. The blade whirled and whined as it tore through the scales and sank deep into the beast. A second later, the lighting was discharged. Morgan leapt back, watching in awe as the electricity crackled over the lizard, but it didn't have nearly the damaging effect he'd been expecting.

Then he remembered that the lizard had a similar ability. Of course, it would be resistant to electrical attacks!

He stopped his retreat a few feet away and took a moment to examine the beast. Its back leg was crushed, its spines were gone, and it was covered in cuts from where his and Sarah's attacks had landed, but all of those wounds weren't enough to kill it outright.

Then it began to glow again.

Morgan's skills were still on cooldown for the next twenty seconds, so he couldn't rely on the extra speed and power they would afford him. He did a quick check of his *RP*. Surprisingly, he had about *1,000*. He had his high *wisdom* to thank for that. Doing some quick math in his head, he figured he would need roughly *15* seconds to regen the *RP* he needed to use his new *starbreak* skill.

The beast was gearing up for a massive attack, though, and he didn't know if Sarah would be able to hold it. She likely didn't have enough *MP* for any of her big attacks, as she'd been using her skills almost non stop.

So, against his better judgment, Morgan used his new divine skill, *shock-blast*.

"Sarah, get back!" he yelled, as his body began glowing a brilliant gold color, and warmth suffused him.

He saw her eyes widen, then she turned and sprinted away from him as fast as she could manage, cursing him all the while.

Morgan grinned, then activated the skill. A massive flash of light lit up the room as the golden energy expanded outward in a ten-foot radius. When the light faded a couple of seconds later, Morgan beheld the lizard and his grin widened.

Maybe the skill wasn't useless, after all.

The lizard was frozen in place, its body locked in the position it had been holding just before the blast had hit. It was still glowing red with chi, and black lightning still coated its body, but even that had frozen. He examined the frozen beast in fascination, wondering just how long the skill would keep it this way.

He remembered the varied duration and was quick to take a few steps back from the beast, circling around it until he met back up with Sarah.

"What did you do to it?" she asked, staring wide-eyed at the frozen beast.

"That divine skill I told you about," he said distractedly, as he watched his *RP* carefully.

"How long will it… never mind."

Morgan's attention snapped back to the lizard as Sarah said this, and saw that it was once again moving.

He gritted his teeth in annoyance. He'd really been hoping that the skill would last longer than that.

The lizard turned to the two of them, eyes gleaming with malice as it dragged its lame leg behind it.

"What's your *MP* look like?" he asked.

"I've got about half."

"Can you block that attack?"

"I don't know."

"Can you delay it for a few seconds?"

Sarah growled low in her throat, then made a slashing movement with her arm. A barrage of *icicle spears* flew outward and began slamming into the lizard. From far away, the spears had appeared to be the same, but up close, Morgan could see that they now all sported three tips, like that of a trident, and they were all wickedly barbed.

"Thanks!" he said, dashing to the side in an attempt to flank the beast.

It was then that he felt his *RP* fill to the max, and the battle came to a head.

The lizard roared in pain as one of Sarah's spears punched into its shoulder, and it decided against trying to defend itself. The crackling electricity built up around it quickly, lashing out every few seconds and shattering stone.

"You'd better kill it!" Sarah yelled, then turned and ran for cover.

"I don't think that'll be a problem," he said to himself as the lizard turned to face him.

He stared the lizard in the eye, and used *starbreak*, feeling his *RP* begin to plummet at an almost alarming rate. At the same time, the lizard opened its mouth, and the lightning that had been gathering over its body began streaming into it, condensing into a crackling ball.

Morgan felt his body float up off the ground, similar to the way *gravity storm* had, but this skill felt quite a bit different. His right hand extended out and he could feel a tiny bead of super-dense gravity begin to form. Then the air around his hand began to rapidly heat, as the gravity pulled *something* in. A moment later, the growing sphere of reddish yellow energy began to glow brightly, slowly rotating on his open palm.

He stared down at it, feeling that the energy seemed to be familiar somehow, but couldn't quite place it. He looked down the lizard and saw that almost all the lightning on its body had now gathered in a sphere before its mouth.

Morgan grinned as he felt his skill finish gathering power. A brilliantly glowing sphere nearly three feet in diameter was floating just an inch above his palm. He stared at it for a second, feeling the power radiating off of it, then his grin widened.

He turned looked back to the lizard, just as it finished gathering the energy for its attack. *Perfect timing,* he thought, *now they'd see who was truly more powerful!*

He pulled his arm back, then threw the glowing ball at the lizard below. At the same time, the lizard fired off its attack. The black, crackling beam of energy impacted against the glowing sphere with a loud boom. The two hung in the air for a second, and Morgan began to worry that his attack would be pushed back. Then, with a sudden whooshing sound, the glowing sphere expanded to ten times its original size.

Morgan watched in awe as the sphere engulfed the lizard, attack and all, in a swirling configuration of gravity and plasma. As he watched the swirling yellow orb, it finally struck him why it had seemed so similar. His attack looked just like a miniature version of the sun.

He laughed to himself, thinking that *starbreak* was an extremely appropriate name for this ultimate skill.

It didn't last nearly as long as *gravity storm*, and the attack rapidly began losing its form. Finally, after only ten seconds, the energy was spent and the attack dissipated. As he floated back to the ground, Morgan noted the damage caused by his attack.

The stone was glowing a cherry red in the twenty-five-foot area the skill had effected. He also noticed, with no small amount of pride, that the only part remaining of the electric-spine lizard was a glowing core.

As he landed, Sarah ran up to him and looked him over, poking at the areas of his shield that were cracked. Morgan let his shield fade and smiled tiredly at her. The attack had taken a surprisingly large amount of energy and now he felt like he needed a nap.

"I'm glad to see that you're not hurt," she said, finally finished with her examination.

She smiled at him then and punched him lightly in the shoulder.

"That was one hell of an attack."

Morgan was about to reply, when a very familiar sounding voice rang out from behind them.

"Yes, a most impressive attack indeed."

Both Sarah and Morgan whirled at the sound of that voice, and both stared as Gold walked into the cavern.

36

"Gold! What the hell are you doing here?"

Sarah, eloquent as ever, was the first to react.

"Who, me?" Gold asked, coming to a stop about twenty feet from them. "Oh, I was just in the neighborhood and decided to drop by for a visit."

Sarah gave him a dead look.

"Really? That's what you want to go with?"

"I agree wholeheartedly. His sense of humor leaves something to be desired," a sultry voice said.

Sarah blew out an annoyed breath, as Katherine emerged from the tunnel as well, dressed in an extremely revealing, skin-tight uniform.

"What are you doing here?" Sarah asked, more than a little annoyed that Princess Busty was here to ruin the party.

"Oh, don't be like that," Gold cut in. "She did go through an awful lot to get you out. The least you can do is thank her."

Everyone, including Morgan, stared opened mouthed at Gold.

"What?" he asked, after seeing everyone's reactions.

"Who are you, and what have you done with Gold?" Sarah demanded, eliciting a snort from Morgan and a laugh from Katherine.

Gold let out a huff and marched away, muttering about ungrateful students.

"You look quite well, Morgan," Katherine said, walking up to him and beginning to prod him in nearly the same fashion as Sarah.

"It looks like you've grown quite a bit in the few days we've been apart." She cupped his face in her palms and examined his violet eyes.

"My, my. Quite a few changes indeed."

By now, Morgan was feeling quite uncomfortable, and Sarah was shaking in anger.

"Do you mind?" she hissed, slapping Katherine's hands away from him and interposing herself between them.

"Oh my, have I offended you in some way?" Katherine asked, quirking a perfectly sculpted eyebrow.

"Yes!" Sarah yelled, going red in the face. "You just barge in here and start manhandling him, after we've been stuck here for over a week! Who the hell do you think you are anyway?"

"The soon to be queen of the North Kingdom," Katherine replied, her tone turning a bit frosty. "And Morgan's future wife."

"Never agreed to that," Morgan cut in.

Sarah flinched a bit when she said this and took a moment to calm herself somewhat. Morgan chose that moment to intercede on her behalf, for which she was very grateful.

"A lot has happened since we last spoke," Morgan said. He was uncharacteristically serious, which immediately got everyone's attention.

"I'd rather we get out of here before we start discussing any of it, though. I'm very hungry and we have been trapped in here for quite some time."

"Of course," Katherine said, dipping her head and removing the key from a small pocket in space.

She plunged the key into the air, and Sarah let out an excited squeak as the portal opened.

"It's about damn time!" she yelled, before jumping straight through.

***

Morgan sat in one of Katherine's comfortable couches. He was dressed in a comfortable pair of silk pajamas, something which he'd considered to be an extravagant waste of money. He still thought they were, but if someone else was going to buy them for him, he wouldn't say no.

He was content and full, having taken another bath and gorging himself on a delicious meal of steak, roasted potatoes and a massive mug of something called root beer. The bubbly liquid had tasted very strange at first, but after a few sips, it had started to grow on him.

Sarah was seated next to him and had taken the liberty of sprawling out on the couch, leaving her legs to rest on his lap, as she reclined back into the cushions. He'd noticed that she'd been

clinging to him ever since they got out, as though afraid of losing
him. He was very happy to actually understand why she was acting
this way and not be completely clueless about the situation.

Katherine was an extremely attractive woman; the most
aesthetically pleasing woman he'd ever seen, in fact. That didn't
change the fact that he still felt no romantic inclination towards her,
but Sarah seemed to be worried that he would. So despite his
discomfort at the contact, he allowed her to keep clinging to him. He
did like Sarah quite a bit and had he had the capacity, he had a
feeling that he would be romantically involved with her.

After Samuel had partially fixed him, Morgan had
understood the basic concept of sex, but none of the nuances that
came with being in a relationship or even the differences between
them. Since his *rank up*, he'd been understanding more and more.
He imagined that he understood better than most people his age, as
where he could examine it from a purely logical view, others tended
to see it through a fog of desire.

He was brought out of his musings as Sarah shifted a bit,
readjusting her legs and eyeing him nervously. He gave her a
reassuring smile, patting her gently. The sound of a door opening
and closing heralded Gold's arrival, along with Katherine. They'd
gone out to give the two of them some time alone after their ordeal
in the *beast zone*, and Katherine had said that she had some business
to discuss with the Assassins Guild, as well as try and locate a
traitorous coward.

"Good, I see that the two of you are rested," Katherine said
as her eyes landed on the two of them.

"Yes, but we have important things to discuss with the both
of you, and not a whole lot of time in which to do it," Morgan said,
sitting up straighter in his seat.

Katherine and Gold both nodded and took a seat opposite
them.

Morgan cleared his throat, trying to find the best way to
broach the subject.

"How close are you to finding a way to overthrow your
father?" Morgan asked.

"Four months at best. Why?"

"We have less than 55 hours if I'm correct. Can you manage
that?" he asked.

Katherine raised an eyebrow but otherwise didn't react. "Explain," she simply said.

So Morgan did. He explained everything Samuel had told them, recounting the story in as much detail as he could. Sarah filled in in a few places but otherwise remained silent.

By the time he was finished, both Katherine and Gold looked extremely worried.

"This isn't good news at all," she said, rising from her seat and beginning to pace. "Not to mention that the timing couldn't be worse."

"How do you mean?" Morgan asked.

"I tried contacting the Assassins Guild to get them to leave you alone, but they flat out refused, saying that once a contract was signed, there was no ending it."

She blew out a breath and sat back down again, rubbing slowly at her temples.

"They're gathering a force big enough to ensure your death. I would normally have you wait here until I can end the contract, but if what you said is true, then I can't afford to keep you locked up here."

"Wait," Sarah cut in. "I thought you said that there was no way to end the contract."

"There is, though the Guild doesn't exactly make it public information," Katherine replied. "If the current head of the Guild dies, then all contracts become null and void."

"Is it even possible to kill the current head?" Morgan asked. "After all, I would assume that the leader of such a powerful and well-placed group would be a terrifyingly powerful individual."

"Normally it wouldn't be. Their leader never leaves the safety of their compound and it's usually guarded very heavily."

"So why is now different?" Sarah asked.

Katherine's lips quirked up a bit.

"Arnold betrayed me while I was fetching the key to rescue you. He fled from the palace, likely to find protection elsewhere. If I don't miss my guess, he was hoping to use the information he had to bribe his way into someone's service."

"I know he's a treacherous snake, but what does that have to do with the Assassins Guild?" Sarah reiterated.

"I may have let slip that he'd been spotted near the border of the South Kingdom," she replied, her smile growing slightly wider.

"You may have forgotten, but your father placed a bounty on his head, as well as Morgan's. Since Arnold has been so successful in killing their members in the past, they've sent every high powered member they currently have in the region after him."

"Meaning that the defense around their base will be severely weakened," Morgan finished for her.

"I would expect nothing less from my future husband!"

"Never said yes," Morgan replied offhand.

"So, we now have a dilemma. Kind Edmund needs to die within the next 55 hours. Morgan can't leave the palace for more than a few hours without the guild catching on. So, we'll have to eliminate their leader first, and only then will we be able to attempt to kill Edmund," Sarah said.

Katherine nodded.

"Why can't anything ever be easy?" Sarah exclaimed, throwing her arms in the air.

"It gets better," Katherine cut in before she could start going on a rant. "If we hope to succeed against my father, I will not be able to go after the Guild. I'll need the time to throw together a plan of action and bring all the forces I have in. The most I can do is provide you with transportation there and back."

"Mother fu..." Sarah began, but Morgan clamped a hand over her mouth.

"None of that. You've got a foul mouth, but that's beneath even you," he said.

Everyone stared at him in shock.

"What?" he asked, slowly removing his hand from Sarah's mouth.

"Since when have you cared what I say?" Sarah asked.

Morgan looked at her for a few seconds in incomprehension, then it hit him. He'd reacted without even thinking about it.

He grinned.

"Looks like my understanding of propriety is improving."

"I'll say!" Sarah said excitedly.

Gold cleared his throat loudly, getting everyone's attention.

"As great as this all is, we're faced with a serious problem here. We have a very short amount of time before a world-destroying beast rises from its ten thousand year slumber. In that time we have to kill the leader of the most powerful group in the five kingdoms, and kill a king in the middle of his war camp."

Gold's uncommonly serious tone put a damper on everyone's spirits until a wide grin spread across his face.

"Sounds like fun. I'm in!"

"That's great and all, but we still need a plan," Sarah said, cutting him off.

"And we'll have one," Katherine said. "For now, you two need some sleep. I'll begin planning now and should have something by morning."

"But..."

"No buts!" Katherine cut her off. "Even if we wanted to act now, we couldn't. We'll need to give it at least 24 hours before we can act against the Guild, and it'll take at least 48 for me to arrange the attack on my father."

"That really won't leave us with a whole lot of time," Morgan said, brow furrowing a bit.

"I know, but it would appear that we no longer have a choice," Katherine said, blowing out a breath.

They were all silent for a few moments until Sarah let out a wide yawn.

"Fine," she replied when Katherine gave her a meaningful look. "We'll go to sleep, but you'd better have a good plan when we wake up."

She stood from the couch, then hesitated.

"Where should we sleep?" she asked, looking around the large room.

Katherine pointed to the far wall on her right, where a long curtain hung.

"There's a sliding panel behind there. You should find a suite with a couple of beds."

Sarah raised an eyebrow at her, and Katherine shrugged.

"This is the only place in the palace that's protected from prying eyes. I needed somewhere for important guests to stay, so I had it built."

"Ah. I was wondering why you seemed to take so many visitors in your bedroom," Gold said with a grin. "I was beginning to think that you just liked inviting strange men in here."

Katherine snorted out a laugh, but Sarah just shook her head. "Come on, Morgan. We should really get some sleep."

"I'll follow you in a minute. I have something I need to talk to them about before I go," Morgan said.

Sarah raised a questioning eyebrow, but he just waved her on. She looked as though she might argue, but then let out another massive yawn.

"Suit yourself," she said, then turned and disappeared behind the curtain.

"What did you need to tell me?" Katherine asked coyly, taking a seat next to him and placing a hand on his lap.

Morgan reached down and very deliberately removed it.

"You might find this hard to believe," he began, ignoring Katherine's incensed look. "I guess I should start at the beginning."

He then explained everything that he'd found out about himself from Samuel and then from Dabu. Surprisingly enough, neither Gold or Katherine seemed shocked when he told them of his memory loss, or that someone had apparently tampered with his mind. He did however, get a reaction when he told them of Samuel's deal.

"So, what you're saying, is that if you manage to fulfill this god's request, he'll fix you?" Katherine asked excitedly.

"That's what he said, and I don't doubt that he can deliver. After all, he's already given me the ability to comprehend things I previously couldn't, though he did suppress my slowly returning memories in exchange," he replied.

Katherine let out an excited squeak and leaned forward to wrap her arms around him.

"Now I have to finish this mission! Once Samuel fixes you, we'll get married and you can rule the Kingdom with me!"

Morgan let out a pained wheeze as she squeezed the air out of him, but he managed to get one thing out before the lack of air forced him to black out.

"Nope."

37

Morgan arose early the next morning feeling refreshed and energized. He checked the small clock on the wall and was surprised to see that it was only six in the morning.

What was going on? He was never up this early, let alone feeling this awake.

He looked over to the bed next to his, to where Sarah had been sleeping when he'd come in the previous night. It was empty.

This was way too weird for him. Sarah wasn't as much of a heavy sleeper as he was, but she'd never been up this early, either.

Morgan quickly rolled out of bed, amazed at how limber he felt. Not even a drop of stiffness in his muscles from the previous day's fighting. How very odd.

Morgan exited the small suite and emerged into the large bedroom. There he saw Sarah, sitting at a table, fully dressed in her armor and eating breakfast.

She looked up as he approached and gave him a wide grin.

"Good morning," she said, more chipper than anyone had a right to be at this hour.

"Morning," he replied back, not feeling at all like his usual cranky self.

"Can you explain why we're both up at the crack of dawn and why I'm not tired?" he asked, taking a seat across from her.

"It's the new *rank*!" she replied excitedly. "It looks like we'll be needing less sleep from now on."

"How do you know that?" he asked, noting that a plate had been set for him as well.

"Gold was here when I woke up and he was nice enough to explain it to me. He and Katherine both left to take care of some things but said they'd be back by mid-afternoon to go over the plans for the evening."

Morgan nodded, then picked up his knife and fork, and cut into the huge stack of pancakes before him.

He wasn't sure how to feel about the change. He liked that he was so much more powerful than he had been, but losing out on sleep seemed like too much.

They ate in silence for the next few minutes, until at last, Sarah spoke up.

"So, what did you talk to Katherine and Gold about last night?" she asked.

"I told them everything that I know about my memory loss. Apparently, they already knew, but they seemed surprised to hear that Samuel said he'd cure me," he answered in between bites.

"And what did Katherine have to say about that?" she asked in a quiet voice.

"She was excited that I was going to marry her," he replied.

"And are you?" Sarah's voice was so low now that he had to strain to hear it.

"You don't have to get all upset," Morgan said, reluctantly setting down his fork. "As I keep telling her, I never agreed to marry her, only to think about it. And since I now understand what that is, I'm even less interested than I was before."

"Really?" Sarah asked, perking up a bit.

"Yes, really. I realize that Katherine is an extremely attractive woman, but I have no interest in any of that. All I want to do is get stronger and I won't be able to do that if there's no world to get stronger in. So for now, I'm focusing on the battles ahead."

"What will you do if we succeed?" Sarah asked, playing with her remaining food.

"Probably go after your father," Morgan replied honestly. "I'm getting sick and tired of him getting in my way. Once this damn war is over, I want to concentrate on getting stronger, and finding the person who erased part of my life. I can't do that while constantly looking over my shoulder."

Sarah nodded, not even in the least bit concerned that her best friend had just casually mentioned murdering her father. She had no love for the man, and wouldn't care either way.

"No matter what happens, I'll be there for you," she said.

"I know," he replied, giving her a smile. "Now please let me finish my breakfast. This may be one of the last I'll ever get to eat."

***

Grub perked up from his slumped position in the horse's saddle.

Aaron Oster

He'd ridden hard over the last few weeks and had reached his home in record time. His eyes were bloodshot and his head pounded something fierce, but he'd made it!

The large gates up ahead were closed, and he could see a couple of guards standing watch to either side.

"Halt! Who goes there?" one of them called out.

"What the hell kind of greeting is that?" Grub shouted back, sitting up straighter in his saddle.

The guards clearly didn't recognize him, as they immediately turned hostile at his reply.

"This is the property of the Merchants Guild. Turn back or we will attack!"

"I am Grub, son of Keet!" Grub yelled, face going red with rage. "Look at my ring, you lowborn shit stains! Now get the hell out of my way, or I'll have your tongues removed for your insolence!"

One of the guards was about to angrily retort, but the other put a hand on his shoulder to stop him. He'd recognized the ring on Grub's finger and realized that he was probably who he said he was.

"Apologies, Lord!" he replied, giving a clumsy bow.

"We didn't recognize you and now we have shamed ourselves greatly. Please, let us escort you inside," he said, bowing deeply, then banging twice on the gate.

"About damn time," he snorted, folding his arms as the gates swung open.

Once they'd opened, he rode in, making sure to take note of both their faces. He'd have them beaten regardless. No one would disrespect him. Not here anyway.

He rode into the main courtyard of the sprawling estate where his family did their business, though it was business in the loosest interpretation of the word. Grub's family, for lack of a better term, was a criminal enterprise. They used the Merchants Guild as a front, of course, but behind closed doors had all sorts of illegal dealings.

They were owed huge sums of money by Queen Beatrice of their own kingdom, as well as several nobles families. That was not to mention all the favors they were owed by the nobility in other kingdoms. If there was one faction that held more power than them in all the Five Kingdoms, it would have to be the Assassins Guild, and even that was a close call.

Grub dismounted as he reached the center of the courtyard and a stable hand scurried out to take his horse's reins.

"Where is my father?" he demanded, as the man tried to leave.

"I believe he's away on business, young master," the man replied in a wheezy voice.

"Then what about my mother?" he demanded, starting to feel more than a little annoyed that he, the heir to the family business, was being so poorly greeted.

He had been willing to overlook their attempt at a rescue. After all, if he were presumed dead, it would be a waste of resources to come look for him, but surely, word of his return must have reached them by now. They were way too well informed for him to think otherwise.

"Your mother is away, as well," the man replied, cringing visibly at his annoyed look.

"Well, tell me who is here, you whimpering shit, or I'll paint the barn a new shade of red with your face!"

"The deputy head is here!" he quickly replied. "She's in her office. That's all I know!" And with that, the terrified man scurried away, bowing hastily and dragging his tired horse behind him.

So, Keldor's been replaced, he thought as he headed into the front door, making sure to take his shoes off before he did.

He sighed as his feet came into contact with the light and springy bamboo mats. He'd really missed this.

The academy had been nice and all, but their floors left something to be desired.

He walked down the long corridor, taking a few turns until he was standing before the sliding door that used to be Keldor's. Steeling himself, he knocked twice on the frame and waited.

"Enter," a very familiar sounding voice called out.

Grub pulled the sliding door to the side, and his suspicions were confirmed.

"Grub! It's so good to see that you made it out alive!" Loquin said, from her seated position behind the low table.

"You're the new deputy head?" Grub asked, completely shocked.

This wasn't right. Loquin wasn't a member of the family. With Keldor's death, the position should have been handed back to his father until Grub turned eighteen. Not to this outsider.

"Do relax and come in. You must have had a long journey. I'll make some tea and explain everything," she said, rising from the floor cushion, and walking over to a small fire pit set against the back wall.

Grub eyed her suspiciously, but eventually gave in, closing the door behind him and taking a seat at the low table. He could see a bunch of official looking documents sitting there, as well as a small inkwell and brush pen.

"So, tell me how you, a complete foreigner, managed to obtain such a high position in our household," Grub asked.

He was feeling a bit calmer now that he was back home, but was still on edge from his long journey and the information he was carrying.

He turned as Loquin set down a small ceramic mug before him, then padded to the other side of the table and had a seat as well.

"That is a very long story, and one which I cannot fully explain myself," Loquin began, taking a sip from her cup.

She held up a finger as Grub opened his mouth, and he held his tongue until she'd finished drinking.

"Your father left a letter before he left on his trip. He told me to be expecting you in the next few days, and to apologize for his absence. The Queen demanded an audience, and one does not deny her wishes."

"And what does the lovely Queen Beatrice want this time?" Grub asked, as Loquin handed him a folded piece of parchment, sealed by a blob of red wax with his father's stamp.

"More money, if my guess is correct," Loquin replied, as he cracked the seal with his thumb and read through the letter.

It was brief and to the point. Loquin had been adopted into the family to replace Keldor, as she had been an invaluable resource to the family for the last twenty years. Grub was to treat her as an equal and trust her with any and all information he'd acquired during his stay at the academy.

Grub folded up the letter and tucked it away with a scowl.

It was typical of his father. He was always abrupt and straight to the point. His mother was quite a bit different. She was a foreigner as well, and was a bit warmer to him.

"So, it would appear that I'm to entrust you with any information I gathered while at the academy," Grub said with a sigh.

He'd wanted to tell his father in person, hoping to receive just a hint of approval from the man, but now he had no choice but to tell Loquin. If he held off after reading the letter, he would only receive his father's ire for waiting.

Looking back to her, he saw her waiting with an expectant expression. He blew out an annoyed breath, then told her everything he'd overhead between Katherine and Arnold. By the time he was done, Loquin was smiling from ear to ear.

Great, he thought. *Now she'll receive all the praise for this, and I'll get nothing.*

"This is some truly excellent information!" Loquin exclaimed. "Your father will be quite pleased when I tell him of your discovery!"

Grub was taken aback.

"You're not planning on taking credit for this?" he asked. Had this been Keldor, he would have expected no less. That was just the way of the family.

"Of course not!" Loquin exclaimed with a laugh. "You will be the head of this family one day, and it would be foolish of me to try and slight you."

Grub felt oddly pleased with those words and nodded.

"Good. At least you're smarter than Keldor was. Now if you'll excuse me, I've had a long journey and would like to take a soak in the hot springs before supper."

"But of course!" Loquin said, rising from her seated position as well. "Enjoy your bath."

***

Loquin's smile slipped as soon as the door closed, and a look of contempt crossed her face.

She'd worked hard to weasel her way into this family, and she wouldn't be put out by some snot nosed brat. Especially not one this dumb.

Her smile was soon back on her face, as the information he'd provided was quite good indeed. This would be the perfect opportunity for her to make the family a vast sum of money, and possibly even secure their place on the South Kingdom's throne, once and for all.

She walked over to the far wall, and slid aside a small wooden panel, revealing an ornately carved mirror sitting in the alcove behind it. She ran her fingers over the gemstones set in its base, in a specific pattern, then waited.

About five minutes later, the face of her most recently acquired favor showed up in the mirror.

"What do you want?" asked Lord Simon, from the North.

Simon had fallen on hard times recently and had borrowed a large amount of money from them to fund a recent project of his, and now he owed them a very large favor.

"Is that any way to talk to the person who gave you so much money?" Loquin asked in a sickly sweet voice.

She relished the struggle on his face as he visibly worked to control his temper. It always made her feel good to put these pompous nobles in their place.

"What can I do for you?" he asked, finally managing to compose himself.

"Oh, nothing major," Loquin replied, toying with a lock of her hair. "I hear that you've gotten in good with King Edmund in recent weeks."

"I have," he replied carefully.

"Excellent! I have some information that might just interest your dear King, so I'd like you to set up a meeting between the two of us."

Simon's face darkened at this.

"Are you mad, woman? Do you know what kind of damage it will do to my reputation if the King finds out I've been consorting with the likes of you?"

Loquin had the good grace to pretend to be offended.

"Well, you didn't seem to mind consorting with us when we handed you that massive bag of money. Now, you can either pay up, with our standard 85% interest rate, or you can set up that meeting. It's your choice," she said, allowing a predatory smile to cross her features.

Starbreak

She saw Simon's face go beet red, then the wind seemed to go out of him.

"Oh, very well," he replied with a sigh.

"Don't look so disheartened, Simon," Loquin cheerily replied. "I assure you that Edmund will be quite pleased with the information we have to offer. Hell, you might even get a promotion. Until we speak again..." Then she cut off the connection.

Loquin closed the small door and went back to sit by her desk. She let out a content sigh as she sat, and stretched her arms over her head.

She had no idea why she'd waited so long to try her hand at this business. It really was so much fun.

38

Morgan put down his knife and fork with a sigh, wiping his mouth with the back of his hand. He burped, earning him a disapproving glare from Sarah, which he completely ignored. Standing from the table, he stretched, wondering what he could do to pass the time.

There were still several things he needed to do, not least of which was figure out exactly what an evolved supermage was and what the extent of his capabilities were. As far as he could tell, everything was still the same. He couldn't really be sure though, as all of his skills had changed once he'd *ranked up*.

He blew out an annoyed breath, prompting Sarah to look up from the book she'd begun reading.

"What's got you so worked up?" she asked with a teasing smile.

"I need to figure out the extent of my ability. Not only that, but I have to figure out what exactly is happening to me."

His brows furrowed in annoyance at the seemingly impossible task before him.

"Why don't you go into a *Beast Zone* to do some training?" Sarah asked. "Maybe while you're there, you can also figure out how to contact Dabu on your own."

Morgan stared at her for a moment, before a wide grin spread across his face.

"Thanks, Sarah. You're a genius!" he said, prompting her to blush.

He quickly dashed back to their room and found the leather bag sitting on her bed. Digging into it, he soon came out with the pouch of keys. Katherine had handed them several more, so he had quite a few to choose from.

Eventually, he settled on a *rank 21 zone*. He quickly stripped out of his pajamas and changed into his enchanted armor. He exited the room a few minutes later, pulling the magesteel gloves on over his hands.

Sarah was reading again, but she looked up as he emerged, giving him an appraising look. He really had filled out since the *rank up.* She could clearly see the definition of his new muscles through the tight material of the armor.

"I'm heading in now. Are you coming with me?" he asked, already sticking the key into the air and turning it.

"I think I'll pass," Sarah said with a wave of her hand. "I've had enough of those damn *Beast Zones* for the next twenty years."

Morgan shrugged.

"Your loss. Just don't complain when I come back stronger than you."

With that, he leapt through the portal.

He emerged a few minutes later into a burning desert. He blinked, immediately squinting as the sun overhead practically blinded him.

Why was he so hot? Shouldn't his new rank afford him some protection against heat like this?

When he stopped to think about it, it did make sense. This was a *rank 21 zone,* so it would be challenging for someone of his level. He opened his eyes again, slowly this time, and allowed them to adjust to the sunlight around him.

The first thing he needed to do was get the lay of the land. Using his *advanced flight,* Morgan shot into the air. After just a few seconds, he was hovering at his maximum height and staring out at the vast rolling dunes of sand around him.

He was in awe at how large the place was. He hadn't even been aware that places like this existed. It made him wonder just what type of beasts would call a place like this home. Despite the heat, his body shivered in anticipation and he landed back on the ground.

Best not to waste any RP when he was out here alone. He wouldn't have Sarah to back him up this time, so he would need to be just a bit more cautious than he normally was.

Morgan began trekking through the sand, feeling his feet sinking in as he walked. He'd spotted a rocky looking outcropping to the north when he'd been in the air. He assumed that was where the *Arc* lived, so he headed in that direction.

It didn't take him long to run into his first beast.

Morgan squinted, using *aura sense* on the spiny shelled creature before him. It's aura immediately flared red and words appeared over the creature's body.

Name: Razor-shell Tortoise
Rank - 20
Ability type - Super

Morgan took up a fighting stance as the beast lumbered up to him.

He'd never heard of a tortoise before, but he guessed that the shell wouldn't be easy to crack.

The beast let out a loud bellow that sounded almost human, then it immediately began glowing red as it prepared to use its ability. Morgan didn't waste a second and activated *storm blade*, forming it into his favorite lance.

A piercing weapon would do well against that thing's shell.

He couldn't help but notice that the amount of gold interspersed with the purple reiki in his blade had increased, if only slightly, since the last time he'd used it.

The tortoise then did something very unexpected. It pulled its head and legs inside the shell. The most alarming part was that it stayed floating in the air, just a few inches off the ground. Then ever so slowly, it began to spin and Morgan immediately saw where this was going.

He wasn't about to wait for that thing to pick up speed.

Morgan darted in, bringing the whirling *storm blade* back to deliver a powerful thrust. His blade impacted against the tough shell but did absolutely nothing.

Morgan cursed, slamming the blade into the tough shell over and over as it picked up speed. After six or seven blows, he could see that his current strength would not be sufficient enough to crack it.

He was about to use *gravity impact* when the beast began to emit a high pitched whining sound. It was only then that he noticed that the tortoise was spinning so quickly, that the spines had become a blur. He leaped to the side without a second thought, sure that the beast was about to attack. He wasn't wrong.

The tortoise shot forward in a blur of motion, slicing through the spot he'd been occupying only seconds before. Morgan thought he'd have a few seconds to recover, but the whirling shell of death abruptly changed directions, and he was forced to once again dive to the side. This time however, he landed on one of his hands, then shoved hard against the ground. The force of the push sent him a good ten feet up, where used his *storm blade's* ability. Purple and golden lightning flashed across the lance as he came down right on top of the spinning shell.

He slammed the blade against the beast, and the lighting discharged with a loud zap. While the blade hadn't penetrated the shell, the lightning had caused some damage, and the tortoise abruptly fell to the ground, twitching and writhing as the electricity coursed through its body.

Morgan landed on the ground next to the beast, then used *gravity impact*. He slammed his blade into the shell and this time the blade punched through with a loud crack. He felt the blade sink into soft flesh, and a moment later the beast stopped moving.

Morgan dismissed his blade, wiping his forehead and letting out a long breath.

That fight had been way tougher than he'd expected. Sure, the beast was a rank above him, but it still shouldn't have been that hard.

Morgan then retrieved the core and examined it.

Name: Razor-shell Tortoise core
Rank - 20
Total available energy: 10,329/10,329

This core was taken from a razor-shell tortoise. As this core was taken from an evolved beast, the amount of available energy has been slightly increased.

Morgan pulled the core he'd taken from the lizard so he could compare the two.

Name: Electric-spine lizard Matriarch core
Rank - 24
Total available energy: 21,006/21,006

This core was taken from an electric-spine lizard. As this core was taken from a zone Matriarch, an intermediate beast, the amount of available energy has been greatly increased.

Morgan let out a low whistle when he saw that.

The lizard was only 4 rank higher than the tortoise, but the energy in its core was more than double.

He quickly absorbed both, feeling a hot flash running through his body. Then, strangely enough, a small screen flashed before his eyes.

Cores absorbed.

Energy to next rank: 31,335/89,000

Morgan blinked and the next moment, the screen vanished. What on earth had that been? It had never happened before.

Morgan's mind began racing as he tried to figure it out. Finally, he decided that it must have either something to do with his new ability or his new divine skill. Either way, he still needed answers. He heard a loud bellow echoing out over the sand dunes, and grinned. He did have to figure it all out, but it could wait until he'd managed to clear this *zone*.

It took him two more hours to make it to the *Arc's* territory, by which point he'd managed to gather enough energy to *rank up*. He held back, though, as he no longer had the luxury of absorbing cores and gaining the maximum attributes per *rank*. He looked up at the massive sandstone formation towering above his head.

The *Arc* was in there, but he wasn't sure if he should go in alone or not. The safe thing to do would be to leave now. He'd already collected a sufficient amount of cores, so he'd technically accomplished what he'd set out to do.

He'd gotten a pretty good understanding of his skills, and was fairly confident that he wouldn't run into any more surprises, though the messages about his progression continued popping up whenever he absorbed a core. He still needed to figure that out.

He debated turning back for just another moment, then he let out a snort. Since when did he take the safe option?

Starbreak

Chuckling to himself, Morgan headed through the tunnel entrance in into the *Arc's* territory. The temperature immediately dropped once he walked in, and he let out a sigh of relief to feel the baking sun finally off his back. He looked around at the oddly shaped stone as he walked, wondering just what could have formed the strange wavy patterns.

He felt a cool blast of air and turned his attention straight ahead. The tunnel opened before him, and he stared, first in confusion, then in utter shock, when he saw the massive three-headed chicken lying at the center of the cave.

39

Morgan rubbed at his eyes a few times, just to make sure he wasn't seeing things.

Nope. The oversized chicken was still there.

He once again had to wonder who in the world had designed these things. Someone had to, and whoever they were, they had a seriously twisted sense of humor.

He crouched in the tunnel, just outside the room, and took his time examining the beast. It was large, about a foot taller than him. Each one of its heads was a different color, and that color carried on down the rest of its body, giving it an odd three-toned appearance. The left head was black, the middle was a light tan and the right, a deep red.

Its feet were a bright yellow and had a set of wickedly curved claws extending outward. He could also spot a smattering of scales throughout its plumage, and they extended in a line from their crests to their beaks, providing a sort of crude armor for their heads.

Morgan focused in, and a blue aura flared around the chicken.

Name: Sonic-Cerberus Chicken Matriarch
Rank - 23
Ability type - Mage

Morgan couldn't decide if he should laugh or take this beast as a serious threat. He still remembered those bloodsucker-chickens he'd fought in a lower *rank beast zone.* They were quite dangerous, and by the looks of it, this was most likely an intermediate beast.

He was tempted to just use *starbreak,* and fry the chicken, but the idea of fighting a three-headed beast was just too exciting an opportunity to pass up. Finally, he made up his mind. Grinning madly, he stepped into the cavern.

The chicken rose as soon as he walked in, and Morgan could see that he'd slightly underestimated its height. It stood around eight feet tall, and six pairs of eyes all locked directly onto him. It was a strange sight, seeing all the heads moving independently from one another, and Morgan wondered how this particular beast made decisions.

Did one head do all the thinking? Or did they all need to make a collective decision before acting?

Morgan then realized that he was overthinking things. It was a freaking chicken. He should be more focused on how to take it down, rather than how it would operate in everyday life. He grinned, then his shield flared to life as he charged in. He noticed almost right away that there were now two golden discs on his shoulders, in addition to the one on his chest, but the rest of his shield was still the same violet he was used to.

Was his divine energy growing? He would have to check once this battle was over.

The chicken then let out an angry squawk, all three beaks opening at once to deliver a stunning sonic attack. Morgan staggered back as his ears came under assault and he grimaced in pain, clutching at his head while the horrible cacophony echoed around the chamber.

He was still clutching at his head when the chicken slammed into him at full force, forming a line of cracks across his shield and sending him into the opposite wall. The air exploded from Morgan's lungs as his back impacted with the wall, and the brittle sandstone shattered under the force.

He gasped, mind still reeling from the sonic attack and he wasn't able to focus for even a moment. Morgan crashed to the ground and the chicken pounced on him, its three heads flashing down to peck at his shield. Luckily for Morgan, the chicken was attracted to the bright golden glow coming from the center of his shield. Otherwise, he might have been killed before his mind could recover from the attack.

He groaned as the ringing in his ears finally abated somewhat, and he was able to focus on the beast standing on top of him. He heard a loud crack and saw that a web-like pattern had formed on the golden disk and the chicken was relentlessly pecking down, widening the cracks with each strike.

Morgan used *gravity impact* and *explosive movement* at once, bucking his hips mightily and watching as the chicken was launched off him in slow motion. He quickly hopped to his feet and delivered five hard blows to the chicken's side. He then finished the maneuver

Aaron Oster

by pivoting on his back leg and swinging it up to slam into the red head closest to him.

Time abruptly sped up as his skills ran out, and Morgan leapt back, covering his ears as the chicken staggered back. The red head had been turned to a bloody pulp under the massive force exuded by Morgan's attack, and it seemed, at least for the moment, to be completely disoriented.

Morgan took his chance, darting in and using *storm blade*. He formed a long, curved saber and slashed out at the chicken's side, but grimaced when the hard scales made it merely glance off.

So blunt attacks are the way to go, he thought.

A thought struck Morgan then, but he was forced to duck as a vicious swipe of the chicken's claws nearly took his head off. It whirled on him and its two remaining heads lashed out, catching him in the right shoulder. He grimaced as his shield finally gave way, and shattered with a flash of purple light. Thankfully, the shield had slowed the attack enough that his armor was able to repel them, but it had been a near hit.

He leapt backward, using his *flight* to assist him. Landing a good forty feet away, Morgan focused in on his *storm blade*, trying out his earlier idea. He let out an annoyed breath when the blade refused to take the shape he wanted.

The skill did say any blade, so it made sense that a blunt weapon like the hammer he'd been trying to make, wouldn't work.

Morgan rolled to the side as the chicken ran past him, blood streaming from the destroyed head.

He idly wondered if his skill might evolve further once he broke through into *rank 29*.

Would he be able to use blunt weapons then?

The chicken whirled back around and began to glow a bright blue, forcing his attention back on the fight. Morgan took a quick look at his *RP*, seeing that it had nearly refilled itself.

He'd had his fun, but he needed to end this before he got hurt. There was a mission he had to complete in only a few hours, and it wouldn't be wise to be injured now.

Morgan grinned at the now two-headed chicken and used *starbreak*. He rose up into the air, seeing the glowing yellow-orange sphere growing in his palm. He looked down at the chicken, just in time to be hit by a wall of sound.

Morgan's eardrums burst, and he lost control of his skill, falling out of the air and slamming hard into the ground. He lay there, stunned as the beast lumbered over to him, the two heads weaving back and forth as it did so.

No time to be in pain, he thought, forcing himself to his feet. That attack had been nasty, leaving blood running from his ears, and a splitting headache in its wake. The chicken dashed over, clucking in a rage that its quarry still wasn't dead. It let out what Morgan assumed was another sonic attack, but seeing as he'd already been deafened, he was completely unaffected.

At least one good thing had come of it, Morgan thought, taking another quick look at his *RP.* He growled, seeing that it was only at about *900.*

That stupid chicken had completely ruined his awesome finishing move and now he would have to wait for his RP to regenerate before he could use it.

He was forced to dodge an incoming peck, and Morgan punched out in annoyance, landing a heavy blow between the middle head's eyes. The middle head went cross-eyed and began looking confusedly around, but its body was still functioning as usual. Even with two heads out of commission, the chicken's foot shot up, claws raking across his chest.

The loud shrieking sound of claws on metal would likely have been extremely unpleasant, but seeing as he was still deaf, Morgan couldn't care less. He grinned, then lashed out with a spinning hook kick, neatly catching the beast behind its knee and sending it toppling to the ground.

It went down with an angry squawk that Morgan couldn't hear. He quickly checked his *RP,* and finally decided that it wouldn't be practical to wait any longer, just to use *starbreak.* Morgan was a little upset, but not overly so. After all, he still had another powerful skill he could use.

He debated whether it was wise to use it in the cave, but in the end, decided that he just didn't care.

Morgan then used his improved *gravity storm.* He hadn't been sure what to expect, so when he rose into the air, and purple and gold lighting began crackling all over his body, he was quite surprised. His hands spread outward, clenching into fists, and the gravity around the chicken immediately intensified. The chicken was slammed to the ground, and judging by the small crater it was beginning to form with its body, the gravity force was extremely intense.

He was wondering what would happen next when there was a massive rumbling crack. The next moment, the cave ceiling exploded and a cyclone of whirling wind slammed into the ground. Morgan's arms shot out and the cracking power that had been dancing over his body connected with the cyclone of air.

He watched in morbid fascination as the *gravity storm* raged on, barely noticing when his feet touched the ground. He just stood and watched, marveling at the storm's terrifying power. After 45 seconds, the storm finally petered out, sending bits of stone and grains of sand raining back to the ground.

Morgan squinted as bright sunlight poured in from the massive hole his attack had left in the cave ceiling. He felt a grin spread across his face, as the last of the rubble showered down around him. Looking toward the center of the attack, he spotted the smoldering, blackened husk that had once been a monster chicken.

He blew out a long breath, then abruptly burst out laughing at the absurdity of the situation. The mighty evolved supermage, being forced to use one of his most devastating attacks to kill a chicken! He was just glad that Sarah hadn't been here to witness it.

He swallowed once, and his hearing abruptly came back in a rush.

That was surprising, he thought, feeling at his ears. His fingers came away, sticky with congealing blood. He was sure he'd been deafened and would need a healer to fix him. Apparently not.

"That was quite the spectacle. I'm glad I made the trip to come watch you."

Morgan whirled on the spot, fists raised as he readied an attack. He pulled up short when he saw who it was.

"Dabu? How the hell did you get in here?"

40

Dabu let out a loud booming laugh, his mirth echoing off the walls of the sandstone cavern as Morgan stared at him in confusion. This only made the man laugh harder, which in turn only, confused him more.

Morgan was beginning to wonder if the man would be okay, when he finally began to calm down.

"Apologies for my rudeness, young supermage," Dabu said, wiping at his eyes. "Your reaction was not one I had been expecting."

Morgan shrugged.

He didn't care either way, but he was glad that Dabu was here. He found it suspicious that he just happened to turn up when he'd been hoping to see him, but Dabu hadn't led him astray yet.

"Yeah," Morgan said slowly, trying to find the best way to broach the subject.

Finally, he just shrugged to himself. If anyone could give him answers, it would be an omniscient supermage.

"Something happened during my last *rank up*," Morgan said, prompting the smile to fade from Dabu's face.

His eyes narrowed for a moment, then widened in the biggest display of shocked amazement he'd ever seen from the man.

Morgan was about to ask him what he saw, when he remembered that Dabu had the *aura sense* skill and that his was far more advanced than his own.

"What do you see?" Morgan finally asked as the silence stretched onward.

Dabu started as if only realizing that Morgan was still there.

"I never thought I'd see the day," Dabu said, his voice trailing off.

There was a sense of awe in his voice that made Morgan feel slightly uncomfortable.

"What's happening to me?" Morgan finally asked, after another minute of silence.

"You have, for lack of a better term, evolved!" Dabu exclaimed. "In all the time I've been alive, I have never once seen an evolved supermage. I had hoped that you might one day advance, but even I didn't think it would be this soon."

Morgan's mind reeled.

He'd evolved? Like a beast?!

"Can you please explain? Ever since my last *rank up*, nothing has felt quite the same. At first, I thought it might just be the increase in my attributes, but Sarah *ranked up* as well and the changes aren't nearly as extreme."

Dabu finally seemed to come to himself then, and his usual smile spread across his face.

"Of course. Apologies for being so rude, please."

He motioned with his hand and Morgan blinked in surprise.

A small table with two chairs now stood on one side of the room. A pitcher of pale blue colored liquid sat in the center, and two glass cups stood next to it. There was also a large loaf of bread, with a log of butter sitting on the side.

Morgan finally grinned back at the man. He hadn't realized how hungry he'd been until he'd seen the food.

Quickly making his way over to the table, he tore a chunk off the bread. It was warm to the touch and crackled wonderfully as he slathered it with butter. Dabu sat down across from him as he took his first bite, washing it down with the sweet pale blue drink.

"What is this?" he asked, taking another sip.

"Ah, that is a cider made from paleberries. They don't grow in this realm, so it's not a surprise that you haven't tasted it before."

"You've hinted at other realms before," Morgan said, latching onto what the god had just said. "Can you tell me about them?"

Dabu shook his head and Morgan sighed.

"I'm sorry that I can't tell you. That would be breaking the rules, and as I've said before, it would not go well for either of us."

Seeing Morgan's disappointed look, he was quick to continue.

"I can, however, answer all your questions regarding your new ability."

Morgan perked up at this and took another huge bite from his bread.

"Now where to begin?" Dabu said, tapping lighting at his chin. After a few moments, he snapped his fingers and began speaking.

"While it is not very well known, people can evolve in a similar manner to beasts, should they meet the correct prerequisites. There are several supers and mages out there that have evolved, and even some that have managed to get to the intermediate level."

"Wait," Morgan cut in. "So what you're saying, is that two supers of equal *rank* can face each other and one will be able to completely annihilate the other?"

Dabu nodded.

"Then why have I never heard of this before?"

Morgan folded his arms, not liking where this was going.

Every time he spoke with Dabu, some new piece of information would be revealed to him. Something that he felt should be known, but for some reason, was not.

"Simple really. Nobody knows about it."

Morgan opened his mouth, but Dabu held up a hand to forestall him.

"Let me explain. All people who awaken an ability have the potential for evolution. The only problem is, is that almost no one manages it. Therefore, it has faded into obscurity."

"What about you then? You're a supermage. You've lived for thousands of years. If there is an evolution, then shouldn't you have reached the pinnacle?"

Dabu looked slightly sheepish at that but answered all the same.

"I actually haven't found a way to evolve yet. It may be hard for you to believe, but some things are beyond even my understanding and this is one of them."

He let out a sigh and leaned back in his chair, staring up through the hole in the ceiling, his mind apparently far away in some distant past.

"So I've met these prerequisites somehow. I'm guessing that it has something to do with the person who screwed with my head."

Dabu opened his mouth to reply, but Morgan was the one to cut him off this time.

"Yeah, yeah. It's against the rules," he said, prompting a snort of laughter from the man.

Aaron Oster

"But tell me, how can I know if I'm up against an evolved mage or super? Are there any out there that are more powerful than the intermediate level? If so, where would they be?"

"To answer your last question, no. There are currently no mages or supers who have managed to advance past the intermediate stage. Normally, there would be no way to tell them apart, but if you advance your *aura sense* skill, the extra information will become available to you."

"Okay, so if there's no discernable difference, why do I have a new source of power? Do all evolved supermages have it?"

"If I'm being perfectly honest, I actually have no idea," Dabu said with a shrug.

He laughed at Morgan's look of disbelief and continued his explanation.

"As I said before, I've never actually met a supermage who's evolved. But just from the look of your aura, I can tell that you've grown significantly in power. You even have a new source of energy other than reiki, which I didn't know was possible."

"So you don't know anything about this *divine* energy either?" Morgan asked, already feeling his spirits sinking.

"I do not," he confirmed, and Morgan felt his frustration growing.

What *did* he know then?

"My skills don't really feel any different, and the way I move and fight hasn't changed. The only difference I can see is in my shield... Oh, and I've had screens popping up every time I absorb a core," he added after a few seconds.

"I don't know much about the differences between the two, but I do know one thing for certain. Evolved supermages have the power of choice. They also get a more in-depth view of the world around them."

Dabu grinned once more.

"I think a demonstration would help you to understand better. How close are you to your next *rank*?"

"I have the cores needed, but I haven't trained enough to gain the maximum attributes for the next *rank*."

Dabu just waved his hand, brushing his concerns aside.

Starbreak

"Once you evolve, you should receive a set amount of attribute points per rank. The tradeoff for this is that it will cost significantly more energy between ranks than it normally would."

"Is that why it cost *380,000 energy* for me to reach *rank 19*?" Morgan asked as he pulled a core from his pocket.

"It was that much?!" Dabu exclaimed, eyes widening in shock.

"Yeah. Isn't that normal for supermages?" Morgan asked, placing the core down on the table.

"No! That's not normal! It should only have cost three times the energy of the previous *rank*. Not ten."

He rubbed at his chin while Morgan picked up the core again, preparing to absorb it.

"Maybe that's how you evolved. When beasts prepare to evolve, they must first store up a massive amount of energy. Once they reach an appropriate *rank*, the energy they've stored up will fuel the changes."

Morgan nodded, remembering that the first beast he'd ever fought had a massive amount of energy for its *rank*. Seeing that Dabu was still lost in thought, Morgan absentmindedly absorbed the core.

The energy flooded into him, but this *rank up* was nothing like the previous ones. Instead of feeling the small increase to his attributes, a purple and gold screen flickered into view before his eyes.

Rank Up!

Congratulations! You have reached Rank 20. You have 18 attribute points to distribute. Would you like to distribute your points now?

Yes/No

Morgan stared at the screen, not believing what he was seeing.

He could choose where his attribute points would go?

His mind began racing, completely ignoring the screen hovering before his eyes. Even if the only perk of evolving was to have the option of placing his points where he wanted, then it would already be worth it. It also hadn't escaped his notice that he had 3 more points than should be possible for his rank.

Was this another perk?

Morgan thought about it for a second, then found he didn't care. He now had the option of placing his points where he wanted. This would give him a huge advantage over anyone, even other supermages.

"So, can you tell me what you see?"

Morgan looked through the translucent screen to see Dabu looking at him with a curious expression.

"You were right," Morgan said. "I have the option to place the attributes where I want."

"Well; go on then," Dabu said, and Morgan turned back to the screen.

Mentally hitting *yes*, a new screen popped up, this one with his attributes.

Strength - 121
Agility - 152
Constitution - 137
Intelligence - 128
Wisdom - 128

That wasn't all that showed up, however.

Skills:
Advanced flight - 1/10
Gravity impact - 1/10
Explosive movement - 1/10
Storm blade - 1/10

Divine:
Shock-blast - 1/15

Traits:
Gravity field - 1/30
Recovery - 1/30
Aura sense (inherited) - 4/50

Extra:
Gravity storm (2ⁿᵈ category) - 1/20
Starbreak - 1/30

Morgan felt his heart rate speed up as he stared at the screen, then a smile crept onto his lips.

If he now had the option to put his attributes into increasing his skill's power before the next breakthrough, then he really could become an unstoppable killing machine. He could imagine himself at his current rank, plowing through supers and mages miles above him.

He had to stop himself from immediately putting all his points into one of his skills to see what would happen. Instead, he forced himself to carefully think through his next decision.

He could upgrade his skills every time he ranked up, but that would leave him physically weak once he got to higher ranks.

Morgan had always been a melee fighter, and no matter how many skills he acquired, that would never change. He thought over what had been his biggest issues in the recent fights and found that he'd been lacking in one area, physical power.

He nodded to himself, happy with his choice, and put *15* of his points into *strength*, and the other *3* into his *gravity impact* skill. He figured that since he'd only been expecting *15* points per *rank*, he wasn't actually losing anything by investing in the skill. A new screen popped up then, asking him to confirm his choice. Morgan selected *yes*, and felt the changes take hold.

Immediately, he felt his muscles ripple under his clothes, as they tightened up, becoming harder and more compact. They didn't actually show any visible sign of growing, but Morgan could feel the effect that it had on his body. Closing the small screen, he opened his status to view the changes.

Name: Morgan
Evolved Supermage: Rank - 20
Energy to next rank - 4,701/109,000
Ability - Divine Gravity & Air
RP - 1,280/1,280 (Regen - 12.8 per second)
DV - 15/15 (Regen - 0.15 per minute)

Aaron Oster

> *Strength - 136*
> *Agility - 152*
> *Constitution - 137*
> *Intelligence - 128*
> *Wisdom - 128*
> *Skills - Advanced flight, Gravity impact, Explosive movement, Storm blade*
> *Divine - Shock-blast*
> *Traits - Gravity field, Recovery, Aura sense (inherited)*
> *Extra - Gravity storm (2nd category), Starbreak*

Morgan grimaced at how much more it cost to move up to *rank 21* but decided that the ability to choose where he put his attributes was ultimately worth the price. He also found that by focusing in on each skill, he could now see how many attribute points he would need to put in to advance them to the next level.

It also didn't escape his notice that his *DV* had gone up by 5 points, and the regen had gone up as well.

Did that have something to do with ranking up?

He idly wondered what kind of power he could have if he somehow figured out how to take his evolved supermage ability and evolve it further to the intermediate class.

"I can already see quite a difference."

Morgan closed his screen and saw Dabu rising to his feet.

"Yes. Thank you for giving me answers to my questions. They were very informative," he replied.

"Of course," Dabu said with a warm smile. "After all, I am invested in seeing you succeed."

"Why is that?" Morgan asked with a raised eyebrow. "And how did you even get in here, or know that I wanted to speak with you?"

"Trade secret, I'm afraid," the man said, winking at him.

He laughed heartily at Morgan's flat expression and backed slowly away.

"I'm afraid that my time here is limited. Just like you, I cannot dally where I do not belong. But don't worry, my young evolved supermage. We will be seeing each other again soon and I will be keeping a close eye on you."

Morgan nodded, rising from his seat and smiling at the man.

Even if he was cryptic, Dabu had helped him more than anyone else in recent months. This conversation had been extremely enlightening, even if he didn't have all the answers he'd wanted.

"A warning before I go. You mentioned the Pinnacle Kings in our last meeting. They are truly terrifying creatures, with all the cunning of an equivalent ranked supermage and twice the power. Be wary of facing them, as you most definitely will not survive at your current *rank*."

Dabu started to fade from view then but said one last thing before he went.

"You didn't hear this from me, but you may want to focus on advancing instead of *ranking up*. You may also be able to gain a few extra attributes by absorbing certain cores, but be careful, as they may be too *advanced* for you."

He winked, and then he was gone.

Morgan stared at the place where Dabu had disappeared, feeling his smile widening at the corners.

He wasn't one hundred percent sure, but he was fairly certain that Dabu had just bent the rules for him.

***

Six years ago...

Sarah watched in horror and amazement as the small boy shoved his arm into Kook's side. She winced in sympathetic pain as the man brought his pommel down on Morgan's head, and was taking a step forward to help, but Morgan miraculously kept his feet.

Sarah stopped, her eyes widening at the sheer display of willpower and perseverance Morgan was displaying. She could clearly see the blood pumping from his shoulder and the blood matting his hair to his skull, yet he hung on, shoving his arm ever deeper into Kook's side.

She was holding her breath, watching the struggle going on between the two of them. As Kook raised his sword to strike again, Morgan's arm suddenly sank deeper into the man's side, and a moment later he let out a howl of pain, the sword clattering from his nerveless fingers. He gasped a few times, face pale and twisted in agony, then he brought his elbow crashing down on top of Morgan's head.

Sarah let out the breath she'd been holding as Morgan staggered back, then fell to the ground. She quickly ran to his side, keeping an eye on Kook, who had sunk to his knees and was clutching weakly at his side.

Bending down next to him, she felt at his neck as she'd seen the healers in the manor do, that one time her mother had passed out. She wasn't even sure if she was doing it right, but she felt a huge sense of relief when she felt a small throb under her fingers.

He was still alive.

Sarah stood, trying to figure out what to do next. The manor was just through the alley up ahead, but Kook still wasn't down and she wasn't even sure if she could trust the guards at the gates.

She looked to the man in question as he let out a long groan and fell to the ground, blood pooling around him in a growing puddle.

Sarah grimaced, deciding that Kook was as good as dead, and she no longer had anything to worry about. She bent down near Morgan and heaved him up from his prone position. She knew it probably wasn't good to be moving him in this condition, but she didn't think she had any choice.

She grunted under his weight as she heaved him over her shoulders, managing to get him onto her back after a few moments of maneuvering. She could feel his blood soaking into her dress, but by this point, it was so filthy that she didn't care.

She staggered forward, stumbling past the dying Kook, not even giving the man a second glance. He didn't deserve that much. He deserved to die out here, alone, for what he'd done to Hint.

Sarah felt tears streaming down her cheeks as she stumbled out of the alley and into the open courtyard. She saw the two guards standing by the gate and was glad to see that they were the same ones as this morning.

Sarah staggered up to the gate, falling gratefully to her knees as the guards rushed forward to meet her, asking questions about her state of wellbeing, Hint, and who the boy was.

Sarah did her best to answer and soon, both she and Morgan had been whisked inside the grounds. Guards had been sent out to purge the city of the gang that had put their Lady through so much, and workmen were sent to clear the rubble and fetch Hint's body. As Sarah lay in bed, watching the healers working over Morgan, she saw him breathing, and she finally felt her sadness abate somewhat.

Today she'd lost a father figure and loyal servant, but she'd gained a friend. She was sure that if there was a heaven, Hint was smiling down on her, glad to see his birthday wish for her finally come true.

41

Sarah looked up from her book as a portal opened in the middle of the room and Morgan walked through. His armor was all scratched up, and there was a trail of dried blood running down from both his ears, but otherwise, he looked to be unhurt.

"Well, don't you just look peachy," Sarah said, as the portal closed behind him and Morgan tucked away the key.

He grinned at her and walked over to flop down on one of the couches.

"You won't believe what happened to me in there," he said, kicking his boots off and sticking his feet up on the couch.

"Really?" she asked, turning to face him with a raised eyebrow. "And what might that be?"

Morgan then spent the next ten minutes shattering every belief she'd once held, about how abilities worked. By the time he was finished speaking, Sarah was on the edge of her seat, wracking her mind to find any way she could become an evolved mage.

"Did Dabu mention any limitations on evolving?" she asked. "Like only being able to evolve during a breakthrough?"

"Not that I can remember," he said with a shrug.

Sarah nodded, mind going over all the information he'd just given her and trying to piece something together. Then she remembered something Samuel had told her before he'd left them in the *Beast Zone*."

"I think Samuel hinted at this when we last saw him," she said with a grin.

"Really?" Morgan asked, sitting up a bit in his seat.

"Yeah. He said that the true path to power does not lie in merely *ranking up*," Sarah said, repeating what the god had said, word for word.

"Why didn't you mention this before?" he asked, quirking a brow.

Sarah shrugged.

"Guess I didn't really think it was that important."

Morgan grunted in reply, then slumped down into the couch.

"I just wish there was a way to figure out how much energy I need to become an intermediate supermage," Morgan idly said.

Starbreak

Sarah sat bolt upright at this, eyes going wide as all her scattered thoughts finally came together.

"Say that again," she said, prompting Morgan to give her a strange look.

She glared at him, and after a few seconds of staring he finally relented.

"I wish there was a way to figure out how much energy I'd need, to become an intermediate supermage," he robotically repeated.

He raised an eyebrow as Sarah's grin widened, and she stood to begin pacing.

"What?" he asked, wondering what she could have figured out.

"How do you know that energy is the path to evolving again?" she asked.

"I don't," Morgan said with a shrug, "I just assumed it was, because of how much energy it cost for me to evolve."

"But it makes sense that it *would* be an energy requirement, though!" Sarah exclaimed.

"Even if it was," Morgan said, "how would you know how much was needed, and how would you even apply the energy?"

His interest was piqued. Sarah wouldn't be talking about this unless she thought she'd figured it out, and he was eager to hear her thoughts.

She stopped her pacing and her grin grew even wider.

"You said that when you ranked up, you got a prompt asking you where you would like to distribute your attributes. Correct?"

Morgan nodded.

"Then it stands to reason that you should be able to apply energy toward your ability if you focus on it."

Morgan's eyebrows shot up and he quickly dug into his pocket to retrieve a core. It was from a razor-shell tortoise and had a little over 10,000 energy. He looked up at Sarah, who nodded eagerly, and motioned for him to get on with it. Doing as Sarah had suggested, Morgan focused on absorbing the energy, but he visualized putting the energy towards advancing his ability, rather than ranking up. To his complete and utter shock, a screen actually popped up before his eyes, giving him the option to do so.

Aaron Oster

Evolved Supermage: Rank - 20 - 55/3,800,000

Would you like to apply 10,022 energy from razor-shell tortoise core towards your ability?

Yes/No

Morgan immediately hit yes, watching as the energy transferred to his ability, bringing him that much closer to his next evolution. He felt the core crumble in his hand, and only then remembered where he was sitting. Closing the screen, he looked down to see a small leather square sitting on his lap. He looked up, and judging by Sarah's smug look, he knew she'd thought ahead where he hadn't.

Normally it would annoy him, but right now he was too excited.

"You were right!" he said, a wide grin spreading across his face. "The cost is astronomical! Ten times more than it was when I moved to *rank 19*, but now I know how to advance my ability!"

Sarah's smug look grew, if at all possible, even smugger. She nodded in a very self-satisfied way and stuck her hand out.

"Give me a core. I wanna try."

Morgan was only too glad to comply, pulling a core from his pocket and handing it over. A look of concentration overtook her face as she focused in on the core. She stood there for a good five minutes without any change, before letting out an explosive string of curses and tossed the core back to him.

"Of course it wouldn't be that easy!" she exclaimed, letting out another long and very explicit string of cursing that made even Morgan quirk an eyebrow.

"You alright?" he asked, trying to hide a grin and failing miserably.

"No! I'm not, Morgan!" she yelled, plopping back down in her seat and looking quite sullen. "Here I was, thinking that I might be able to find a way to evolve, and it just refuses to work!"

She glared at him, as though it were his fault that it wouldn't work for her, when it had for him.

"Don't blame me," Morgan said. "If it were that easy to evolve, don't you think everyone would know how to do it by now?"

Sarah thought about it and eventually nodded.

"I only evolved by accident," Morgan continued. "I don't even know how it happened, or if this was just part of the modifications done to me by whoever messed with my brain."

Sarah nodded again, and the two of them fell into a contemplative silence, as they both bent their minds towards figuring out what the issue could be.

"What were Dabu's exact words regarding the evolution of mages and supers?" Sarah finally asked.

"He said that everyone's path to evolution was different. That it was the main reason why no one even knows about it because the only people who evolved have done so by accident."

Sarah nodded slowly, thinking over the events leading up to Morgan's evolution, and a crazy idea began to take shape in her mind.

"If we went into another *Beast Zone* right now, how much rest will we need before tonight's attack?" she asked, sitting up again and feeling her heart rate increase at the sheer stupidity of what she was about to suggest.

Morgan checked the clock against the far wall, surprised that it was still relatively early.

"It's not even eleven yet." He shrugged. "I'd say that we'd probably only need about three hours rest, so it's doable. Why? Did you want to get in a little extra training?" Morgan asked, the usual battle hungry grin coming to his face.

"Something like that," Sarah said, getting up and heading to change. "I want you to try and find a key to an *advanced zone*. I know that there should be a few in the pouch, and there might be one that's on our level."

Morgan's eyebrows shot up for what felt like the hundredth time that morning.

"Who are you and what have you done with Sarah?" he asked.

Normally he was the crazy one.

Sarah flashed him a grin, but left his question unanswered.

Morgan just shook his head, but headed to the room while Sarah headed to change.

"Oh, one last thing," Sarah called out, getting his attention before he went into the room.

"Try and see if you can find a healer for when we get back. I have a feeling we might need one!"

***

Morgan looked around at their new surroundings, getting a strange foreboding feeling. The landscape before them was blackened and charred, and he could see a smoking volcano in the distance. He looked over at Sarah and saw the same look of unease he felt reflected on her face.

He'd managed to find a *rank 22 advanced beast zone* key. It hadn't been hard to find, as all *advanced zone* keys were black, instead of silver, and marked with red numbers. He'd contacted Katherine and told her of their intentions, asking her to send a healer to wait for them. She'd tried to talk him out of it, but Sarah had insisted and Morgan wasn't about to let her go in alone. After a few minutes of argument, Katherine had finally relented, sending for a healer she trusted.

She'd wanted to come with, but was otherwise occupied. She did scold them both for being so reckless and putting the whole plan at risk. After she'd cut the connection, Morgan had given Sarah an odd look. This was very unlike her. She was normally the one who preached caution, and here she was, throwing herself into an extremely dangerous situation without explaining why.

"I know that I'm not supposed to be the voice of reason, but I don't think this is a good idea," Morgan said, feeling the somehow oppressive feeling of this zone bearing down on him.

This place was filled with beasts that they could technically defeat, but they would all be either intermediate or advanced beasts. This meant that every single fight would be extremely difficult, if not outright deadly.

Sarah grimaced, but just shook her head.

"This is necessary. Just trust me on that."

Morgan hesitantly nodded.

She'd gone along with almost all of his insane ideas, so he would support her in this, no matter how much his instincts screamed for him to leave.

"There's a healer waiting for us, correct?" she asked, and Morgan noticed a slight tremor in her voice.

Morgan nodded. He'd seen her come in right as he was stepping through the portal.

"Good," she said, blowing out a breath. "Good." She said this as though giving herself courage for what they were about to do.

"Alight," she said, voice just a bit too loud for Morgan's comfort. "Let's go."

Morgan nodded, immediately using his *storm blade* and forming a lance of whirling purple and gold. Sarah jumped at the sudden sound of rushing air and glared at him before turning her attention forward again.

She's really on edge, Morgan thought, walking just behind and to the right of her. His eyes started scanning their surroundings for any sign of movement. The crunching sound of the porous stone underfoot was the only sound they made as they waded deeper into the *advanced zone.*

Every time Morgan thought he saw something, his heart would jump into his throat. After the fifth time this happened, he forced himself to take a few deep breaths.

He was too much on edge. His muscles were tensed and his breathing irregular. He had to relax, otherwise, he wouldn't be able to fight at peak performance when they did eventually run into something.

Just as he'd managed to get his heart rate down, Sarah abruptly halted, forcing Morgan to stop as well.

"What is it?" he asked, but as he looked past her, it became glaringly obvious as to why she'd stopped.

A massive lumbering creature crested the rise ahead of them, and Morgan felt his recently slowed heart rate spike in fear. Every instinct in his body screamed at him all at once.

This was not a beast they should be fighting. They should just open the portal right now and leave.

Then the beast let out a roar that shook them both down to their very cores and charged.

42

"Morgan," Sarah said, her voice carrying an edge of panic. "What are we looking at?" She was already conjuring two *ice golems* and sent them to hold off the monster.

The beast was huge and had a vaguely bearlike face, but that was about the only similarity it had to one. In fact, the dire-flame bear they'd fought back in the North Kingdom was just a cuddly puppy compared to this monstrosity.

It was massive, quite a bit larger than the aforementioned bear. Standing around fourteen feet at the shoulder and at over twenty feet long, the beast was extremely intimidating. Its fur was colored a deep black, streaked through with a swirling pattern of red and orange. Its body was a mix of ape and wolf, and it ran forward with the gait of an ape.

Its front paws were a pair of massive fists, and Morgan could spot the glint of metallic claws every time it lifted them. The rear wolf's paws didn't look any less terrifying. Pitch black, with lines of red swirling through in a flame-like pattern, they were tipped with a gleaming pair of red claws that glowed with an eerie light. As it drew nearer, he could begin to see the rippling muscle that covered it from head to toe.

The beast had the massive biceps and pectoral muscles of an ape, and he could see them rippling and flexing with each step. It roared again as the *ice golems* crashed into it, slowing it for only a moment. Then it swung out with a glowing red fist, shattering both constructs into a million tiny fragments. Then it turned its gleaming blue eyes on them, its shortened bear-ape muzzle bunching up in a snarl.

"Morgan! Stop admiring the damn thing and tell me what we're fighting!"

Morgan was snapped out of his stupor as Sarah shouted at him, sending another pair of *ice golems* at the beast.

"Right. Sorry," he sheepishly said, using *aura sense* on the beast.

Name: Chimera-flame ape
Rank - 21

Ability type - Super

A red light flared around the beast as he examined it, and judging by its density, as well as the monster's appearance, Morgan had no doubt in his mind that they were facing an advanced beast.

And one that was a full rank above him, and two above Sarah.

Morgan answered Sarah's question as the ape tore through the newest set of golems and continued on towards them.

"So, you got a plan?" Morgan asked. This was her idea, after all.

"Yes," Sarah answered, lifting her arms and grimacing for a moment.

Morgan was about to ask what she was doing when a massive block of ice began rapidly forming the air. His eyes widened as he realized she was using her most powerful skill right at the start.

Likely trying to end the fight quickly, he thought, watching the iceberg growing larger and larger by the second. He just hoped it would be enough.

Morgan saw the ape's eyes flick upward, then it stopped its charge. It rose on its hind legs, letting out a massive bellow and pounded its chest in challenge, sending huge shock waves over the open area between them.

Its entire body began glowing red, then it crashed back on all fours and ran towards them, now twice as fast as before.

"Shit!" Sarah yelled, seeing that she wouldn't have her attack ready in time.

"I'll try and buy you a few seconds!" Morgan yelled, flashing past her and activating *advanced flight.*

As he drew near the ape, he simultaneously used *gravity impact* and *explosive movement.* Time slowed to a crawl, and he lunged for the ape's neck with his lance, charging it with lightning as he closed the distance. Purple and gold electricity flared across his lance just before impact, and Morgan was sure the attack would do some significant damage.

Advanced beast or not, his attack would probably be strong enough to kill someone even over rank 29. Probably.

But his attack didn't hit its intended target. Morgan's eyes widened as the ape's glowing blue orbs suddenly swiveled, locking onto him. Then it shifted its body, not quickly enough to completely avoid the attack, but enough to avoid a fatal blow.

Morgan's lightning charged lance punched into the ape's shoulder, tearing a bloody chunk from its hide and sending lightning coursing through its body. Morgan could already tell that the wound was superficial for a beast this size. He felt his skill timer run out, and just managed to throw his shield up before a massive glowing red fist collided with the side of his head.

That one punch was enough to completely shatter his shield and send him flying more than a hundred yards through the air. He let out a pained gasp, as he heard a loud crunch when his body slammed into the rocky ground. The sharp stones turned into razors, slicing through his armor, and opening deep gouges in his skin as he bounced and rolled. He grunted in pain as his body finally came to a rest, and he began doing a mental check of his faculties.

Both his arms and legs still worked, so at least there was that, but his entire body was covered in bruises and lesions. He was fairly certain that a couple of ribs were broken and judging by the blood pumping from his head, he may very well have a skull fracture.

He winced, getting slowly to his feet and examining the damage that had been done.

Yup. He looked as bad as he felt.

His armor was completely shredded, the metal plates being the only part that still looked to be functional. He winced, feeling gingerly at his skull and finding the tender spot where the ape's fist had connected.

If I hadn't thrown my shield up, that one attack would have blown my skull to bits, Morgan thought, as he tore one of the shredded sleeves off and wrapped it tightly around his head. He was still a bit groggy, which meant that he likely had a concussion on top of everything else.

Sarah was definitely going to need to make this up to him when… Sarah!

Morgan's eyes snapped to where his friend was now facing down the towering ape alone, the massive block of ice hovering up in the air between them. Sarah's face was pale but determined. She screamed something at the ape, likely some expletive about its mother, then brought her arms down, sending the massive iceberg at the towering beast.

***

Sarah watched Morgan's body go skipping across the ground, in a similar fashion to a stone skipped over a pond and felt her heart seize up. Then she shook herself. Morgan would be fine. He'd survived worse than that, and she had something to finish.

The ape turned to her then, and reared up again, pounding its glowing fists into its chest. Sarah felt her skill finish charging then and shouted back.

"Take this, you overgrown ass! It'll probably improve your looks!"

Sarah knew that what she'd said made absolutely no sense, but she was so full of adrenaline that she could barely think straight, let alone come up with a proper insult for the towering monster.

She brought her arms down, sending the massive ice block crashing down on the ape. She watched with a sense of pride as the huge mass of ice and freezing water crashed down on top of the roaring ape, burying it in more than ten tons of the stuff. She sagged slightly as the skill released, and was forced to lock her knees to prevent them from buckling.

She'd used nearly all her mana on that attack. She just hoped it had been enough to kill it, or at least weaken it enough that Morgan could finish it off.

She watched the ice block tear a massive furrow through the ground, as momentum drove it forward. She then turned to see what had happened to Morgan and felt a huge sense of relief as she spotted him on his feet. He looked quite worse for wear, but he was alive.

She grinned at him, but he didn't grin back. She watched as his eyes widened and he launched himself in her direction. Sarah activated her shield, blue light flaring around her, even as she turned to face what she knew to be coming. A glowing red fist crashed into her right side, and pain, like she'd never felt before in her life, flared throughout her body.

She screamed as her shield shattered under the monstrous force of the attack and she felt bones beneath grind and snap. The next moment, her broken body was sailing through the air, barely conscious. *This shitty plan better work,* was her last coherent thought before she passed out.

***

Morgan, who had a better view of the ape, saw Sarah's attack hit, but her aim seemed to have been slightly off. Instead of burying the ape under the ice, it hit the ground just a foot away from it. The momentum from the gigantic block, as well as the protruding icicles were enough to cause some damage, but it was not nearly the devastating attack that it should have been.

Sarah looked over at him and grinned, but he could already see that the ape had worked itself free of the attack and was sprinting towards her, streaming blood from numerous cuts, but still very much alive.

He launched himself at her, desperately trying to use *explosive movement*, but it was still on cooldown for the next 5 seconds. He growled in annoyance, feeling his heart leap into his throat as he watched Sarah's shield flare the second before the ape's fist connected with the side of her head. He watched in horror as her body was sent flying through the air in a similar manner to his, but she was undoubtedly far more hurt than he had been.

Her ability didn't lend itself to soaking up attacks the way his did, so the attack would have done a lot more damage to her much more fragile body. Morgan clenched his teeth, forcing his burning legs to move faster as he launched himself into the air, catching the ape in the side of the head and sending it flying.

He thought he'd heard a crunch when his foot connected, but he didn't look. Having used the ape as a springboard and launching himself in Sarah's direction, he used *advanced flight*, rocketing toward Sarah's broken form. He managed to catch her right before she hit the ground, grunting as her weight slammed into him.

He drifted slowly down and placed her gently on the ground, feeling his heart seize up as he brushed her blood-soaked hair away from her face. Her eyes were closed, her face matted with blood, and her body twisted in a way that made his stomach clench in sudden fear.

He quickly placed his head to her chest, grabbing at her wrist at the same time to feel for a pulse. He waited for what felt like hours, but in reality were just seconds, hoping to hear something. Finally, when he was about to lose hope, he heard a slow thump, followed by a light pulse under his fingers.

He blew out a sigh of relief, feeling the fear that had been closing like an icy claw around his heart ease somewhat. He quickly straightened, pulling the portal key from his pocket.

She might still be alive, but she wouldn't be for too much longer if he didn't get her to the healer quickly.

He was about to stick the key into the air, when a bellow of rage caught his attention. Turning his head, he saw the ape charging at him once more, blood streaming from where his foot had impacted. In a split second, Morgan realized that he wouldn't have enough time to open the portal and get them through before the ape reached them. Then he felt something that he never thought he'd feel again. Rage.

Boiling anger started up in his chest and quickly spread through his entire body. He stood from Sarah's prone form, vision becoming red tinged around the edges, and his pulse pounding in his ears.

This ape had nearly killed Sarah, and now it was trying to prevent him from saving her. No one would hurt her like that and get away with it. He would show this beast who the real monster here was.

Morgan let out a roar, loud enough to match even that of the ape's. He didn't know it, as he couldn't see, but his body began to give off a bright purple and gold glow that had nothing to do with his shield. The ape actually faltered for a second as it beheld the glowing human before it. Its instincts warned it that this was a rival predator, one with far more power than its own, but the magic of the *zone* quickly overrode those instincts and the ape roared back, continuing its charge.

Morgan flashed forward, covering the distance far quicker than should have been possible without the aid of his skill. He slammed a glowing fist into the ape's abdomen and he felt bones crack under that blow, but the ape roared. Striking back, it sent its claw-tipped fingers tearing into Morgan's exposed skin, and began ripping massive chunks of bloody flesh from his side.

Morgan ignored the horrendous injury, spinning in place and slamming his leg into the ape's grounded arm. There was a loud

Aaron Oster

crunch as the limb snapped, and Morgan grinned, his blood-flecked face appearing almost demonic as he did so. The ape bellowed, staggering back and clutching at its broken limb.

It stared at the human in incomprehension. Its instincts told it that the animal before it should be close to death after all the damage it had inflicted, but it appeared to be whole and undamaged.

Morgan roared again, reiki and divine energy mixing together in a glowing sphere before him and blasting out in a wide cone. The ape roared back, rearing up on its hind legs and baring its chest. It opened its mouth, using another ability, this one from its wolf aspect. A glowing lance of freezing flames shot from its mouth. The two attacks collided, sending smaller beams firing off in all directions.

A ring of blue flames sprang up around the pair, burning with such intense heat, that the stone itself caught aflame. Where the ape's flames touched, the ground writhed with blue fire, and the stone melted and solidified under the intense heat and coldness. When Morgan's attack hit, the ground exploded, sending showers of shrapnel in all directions. The ape roared and intensified its attack and Morgan yelled back, grinning madly the entire time. He let off on his attack and allowed the ape's beam to come flying at him, then he ducked under it, flashing forward in an instant and stopping before the ape.

Both his fists glowed with gold and violet light, then he slammed both palms into the ape's chest. The ape roared in pain as a ripple flowed out from where his hands had made contact. Morgan stared it straight in the eye, meeting the ape's blue ones with his mismatched gold and purple ones. His wild grin widened and he said one word.

"Die!"

The voice that came from his mouth sounded nothing like his usual one. It was high pitched and reeked of madness.

The ape only had the chance to roar one more time before two massive holes were punched straight through its chest and out its back, twin beams of gold and purple emerging from the other side. The ape staggered back, with blood streaming out of its chest. It stared down in incomprehension as Morgan's fist slammed into its chest one last time. His hand came back clutching something that glittered blue and red, and the beast crashed to the ground, dead.

Morgan stared down at the glittering core in his hands, then tossed it over his shoulder. His heart racing, his body thrumming with power and the mad grin still plastered on his face.

This wasn't enough. He had to do more. He had to kill more!

He turned, looking for something else to fight when his eyes landed on Sarah's prone form. Her body flashed blue in his vision, and his grin widened.

Another challenger! And a powerful one at that!

He took a step toward her, preparing a glowing sphere of gold and violet in his hand, when a heard a voice off to his left.

"My, my. It would appear that you're progressing nicely, but I can't have you killing her just yet. We still need her alive."

Morgan's eyes landed on a woman standing just a hundred feet from him. Long black hair was whipped around a heart-shaped face by a breeze that had sprung up around her. Bright green eyes showed through the dark strands of her hair, and her red painted lips were turned up in a smirk.

Her aura flashed gold and black to his vision, and Morgan grinned, turning away from the much weaker opponent to his back, and faced his new opponent.

She was strong. Stronger than anyone he'd ever met. Killing her would be fun!

He let out a loud cackle and launched himself at her, using the same attack he had used earlier. Gathering his power around himself, he used a tremendous amount of gravitational force to warp the space between them and appeared before her in an instant, slamming a glowing fist right into her face.

"Are you quite finished?"

Morgan pulled his fist back to see the woman regarding him with a bored expression. She was completely unharmed, but instead of deterring him, this only encouraged him more.

"Not even close!" he yelled, then unleashed a barrage of attacks, each one aimed at a vital area.

The woman watched him in amusement. On anyone else, these would be crippling blows, but not to her.

Morgan pulled his fist back for another attack, just as the woman finally struck back with two simple movements. She knocked his fist casually to the side, then flicked him in the center of his forehead. She was careful to hold back, but the blow still sent him flying with enough force to break the sound barrier.

She let out a long sigh as Morgan's body tore a long furrow in the ground, finally coming to rest near his friend's still unconscious form.

Should have kept a closer eye on him, she thought, walking over to him and examining his unconscious form. She wouldn't make that mistake again.

She bent down, retrieving the key from his pocket and opening the portal back to Katherine's room.

At least the girl had had the foresight to get a healer ahead of time. She could spot her waiting on the other side, ready to tend to them as soon as they came through.

She squatted, getting a grip under both their collars and hauling them up off the ground. She saw a glittering core lying on the ground, and levitated it off the ground and into Morgan's pocket. She took one more look down at him. His features had returned to normal and his core looked to have calmed down.

She grimaced as she tossed them both through the portal, throwing the key in after them.

He wouldn't remember the fight, but the skill would show up in his status as soon as he opened it. She just hoped he wouldn't use it again before he could control it. She'd worked too hard to have him ruin all her plans now.

She silently cursed at the rules that wouldn't allow her to block the skill, knowing that she'd already stretched them as far as he'd allow.

She took one last look through the portal, seeing a very confused looking healer tending to both Morgan and Sarah. The next moment, the portal snapped shut, cutting them off from her sight.

She took one last look at the damage Morgan had done to the beast and felt her sour mood lift slightly.

At least she now had a small taste of the kind of power he'd be able to wield in the future.

43

Morgan slowly came to, feeling a warm sensation running through his body. Squinting his eyes, the healer that Katherine had sent for slowly came into view. He blinked a few times, focusing in on the woman for a few seconds, confused as to where he was.

"What happened?" he asked, sitting up and examining himself, noticing the state of his armor.

"You tell me," the woman said. "The two of you came through the portal not five minutes ago. You were both unconscious and your friend over there was in pretty rough shape."

Morgan looked over to see Sarah sitting with her back against one of the couches. She had her knees pulled up, arms wrapped around them and hiding her face behind them.

"I'm not sure," Morgan said, feeling gingerly at his head.

He remembered bits and pieces of the fight, but it was so disjointed that he couldn't make any sense of it.

The healer gave him an understanding look.

"Head injuries often result in short-term amnesia. Don't worry, though. It'll come back to you," she said, patting him lightly on the arm.

She rose to her feet and headed to the door.

"Wait," Morgan called out, as she was opening the door.

The woman stopped, turning to give him a questioning look.

"Thank you," Morgan said. "Can I have your name?"

The woman smiled at him but shook her head before leaving, closing the door behind her with a click.

Morgan stared after her for a few seconds before shrugging. Some people preferred to keep to themselves. He wouldn't fault her for doing what he'd done many times before.

He then noticed that Sarah had lowered her knees to the floor and was looking at him with a guilty expression.

"What?" he asked, rising to his feet and going over to sit next to her on the floor.

The fight was still disjointed, especially towards the end, but it was slowly coming back to him.

"I'm sorry."

Her voice was so low that he could barely hear her.

Aaron Oster

"For what?" he asked, genuinely confused.

She motioned to the state of his clothes.

"You must have been pretty badly hurt for your clothes to look like that."

Morgan shrugged.

"So were you," he said, gesturing to her equally tattered clothes, surprised that she wasn't attempting to cover herself up more, with the state her clothes were in.

"Yeah, but it's my fault. I dragged you in there, knowing that I'd be horribly hurt, and you'd need to finish the beast off on your own." She buried her face in her knees again, as Morgan tried to wrap his head around what she was saying.

"I don't understand. We both knew we would be hurt, that's why we had a healer waiting."

But Sarah was already shaking her head.

"I went in planning on getting hurt. I thought that your near-death experience might have been what caused your evolution, so I decided to try it for myself."

Morgan's eyes widened when he heard this. Was that why she'd insisted on trying to kill the ape herself?

"You know that my near death experience only came *after* I discovered the massive energy cost to my next *rank*."

Sarah bit her lip, then slowly nodded, burying her face into her knees once more.

How could she have been so stupid?

A memory flashed through Morgan's mind, of Sarah's attack missing the ape by a hair, just injuring instead of killing it.

"Did it work?" he asked, prompting Sarah to look up in surprise.

He could see tears at the corners of her eyes and understood that she felt responsible for his injuries, but it made no sense. He'd gone in there willingly, so she had nothing to feel guilty about.

"Aren't you angry at me?" she asked.

Morgan shrugged.

"It's not your fault. I went in willingly. It was a stupid plan, but if it worked, then it might have been worth it."

Sarah flinched a bit at his admonishment. He didn't raise his voice or even say it in an accusatory tone, but it hit her hard all the same.

"I don't know," she said with a shrug.

Morgan dug into his pocket to retrieve his last core and was surprised when he came out with two.

He must have killed the ape and taken its core, though he couldn't remember doing it.

He handed one of the cores over to her.

"Will this be enough to get you to the next *rank*?" he asked.

Sarah took it and examined the core for a second, then nodded.

She was about to absorb the core, when Morgan stopped her.

"Don't wanna make a mess," he said with a grin, rising from his seated position and going to get the folded square of leather.

When he came back, he was relieved to see that her mood had improved somewhat, and she gave him a weak smile as he placed the leather on her lap. She turned her attention back to the core, taking a deep breath before absorbing its energy. The core crumbled and Sarah's body shuddered with the *rank up*.

"So?" Morgan eagerly asked.

Sarah's eyes flickered through the air as she read over her status, and slowly, a smile spread across her face.

"It worked!" she said, closing her status and beaming up at him.

"How do you know?" he asked, not noticing any physical changes.

"I haven't evolved yet, but the energy cost to my next *rank* jumped from 80,000 to 320,000!"

Morgan noted that the cost of evolving a mage ability seemed to be less than that of a supermage ability, though it did make sense.

"So, all we need to do is gather enough energy to get you to *rank 21*," Morgan said, examining the core clutched between his fingers.

In truth, he'd wanted to use the energy for himself, but the amount contained in this core would be significant and would help Sarah on her path to evolution.

Before he handed it over, though, he opened its stats so he could check something that Dabu had mentioned.

Name: Chimera-flame ape core
Rank - 21

Aaron Oster

Total available energy: 42,217/42,217
Total available AP: 12/12

This core was taken from a chimera-flame ape. As this core was taken from an advanced beast, the amount of available energy has been massively increased.

Morgan grinned as he saw that Dabu had been telling the truth. He could let Sarah have the energy, but he would take the attribute points before handing it over. He remembered that the azure-crystal wyvern core had shattered when he'd absorbed all its energy and he had a feeling that it had had a few attribute points as well.

He focused in on the attribute points and thought about absorbing them.

Would you like to absorb 12 AP from the chimera-flame ape core?

Yes/No

Hitting yes, Morgan saw the *AP* go down to zero. He held his breath for a moment, but thankfully, the core didn't shatter. He'd been afraid it might, but even if it had, it would have been worth it. The *AP* in the core was far more valuable to him than the energy would have been.

"Here," he said, handing the core over to Sarah with a grin. "I think this should be yours. It'll definitely help you to your next *rank.*"

Sarah took the core and let out an excited gasp, absorbing it immediately, and she started going through her status.

Seeing that she was now busy with her status, Morgan decided that he'd use the *AP* he'd received from the core. Grinning to himself at the thought of upgrading one of his skills, Morgan thought about using the *AP* he'd collected, and a status screen flickered into view.

You have 12 attribute points to distribute. Would you like to distribute them now?

Yes/No

Mentally selecting *yes*, Morgan watched as a new screen popped up.

Strength - 119
Agility - 150
Constitution - 135
Intelligence - 126
Wisdom - 126

Morgan stared at his attributes, extremely confused by what he was seeing.

All his attributes had dropped by 2 points each. This had to be some kind of mistake.

He decided to look at his skills, hoping that they might have some kind of answer for him.

Skills:
Advanced flight - 1/10
Gravity impact - 4/10
Explosive movement - 1/10
Storm blade - 1/10

Divine:
Shock-blast - 1/15
Rage of the Gods - 5/1,000

Traits:
Gravity field - 1/30
Recovery - 1/30
Aura sense (inherited) - 4/50

Extra:
Gravity storm (2nd category) - 1/20
Starbreak - 1/30

Aaron Oster

Morgan's eyes widened when he saw the new skill and immediately examined it for more information.

Rage of the Gods - Reiki and divine power flood your body, massively increasing all of your stats (Currently X5). Your body will also rapidly regenerate any damage done to it, so long as your heart remains undamaged. The strain of the power on your mind will cause you to lose control and attack anything in sight (increasing your intelligence may help to mitigate this effect). You are unable to use skills while this skill is active, but you gain the ability to use pure reiki and divine power.
Cost - (-2) AP to all stats
Duration - N/A

Morgan gawked.

Was this what had happened in the beast zone? Had he somehow activated this skill and beaten the ape?

He clutched at his head as everything suddenly snapped into place. Everything up until the point where he'd turned to face the ape after it had attacked Sarah. After that, everything was a blank.

How had he stopped once he'd activated the skill? According to the description, it didn't have a timer, which meant he would have kept rampaging after the ape was dead. He then remembered what the healer had said.

She'd said that they both came through unconscious, which could only mean that someone had stopped him.

Morgan felt a chill run down his spine.

Someone had stopped him, but who?

He shook himself, dispelling the sudden feeling of unease that had settled over him.

Whoever it was, he either owed them or should be afraid of them. Regardless of which it was, he had a feeling he'd be finding out soon enough.

He took a few minutes to carefully re-read the skill description, which was by far the most informative out of any of his skills. From what he could see, the skill was the most powerful one in his entire arsenal. It would quintuple all of his stats, making him five times as powerful as he was now. It would also rapidly heal him, so he could take on grievous injuries and continue on fighting.

Losing *2 AP* from each attribute would have been rough, but so long as he had a core to replenish them, it could have been manageable. If he would lose his mind every time he used it, though, it wasn't worth it.

He blew out a long breath, then used *10* of his *AP* to restore his attributes to where they were before, watching sadly as his available points dropped to *2*. He then dropped into his *gravity impact,* bringing it to *6/10.*

If worst came to worst, then he could always upgrade when he *ranked up* next time. He then took a look at his status to see what changes had occurred.

Name: Morgan
Evolved Supermage: Rank - 20
Energy to next rank - 4,701/109,000
Ability - Divine Gravity & Air
RP - 1,280/1,280 (Regen - 12.8 per second)
DV - 30/30 (Regen - 0.3 per minute)
Strength - 136
Agility - 152
Constitution - 137
Intelligence - 128
Wisdom - 128
Skills - Advanced flight, Gravity impact, Explosive movement, Storm blade
Divine - Shock-blast, Rage of the Gods
Traits - Gravity field, Recovery, Aura sense (inherited)
Extra - Gravity storm (2nd category), Starbreak

It looked the same as last time, but now there was the added *rage of the gods* skill. His *divine energy* had also increased for some reason, which he could only assume had something to do with using his new skill.

The skill was extremely powerful, and the cost to upgrade it was astronomical compared to the rest, which made him wonder if upgrading the skill would give him conscious control over it. Then again, the skill had said that increasing his intelligence would help with that. He just wondered by how much.

Aaron Oster

He blew out a long breath, sighing for what felt like the tenth time in the last minute.

"Is something wrong?" Sarah asked.

She'd closed her status and was watching him with a worried expression. Morgan debated keeping it to himself, but decided that if he could trust anyone, it would be Sarah. They had gone through an awful lot together, and she might have some insight into his new skill.

By the time Morgan had finished explaining, Sarah was staring wide-eyed. Then she put on a mock scowl and let out a loud huff.

"Every time I catch up, you get some cool new power that pushes you far ahead. It's not fair!" she exclaimed, kicking her feet in a way that he hadn't seen her do since the day they'd met.

Morgan snorted, then began laughing. Sarah glared at him for a few more seconds, then joined him, leaning against him and laughing right along with him.

Morgan felt his worries melting away as he sat on the floor of Princess Katherine's room in the North Kingdom palace.

He might not know what would happen next. He wasn't even sure if they would survive the next 48 hours, but right now, everything was okay.

***

It was nearly four o'clock when a portal opened in the center of the room and Gold stepped through, followed closely by Katherine.

Morgan had been doing push-ups in the far corner, while Sarah had been reading. They both stopped what they'd been doing as soon as the portal appeared.

"Oh good. You're both awake!" Gold said, striding up to a couch and unceremoniously plopping down into it.

"I don't understand where you get the idea of us being so lazy," Sarah replied, her lips pinched in annoyance.

"Well, if I recall correctly, you two were always sleeping when I came to get you for our afternoon lessons," Gold replied with a grin.

"That was because we were exhausted from the torture you called training, you sick bastard!" Sarah exclaimed, slamming her fist down on the table.

"Now there's the Sarah we all know and love!" Gold exclaimed, kicking off his boots and propping his feet up on the couch.

Sarah's eye had actually begun twitching and Katherine mercifully cut in.

"There's no time for whatever this is," she said, as Morgan approached.

He was covered in a light sheen of sweat, which Sarah found surprising as he'd been going at it for nearly an hour.

Wasn't he tired after the day they'd had? How could he keep going?

They'd already changed and had decided to keep what had happened to themselves, once again deciding not to trust anyone else, unless Dabu decided to pop by for another visit.

She'd never met the man, but she really hoped she'd be able to soon.

She was snapped from her thoughts as Katherine continued speaking.

"We have plans to discuss, so if you'll please all sit down, we can begin."

Gold spread his arms out, motioning to his sprawled out position on the couch, prompting a snort from Sarah and an eye roll from Katherine.

Morgan took a seat on a plush chair, wiping his brow with a towel and waiting for Katherine to begin.

"I just heard back from my informant in the guild. The attack on Arnold will be happening tonight. They have indeed tracked him to the South Kingdom border and plan to ambush him on an abandoned stretch of road near the border wall."

"Glad to hear some good news," Sarah said.

She'd been wanting to see Arnold dead for years now and was glad that someone was going after him in force, even if it was the Assassins Guild.

"Yes, that traitor should be dead by the end of the night, which brings us to our plans for tonight. Unfortunately, I cannot go with you, as I'm still trying to reach my contacts in the other kingdoms. Lucky for us, Gold has agreed to join you two."

They both looked to Gold, who twiddled his fingers at them in reply.

"Do you have any information on what kind of opposition we'll be facing?" Morgan asked.

"As far as I can tell, there will only be a total of eight guards in the compound between eight and nine o'clock tonight. We estimate them to be from *ranks 25* to *32*, not including their current head, a woman by the name of Swan."

"That really isn't a whole lot of time," Morgan said, brows creasing. "Not to mention that we'll be severely outmatched."

"Aren't you forgetting someone?"

Morgan turned to see Gold, still twiddling his fingers with that same slightly sadistic smile on his face.

"How could we forget, with you interrupting every minute to remind us?" Sarah asked dryly.

"Yes. Gold will be there, so there's no need to worry about being overpowered. You will need to be careful not to trigger any alarms, though. You'll have to be quick and make sure none of them get the chance to alert the others."

Sarah and Morgan both nodded, and Katherine continued.

"We'll be going through a portal to another location in three hours' time. After which, I'll open a portal to the guild's headquarters. As soon as you've killed Swan, contact me, and I'll open a portal in your location. Every member of the Assassins Guild will know as soon as she's dead and will return to their headquarters, so it's vital that you don't delay for even a second."

It was a relatively simple plan, but simple plans were often the best. It left little room for a mistake, and if something went wrong, they could figure it out on the go.

"Now, for what will happen after," Katherine continued. "As we're working on such a tight schedule, we'll need to attack my father by tomorrow night. As it stands, we only have about 38 hours until this first Pinnacle King awakens. I'm not sure exactly what will happen when he does, but I'd rather not find out.

"As of right now, I've only managed to secure the help of two people," she said with a grimace. "All the others were too afraid to act this soon, so it looks like we won't have the support we need.

This will have to be done quickly so that there's no time for my father to react.

"Right now, we have the element of surprise, as he isn't counting on an attack from within his own forces. The plan is for me to portal straight in to give him a quick report. I do it all the time, so he won't be suspicious if I leave the portal open while we speak. Then, you'll come through. I have someone who will keep the attack silent, so as not to attract attention, but we'll have at least six guards who will be over *rank 40*, as well my father himself, who is at the *maximum rank* of *50*."

Morgan winced when he heard that.

"Do you really think we can beat those odds?" he asked.

Katherine shrugged.

"If I'm being perfectly honest, our chances of success aren't that great, but we don't have any other choice. Luckily for us, we'll have our own *maximum ranked* fighter coming along with us."

"Who?" Sarah asked, sitting up straighter in her seat.

"King Herald," Gold cut in with a grin. "I had a little chat with him last night while the two of you were being lazy. He normally wouldn't take this kind of risk, but apparently, Samuel's warning was a good enough cause for him to do it."

"If Herald is going, shouldn't he be able to bring along some of his guards?" Morgan asked.

Gold shook his head.

"According to his intelligence, Edmund is planning a massive raid on his camp tomorrow night. The timing couldn't have been worse."

"Yes, it's bad timing," Katherine said, "but tomorrow night is still our best chance. Since there will be that massive raid, the camp will be mostly empty. Not completely, mind you, but there will probably only be a token force of around a thousand or so."

"Oh, that's all good then!" Sarah replied sarcastically. "Only a thousand soldiers. We can take that many."

"As I said, we'll only need to deal with him and his guards."

"If I may ask, what's the point of us going along?" Morgan asked. "If all the guards will be over *rank 40*, then there really isn't much the two of us can do."

Aaron Oster

"You'll be our backup, in case anyone comes to visit while we're taking care of the king," Katherine replied. "It'll be four against six, so we'll have our hands full."

Morgan nodded. That made sense. They couldn't count on everything running smoothly, so they would bring the two of them along just in case.

"Are there any other questions? I haven't slept in four days and really need at least a few hours before tonight," Katherine said.

"Why do you need to sleep?" Gold asked, his innocent expression giving away his intention of a wisecrack before he even said it. "After all, you won't be doing anything tonight."

***

Morgan stepped through the swirling portal and emerged into a wooded clearing. He had no idea where he was, but apparently, this was the staging point for their assault on the guild. Katherine's informant had contacted her five minutes ago, saying that the compound had emptied out, and now they were preparing for the attack.

He pulled his magesteel gloves from his belt and began pulling them on, as Sarah, then Gold, stepped through the portal. A few seconds later, Katherine stepped through and the portal closed behind her.

They were all dressed for combat, aside from Katherine, and were already geared up for the attack.

"Where are we?" Morgan asked in a low voice.

He wasn't sure why, but he felt that speaking too loudly wasn't appropriate at a time like this.

"We're on the fringes of the Central Kingdom, near the border to the West. The Guild's main compound is located just a few miles east of here, but we're far enough away not to trip any alarms."

"Aren't you worried that your portal opening will trip some sort of alarm?" Morgan asked as she looked down to her wrist.

"As I said before, this normally wouldn't be possible, but we'll have a small window in which to get you in."

"How small are we talking?" Sarah asked.

She was wearing her tight-fitting armor and had her combat knife strapped to her belt.

"Ten seconds, but you shouldn't need more than that if you all go at once."

"You weren't kidding when you said the time frame was small," Gold said, talking at a regular volume.

Everyone winced, and they all turned to glare at him.

"What? You said that we were far enough away to avoid detection," he said with a shrug.

Sarah had opened her mouth to deliver what would likely be a stinging retort when Katherine suddenly held her hand up for silence. They stood like that for several seconds, then she lowered her hand and opened a portal.

"On my say, go in and move quickly."

They all nodded and Morgan could feel his heart rate increase with excitement.

He wondered what kind of enemies he'd get to face in there.

"Five, four, three, two... Now!" Katherine said, and Morgan lunged forward, darting through the portal before anyone else got the chance.

There was a moment of disorientation, then he was sprinting across an open field, toward a small shack. He wondered for a moment if they might have the wrong place, but suddenly he caught a flash of movement from the corner of his eye.

He rolled, avoiding something flying through the air at eye level, then sprang back up to his feet.

His eyes locked onto a black-clad figure, who was running at him and closing the gap with astonishing speed.

Wasn't this supposed to be an open window where they could get in?

Morgan quickly focused on the figure, using *aura sense.* Immediately, a blazing red aura surrounded the figure and letters floated up above his head.

Name: Melvin
Rank - 27
Ability type - Super

Aaron Oster

Morgan blinked, releasing the skill and gearing himself up for a fight. Then, something slammed into the man's side, hurling him through the air. He landed with a muffled thump a few hundred yards away and a massive ice block fell on his head.

He heard a sickening crunch, and knew the man had met his end. Looking over his shoulder, he saw Sarah giving him a self satisfied smirk, while Gold just shook his head.

Had Sarah really just taken out a rank 27 super in two blows?

Then he noticed the bloody stone spike sinking back into the ground to his left.

Now that made more sense.

"Where is the compound?" Morgan asked in a hushed tone, as Sarah and Gold jogged up to him.

"You're looking at it," Gold replied, pointing to the small shack.

"That's the headquarters of the largest guild in all the Five Kingdoms?" Sarah asked, incredulity written all over her face.

"No time to talk out in the open. Follow me, and I'll explain," Gold said, taking off at a sprint.

Sarah looked to Morgan and he shrugged, then took off after the man. Sarah let out a snort but followed all the same. It only took them about thirty seconds to reach the shack, and Gold stopped before the door, holding his hand up to stop them from advancing any more.

He pressed his ear to the door and waited for a few seconds, then straightened up and gently eased the door open.

"After you," he said, motioning them in.

Already being used to this from their time at the academy, both Sarah and Morgan walked into the small shack, still wondering how an entire clandestine organization would fit inside.

Their answer came the second they walked in. A long, concrete corridor stretched before them, continuing on for what seemed like miles.

"Yup, much bigger on the inside," Gold said, pulling the door shut behind them with a light click.

"Any idea where we're supposed to go?" Sarah asked.

"Only one tunnel," Gold said with a shrug.

Sarah glared at him, but Morgan placed a calming hand on her shoulder.

"He's right. We only have 55 minutes until our window close. We need to hurry."

Sarah nodded, deciding to save all of her aggravation for Gold until their mission was complete.

"Tread lightly if you can. Sound will carry for a good distance in here," Gold advised, then took off at a sprint down the tunnel, feet barely making a whisper on the ground as he went.

Morgan was quick to follow and Sarah was right on his heels. Neither of them was nearly as silent as Gold, but they moved with more stealth than would have been possible before their *rank ups*.

They ran on for a good five minutes, the concrete tunnel bare of anything other than small lamps set at intervals to light the long corridor. At last, Morgan could spot light up ahead, and Gold held up a hand, slowing their pace to a normal walk.

They crept to the end of the tunnel and placed their backs to the wall, then slowly peeked out. They saw a large concrete room, similar to the tunnel. It was mostly bare, with only a small table pushed up against one corner. This was likely a checkpoint and a way to make sure no one got in without permission.

The problem was that neither he nor Sarah could spot any way to continue. They each carefully examined the walls, floor, and even ceiling, but there was no evidence to indicate that there was a way forward.

"Do you see anything?" Morgan asked Gold, as he scanned the room.

"There," Gold said, pointing to a blank spot on the wall. "That's our way in."

"How do you know?" Sarah asked skeptically.

Gold flashed her a grin, then darted out from the tunnel exit and ran straight for the section of wall he'd pointed out.

Sarah opened her mouth to say something, then he dove forward and vanished.

"What the…" Sarah began, but a light scuffing coming from the tunnel quickly had her moving to the spot Gold had just vanished through.

Morgan was close behind her, fascinated at the concept of hiding an entrance in plain sight. Sarah winced as she slammed her shoulder against an invisible doorframe, but Morgan, seeing where she'd impacted with the wall, was able to avoid it.

They emerged into a well-lit hallway that looked nothing like the sparse, concrete-lined one they'd been walking through. Black and white marble tiles lined the floors, and the walls were lined by rich mahogany panels. Suits of armor stood in a neat line on either side of the hallway, and Morgan could spot well over thirty doors just from where he was standing.

"How big is this place?" Sarah asked, wonder in her voice.

"No clue, but my best guess," Gold paused, looking down the hallway and squinting slightly, "would be somewhere in the five square mile area."

They both turned to stare at him in shock.

"And we're supposed to locate *one person* in an hour?" Sarah exclaimed.

"Forty-three minutes," Gold corrected cheerily. "Let's get moving!"

44

Arnold walked swiftly down the abandoned stretch of road between the last town of Kerg and the South Kingdom border. He'd debated spending the night in town but had ultimately decided that it was best to escape the North Kingdom as soon as he could.

His eyes flitted nervously around the wide open area. He didn't know why, but he suddenly felt distinctly uneasy.

His feet moved just a bit faster as he subconsciously sped up his pace, and he clutched at the short sword buckled at his belt.

He'd been unable to find a proper replacement for his massive two-handed one, but this toy was better than nothing. While some supers preferred to fight bare handed, he had always preferred a sword. He found that it greatly increased his chances of winning a fight and who wanted to take the time to learn a martial art? The art of the sword was all he'd needed to know.

Arnold felt his pulse quicken a bit as he continued running. He was headed for the Merchants Guild in the South. The information he had was extremely valuable and he had no doubt that if anyone had the power to hold back the Assassins Guild, it would be them.

The night was silent, and the only sound to be heard on the dusty road was the sound of his boots scuffing lightly against the gravel underfoot. There was a half moon in the sky, giving less light than Arnold felt comfortable with.

His eyesight was normally impeccable, but the moon had been drifting in and out of clouds for the last hour. Even when it was showing, it would cast weird shadows on the barren landscape, making details hard to judge.

The only warning Arnold received was a light swish of air. The next moment, he was sent bouncing across the hard-packed earth, wincing at the force of the blow. He slammed a fist into the ground as he came out of a particularly nasty impact with a prickly cactus. The force of the blow launched him a few feet into the air, and he was finally able to orient himself enough to manage a landing.

His feet plowed deep furrows in the ground as he slid back, and Arnold's breath caught in his throat at the sight before him. Over

Aaron Oster

a hundred black-clad men and women were now standing on the open stretch of space. His momentum finally ran out then and he came to a full stop, eyes scanning over the gathered assassins.

He caught a flash of movement from his right, but he wasn't quick enough to dodge as something hard slammed into his ribs. Arnold grunted as he felt something snap, then he was once again sent bouncing over the hard ground.

He let out a howl of anger and smashed his fist into the ground again, this time using his *concave* skill. There was an earth-shattering boom and a massive crater formed where his fist impacted. The force threw him upward a good twenty feet, and when he looked down, was glad to see that at least three people had been caught in the blast.

His pleasure vanished in an instant, when they all stood up as one, seemingly unhurt. Arnold came back to the ground, landing hard and taking off at a sprint for where the assassins seemed to be spread the thinnest. He caught a flash of movement again, and this time he managed to throw a hand up to block.

He howled in pain as his forearm shattered, the force of the attack spinning him violently around and sending him to his knees. Arnold gritted his teeth, as hot blood poured down his arm, and he forced himself back to his feet.

Apparently, the assassins were no longer taking any chances with him. This was an all-out war, one that he stood no chance of surviving.

He looked up at the black-clad figures. So far, he had yet to spot a single one move to attack, yet he'd been hit hard enough to break bones more than once. This could only mean that the assassins here were their best.

If he was going to die here, he may as well try and kill as many of them as he could. If for no other reason than to spite the people that had set out to end him.

Arnold coughed, tasting the coppery tang of his own blood, and grinned.

"Well, then. Let's dance!" he roared, pulling his short sword from the scabbard and twirling it in the air.

***

"Not here," Sarah said, closing another door and jogging to catch up with Morgan and Gold.

They'd been at this for the past twenty minutes, without even a shred of luck. Their time was ticking down fast and they were no closer to finding the head of the Guild than they had been before they'd left.

"No luck here, either," Morgan said, closing another door and moving to follow Gold.

He sounded a lot less frustrated than her, but he'd always been good at hiding his emotions.

Then again, she thought, *maybe he's so good at hiding them because he simply didn't feel them at all.*

"How much time do we have left?" Sarah asked as the three of them stopped in the middle of the hall.

"Twenty-one minutes," Gold replied.

He was actually beginning to look a bit worried, not that Sarah could blame him. This was their best shot at stopping the assassins from coming after both of them, and they were likely going to fail because this place was so damn big.

"I don't think we'll find anyone in this hallway," Morgan said, after they'd been silent for a few seconds.

"Where, then?" Sarah asked. "This hallway is all I can see in either direction!"

"I think I have a theory about that. We've been seeing the exact same room duplicated every time we open a door. So what if the hallway is also an illusion and we've been searching the same rooms over and over?" Morgan asked.

There was a loud slapping sound, and they both turned in surprise to see Gold had whacked himself on the forehead.

"Of course! Silly me. It's been so long since I've done this sort of thing that it completely slipped my mind."

"So if we're trapped in an illusion, how do we get out?" Sarah asked.

"Simple. We spread out," Gold replied with a grin.

"How will that help?" she asked.

"While illusions are a very powerful type of magic, every single illusion based skill has some limitation, and the biggest limitation of any illusion is space."

Sarah opened her mouth, but Gold held up a finger.

Aaron Oster

"No time for the full lesson, so I'll give you the cliff notes. Illusions can only cover a certain amount of space, but an illusionist can keep it moving so long as we're clumped together. If we move far enough apart, it'll begin fraying and eventually fail."

"Sounds pretty straightforward," Morgan replied with a nod, and without another word, took off at a full sprint down the hallway.

"He's got the right idea!" Gold said with a grin. "You stay here."

He took off in the opposite direction, leaving Sarah all alone.

She growled under her breath at their eagerness, and in her opinion sheer stupidity, at splitting up in hostile territory. She clenched her fists, then activated her mage shield, conjuring a floating ice shield at her back, and a few *icicle spears* just in case.

She then began to notice that the walls were beginning to look odd. She blinked a few times and rubbed at her eyes as it seemed to swim before them. She was beginning to wonder if she was seeing things, when the elaborate and richly decorated hallway vanished, only to be replaced by the uniformly gray concrete.

Looking down to both ends of the hall, she could now spot where both exits were and headed in the direction Morgan had taken. No doors lined the hallway, leading her to wonder just what they'd been opening and looking into for twenty minutes. Then she heard a loud clang from up ahead, and quickly broke into a run, fearing the worst.

Sarah barreled out of the tunnel exit, emerging into yet another concrete room. This one was very different than the first one they'd entered. For one, there were a few pieces of actual furniture, such as tables, chairs and a large bookcase. For another, there were the two black-clad assassins that Morgan was currently fighting.

She froze in place, trying to assess the situation. Morgan was on the defensive, but managing to hold them off, if just barely. This meant that while they were powerful, they were not powerful enough to completely overwhelm him. She could see that this wouldn't be the case for long, however.

Quickly, she targeted the one on the left and sent all her *icicle spears* into the man's back. By the cry of pain that left the figure's throat, she realized that it was not a man at all. The woman whirled around, a pair of gleaming daggers flashing in the lantern light as she glared at her.

Sarah's attack, while not lethal, was undoubtedly causing her a great amount of pain. She could clearly see the tips of at least four icicles poking out of her back, and knew that this fight would be made a lot easier due to her sneak attack.

"I'll get you for that you, sneaky bitch!" the woman yelled, launching herself at her.

Sarah quickly back-peddled, throwing a wall of ice in the woman's way, then used her *bitter frost* skill just as she vaulted over the wall. Then woman visibly slowed, and Sarah was quick to pin her leg in a block of ice.

The assassin wasn't about to go down that easily. Her fists glowed brightly for a moment, then her hands flashed out, sending a shower of needles right at her. Sarah threw up another ice wall, hearing a loud crunch as the needles impacted with the wall.

"She's *rank 26!*" Sarah heard Morgan yell.

Well, that was a relief, Sarah thought, whirling around from behind her ice wall and throwing a barrage of *icicle spears* at the assassin.

To her credit, she managed to avoid most of them, even with Sarah's skill reducing her speed by nearly half. The woman cried out as two of them found their mark, their three pointed tips burying themselves deeply into her right thigh.

She then conjured a massive ball of ice and sent it flying right at the assassin's head. The ice shattered when Morgan's opponent disengaged and intercepted the attack, slicing right through it with a curved sword.

"Thanks for that," the woman called out before her head was abruptly blown off as Morgan seemed to simply appear behind her, fist extended outward.

He nimbly dodged back as the other assassin swung around at him, and Sarah used the opportunity to use one of her powerful skills.

Her *icy wave* tore up the ground before impaling the assassin right through. He let out one final yell of agony, before he slumped, blood running down the razor-like icicles and pooling on the ground beneath him.

"That was quite the show," Gold said, emerging from the tunnel and clapping slowly.

Sarah was so used to this by now, that she would have been surprised if he *hadn't* shown up as soon as the fight was over.

"Where have you been?" Morgan asked.

"Oh, just taking care of the other four that were sneaking up behind us."

Of course, he was.

"How much time have we got?" Sarah asked, reminding them that they were on a tight schedule.

Gold looked down at his watch and winced.

"Eight minutes. But don't worry. I think I know where to go now. Follow me," he said, moving quickly around the field of razor ice, and darting down the opposite hallway.

Since neither of them had any idea where they were, they were quick to follow.

Sarah could feel her heart pounding faster as she counted down the time in her head. They wove their way through an intricate system of corridors that all looked exactly the same, but for some reason, Gold seemed confident about where he was going.

She began to panic when they reached the five minute mark and had yet to find the leader.

"Hey, Gold, are you sure you know where we're going?" she asked, panting lightly from exertion.

She may have been in good shape now that she'd made it to rank 20, but they were moving at a pace which would have probably killed a normal person, and she was beginning to feel it.

"Just one more minute!" Gold replied, speeding up just a little more, and making her stumble slightly as he did.

They took one turn after the next, Sarah continuing to count the seconds as they moved. She was beginning to panic when she hit the three and a half minute mark, but the end of the hallway came into sight. There was a heavy steel bound door set into the wall and two assassins stood guard.

"I can't read their *ranks!*" Morgan called out as the assassins took up a battle formation.

That wasn't good. If Morgan couldn't read their ranks, it meant that they were at least ten ranks above their own.

A split second later, there was a whoosh of air and Gold seemed to appear before them.

"I'll take care of these two. You handle the boss!"

Starbreak

"Are you nuts?" Sarah yelled, even as Morgan used his *storm blade* and slashed the handles from the massive door.

"I'm sure you can handle it," Gold replied, as two stone golems rose from the ground.

Sarah gritted her teeth as Morgan tore the door from its bearings and threw it to the side.

He really had gotten strong. Evolution was no joke.

She took one last look back at Gold, then swiftly followed Morgan into the room.

45

Morgan entered the dimly lit room, followed closely by Sarah. The room was sparsely decorated, with only a small desk and chair, and a bed in one corner.

He looked quickly around the room, looking desperately for his target, when a small movement from the bed caught his attention. He was there in a flash and staring down an old, fragile looking woman. Her cheeks were sunken with age and she looked for all the world, to already be dead. The only sign of life was the slow rise and fall of the blankets around her.

Sarah walked up next to him, staring down at the old wrinkled woman in confusion.

"Is this her?" she asked.

Morgan shrugged and used *aura sense.*

Name: Swan
Rank - 6
Ability type - Mage

"That can't be right," he said, brows knitting together in confusion.

"What can't be right? What did you see?" Sarah asked, leaning in closer to him.

"It says here that her name is Swan, but she's only *rank 6.* Do you think we got the wrong person?"

Sarah bit her lip nervously, wondering if they had indeed been tricked, when the woman let out a loud rattling cough and her eyes blinked slowly open.

"So, you've come to kill me," she said, voice harsh and raspy.

"Are you the leader of the Assassins Guild?" Morgan asked, ignoring her words.

"Would you be here if I wasn't?" she asked, coughing a few times.

"But that doesn't make any sense!" Sarah exclaimed. "How can a fragile old woman, who's only *rank 6,* be the leader of the assassins guild?"

Swan actually looked surprised when Sarah mentioned her *rank*, but didn't otherwise move to answer her question.

"Well, if she's who she says she is, then all we have to do is kill her, right?" Morgan asked, raising his *storm blade* to end her.

"Wait!" Sarah yelled, grabbing his arm and preventing him from attacking.

"We can't wait, Sarah," Morgan said, attempting to pry her fingers free. "We only have ninety seconds before our time runs out. We can't afford to be weak, just because she's not what we expected."

"It's called compassion, Morgan!" Sarah yelled, face going red. "You do know what that is, don't you?"

Morgan shrugged in reply.

He understood the concept, but compassion was for the weak, not for those who wanted to survive.

"Ah, so you're the ones Simon was after."

Morgan and Sarah both turned their attention back as the old woman finally spoke up.

"How did you.."

"Know?" Swan chuckled lightly, but it turned into a racking cough halfway through, and it took her a few moments to catch her breath.

"I am the leader, after all. I know the names of every single person who I've sentenced to die, though your case was a rare one, Sarah, as you were asked to be brought back alive."

"How is it that you're the one in charge?" Sarah asked, trying to keep her tone soft.

Swan looked as though she wasn't going to answer but eventually seemed to decide to indulge them.

"The leader of the guild is chosen by three very specific rules. One: they must have been a part of the guild for at least twenty years. Two: they must be voted in by at least an eighty percent majority, and finally, they must be below *rank 9*. This is to ensure that no leader will rule for too long, and if too many become unhappy with their leadership, can be easily removed."

"Wait, so what you're saying is that you'll be dead soon anyway?" Morgan asked.

Aaron Oster

"For lack of a better term, yes. I likely won't survive the night. I've been feeling my end coming for quite some time," she said, turning her eyes up to the ceiling.

"So we wasted all this time and effort, for nothing," Morgan said, allowing his blade to disappear and reaching for Katherine's pendant.

"I daresay you have," Swan replied weakly.

Just then Gold strode into the room. He was chipper as always and his boots left bloody footprints on the ground below.

"She dead yet?" he asked, walking over and examining the decrepit old woman.

"You!" Swan exclaimed, her face going red. "What are you doing here?"

She attempted to rise from her bed and reached out with claw-like fingers for Gold's throat.

"Keeping a promise," Gold replied.

Sarah shivered at the tone of his voice. It was nothing like the tone he'd been using until now. It was cold.

"I might be dying, but you won't escape from here alive!" Swan hissed, reaching for something at her bedside.

There was a loud, wet crunch and Swan's hand went limp.

"Why did you do that?" Sarah demanded, looking down in horror at the stone spike protruding from her chest.

Blood was already beginning to soak the front of her shirt, and her eyes had clouded over with death.

"I did what was necessary," Gold replied, rising from the bed. "Now call our ride. We're out of time."

Morgan nodded, pressing the button on the side of the pendant, and a second later a portal opened. Sarah was the first one through, her back rigid as she held back tears of anger and frustration. Morgan was next, stepping through the swirling portal and leaving Gold alone with the cooling corpse of the Guild's former leader. He looked her over one last time, then he turned and walked through the portal.

***

Arnold grunted as a few more ribs cracked under the massive force of an attack. He quickly spun, lashing out with his crimson blade. He felt it nick something but failed to feel the satisfying blow he'd been hoping for.

He cried out as something sharp slashed across his side, opening a fine line from his shoulder to his lower back. He staggered, dropping to one knee and coughing up huge globs of blood.

This wasn't going at all how he'd hoped. Though, in hindsight, he guessed he shouldn't be surprised.

He forced himself back to his feet, vision going a bit fuzzy around the edges, and staggering slightly as his head swam.

He heard a light swish of movement, and threw himself to the side, feeling something sharp tear through his right earlobe. He grimaced as he rolled back to his feet, feeling at the cut and realizing that had he stayed still, his head would no longer be attached to his body.

His eyes flicked around to the numerous assassins, every single one of them still and unmoving.

He gritted his teeth, then slammed his foot into the ground and used the last of his chi to activate his *eruption* skill. There was a loud rumbling, then a gout of molten lava spewed from the ground, covering a fifty-foot radius in molten rock.

He finally saw the assassins move then, darting quickly back from the growing pool of glowing stone. He coughed again, blood splattering and hissing against the lava underfoot. He grinned, despite the agony and took a step forward. Suddenly, something slammed into the back of his head and sent him flying.

He felt bones grind and break as he slammed into the ground, hard enough to leave a small crater. He skidded for at least a few hundred yards, the rough gravel tearing up his skin and lodging inside. Something like this normally wouldn't have been possible, but the damage that had been done so far had severely lowered his resistance to damage.

He came to a halt, groaning and barely conscious. He blinked, as blood streamed into his eyes from a gash in his scalp, and he forced himself to roll onto his back.

Staring up at the starry sky above, Arnold could feel the life flowing out of him. Then a shadow passed over him and he saw a figure clad in black.

So this is it, he thought bitterly.

He tried to say something, but all that came out was a rasping gurgle. His vision swam once more as the blood loss and shock finally sank in, in the absence of adrenaline. Arnold took one last rasping breath. Then he blacked out.

***

Morgan stepped through the portal, followed closely by Sarah and Gold. All signs of his earlier seriousness were gone, now replaced by his usual easygoing look, but Morgan couldn't forget the look on his face when he'd killed Swan.

He would have killed the woman in a heartbeat, but only out of necessity. Gold had seemed to enjoy it somehow.

He wondered what sort of history the two shared, but decided that it was none of his business. He felt something soft crash into him and a second later, the air was being squeezed from his lungs.

"It's good to see you made it out alive, husband!" Katherine's sultry voice sounded near his ear.

"Not your husband," he managed to croak out.

He felt her warm lips brush against his cheek. Then, mercifully, he was able to breathe again as she let go.

He turned to see Katherine beaming at him.

"Your mission was a success!"

"Yes," he said, rubbing at his sore ribs.

Shouldn't his strengthened body be able to handle Katherine's over-enthusiastic greetings?

He looked around then, noticing that they were in the same clearing they used as a staging ground for their attack on the guild.

"Are we heading back to the palace now?" Morgan asked.

Katherine shook her head.

"It's too risky when we're so close to the attack."

"So will we be staying here until tomorrow night?" Sarah cut in, walking up to them and placing her hands on her hips.

It was clear to Morgan that she had seen Katherine's greeting and was not at all pleased by it.

Why couldn't life be simpler? he asked himself with a sigh.

"No," she answered. "We'll be heading to meet Herald and finalize our plans for the attack."

"What about the other people you said would be joining us?" Morgan asked.

"The others are already waiting for us," she said, holding her hand out to open a portal.

Nothing happened.

Katherine's brows came together in confusion, and she tried again, without success, to open a portal.

"What's going on?" Morgan asked, seeing the worried look on her face.

"The portal. It's refusing to open," she said, taking a step back and staring at the space in confusion.

A loud crack sounded off to their left, and all three of them turned in that direction.

Morgan's eyes swiveled back and forth, trying to pick anything out of the surrounding darkness, but not seeing anything out of place.

"Do you see any…" He stopped as his eyes fell on her, eyes widening in shock.

Katherine stared back at him for a long moment, eyes wide, then slowly, her eyes lowered down to the massive diamond spike protruding from her chest.

She looked back up to him, blood frothing at the corners of her lips as she tried to say something. Then the spike was torn from her back and she staggered forward into him, blood gushing from the gaping wound.

He stared down at her for a long moment, then looked up to the man standing behind her. He was wearing the same casual smile as he always did, but it just didn't seem to fit. It was wrong.

He heard a loud gasp, and turned to see Sarah staring at him, eyes wide in shock and fear.

"Morgan."

The voice was faint, but Morgan quickly looked down to Katherine. He could see the light in her eyes dimming, as her blood soaked through his armor.

She smiled up at him, her teeth stained red with her blood, and tears leaking from the corners of her eyes. She reached out a trembling hand and stroked his cheek gently. Then, she leaned up and kissed him. He could taste her blood on his lips, but he didn't push her away. He would at least let her have that much before she died.

He felt her body tremble one last time, then go still in his arms. He gently lowered her to the ground, feeling his chest constricting in a way it never had before.

It hurt.

He looked up to the man he had once counted on, both as a mentor, and a trusted friend.

Why did it hurt so much?

"Why did you do that?" he asked, in a surprisingly calm voice.

He could hear Sarah crying next to him, and wondered why.

She hadn't seemed to like Katherine at all, so why was she so upset at her death?

"She was going to ruin my plans. I couldn't very well have her do that."

"And what exactly are your plans?"

"My plans are my own, but suffice it to say that none of you will be getting in my way. With Katherine out of the way, and you more than a week's journey from the battlefield, there's no way you can stop them in time."

"You want the Pinnacle Kings to awaken," Morgan said, the realization hitting him almost immediately.

"Yes! Give the man a prize!"

"But why? None of this makes sense!" They both turned as Sarah spoke up for the first time.

"Why would you do this? For what possible reason?"

Gold grinned then and gave them both an exaggerated bow.

"While I would love to tell you, I'm afraid that would be *against the rules.*"

They were both struck dumb by his reply, and Gold twiddled his fingers at them before abruptly vanishing, leaving the two of them and Katherine's now cooling body, alone in the dark.

Epilogue

Six Years ago...

Simon slammed his fist angrily into his desk, cracking the wood and splitting it in half. The man standing by the door jumped nervously as he did so, but he hardly took notice.

How had all his carefully crafted plans gone so horribly wrong? He'd worked on them for months, carefully bribing the correct guards, hiring those street thugs and making sure that the guard rotations would include only those privy to his plans.

He growled to himself, and only then seemed to notice the man still standing in the doorway.

"What?" he asked, making the man jump once again.

"T-The workmen just finished clearing the rubble away, my Lord," the man said, sweat clearly beading his brow.

"And?!" he thundered.

"They didn't find anything," the man replied, earning another glare from Simon.

He stared the man down for a few more seconds, relishing his fear, despite the foul mood he was in.

"Very well. You may go," he said, waving a dismissive hand.

The man scurried away, without so much as a backward glance, slamming the door shut behind him.

Simon rose from his ruined desk and began pacing his office, mind whirling with unanswered questions.

Hint was supposed to die in that attack, but seeing as every other aspect of his carefully crafted plan had failed, that was no surprise.

Sarah was supposed to be kidnapped, then ransomed back to him. She was supposed to be terrified and never want to leave the manor again, thereby giving up what little freedom he'd promised her willingly. She would then obey his wishes without question, and all he would have to do to keep her in line was remind her of that horrible day when she didn't listen to him.

Hint was a bad influence on her and he'd suspected that Sarah had been acting out, due to his interference. So he had arranged it that Hint would meet with an untimely death, serving the dual purpose of ridding him of a bothersome pest, and further cementing into Sarah's mind the dangers of the outside world.

Simon stopped his pacing and watched through the windows of his office as his daughter escorted a small boy out of the manor grounds. He grimaced as she leaned in and hugged him, watching the joyous smile on her face as the boy headed towards the city.

That boy! He had been the one to ruin everything.

Simon slammed his fist into a very expensive mahogany bookcase, shattering it and sending tomes bouncing to the floor.

"Whoever that boy is, he's going to pay!" he vowed.

***

Arnold awoke with a loud gasp and sat bolt upright. He flailed about for a few seconds, as his mind tried to catch up with his body.

"Do calm down. You're not in any immediate danger," a very familiar sounding voice said from his left.

Arnold took in a few deep breaths, then turned to face the man who had most likely saved his life. It hadn't escaped his notice that his body had been completely healed. There wasn't so much as a scratch on him.

His eyes locked onto the man. He looked vaguely familiar, but he couldn't place exactly where he'd seen him before. One thing was certain, however. This man was extremely powerful if he'd managed to chase off all those assassins.

"How did you do it?" he asked.

He knew this man was powerful, but he just had to know.

"You were pretty banged up, but healing wounds such as yours really isn't a big deal," the man replied with a wave of his hand.

"No. How did you chase off the assassins?"

The man looked genuinely surprised.

"What assassins? I didn't see any around here."

Arnold stared at him suspiciously for a few moments, but not detecting any lie in the man's face or posture, he shrugged and forced himself onto his feet.

Why would the assassins have left him alive? Sure, he was on the verge of death, but he didn't think they would just up and leave before confirming that he actually was dead.

"So who are you anyway? And why did you heal me?" he asked, folding his arms and staring down at the man.

Now that he knew the man wasn't all powerful, he was more confident in dealing with him.

"I'm actually here on orders," the man replied.

"Whose orders?"

"The Merchants Guild," he replied, eliciting a raised eyebrow from Arnold.

He'd been heading to them anyway, but they wouldn't have known that. Something wasn't quite right with this situation.

"How did you know I was coming, and why would the Merchants Guild be interested in me?"

The man shuffled nervously but answered all the same.

"We have a number of informants in the North Kingdom who placed you at the side of Princess Katherine. From the reports, we had assumed that you were working for her directly, but when you left the palace without your possessions and began running south like the devil himself was chasing you, we figured that the two of you had had a falling out."

Arnold blinked.

That was one hell of a deduction. The people that they had working for them must be top notch.

"Seems you've figured me out, but you still haven't explained why you came after me."

The man blinked in surprise.

"We assumed that you were coming to us, so I was sent out here to fetch you."

"And they just so happened to send a healer?"

He wasn't buying any of this.

The man shrugged.

"I only do as I'm ordered. The person who gave me the orders is the one you should really be talking to. She can provide you with all the answers you'll need. Now, do you want to come with me or not?"

Arnold thought about it for a few seconds, before nodding.

He was heading to the guild anyway, so he might as well.

"Very well then. Stand back."

The man pulled a parchment scroll from his pocket and placed it on the ground. Then he pulled a small vile of glowing blue liquid from another pocket and upended it on the parchment. A moment later, a swirling portal appeared over the paper. It looked similar to one of Katherine's, but it wasn't quite the same.

"Impressive," Arnold said with a nod.

He wasn't even aware that magic like this existed.

"We expect you to keep quiet about this, of course, as it's information the guild would rather not get around."

Arnold nodded his agreement.

Magic like this could change everything in the Five Kingdoms, so it was best to keep quiet about it. For now.

"So do I just step through?"

"Yes. I take it you've used portals before?"

Arnold let out a snort, then stepped through the portal. He emerged a moment later into a well-lit room. The floors were lined with some sort of springy material, and the walls seemed to be made of panels of waxed paper.

The man stepped through the portal a moment later and it snapped closed behind him.

"I must ask you to remove your boots," the man said.

Arnold turned to him and noticed that his boots were tucked under his arm.

"Strange custom," he said, leaning down and unlacing his boots.

"You'll get used to it very quickly if you live here. It is considered common courtesy."

Arnold managed to work his boots off and tucked them under his arm.

"Very good. Follow me," the man said, sliding one of the panels aside and walking down a narrow corridor.

Arnold followed him, eyes roaming over the stage décor lining the walls.

He'd never been to the South Kingdom before, but he'd heard they were a bit different. Then again, it would be an extremely boring world if everyone was the same.

He followed the man through a maze of turns, and took the time to examine him more closely.

He was sure he'd seen him somewhere before. But where? The answer was on the tip of his tongue, but he just couldn't figure it out.

They stopped before another sliding door, and the man knocked three times on the wooden frame.

"Enter," a feminine voice called out from within.

The man slid the door aside, and Arnold followed him in, eyes widening in recognition at the woman sitting behind a low table.

"What are you doing here?!"

Arnold was so shocked, that the words slipped out before he could think better.

The woman laughed, however, a light airy sound that put him somewhat at ease.

"It's quite a surprise to see you here as well, Arnold," Loquin said, placing her chin on her hands and leaning forward a bit. "The last time I saw you, you were on a killing spree in the academy."

"Oh, well you see…" Arnold began.

He was so off balance that he didn't even know what to say. It didn't help that the woman sitting before him had beauty, enough to even rival that of Katherine's. The whole thing was enough to leave him tongue-tied.

"Don't worry about that," she said, flashing him a smile. "That was then, and this is now. How about you have a seat, and we can discuss your future."

Arnold nodded, feeling an odd mixture of excitement and trepidation as he took his seat across the striking woman.

*** *

Loquin grinned as King Edmund's face appeared in her mirror.

"King Edmund, I'm glad you could take the time to speak with me," she said, pitching her voice just enough to make him think she was interested in more than just a meeting.

"Headmistress Loquin, or should I say, *former* Headmistress. To what do I owe the pleasure?" His voice was hard, just like the rest of him.

Aaron Oster

His face was set in a neutral expression, but his violet eyes bore into her with all the intensity of a predator examining his next kill.

"Yes, I am the former Headmistress of the academy, but I now hold another prestigious title," Loquin fired back, not even showing a hint of discomfort.

"So I've heard," he replied. "Get to the point, then. I have a war to win."

"But of course," she replied, grin widening just a touch.

"What would you say if I had some information regarding someone close to you, someone who may be plotting something nefarious?" Loquin dragged out the *S*, so it came out as more of a hiss than an actual word.

"I would ask for proof of this supposed elicit activity," he said, folding his arms, but seeming to take a greater interest in what she had to say.

"But of course. Arnold, why don't you come and say hello to your old King?"

Loquin had to suppress a laugh at Edmund's expression as Arnold came into view.

"Hello, Edmund," Arnold said, keeping his tone even despite the urge to curse and rail at the man who had broken his promise to him.

"My, my. Aren't you full of surprises?" Edmund replied. "I take it that he is your informant?"

"Him, and another," Loquin replied. "I assure you that the information is accurate. We even had a diviner listen for any falsehood and they found none."

"Very well," Edmund replied.

He didn't honestly think that the Merchants Guild would provide him with false information. He'd just wanted to see who their informant was, and now he had.

Loquin grinned.

"I'm sure we can come to some sort of arrangement for this information. Don't you?"

Edmund's eyes glittered for a moment, then a small smile cracked across his granite-like features.

"Very well. Let's make a deal."

***

Loquin sat back with a sigh of contentment. Her dealings with Edmund had gone quite well, all things considered. She'd told him of his daughter's plans to overthrow him, and in exchange, he'd offered his aid when she called upon him.

She grinned to herself, knowing exactly what she'd be asking for.

It was about time for a new Queen to rule the South, and she just happened to know the perfect candidate.

"My, my Locky. Aren't we having fun today?"

Loquin froze, blood running cold when she heard that voice. Slowly turning in place, she saw a man emerge from a shadowed corner of the room and stride casually over to lean against the far wall.

"What?" Loquin swallowed hard, trying to get some moisture down her suddenly very dry throat.

"What are you doing here? I haven't broken any of the rules," she said, feeling her body trembling.

"Oh, I know," he replied with a wide grin. "If you had, you would already be dead. After all, no one breaks the rules and lives. Not even gods."

The man stopped speaking for a moment and examined her features with a slight frown.

"Please take your original form. It just doesn't feel right speaking to you like this. It's as though I'm talking to a whole other person."

Loquin's throat bobbed once, then her features abruptly shifted. Long black hair replacing the brown, and piercing green eyes showing through. Her red painted lips were trembling slightly, but she did her best to keep her features composed.

"Much better," the man replied, sending a shiver down her spine.

"So what do you want?" she asked, still trembling, despite the knowledge she was safe.

"Just curious, I suppose."

He pushed himself off the wall and began pacing back and forth.

Now that he had moved into the light, Loquin could now see him clearly, noting that the outfit he was wearing was one that she hadn't seen in many years.

He was dressed in a crisp three-piece business suit that did not match the style of the Five Kingdoms in the slightest. A gold chain looped at his waist, to the pocket watch he always kept with him, and his brightly polished shoes contrasted visibly with the bamboo matting underfoot.

"Why tell Edmund about his daughter, but leave out the other vital piece of information you had? You know. The one about our young supermage."

"That's none of your business," she replied, trying to feign annoyance. "Now if you don't want anything else, please leave."

The man paused his pacing, tapping his finger against his chin.

"I'm hurt, Locky. I thought we'd grown pretty close in our time together at the academy."

"You ruined my plans. Now leave," she said, now feeling her fear being replaced by anger.

"Fine. I'll go, but just a little warning before I do. You came very close to breaking the rules with that stunt you pulled with Morgan."

His voice hardened and his eyes gleamed with golden light.

"Make sure it doesn't happen again, or I'll be back for a less pleasant visit."

He gave her one last grin, then vanished into thin air.

Loquin slumped down into her seat and let out a long shuddering breath. Her earlier excitement at successfully maneuvering Edmund was now gone, replaced by a feeling of dread.

Why had he come here? There was no way it had just been to issue her a warning. This could only mean that he was planning something. But what?

Loquin blew out another breath, feeling her heart rate slowly going down. She may not know what he had planned, but she knew one thing for certain.

Gold truly was a terrifying man.

***

Morgan stared down at Katherine's body and Sarah clung to his arm, as much to support herself, as to support him.

"What do we do now?" she finally asked.

"I don't know," he replied.

Gold had been right. Without Katherine, they stood no chance of killing Edmund or even making it there in time to stop the Pinnacle Kings from awakening.

"I just can't believe she's dead," Sarah said. "She seemed too powerful to die."

Morgan knew what she meant, but a life of hardship had already taught him that no one was truly invincible.

He noticed something glittering on the ground near her. He'd nearly missed it, as her body had landed on top of it, but he was now glad he hadn't.

Reaching down, his fingers closed around the largest core he'd ever seen. He hadn't noticed this anywhere on her, which meant that she'd removed it from a spatial tear before she'd died.

Taking a deep breath, Morgan opened the core's status.

Name: Infernal-Bane Lyvern Patriarch Core
Rank - 49
Total available energy: 431,932/431,932
Total available AP: 58/58

This core was taken from an infernal-bane lyvern. As this core was taken from a zone Patriarch and an advanced beast, the amount of available energy has been massively increased.

"Holy crap," Morgan whispered, getting Sarah's attention.

"What?" she asked, wiping at her eyes.

Morgan quickly absorbed all the available *attribute points*, then handed the core over to her.

Sarah took the core, eyes widening as she examined it. "This is…"

"I know," Morgan said. "I think she wanted us to have this, to help us against her father."

"With this much energy, I can…" Sarah trailed off again.

"Yes; you can evolve," Morgan replied, giving her a weak smile. "Go ahead. Do it."

Aaron Oster

Sarah nodded, letting out a shaky breath as she absorbed the 280,000 energy she needed to move up to the next *rank*."

Morgan watched her closely.

Neither of them had seen him evolve, so he was curious how it would look.

Sarah stared at the core for a second, then her body went rigid and she began emitting a bright blue light. Morgan was forced to cover his eyes as the light flared brighter and brighter. The entire thing lasted only a few seconds, but when the light faded, Morgan noted some significant changes to his friend.

For one, she'd grown a couple of inches taller, putting her once again at eye level with him. Her arms had become more toned and her body had slimmed down, and the new muscle definition was giving off the impression of coiled power just waiting to be unleashed. The strangest part about it to Morgan was that her breasts and hips had actually grown a bit.

He knew that women liked having those traits accentuated, but always thought that having a slimmer figure would make fighting easier. Regardless, he was sure Sarah would be happy with the change.

Then she opened her eyes, and the most notable change became apparent to him. Her eyes were now a bright emerald green, as opposed to the darker leaf green it had been before. A bright blue ring surrounded each of her pupils, the same way Morgan had gold around his.

"How do you feel?" Morgan asked as she examined herself.

He noted with some satisfaction that she did indeed seem pleased with the cosmetic changes.

"Just give me a second," she said, flashing him a grin, and looked over her status.

After a few moments, she closed it. She seemed slightly disappointed, but not overly so.

"It doesn't look like I have the option to assign my attribute points, but they've all increased by 18! My ability has also changed to *evolved mage,* and I can see how much energy I'll need to move up to intermediate. I also got a new skill, *storm cyclone,* which lets me conjure a massive ice storm full of cutting water and ice.

"Oh, and that's not even the best part," she said with a grin, then her mage shield flared up around her.

Morgan stared at the construct of pure mana that surrounded her body like armor. It looked as though she were standing inside a slightly larger version of herself, and he tapped his fingers against it, feeling how solid the barrier actually was.

"Looks like evolution is different for mages," he said, a little disappointed that she wouldn't be able to place her attribute points, but glad that her shield had improved this much.

It would definitely help her if an enemy got in close as that ape had. He wasn't even sure he could burst through that without using his gravity impact skill.

"It looks like we owe Katherine a lot," Morgan said, feeling his chest tighten again as he looked back to the woman's prone form.

Sarah's happy expression vanished, and she dismissed her new shield.

"Why do you think he killed her?" she asked in a quiet voice.

"She's not dead."

Both Morgan and Sarah jumped, whirling at the unfamiliar voice that rang out across the clearing.

A woman strode out from between the trees, a serious expression on her very plain looking face.

"Who are you?" Morgan asked, pulling away from Sarah and taking up a fighting stance.

He'd been surprised too many times tonight to take any chances.

"What do you mean, 'she isn't dead?'" Sarah asked.

"Katherine knew me as Vivian, a talented healer, but that isn't who I really am."

She then bent down near the Princess' prone form and laid a hand over her ruined chest. A pulse seemed to flow out from her palm, and then she rose, dusting off her pants.

Morgan and Sarah then stared in dumbfounded shock as the pool of blood around Katherine suddenly began moving in reverse, flowing back into her body. Her skin began reknitting itself, and soon Katherine was lying whole and undamaged once more. Even her clothes had stitched themselves up, and after a few breathless moments, her chest began to slowly rise and fall.

"How did you do that?" Sarah asked, awe tinting her voice.

"That was way beyond healing," Morgan cut in, looking from Katherine to the woman who had called herself Vivian. "She was dead, no two ways about it."

"That she was," the woman admitted, contrary to her earlier statement, but she didn't offer any further explanation.

"Who are you really?" Morgan asked, eyes narrowing.

It didn't escape his notice that despite Katherine's healthy complexion, and obviously beating heart, she had yet to awaken.

As though in response to his question, Vivian's form began to change, shifting and ripping. They both stared, as her features rearranged themselves until the person standing before them barely resembled the woman who had been there, just a moment before.

Morgan's eyes widened as he took in her features, and he felt his stomach drop.

She was tall and slender, with a lithe and athletic build. She had a tanned complexion and slightly upturned brown eyes. Her black hair was short and choppy, and a silver stud pierced her left ear.

"I know you!" Morgan said, in a half whisper, half shout.

"Wait, you do?" Sarah asked. "Who is she?"

"She's the woman from my memories!" he said, instantly on guard.

Had she been the one who modified him?

Sarah's eyes widened as well, and she turned back to look at the mystery woman.

The woman didn't seem surprised to be recognized and nodded her head sharply.

A lance of whirling purple and gold-tinged wind flared around Morgan's arm, and he took a step forward.

"Tell me who you are. Are you the one who messed with my head? Why can't I remember anything?" His violet eyes began glowing as reiki flooded his body, and he prepared himself for a fight.

The woman didn't budge, staring him down without a trace of fear in her eyes.

"We have no time for this right now."

Her voice even sounds different than it had, Sarah noted as her eyes flicked between Morgan and the woman, wondering if a fight was about to break out.

"Then make time," Morgan replied, lightning now crackling across his glowing lance.

The woman opened her mouth to reply when a loud echoing boom rang out through the night. The next moment, they were all thrown off their feet as a massive shockwave ran over the ground beneath them.

Morgan was so surprised, that his lance disappeared, fading away into nothingness.

"What the hell was that?" Sarah exclaimed, getting slowly to her feet.

"That," the woman replied, getting to her feet and lifting Katherine in her arms, "was the awakening of the first Pinnacle King."

Both Sarah and Morgan stared at her.

"Wait. How do you even know about that?" Morgan demanded, debating whether to just attack this woman right now.

"I thought we still had twenty-four hours!" Sarah exclaimed at the same time.

The woman just shook her head and turned to leave the clearing.

"As I said before, we have no time for that now. Katherine will need a few more hours to recover, and we're too exposed out here. So you can either come with me or stay here. Your choice."

Morgan stared after the woman, mind racing with all the disparate pieces of information he'd collected thus far. He gritted his teeth in annoyance.

This woman had the power to bring the dead back to life and had knowledge of things that were given to him by a god. She may also have had something to do with his memory loss, and somehow knew Katherine.

None of it added up.

Morgan was never one to dally, however, and quickly made his decision.

"Fine. We'll go with you, but on one condition," Morgan said.

The woman turned her head back and quirked an eyebrow at him.

"Who are you really?" he asked, folding his arms and daring her not to answer.

Aaron Oster

The woman seemed to consider her answer for a moment before she shrugged, the corners of her lips quirking up slightly.

"Very well, I suppose it's only fair. My name is Gwendolyn, and I am a supermage."

Continue reading after the credits for an exclusive preview of:

SOMERSET: THE RULES (BOOK ONE)

Afterword

What's up Super-People. For reaching the end of book 2, I award you with 5 attribute points (assign them as you will). I've had an absolute blast writing this book! If you love GameLit or LitRPG as much as I do, then you should check these amazing pages out! You can keep up with your favorite genre of books, all while being part of an awesome community.

GameLitSociety
Spoiled Rotten Readers
Soundbooth Theater Live

You can support me on Patreon if you want some exclusive previews and benefits. You can also follow me on my various social media, as that is where I do giveaways, and release all news on my upcoming books.

Patreon: Rise To Omniscience
Instagram: Aaron Oster
Facebook: Aaron Ostreicher

Upcoming releases:

Somerset: The Rules (Book One) June 2019
Rise To Omniscience (Book Three) Summer 2019

Out Now:

Supermage: Rise To Omniscience (Book One)
Starbreak: Rise To Omniscience (Book Two)

ONE

Sam slowly cracked his eyes open, and immediately shut them against the bright, fluorescent light shining right into them. He groaned, feeling the pounding in his head intensify for a brief instant, before receding back to a dull throbbing, ache.

What the hell happened last night, he thought to himself, attempting to open his eyes once again.

He groaned in protest as the fluorescent lights shone into his eyes once more, piercing into his brain and making him wince.

Maybe drinking an entire cup of vodka on that stupid dare, hadn't been such a great idea.

He rolled to the side, and tried opening his eyes once more; only to once again, be greeted by the bright light.

"Alright Greg, you can stop now. This isn't funny man!" Sam groaned, putting his hand up in front of his eyes in a feeble attempt to block it out.

When the light didn't stop shining however, he started to become annoyed.

"Look man, I've got a wicked hangover and this shit ain't funny anymore. Now get that damn light out of my face, or I'll seriously fuck you up!"

This was of course, an idle threat. Greg had a full ride at Penn State, and was on track to become a pro boxer. Sam had as much chance of beating him up, as a five year-old had against him. The light still did not move however, despite Sam's very intimidating threat of physical violence. So, letting out an explosive string of curses that would have made even his mother cringe, he forced his eyes open.

Slowly, the world came into focus, and blurry outlines formed into recognizable shapes. Sam could now see that it hadn't been an overhead light that was blinding him, but rather, a floating blue screen hovering in front of his face. The letters swam before his eyes for a few moments, before his vision finally focused enough for him to read it.

WELCOME TO SOMERSET

Aaron Oster

> *A land of mystery, and magic! You have been chosen by our Illustrious Overlord to take part in The Rules; a no holds barred death-match, to see who among you is the most powerful.*
>
> *You have been transported here against your will. The only way back, is to reach level 100, and defeat the final boss.*
>
> *Please do be careful with your life, as it is the only one you'll get.*
>
> *Have a pleasant match; and remember, we're always watching...*

Sam stared at the box of text for a few more moments, having a hard time understanding what was going on; then, the box abruptly vanished, leaving him staring up at a cloudless, blue sky.

"What the actual fuck!" He yelled, jumping to his feet and groaning as the sudden movement made his head swim.

How the hell had he gotten outside?

He quickly scanned his surroundings, noting that he was in a wide open field of swaying grass. He could see a distant tree line to the south - *or at least he thought it was south* - but other than that, it was just grass for miles around.

"God dammit Greg!" Sam yelled as his mind came to the only rational conclusion it could.

Greg had gotten him piss drunk, then driven him out into the middle of this field and left him here! The smug bastard was probably sitting back in his room, laughing with his other buddies at his predicament right now.

Then, someone with a very proper sounding voice carrying just a hint of a European accent, spoke up.

"I do not know who this Greg fellow is, but I can assure you that he had nothing to do with this."

Sam's head whipped around at the sound of that voice, his eyes scanning frantically over the surrounding grassland, but not spotting anything to suggest there might be someone nearby. He placed a hand to his forehead, wondering if he might just be losing it; when the voice spoke yet again, this time carrying just a hint of exasperation.

"Down here; I swear you humans have the brain capacity of a squirrel sometimes."

Sam lowered his gaze, and his eyes finally came to rest on a medium-sized black and brown dog. Its color and size matched that of a Shepard, but it had fur and facial features more akin to that of a Collie.

Never seen a dog like that before, Sam thought.

The dog, for his part, was sitting neatly on its haunches and staring up at him in amusement.

Then, the fact that the dog had spoken to him, hit Sam like a freight train.

"Oh no! I must be tripping!" Sam groaned, reaching up and clutching at his head again.

"I know that Greg had some shrooms at that party last night, but I'm sure that I didn't touch them. That sneaky bastard must have slipped some into my food when I wasn't looking!"

Sam sat down, and began rocking back and forth, looking wildly around for any gigantic pink elephants that may have decided to go out for an early morning stroll.

"I can assure you that I am quite real; and that you are not, as you say, tripping." The dog said again, still looking at him with that same amused expression.

"Well then, what other explanation can you offer Sparky?" Sam asked, cracking a smile of his own.

Oh crap, he was talking to his hallucinations now; he really hoped he wasn't back in his room right now. He could imagine Greg standing over him right now; recording this whole thing so he could use it against him for the next year!

"First of all; my name is Gordon, not Sparky!" The dog said with a huff; "and secondly…"

"Ow!" Sam yelled, as a small pebble whizzed through the air and struck him on the forehead.

"What the hell was that for you dumb mutt!?" He exclaimed, rubbing at the spot where the stone had impacted.

"That," Gordon said, padding over to sit right before him, "was to prove that this place is as real as your world. If you can feel pain, you are very obviously, awake."

Sam stared at the dog for a few seconds, eyes going wide. Then he pulled his fist back and punched himself in the face. Hard.

"Mother fucker!" He yelled, rolling on the ground; eyes streaming as blood ran from his nose.

It didn't escape his notice, even through the blinding pain, that a message had popped into his field of vision as soon as his fist made contact.

You Deal: -3 Damage to yourself (Blunt).

"Oh dear; it would appear that I have been saddled with an absolute moron," Gordon said, shaking his head sadly.

"Don't talk down to me dog!" Sam yelled, sitting up slowly and pinching his nose.

This couldn't be happening! It just couldn't! Messages didn't float in the air, and dogs didn't talk; this was all just a dream. Right?

Sam was snapped from his downward spiral into madness, when the dog spoke up yet again.

"You do realize that you do not need to do that; correct? If you have not noticed, the bleeding debuff should already have worn off."

Sam didn't understand half of what the dog said, but when he let go of his nose; the bleeding had indeed stopped. He was, once again, completely shocked. Feeling at his whole, and undamaged nose, Sam couldn't understand how this was possible.

If this wasn't a horrible trip, could that floating blue box have been right?

"Alright dog; where the hell am I, and how do I leave?"

Gordon's ears stiffened at that and he turned his nose up at him.

"I have a name you know; address me as Gordon, or not at all you primeval simian!"

Sam wasn't entirely sure what the dog had just called him, but he was pretty sure it had been an insult.

"Fine you pompous mutt, I'll call you by your damn name, if you tell me how to leave!"

"Did you not read the welcome message?" Gordon asked with a sigh. "You cannot leave until you have reached *level 100*, and defeated the final boss. Can you not read, simian?"

"Quit calling me a simian!" Sam yelled, feeling his very limited patience severely straining with this unhelpful, and insulting dog.

"I will, just as soon as you stop calling me; mutt," the dog replied in kind.

Sam let out an explosive breath; then took a few moments to calm himself.

"Fine. Gordon. Can you please tell me where I am, and how to get home?" Sam tried once again.

"Yes Sam. You are in Somerset, a world of mystery and magic, and as I stated previously; you can only go home by reaching *level 100,* and defeating the final boss."

Sam's face turned a deep shade of red, and he let out another explosive string of curses.

So, he was trapped in some unknown world, his only company was a talking dog; and the only way home was to reach level 100. Whatever the hell that meant.

"Who exactly is the final boss; and how do I reach *level 100?*" Sam asked.

"An excellent question!" Gordon replied, his tail beginning to wag. "The final boss is our illustrious Overlord. You can reach *level 100,* by completing quests, fighting challenging opponents or doing a dungeon dive!"

"Great; so we're in a video game then?" Sam asked.

Though he'd never actually been a gamer, Sam had been an avid reader; or should he say, listener, of fantasy novels. Audiobooks were very popular, and who the hell had the time to read in this day and age? He must have listened to hundreds of books about people getting stuck in video games, though he'd always imagined that if it happened to him, it would be as a jacked warrior; not as... well, himself.

He wasn't bad looking. Standing at just over five feet, nine inches tall; he had longish sandy-blond hair, light gray eyes and a clear complexion. His skin was lightly tanned, and he had a small amount of lean muscle on his skinny frame; but he was nothing remarkable. He'd only ever kissed a few girls, and at nineteen years old, was still a virgin.

Not that he'd ever admit that to his friends.

"It is sort of like your Earth video games; but with a few... shall we say... twists." Gordon said, his large canine teeth showing in an approximation of a smile.

"Like what?" Sam asked, now feeling distinctly uneasy.

"Well for one, there are no, as you Earth people say, respawn's. If you die, that is it. Game over."

Sam audibly gulped when he heard that.

So not only did he have to level up while fighting dangerous monsters, but he had to do so with the knowledge that if he died, it would be permanent.

"You mentioned some other differences?" Sam hedged, noting that his voice was pitched just a bit higher than it normally was.

"Ah, yes. Take a look at this."

Gordon then waved a paw, and a new translucent screen flashed before his eyes.

THE RULES

Each day a new rule will appear in your character status. The rules can be as simple as not dying, or as severe as taking on a boss monster 30 levels above your own. Failure to follow these rules will incur a severe penalty.

Sam quickly read over the message, the screen disappearing almost as soon as he was finished.

"Wait! So if I don't follow the rules; I'll die!?" Sam asked, feeling his heart rate increasing at a rapid pace.

"Though it is a possibility; I do not think you will die if you break a rule. You will however, very much regret doing so."

Sam blew out a long breath, leaning back on his palms and staring up at the cloudless, blue sky above. A light breeze blew over him, tickling his skin and setting the long grass swaying with a loud rustling sound.

It was nice out, probably around 70 degrees Fahrenheit, and with the sun warming his face, he could already feel his headache receding.

So, he was trapped in a videogame-like world, and the only way out was to kill some douchebag Overlord... That sounded like more fun then he'd had in his entire life!

"Alright," he said, finally beginning to accept that this might actually be real. "Where do we begin?"

Printed in Great Britain
by Amazon